TEEN TITANS™ GO!

ROLL WITH IT!

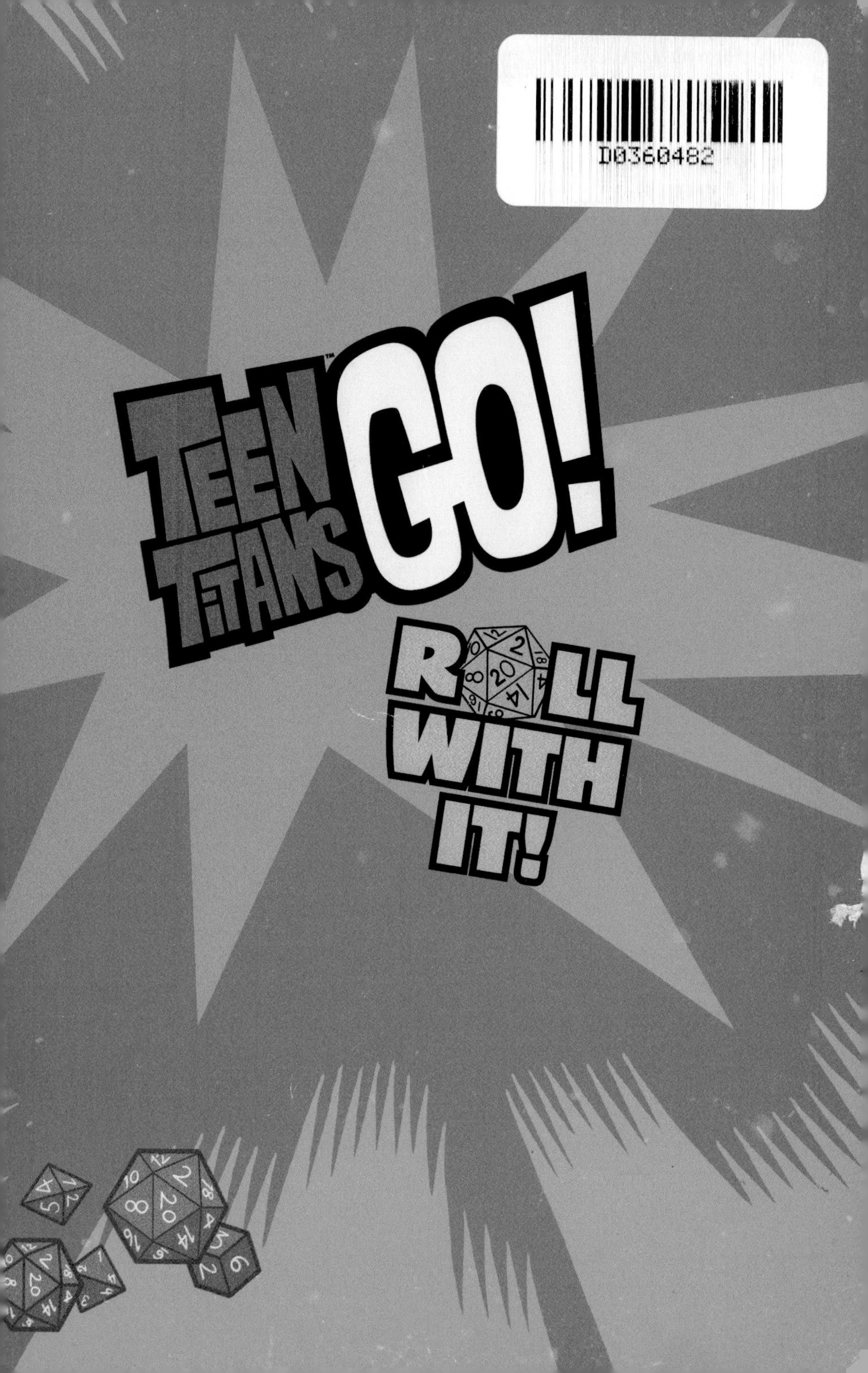

Written by
Heather Nuhfer and **P.C. Morrissey**

Jump City
drawn by **Agnes Garbowska**
and colored by **Silvana Brys**

Basements and Basilisks **world**
drawn by **Sandy Jarrell**
and colored by **Wendy Broome**

Lettered by **Wes Abbott**

Cover by Garbowska and Brys

TEEN TITANS GO!

ROLL WITH IT!

KRISTY QUINN Senior Editor
STEVE COOK Design Director - Books
AMIE BROCKWAY-METCALF Publication Design

BOB HARRAS Senior VP - Editor-in-Chief, DC Comics
MICHELE R. WELLS VP & Executive Editor, Young Reader

JIM LEE Publisher & Chief Creative Officer
BOBBIE CHASE VP - Global Publishing Initiatives & Digital Strategy
DON FALLETTI VP - Manufacturing Operations & Workflow Management
LAWRENCE GANEM VP - Talent Services
ALISON GILL Senior VP - Manufacturing & Operations
HANK KANALZ Senior VP - Publishing Strategy & Support Services
DAN MIRON VP - Publishing Operations
NICK J. NAPOLITANO VP - Manufacturing Administration & Design
NANCY SPEARS VP - Sales
JONAH WEILAND VP - Marketing & Creative Services

TEEN TITANS GO! ROLL WITH IT!

DC – a WarnerMedia Company

Printed at LSC Communications in Crawfordsville, IN, USA.
10/2/20. First Printing.
DC Comics, 2900 West Alameda Ave., Burbank, CA 91505
ISBN: 978-1-77950-430-2

PEFC Certified
This product is from sustainably managed forests and controlled sources
PEFC/29-31-337   www.pefc.org

Library of Congress Cataloging-in-Publication Data
Names: Nuhfer, Heather, writer. | Morrissey, P. C., writer. | Garbowska, Agnes, illustrator. | Brys, Silvana, colourist. | Jarrell, Sandy, illustrator. | Broome, Wendy (Comic book illustrator), colourist. | Abbott, Wes, letterer.
Title: Teen Titans go! roll with it! / written by Heather Nuhfer and P.C. Morrissey ; Jump City drawn by Agnes Garbowska and colored by Silvana Brys ; Basements and Basilisks World drawn by Sandy Jarrell and colored by Wendy Broome ; lettered by Wes Abbott.
Other titles: Roll with it! | Teen Titans go! (Television program)
Description: Burbank, CA : DC Comics, 2020. | Audience: Ages 8-12 | Audience: Grades 4-6 | Summary: "The Teen Titans have a regular game of Basements and Basilisks, but when the Basement Boss (Robin, of course) tries to make the game super fun by making it super impossible to win, the team rebels. Their new BB is much more enjoyable-and she actually lets them complete their quests, which is excellent motivation to keep playing. But the Boy Wonder begins to worry the Titans will be trapped in their imaginations forever, going on endless, breezy-easy quests, neglecting their duties in Jump City. There might also be problems with the campaign's most important relic, the "Anklet of Extreme Crushing (and Chafing)" that Robin has tightly clasped to his leg."-- Provided by publisher.
Identifiers: LCCN 2020026176 (print) | LCCN 2020026177 (ebook) | ISBN 9781779504302 (paperback) | ISBN 9781779504388 (ebook)
Subjects: LCSH: Graphic novels.
Classification: LCC PZ7.7.N84 Te 2020 (print) | LCC PZ7.7.N84 (ebook) | DDC 741.5/973--dc23
LC record available at https://lccn.loc.gov/2020026176
LC ebook record available at https://lccn.loc.gov/2020026177

Chapter One

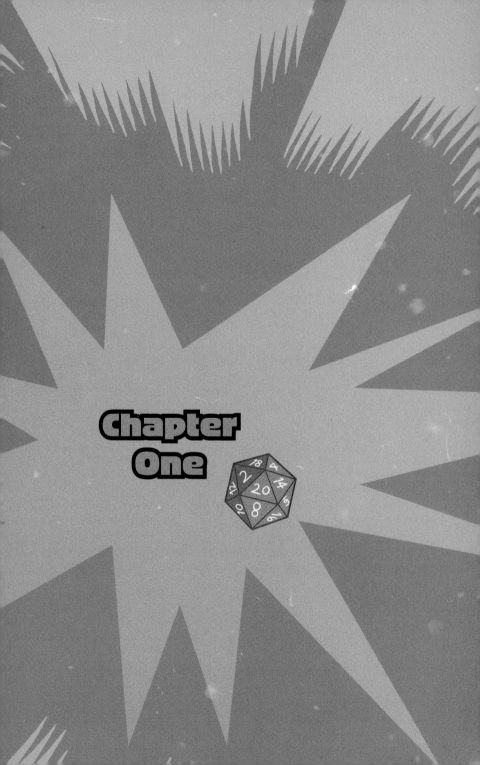

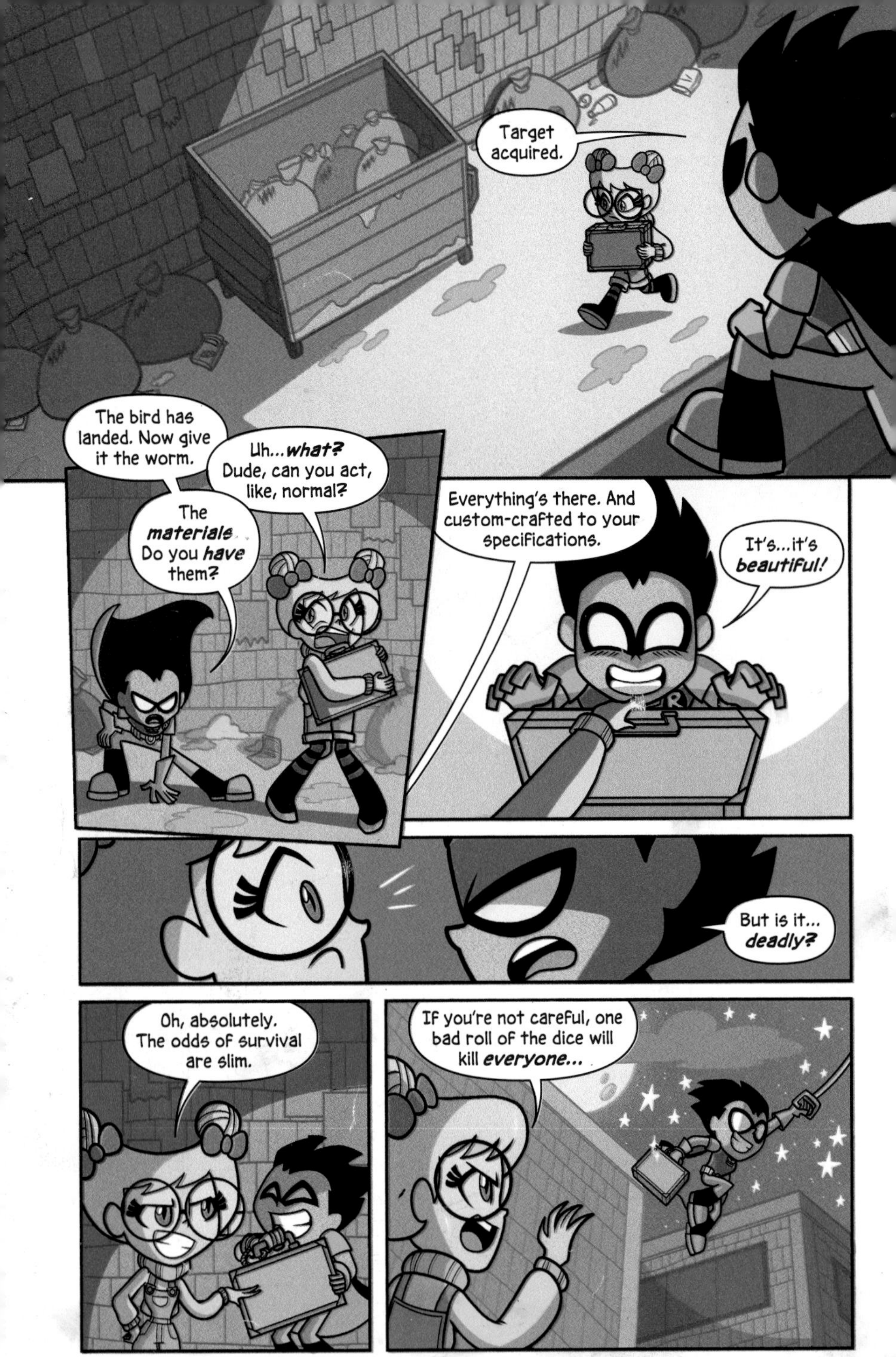
Target acquired.
The bird has landed. Now give it the worm.
The materials. Do you have them?
Uh...what? Dude, can you act, like, normal?
Everything's there. And custom-crafted to your specifications.
It's...it's beautiful!
But is it... deadly?
Oh, absolutely. The odds of survival are slim.
If you're not careful, one bad roll of the dice will kill everyone...

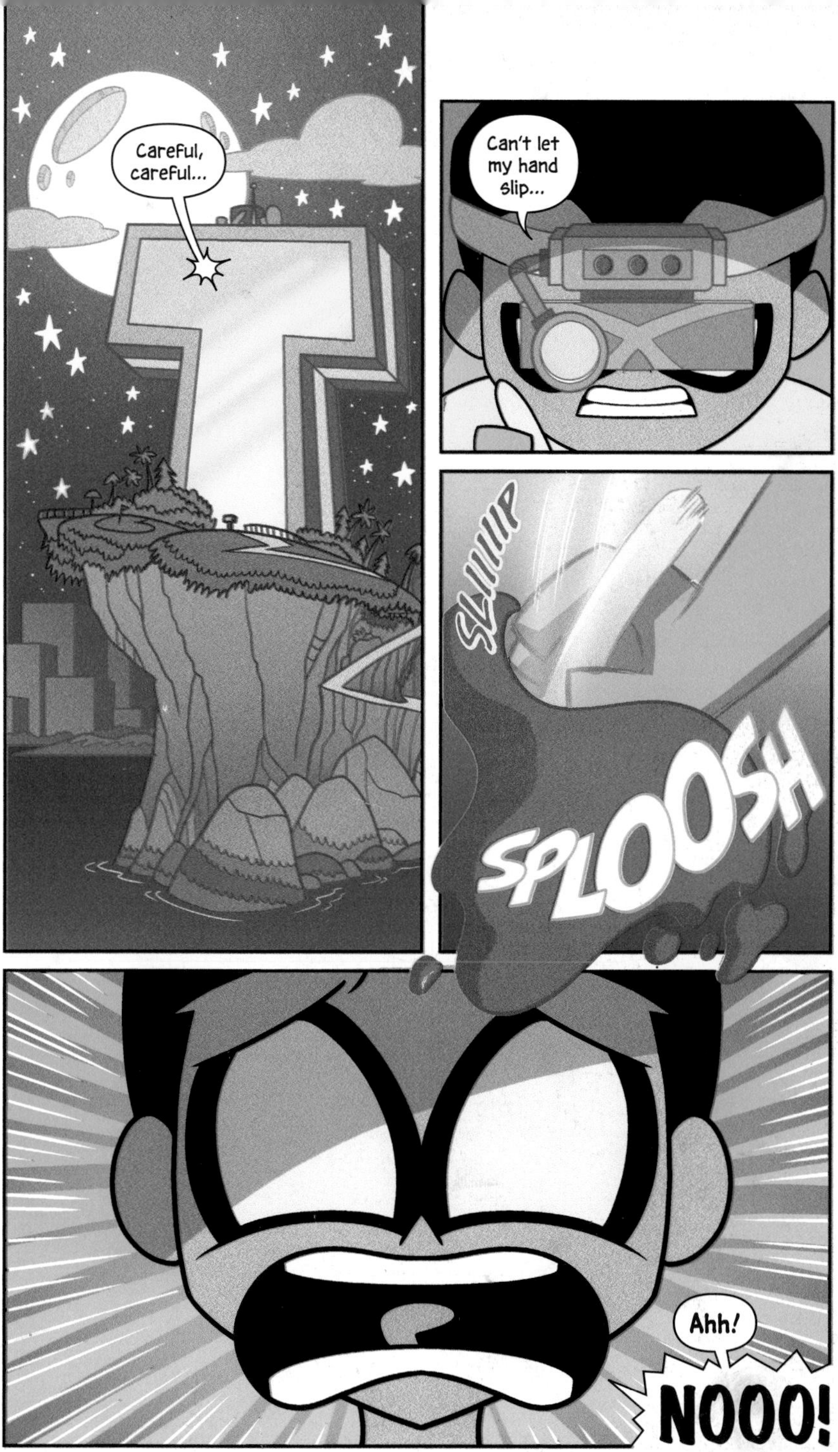
Careful, careful...
Can't let my hand slip...
SLIIIIIP
SPLOOSH
Ahh!
NOOO!

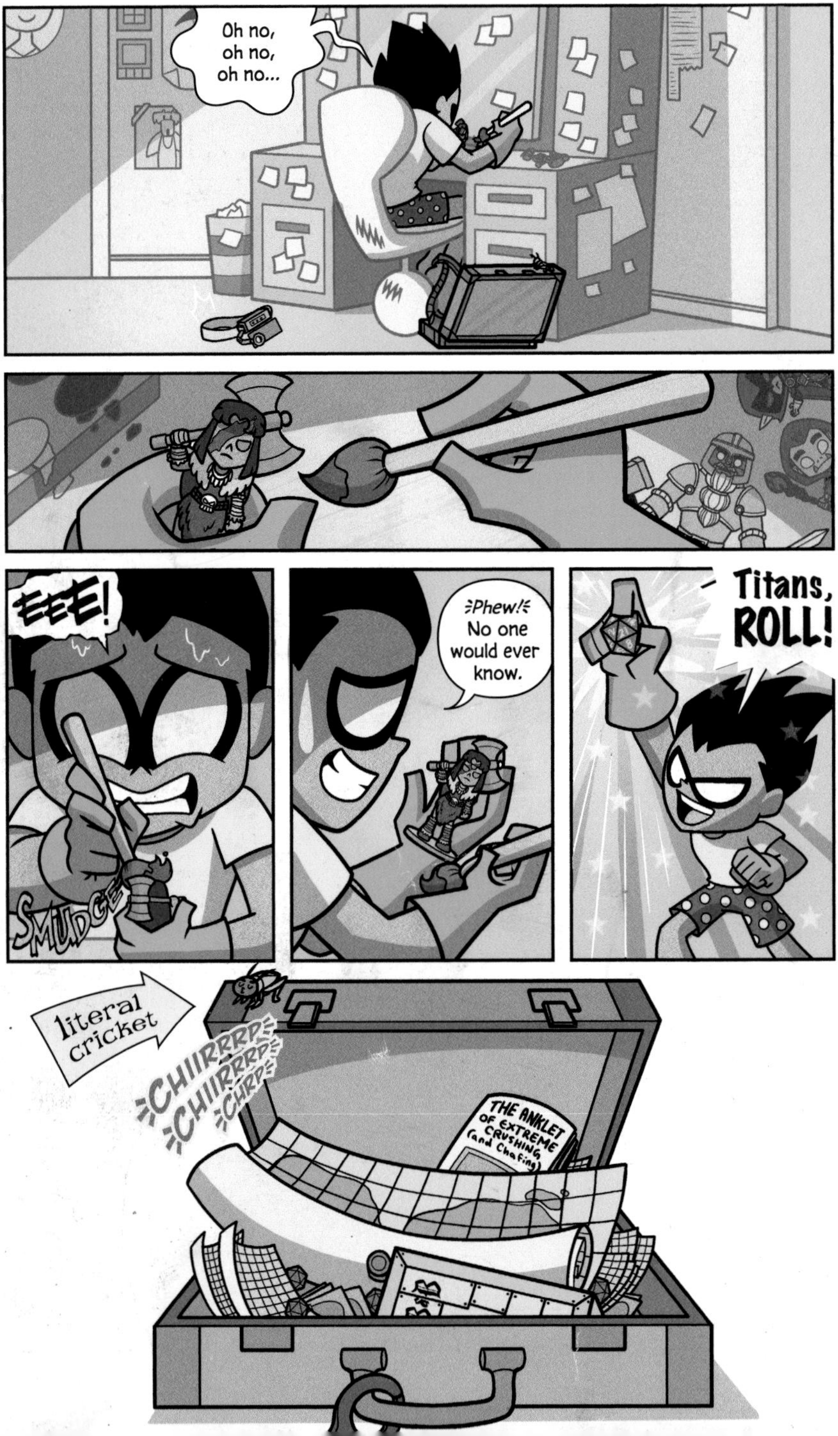
Oh no,
oh no,
oh no...
EEE!
SMUDGE
Phew!
No one would ever know.
Titans,
ROLL!
literal cricket
CHIIRRRP
CHIIRRRP
CHIRP
THE ANKLET OF EXTREME CRUSHING (and Chafing)

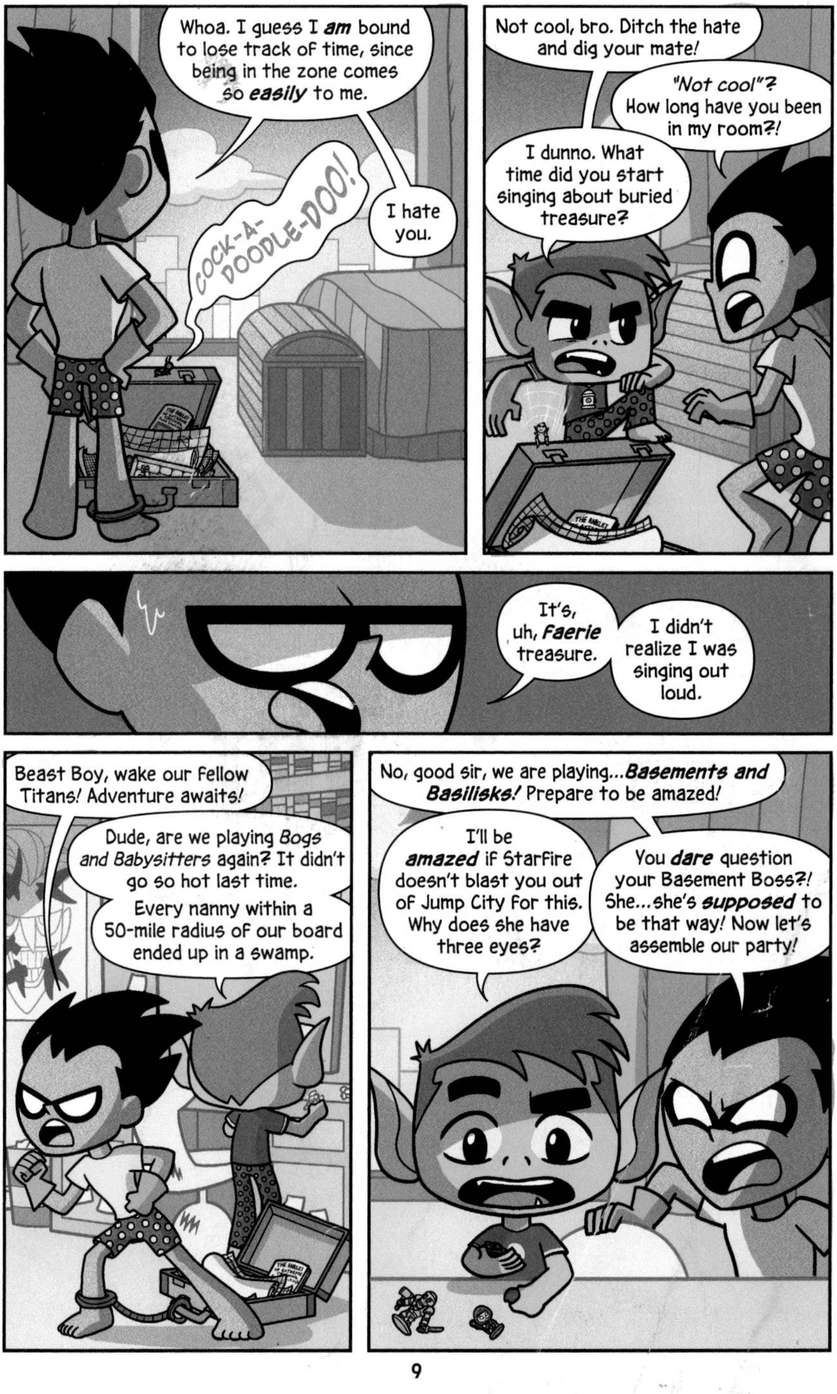

Whoa. I guess I **am** bound to lose track of time, since being in the zone comes so **easily** to me.
COCK-A-DOODLE-DOO!
I hate you.
Not cool, bro. Ditch the hate and dig your mate!
"Not cool"?! How long have you been in my room?!
I dunno. What time did you start singing about buried treasure?
It's, uh, **faerie** treasure.
I didn't realize I was singing out loud.
Beast Boy, wake our fellow Titans! Adventure awaits!
Dude, are we playing *Bogs and Babysitters* again? It didn't go so hot last time.
Every nanny within a 50-mile radius of our board ended up in a swamp.
No, good sir, we are playing... ***Basements and Basilisks!*** Prepare to be amazed!
I'll be **amazed** if Starfire doesn't blast you out of Jump City for this. Why does she have three eyes?
You **dare** question your Basement Boss?! She... she's **supposed** to be that way! Now let's assemble our party!

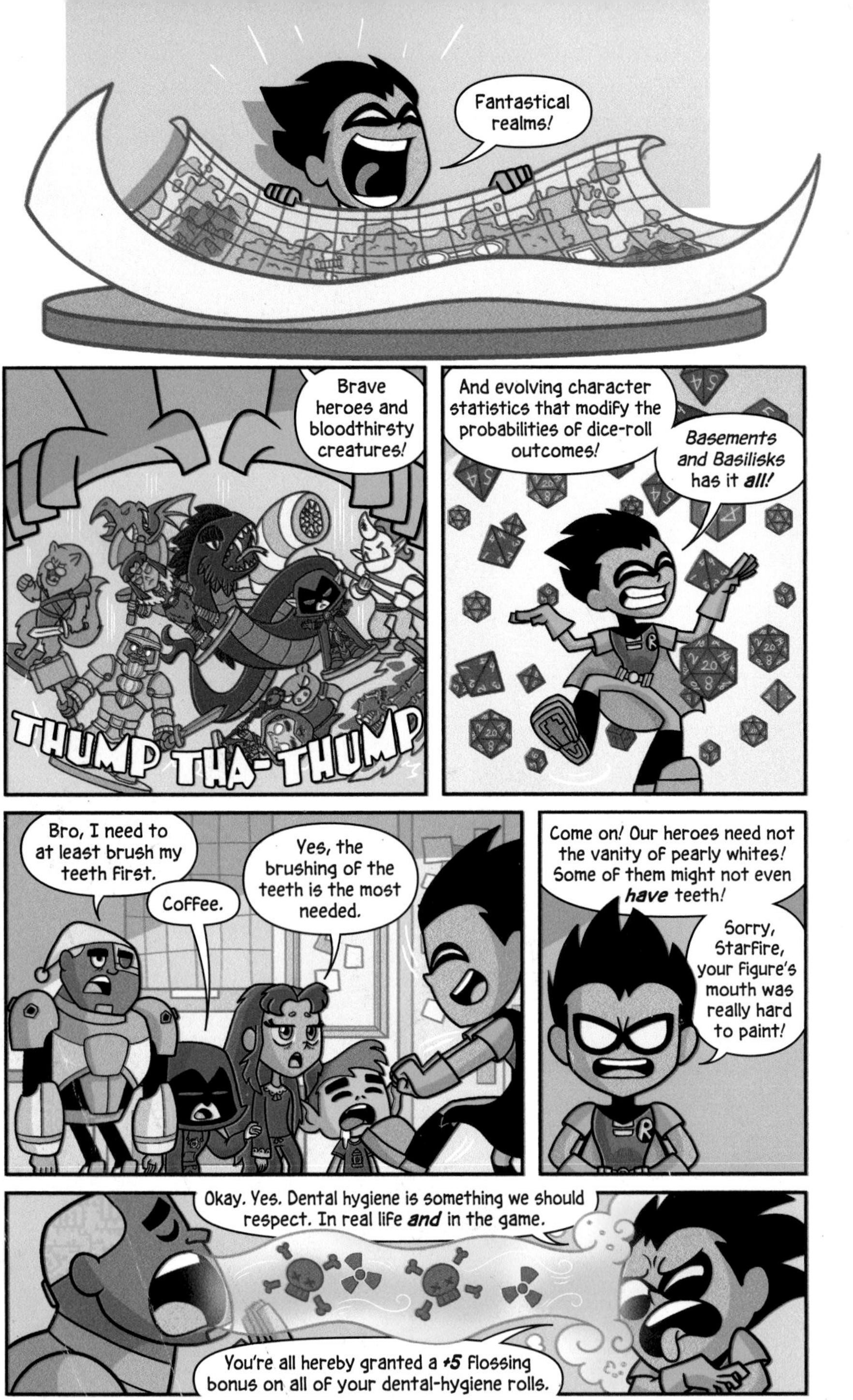
Fantastical realms!
Brave heroes and bloodthirsty creatures!
THUMP THA-THUMP
And evolving character statistics that modify the probabilities of dice-roll outcomes!
Basements and Basilisks has it ***all!***
Bro, I need to at least brush my teeth first.
Coffee.
Yes, the brushing of the teeth is the most needed.
Come on! Our heroes need not the vanity of pearly whites! Some of them might not even ***have*** teeth!
Sorry, Starfire, your figure's mouth was really hard to paint!
Okay. Yes. Dental hygiene is something we should respect. In real life ***and*** in the game.
You're all hereby granted a ***+5*** flossing bonus on all of your dental-hygiene rolls.

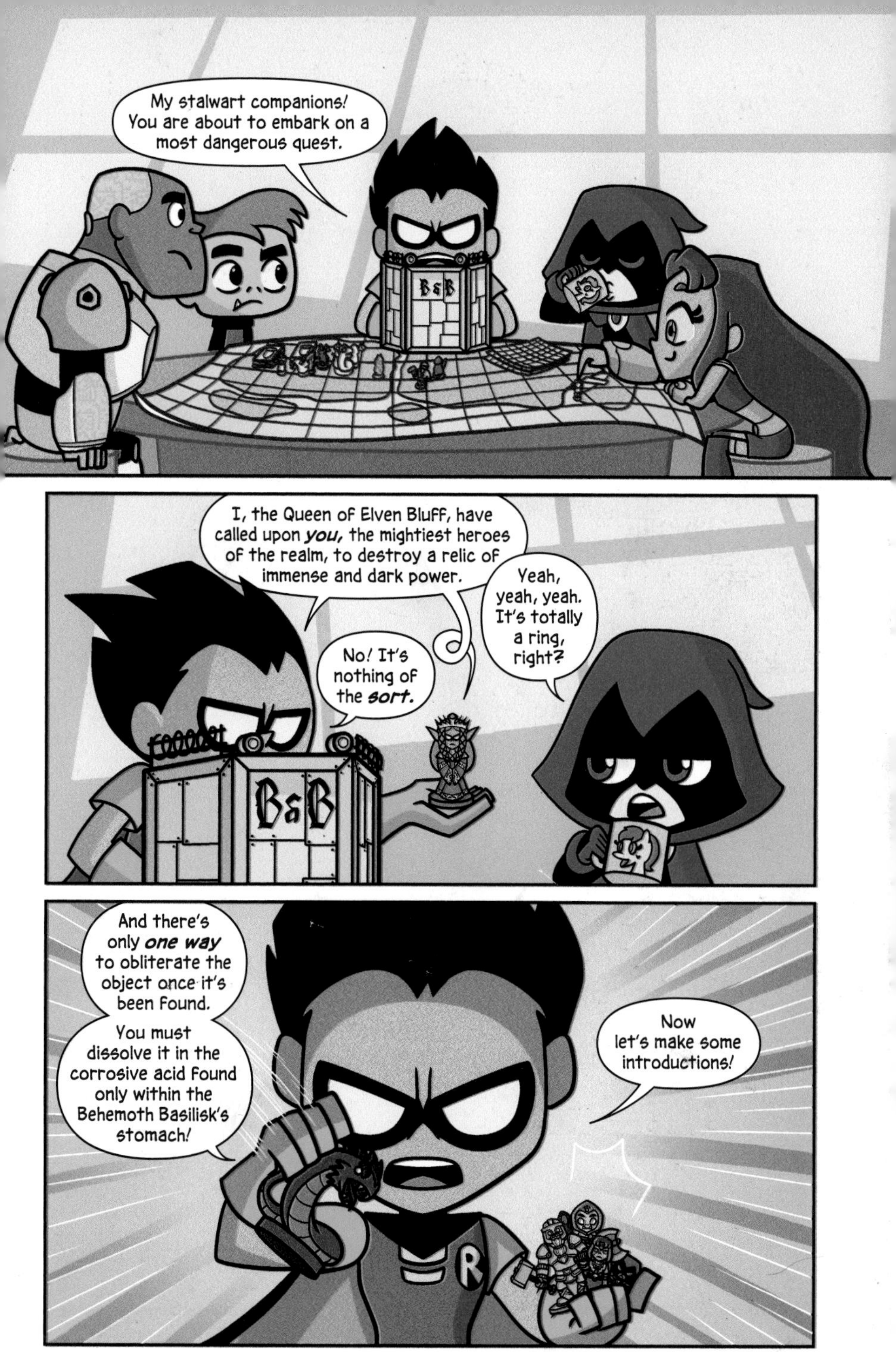
My stalwart companions! You are about to embark on a most dangerous quest.
I, the Queen of Elven Bluff, have called upon *you,* the mightiest heroes of the realm, to destroy a relic of immense and dark power.
Yeah, yeah, yeah. It's totally a ring, right?
No! It's nothing of the *sort.*
B&B
And there's only *one way* to obliterate the object once it's been found.
You must dissolve it in the corrosive acid found only within the Behemoth Basilisk's stomach!
Now let's make some introductions!

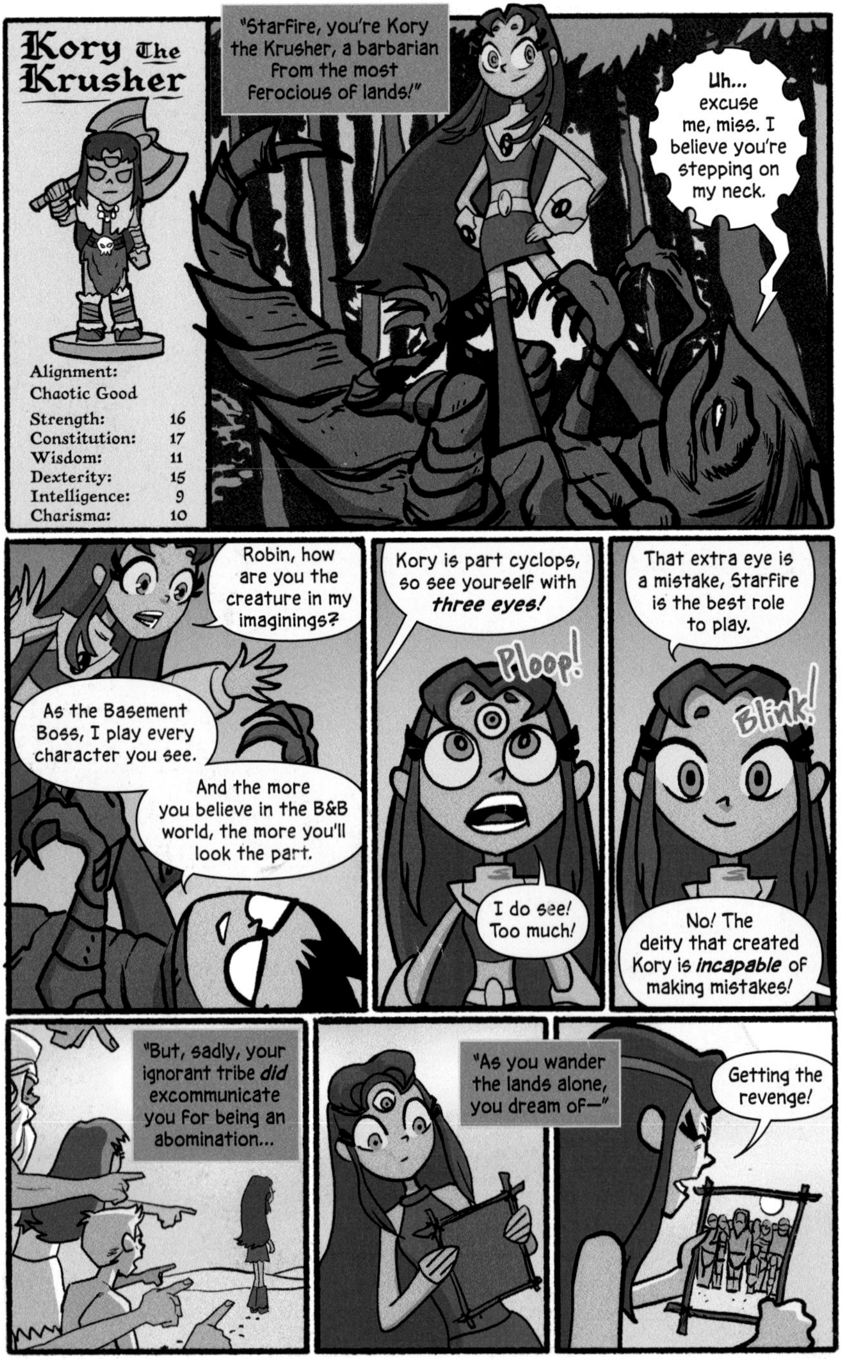
Kory The Krusher
Alignment: Chaotic Good
Strength: 16
Constitution: 17
Wisdom: 11
Dexterity: 15
Intelligence: 9
Charisma: 10
"Starfire, you're Kory the Krusher, a barbarian from the most ferocious of lands!"
Uh... excuse me, miss. I believe you're stepping on my neck.
Robin, how are you the creature in my imaginings?
As the Basement Boss, I play every character you see.
And the more you believe in the B&B world, the more you'll look the part.
Kory is part cyclops, so see yourself with three eyes!
Ploop!
I do see! Too much!
That extra eye is a mistake, Starfire is the best role to play.
Blink!
No! The deity that created Kory is incapable of making mistakes!
"But, sadly, your ignorant tribe did excommunicate you for being an abomination...
"As you wander the lands alone, you dream of—"
Getting the revenge!

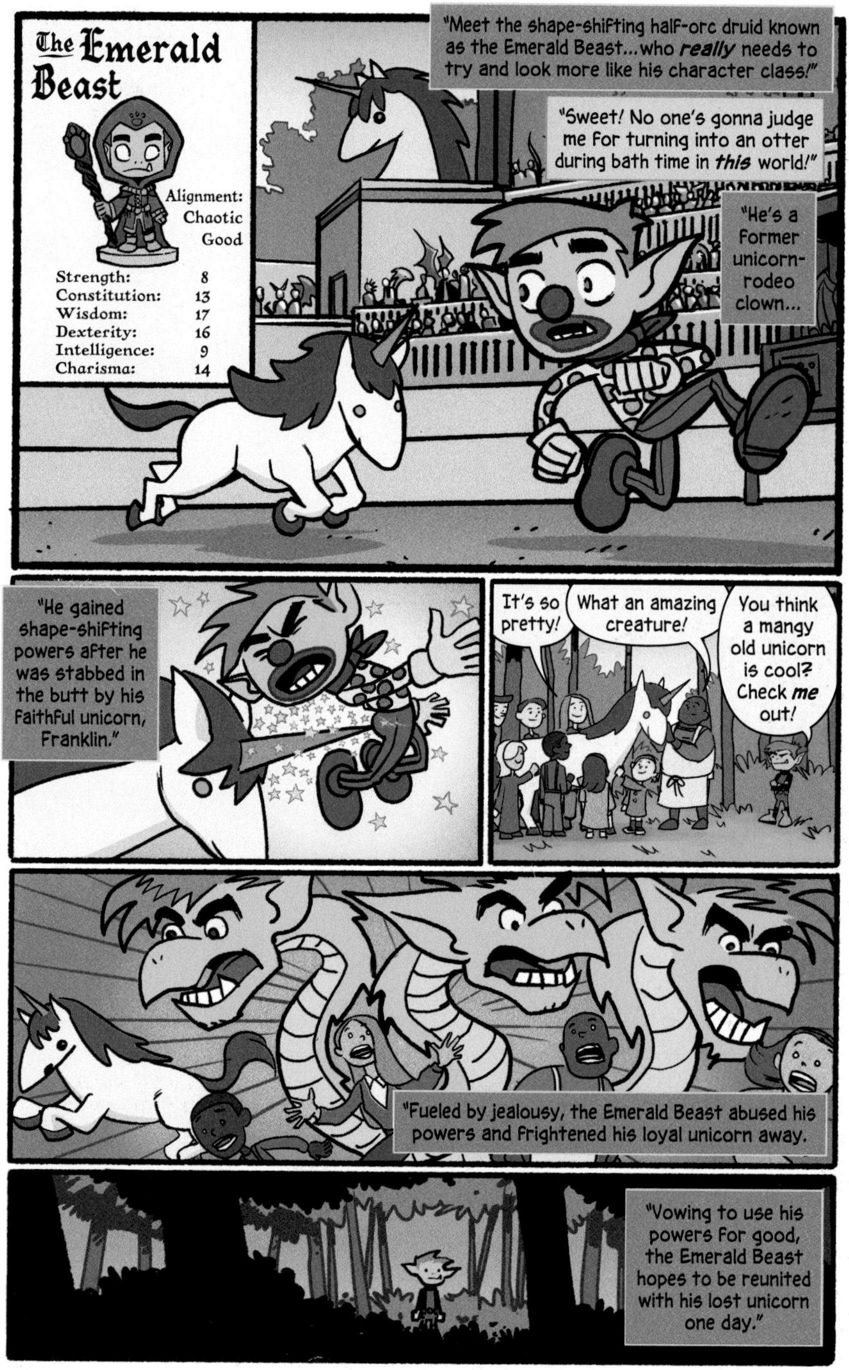
The Emerald Beast
Alignment: Chaotic Good
Strength: 8
Constitution: 13
Wisdom: 17
Dexterity: 16
Intelligence: 9
Charisma: 14
"Meet the shape-shifting half-orc druid known as the Emerald Beast...who *really* needs to try and look more like his character class!"
"Sweet! No one's gonna judge me for turning into an otter during bath time in *this* world!"
"He's a former unicorn-rodeo clown...
"He gained shape-shifting powers after he was stabbed in the butt by his faithful unicorn, Franklin."
It's so pretty!
What an amazing creature!
You think a mangy old unicorn is cool? Check *me* out!
"Fueled by jealousy, the Emerald Beast abused his powers and frightened his loyal unicorn away.
"Vowing to use his powers for good, the Emerald Beast hopes to be reunited with his lost unicorn one day."

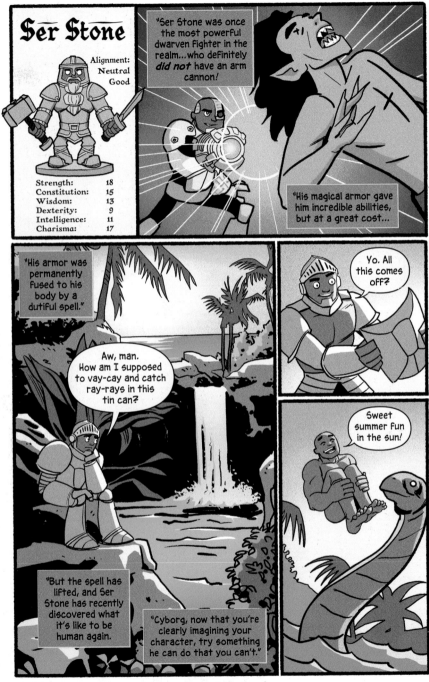

Ser Stone

Alignment: Neutral Good

Strength: 18
Constitution: 15
Wisdom: 13
Dexterity: 9
Intelligence: 11
Charisma: 17

"Ser Stone was once the most powerful dwarven fighter in the realm...who definitely *did not* have an arm cannon!

"His magical armor gave him incredible abilities, but at a great cost...

"His armor was permanently fused to his body by a dutiful spell."

Aw, man. How am I supposed to vay-cay and catch ray-rays in this tin can?

"But the spell has lifted, and Ser Stone has recently discovered what it's like to be human again.

"Cyborg, now that you're clearly imagining your character, try something he can do that you can't."

Yo. All this comes off?

Sweet summer fun in the sun!

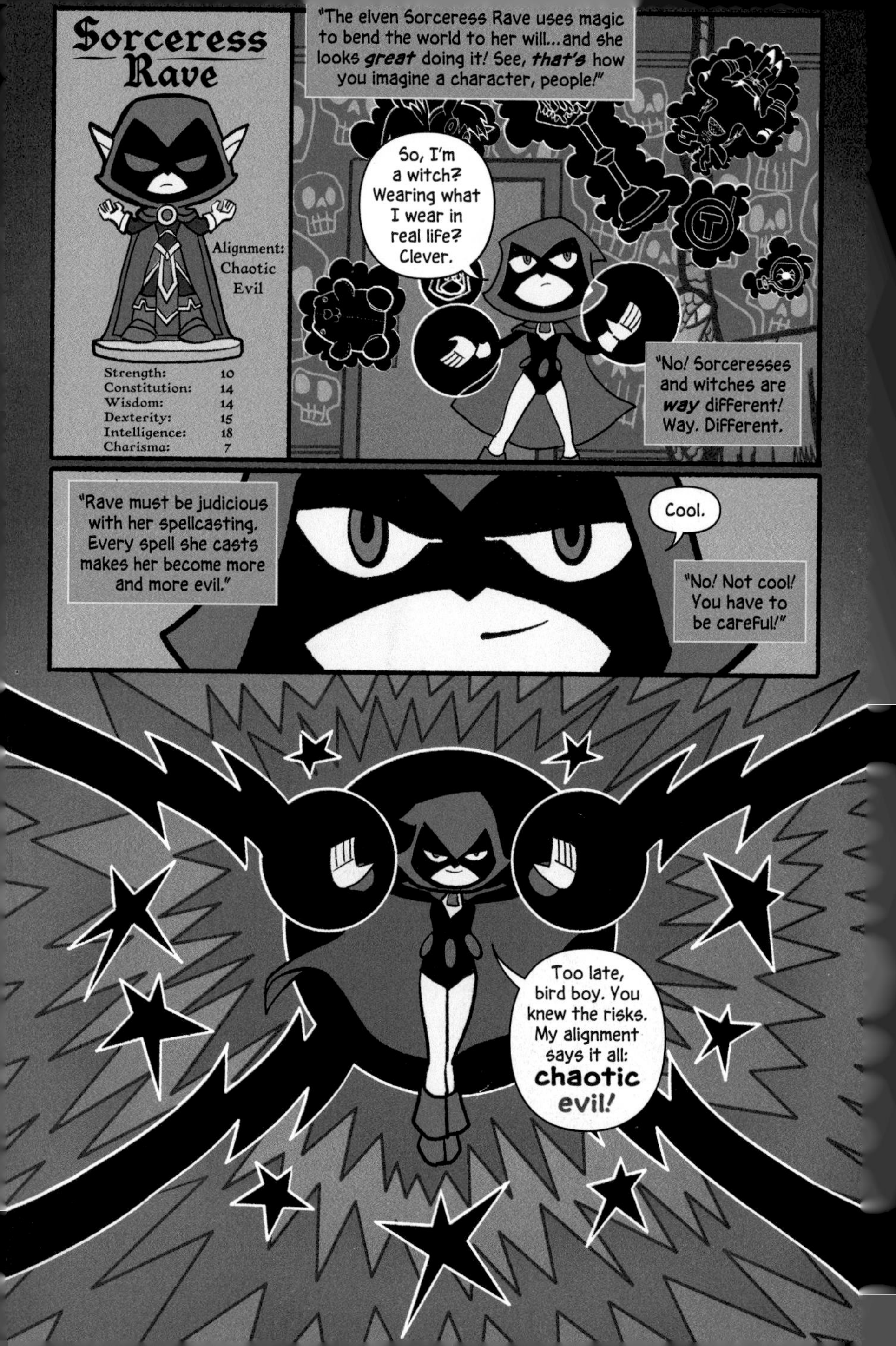

Sorceress Rave
Alignment: Chaotic Evil
Strength: 10
Constitution: 14
Wisdom: 14
Dexterity: 15
Intelligence: 18
Charisma: 7
"The elven Sorceress Rave uses magic to bend the world to her will...and she looks great doing it! See, that's how you imagine a character, people!"
So, I'm a witch? Wearing what I wear in real life? Clever.
"No! Sorceresses and witches are way different! Way. Different.
"Rave must be judicious with her spellcasting. Every spell she casts makes her become more and more evil."
Cool.
"No! Not cool! You have to be careful!"
Too late, bird boy. You knew the risks. My alignment says it all: chaotic evil!

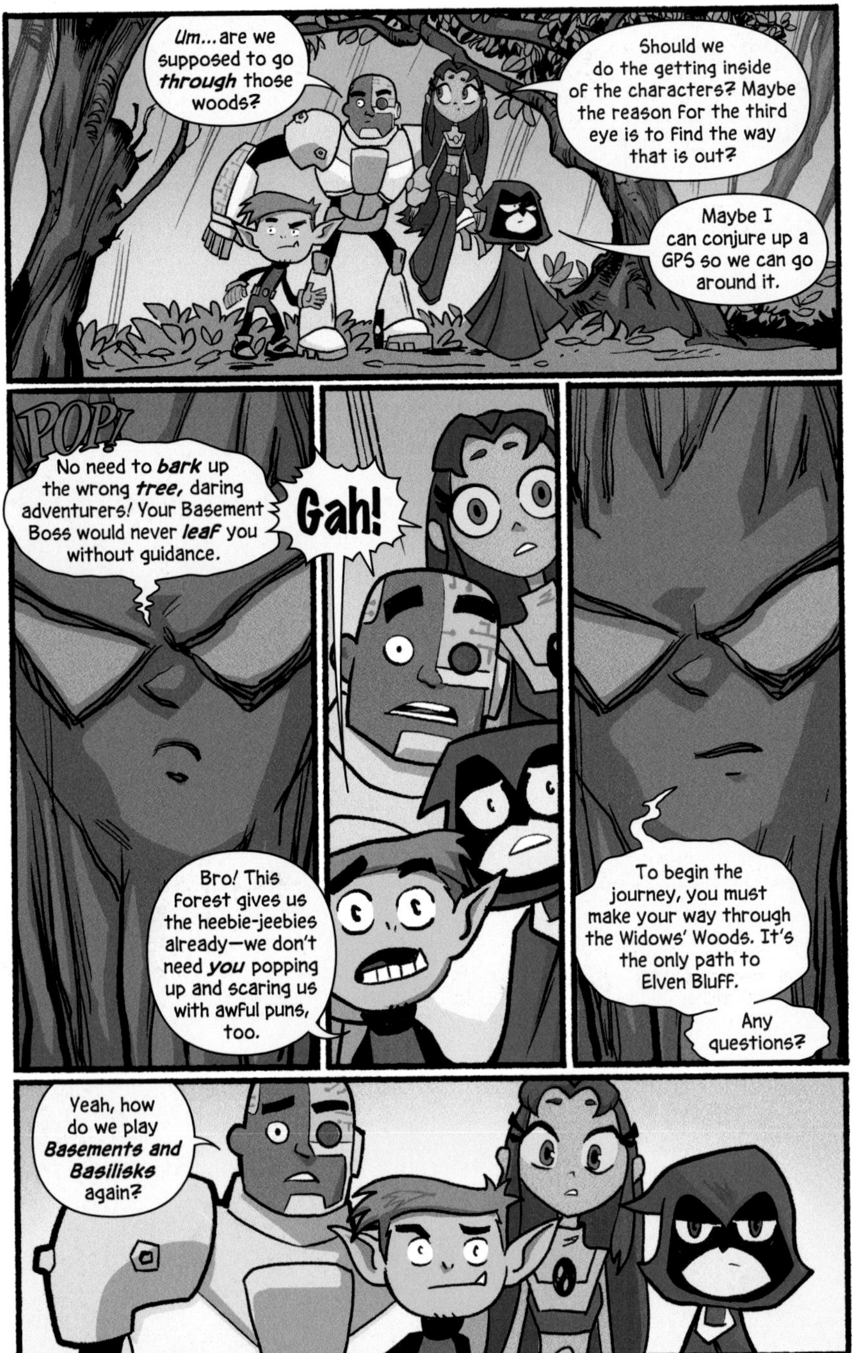

Um... are we supposed to go ***through*** those woods?
Should we do the getting inside of the characters? Maybe the reason for the third eye is to find the way that is out?
Maybe I can conjure up a GPS so we can go around it.
POP!
No need to ***bark*** up the wrong ***tree,*** daring adventurers! Your Basement Boss would never ***leaf*** you without guidance.
Gah!
Bro! This forest gives us the heebie-jeebies already—we don't need ***you*** popping up and scaring us with awful puns, too.
To begin the journey, you must make your way through the Widows' Woods. It's the only path to Elven Bluff.
Any questions?
Yeah, how do we play ***Basements and Basilisks*** again?

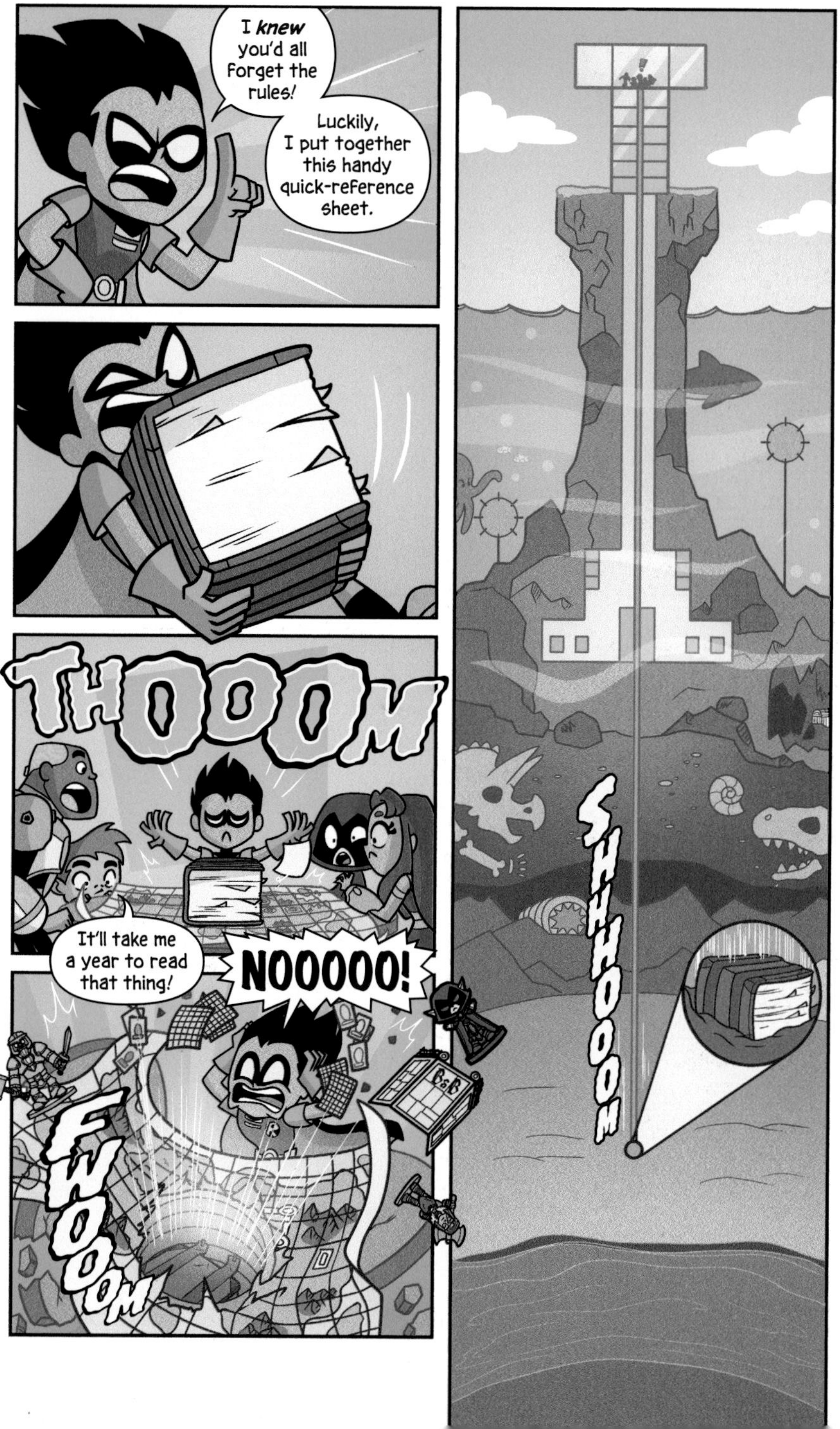
I *knew* you'd all forget the rules!
Luckily, I put together this handy quick-reference sheet.
THOOOM
It'll take me a year to read that thing!
NOOOOO!
FWOOOOM
SHHHOOOOM

Chapter Two

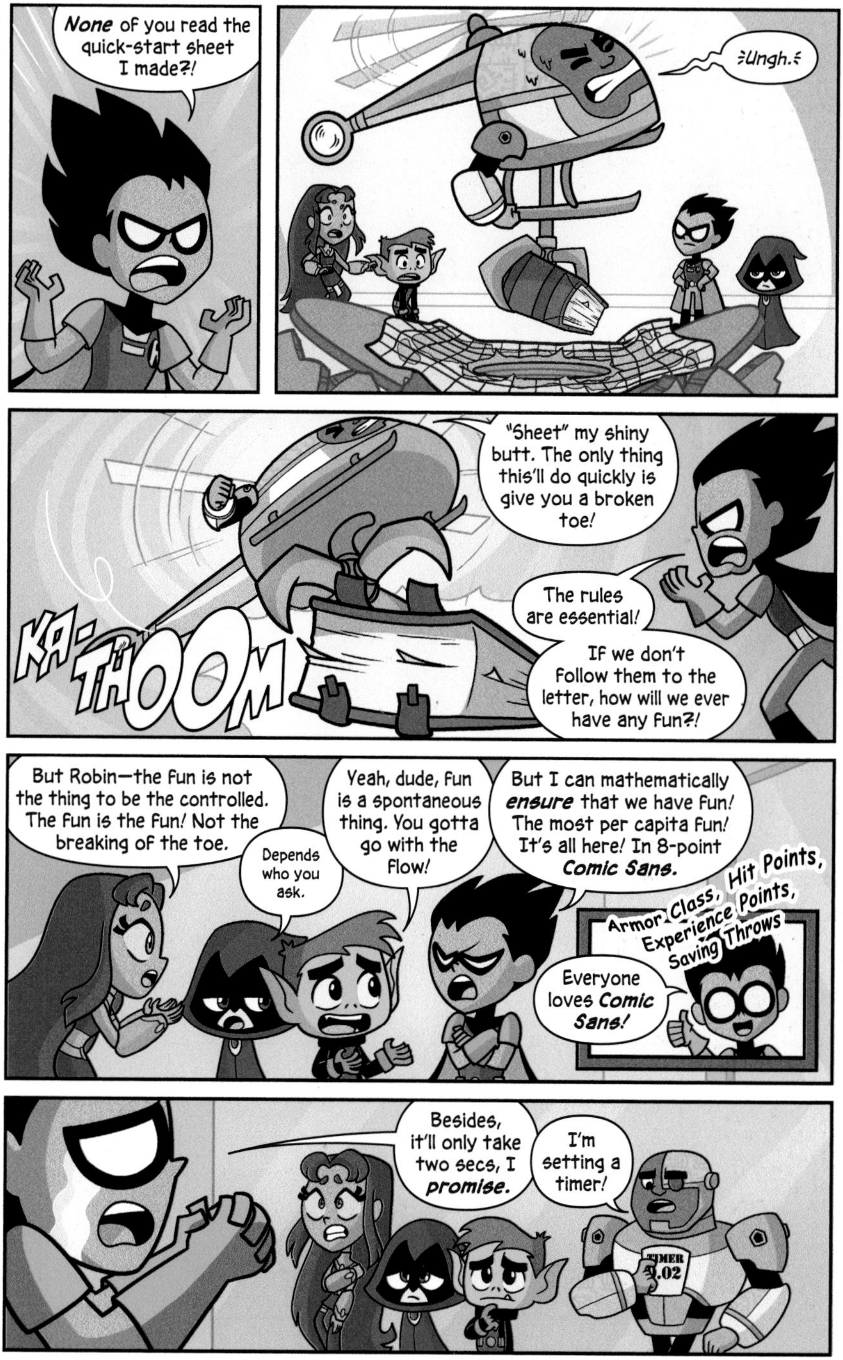
None of you read the quick-start sheet I made?!
Ungh.
"Sheet" my shiny butt. The only thing this'll do quickly is give you a broken toe!
KA-THOOM
The rules are essential!
If we don't follow them to the letter, how will we ever have any fun?!
But Robin—the fun is not the thing to be the controlled. The fun is the fun! Not the breaking of the toe.
Depends who you ask.
Yeah, dude, fun is a spontaneous thing. You gotta go with the flow!
But I can mathematically ensure that we have fun! The most per capita fun! It's all here! In 8-point Comic Sans.
Armor Class, Hit Points, Experience Points, Saving Throws
Everyone loves Comic Sans!
Besides, it'll only take two secs, I promise.
I'm setting a timer!
TIMER

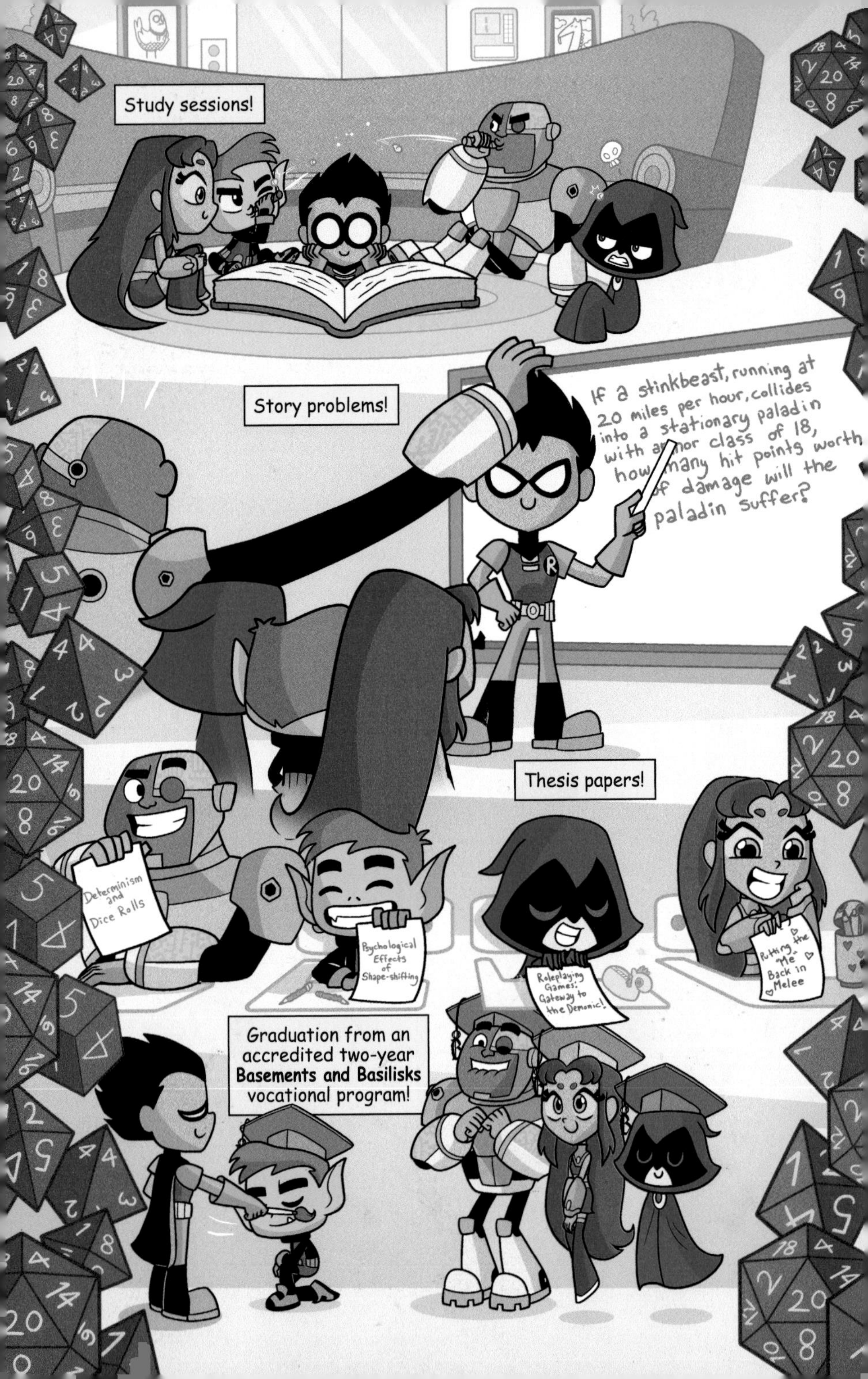

Study sessions!
Story problems!
If a stinkbeast, running at 20 miles per hour, collides into a stationary paladin with armor class of 18, how many hit points worth of damage will the paladin suffer?
Thesis papers!
Determinism and Dice Rolls
Psychological Effects of Shape-shifting
Roleplaying Games: Gateway to the Demonic!
Putting the "Me" Back in Melee
Graduation from an accredited two-year **Basements and Basilisks** vocational program!

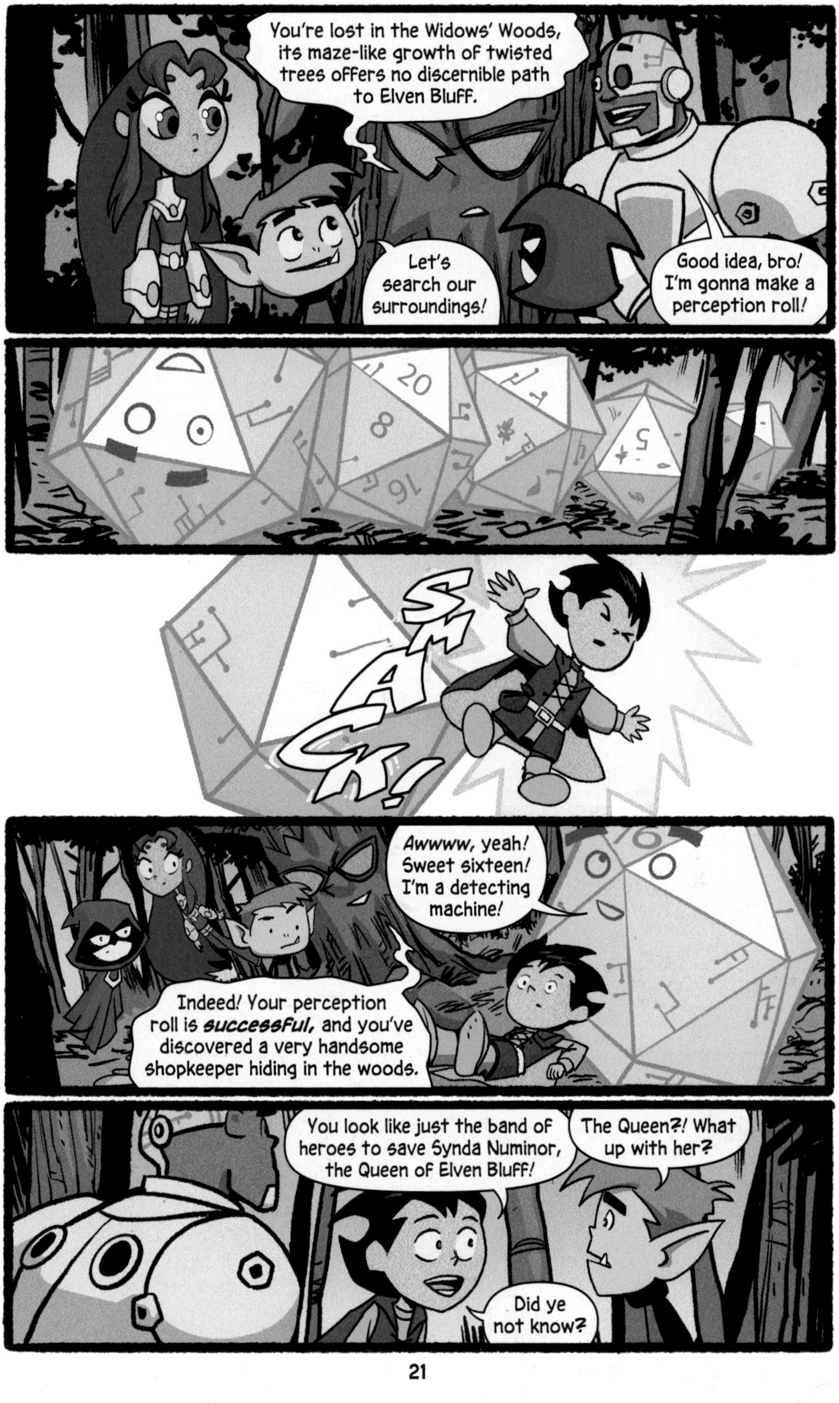
You're lost in the Widows' Woods, its maze-like growth of twisted trees offers no discernible path to Elven Bluff.
Let's search our surroundings!
Good idea, bro! I'm gonna make a perception roll!
SMACK!
Awwww, yeah! Sweet sixteen! I'm a detecting machine!
Indeed! Your perception roll is *successful,* and you've discovered a very handsome shopkeeper hiding in the woods.
You look like just the band of heroes to save Synda Numinor, the Queen of Elven Bluff!
The Queen?! What up with her?
Did ye not know?

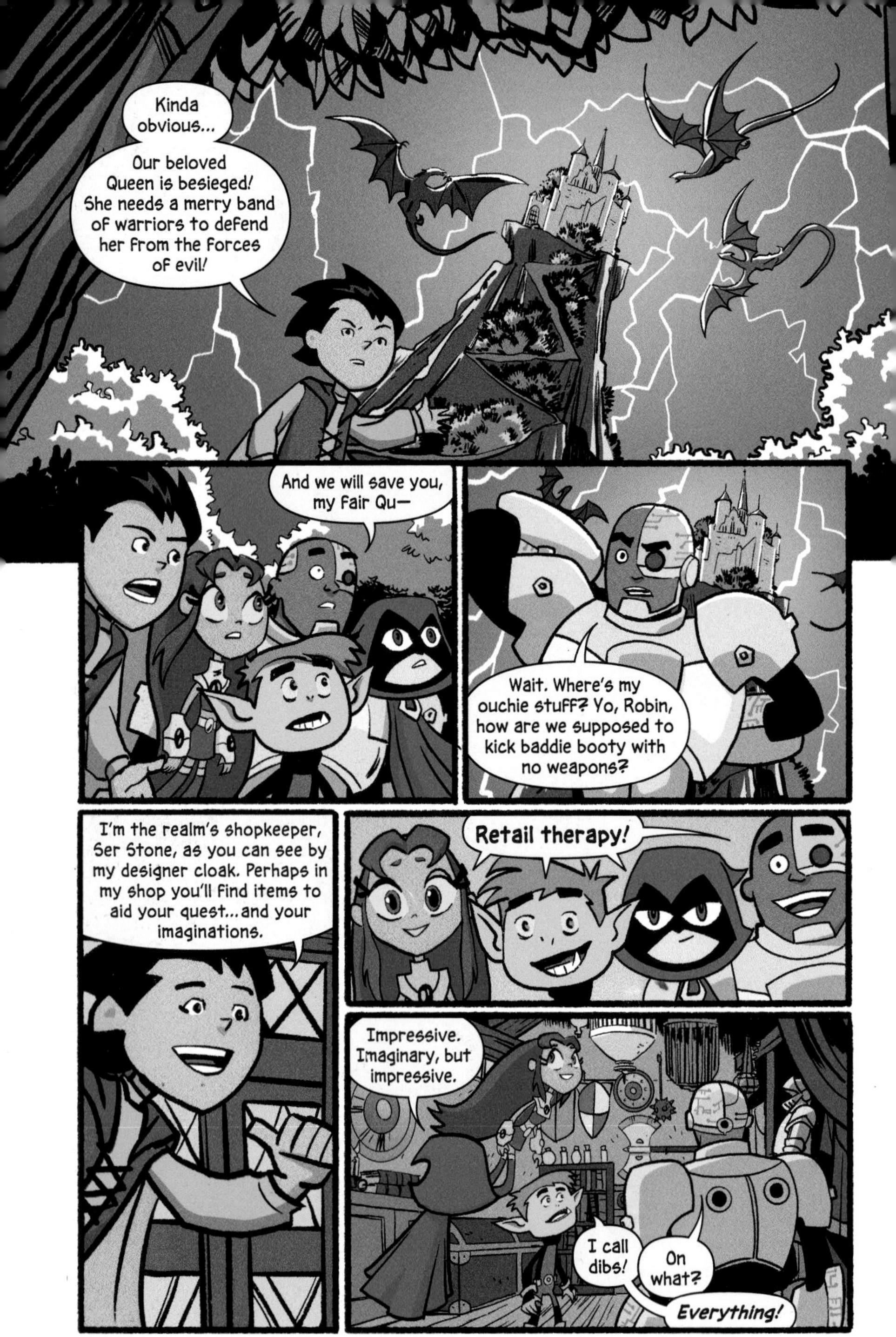
Kinda obvious...
Our beloved Queen is besieged! She needs a merry band of warriors to defend her from the forces of evil!
And we will save you, my fair Qu—
Wait. Where's my ouchie stuff? Yo, Robin, how are we supposed to kick baddie booty with no weapons?
I'm the realm's shopkeeper, Ser Stone, as you can see by my designer cloak. Perhaps in my shop you'll find items to aid your quest...and your imaginations.
Retail therapy!
Impressive. Imaginary, but impressive.
I call dibs!
On what?
Everything!

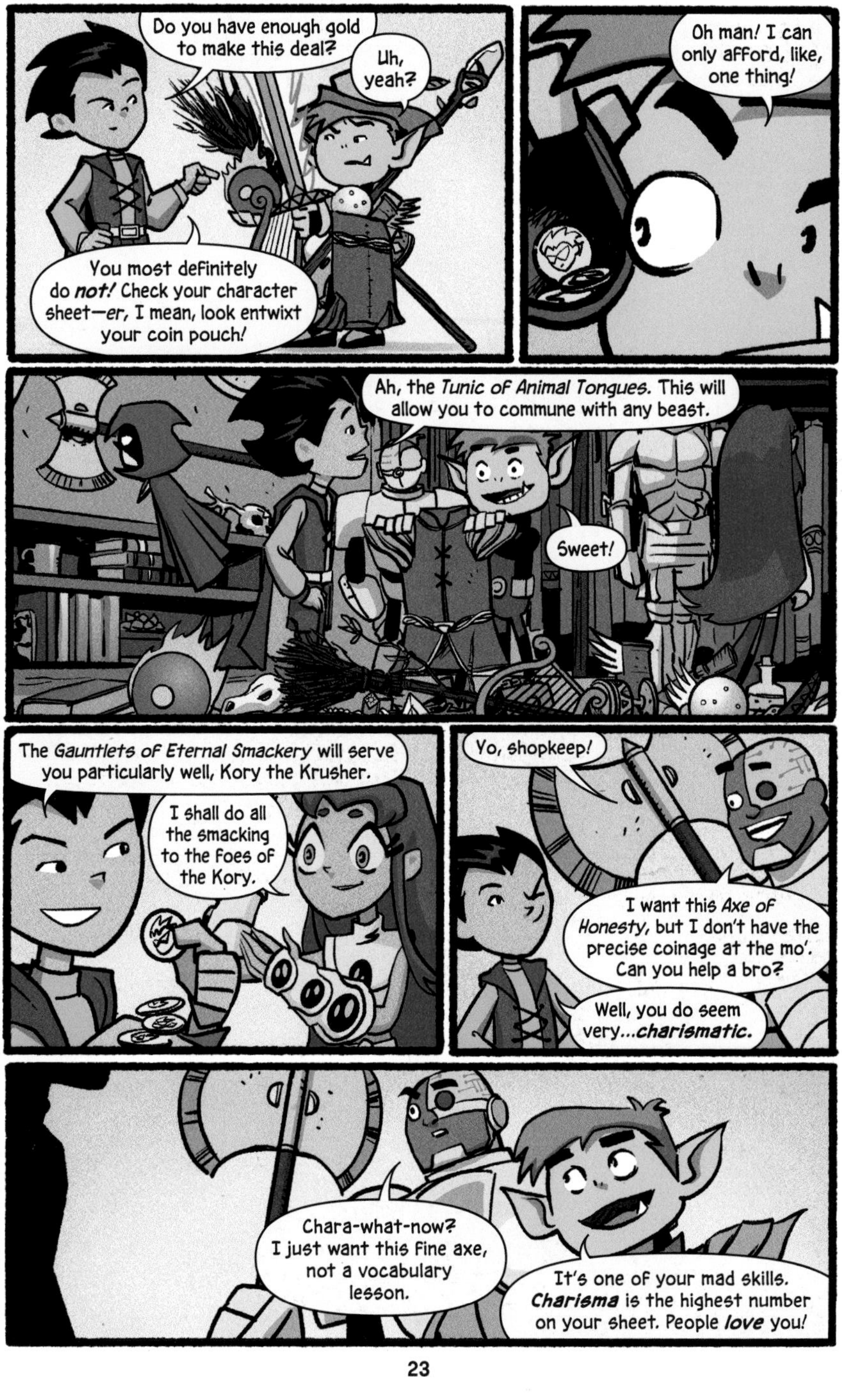

Do you have enough gold to make this deal?
Uh, yeah?
You most definitely do *not!* Check your character sheet—*er,* I mean, look entwixt your coin pouch!
Oh man! I can only afford, like, one thing!
Ah, the *Tunic of Animal Tongues.* This will allow you to commune with any beast.
Sweet!
The *Gauntlets of Eternal Smackery* will serve you particularly well, Kory the Krusher.
I shall do all the smacking to the foes of the Kory.
Yo, shopkeep!
I want this *Axe of Honesty,* but I don't have the precise coinage at the mo'. Can you help a bro?
Well, you do seem very...***charismatic.***
Chara-what-now? I just want this fine axe, not a vocabulary lesson.
It's one of your mad skills. ***Charisma*** is the highest number on your sheet. People ***love*** you!

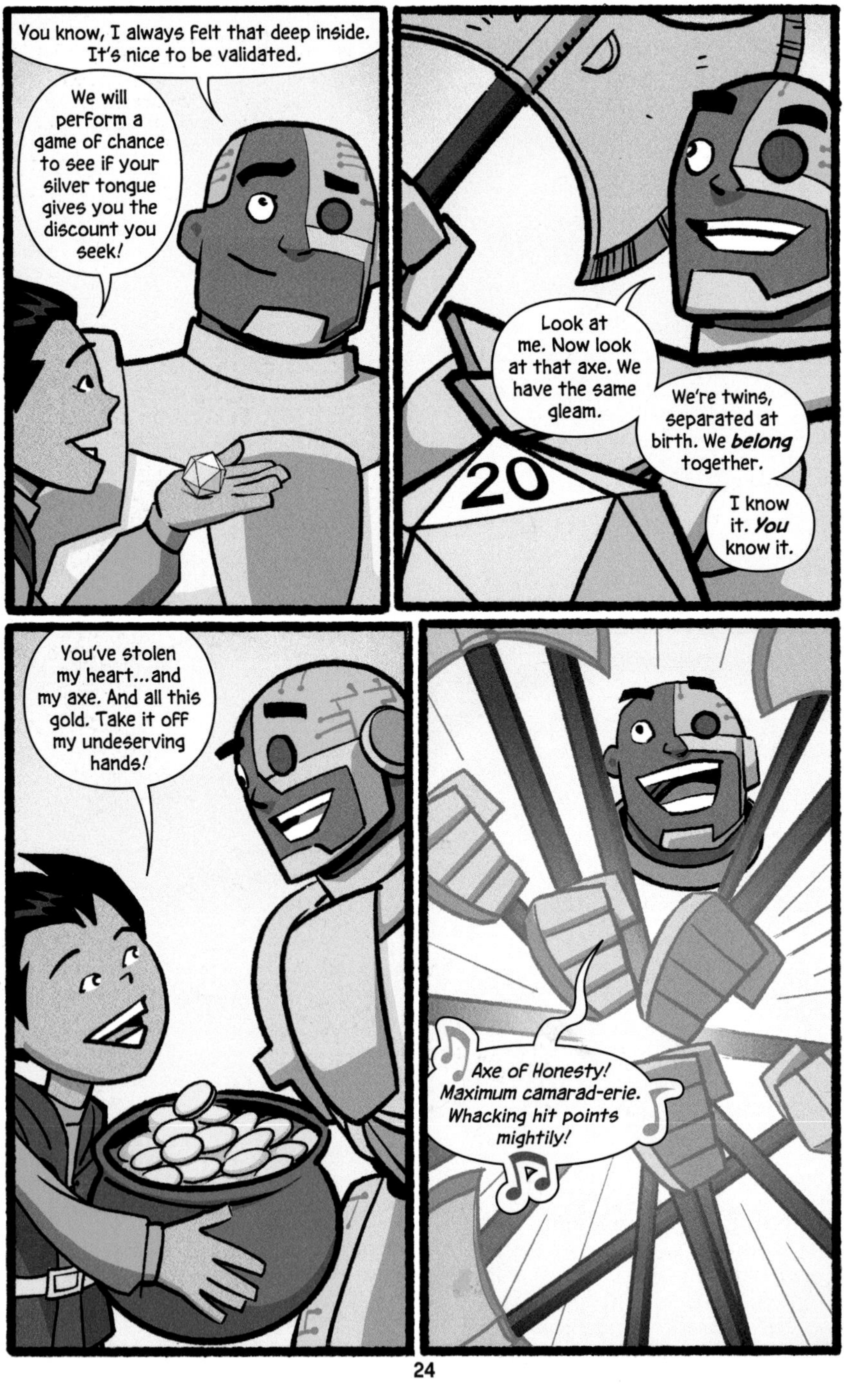
You know, I always felt that deep inside. It's nice to be validated.
We will perform a game of chance to see if your silver tongue gives you the discount you seek!
Look at me. Now look at that axe. We have the same gleam.
20
We're twins, separated at birth. We *belong* together.
I know it. *You* know it.
You've stolen my heart...and my axe. And all this gold. Take it off my undeserving hands!
Axe of Honesty! Maximum camarad-erie. Whacking hit points mightily!

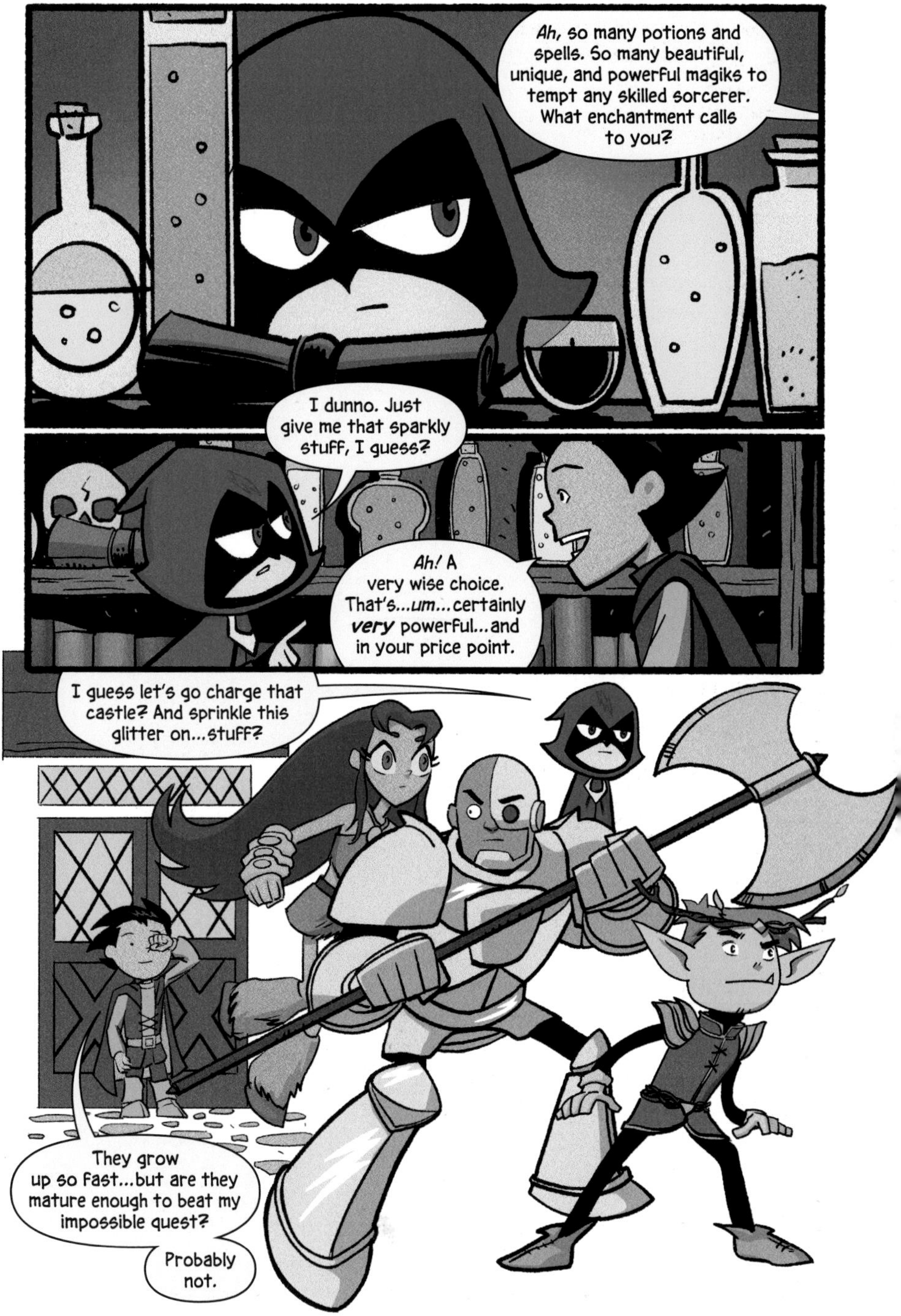
Ah, so many potions and spells. So many beautiful, unique, and powerful magiks to tempt any skilled sorcerer. What enchantment calls to you?
I dunno. Just give me that sparkly stuff, I guess?
Ah! A very wise choice. That's...*um*...certainly ***very*** powerful...and in your price point.
I guess let's go charge that castle? And sprinkle this glitter on...stuff?
They grow up so fast...but are they mature enough to beat my impossible quest?
Probably not.

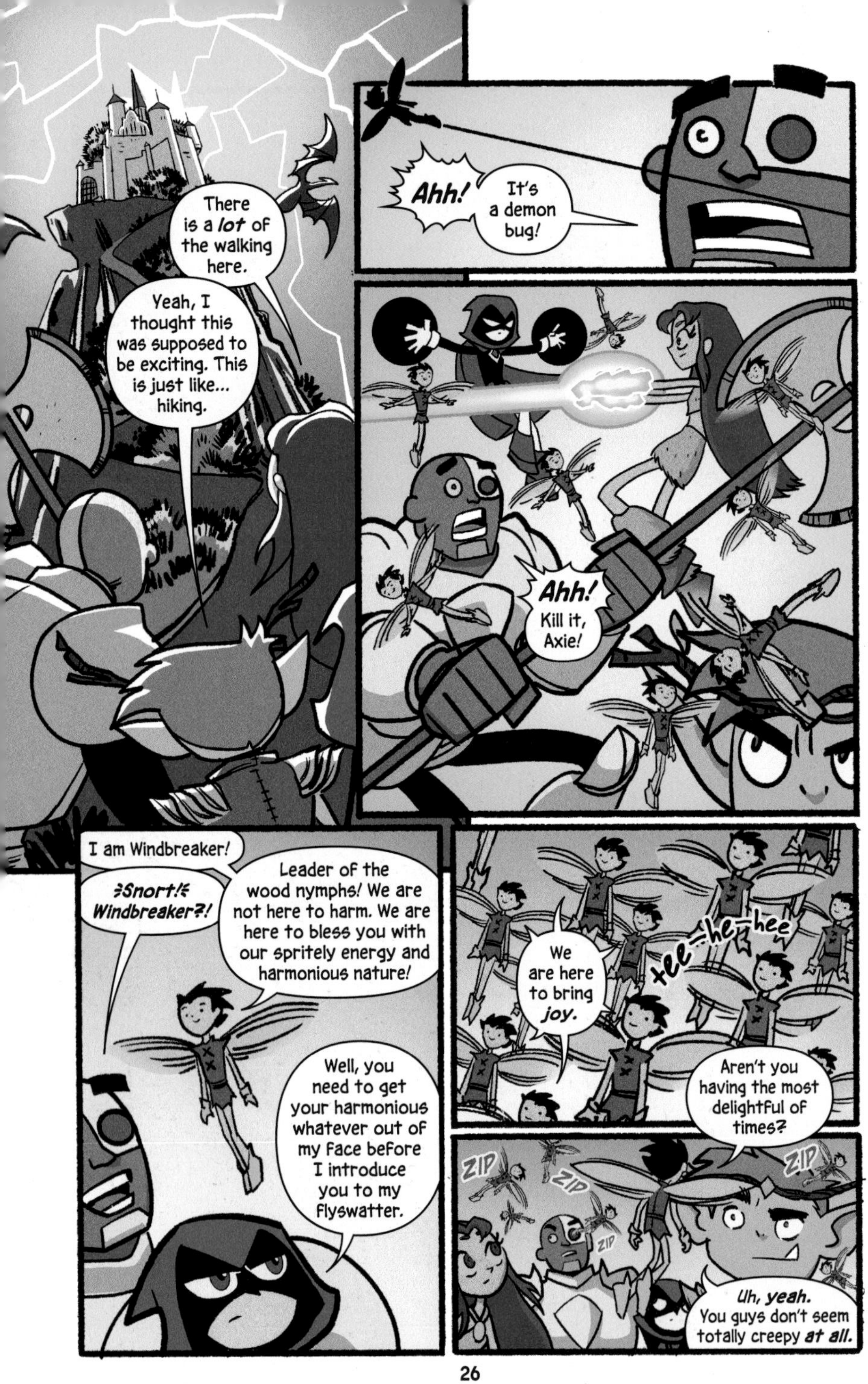
There is a *lot* of the walking here.
Yeah, I thought this was supposed to be exciting. This is just like... hiking.
Ahh!
It's a demon bug!
Ahh! Kill it, Axie!
I am Windbreaker!
Snort! Windbreaker?!
Leader of the wood nymphs! We are not here to harm. We are here to bless you with our spritely energy and harmonious nature!
Well, you need to get your harmonious whatever out of my face before I introduce you to my flyswatter.
We are here to bring *joy.*
tee-hee-hee
Aren't you having the most delightful of times?
ZIP
ZIP
ZIP
ZIP
Uh, yeah. You guys don't seem totally creepy *at all.*

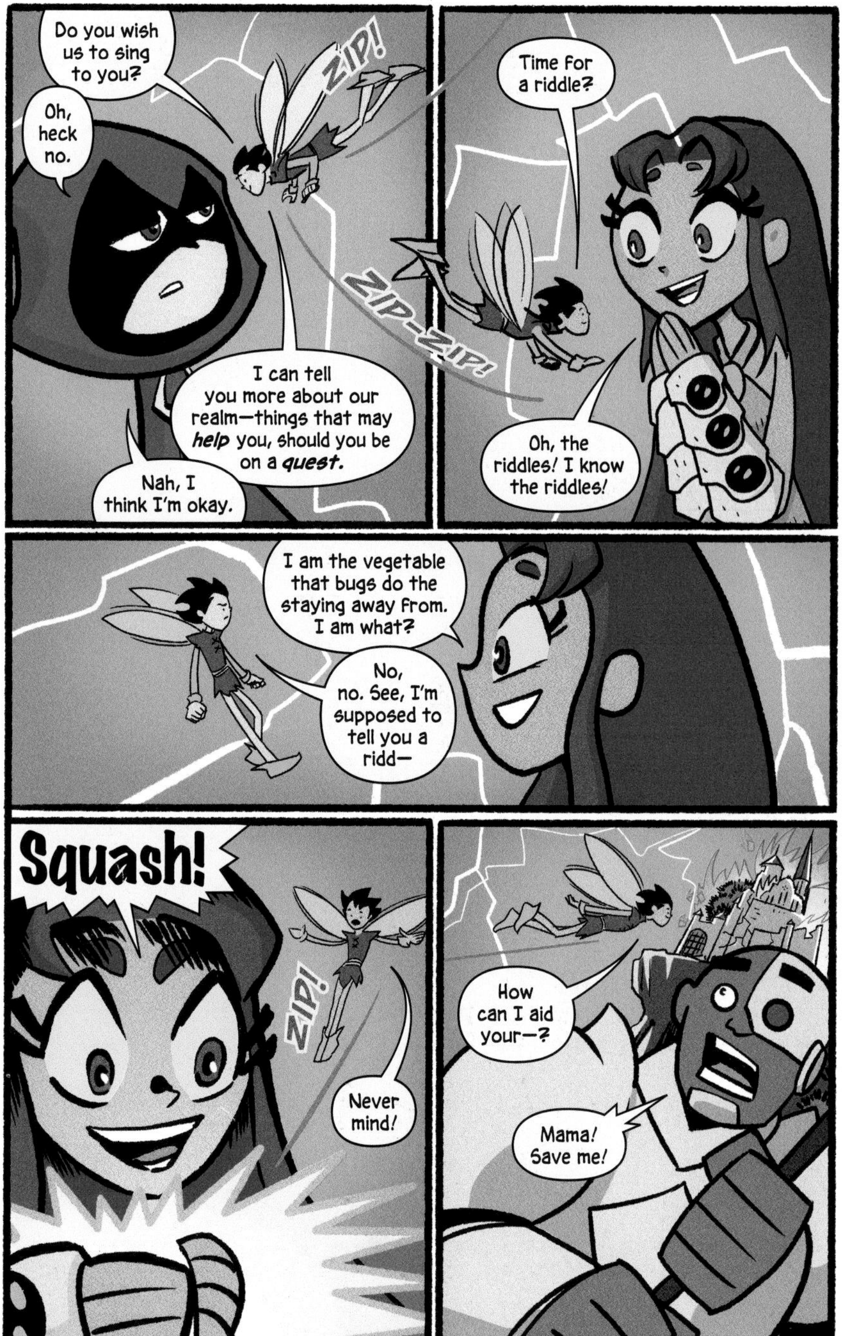

Do you wish us to sing to you?
ZIP!
Oh, heck no.
I can tell you more about our realm—things that may *help* you, should you be on a *quest*.
Nah, I think I'm okay.
Time for a riddle?
ZIP-ZIP!
Oh, the riddles! I know the riddles!
I am the vegetable that bugs do the staying away from. I am what?
No, no. See, I'm supposed to tell you a ridd—
Squash!
ZIP!
Never mind!
How can I aid your—?
Mama! Save me!

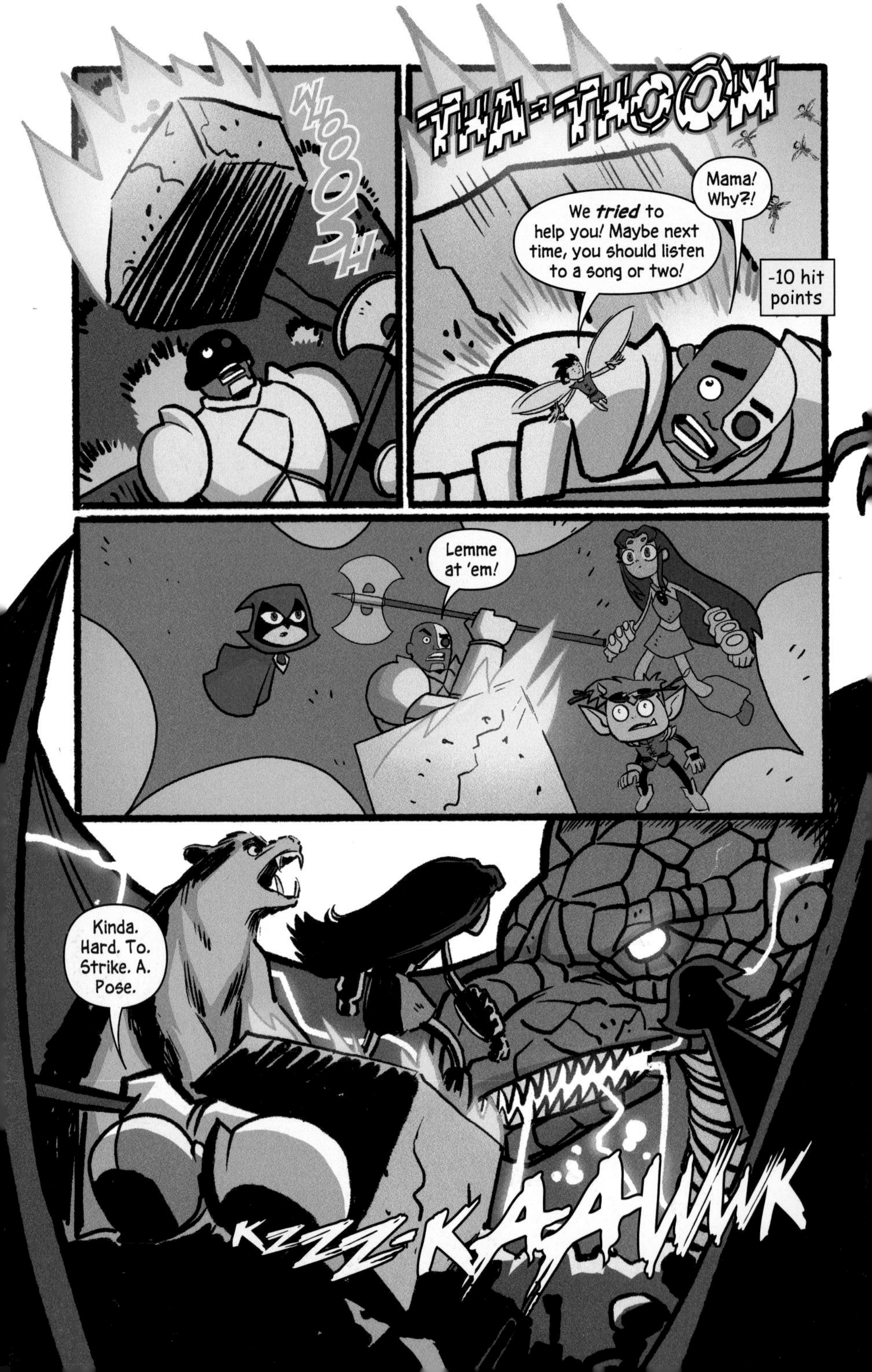
WHOOOMH
THA-THOOM
Mama! Why?!
We tried to help you! Maybe next time, you should listen to a song or two!
-10 hit points
Lemme at 'em!
Kinda. Hard. To. Strike. A. Pose.
KZZZZ-KAAWWK

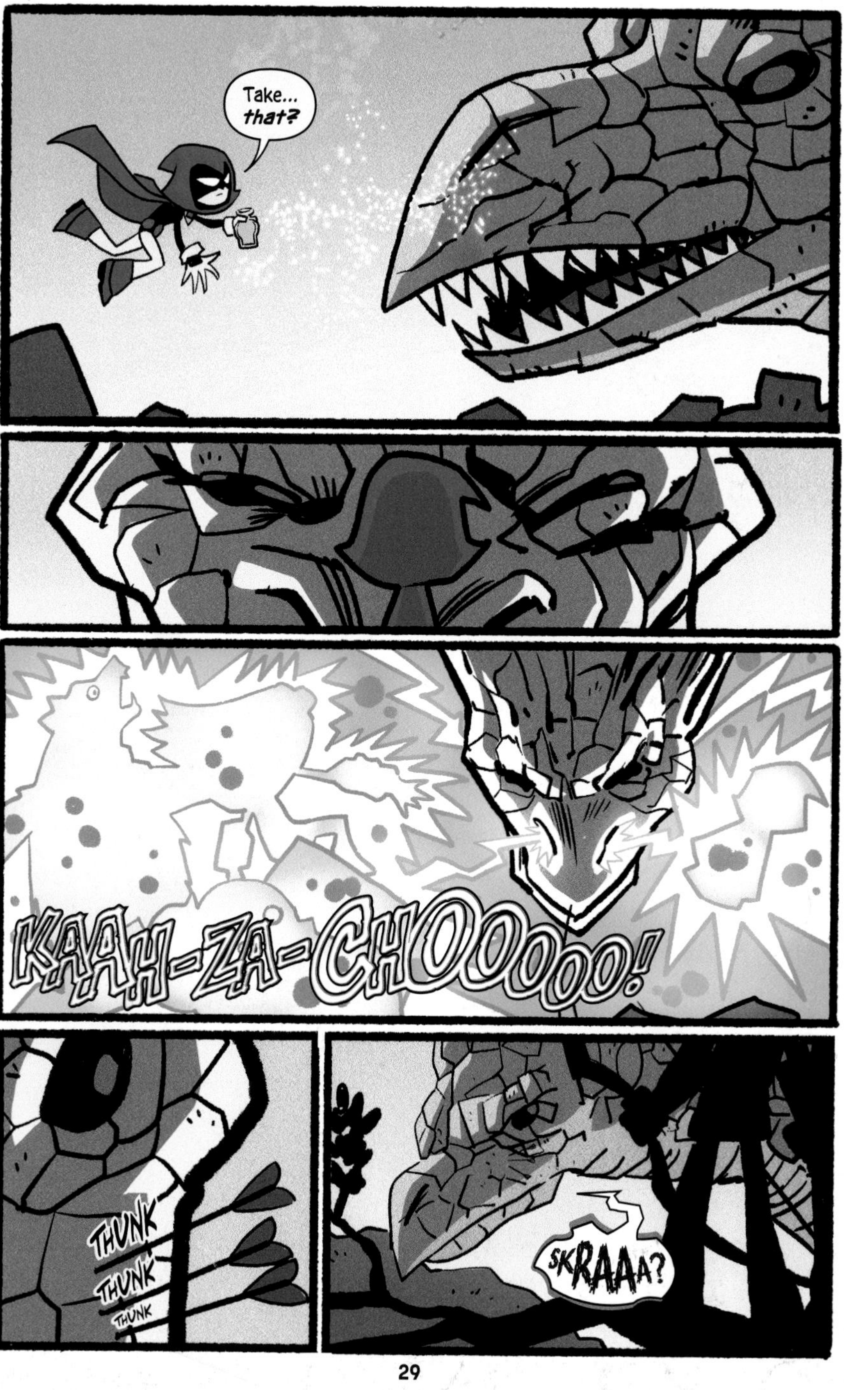

Take... *that?*
KAAH-ZA-CHOOOOOO!
THUNK
THUNK
THUNK
SKRAAAA?

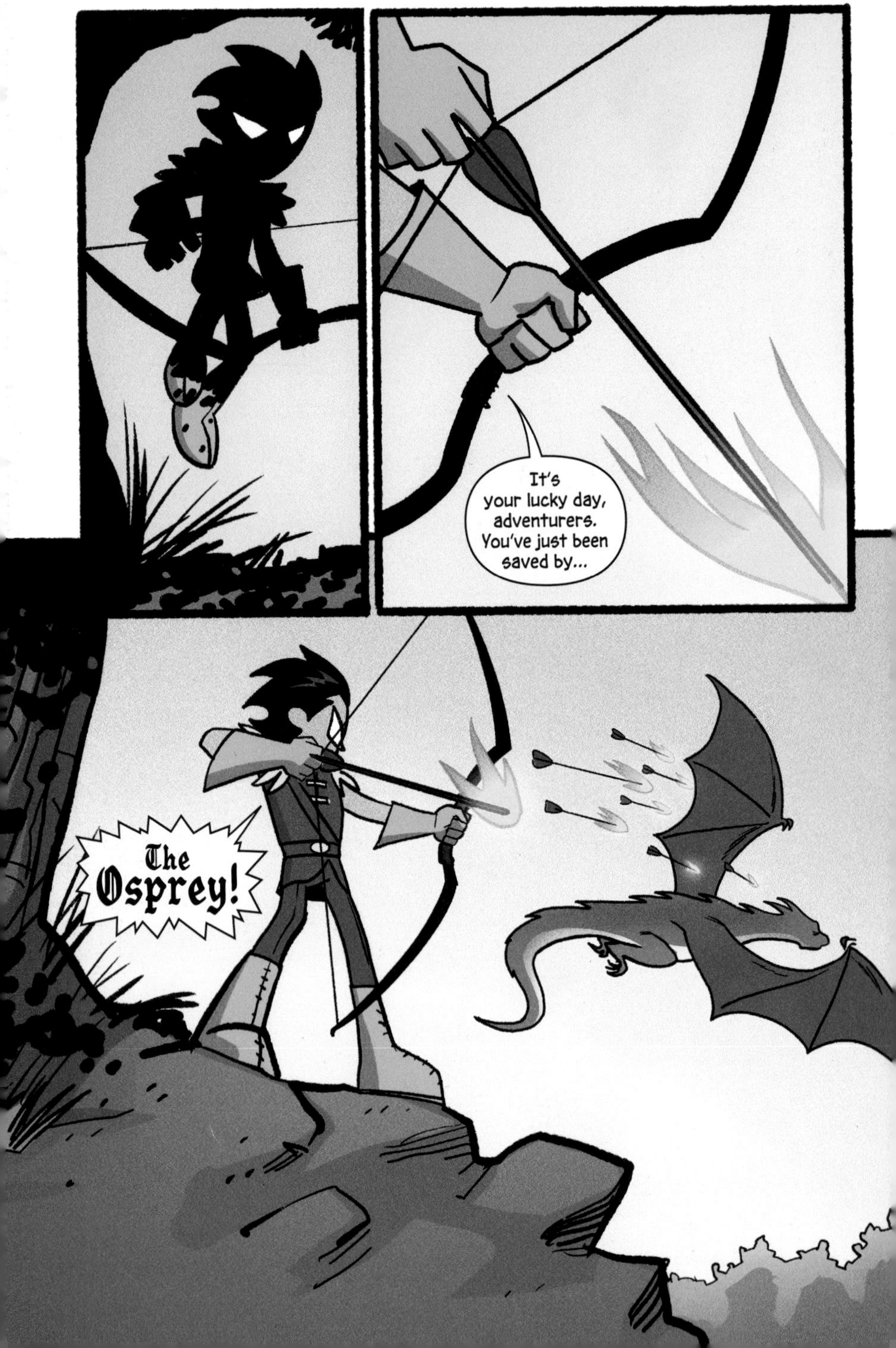
It's your lucky day, adventurers. You've just been saved by...
The Osprey!

Chapter Three

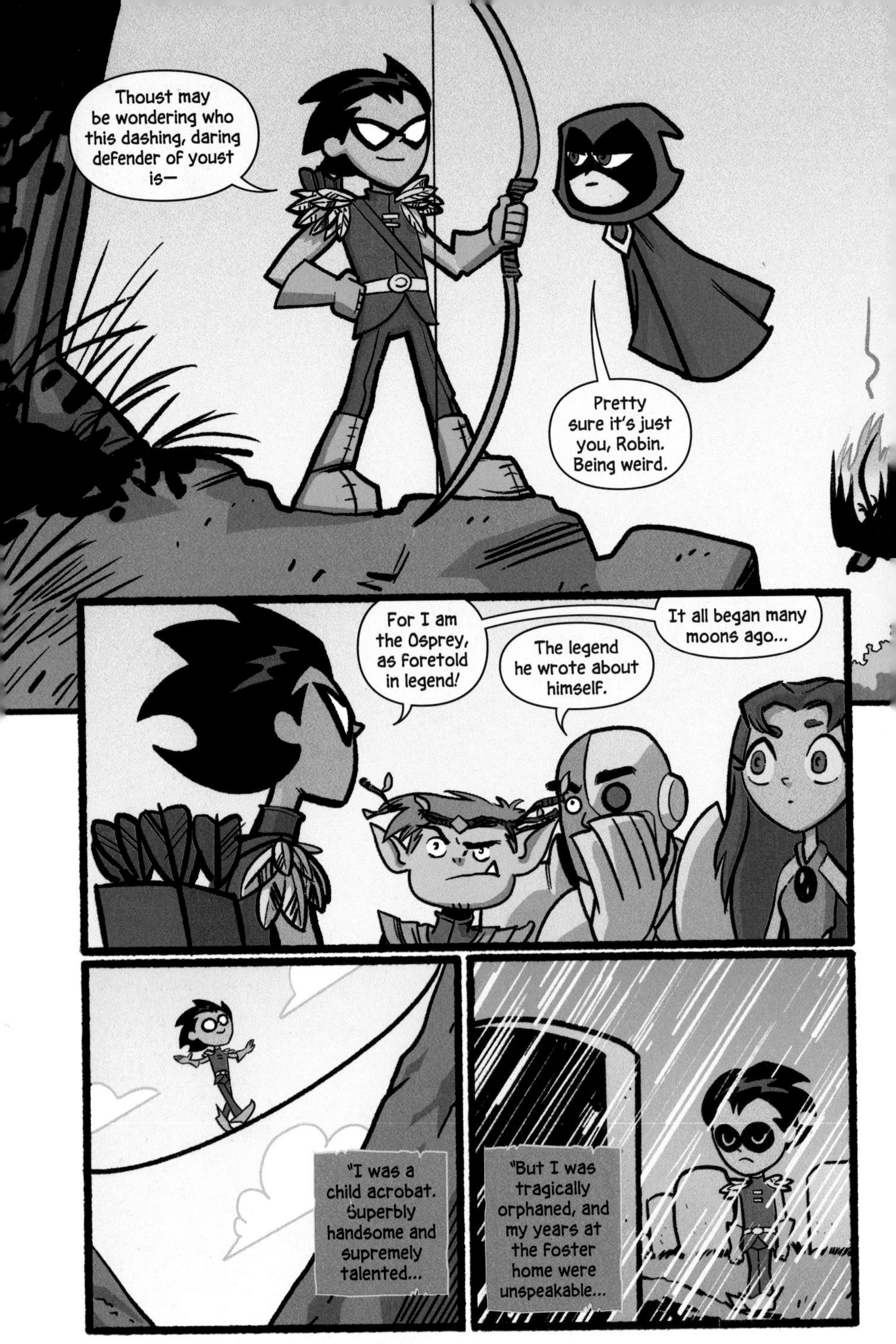
Thoust may be wondering who this dashing, daring defender of youst is—
Pretty sure it's just you, Robin. Being weird.
For I am the Osprey, as foretold in legend!
The legend he wrote about himself.
It all began many moons ago...
"I was a child acrobat. Superbly handsome and supremely talented...
"But I was tragically orphaned, and my years at the foster home were unspeakable...

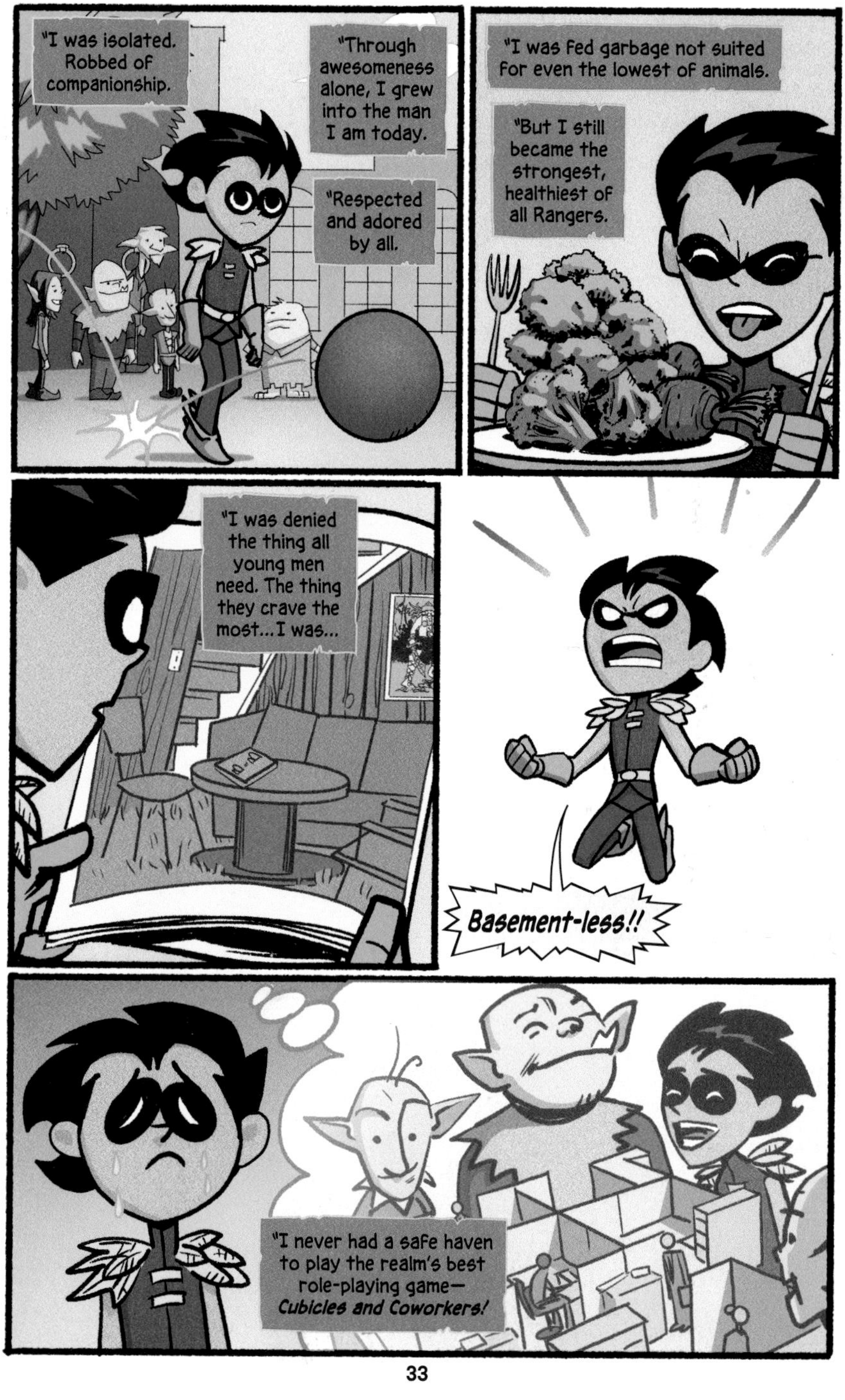
"I was isolated. Robbed of companionship.
"Through awesomeness alone, I grew into the man I am today.
"Respected and adored by all.
"I was fed garbage not suited for even the lowest of animals.
"But I still became the strongest, healthiest of all Rangers.
"I was denied the thing all young men need. The thing they crave the most...I was...
Basement-less!!
"I never had a safe haven to play the realm's best role-playing game—*Cubicles and Coworkers!*

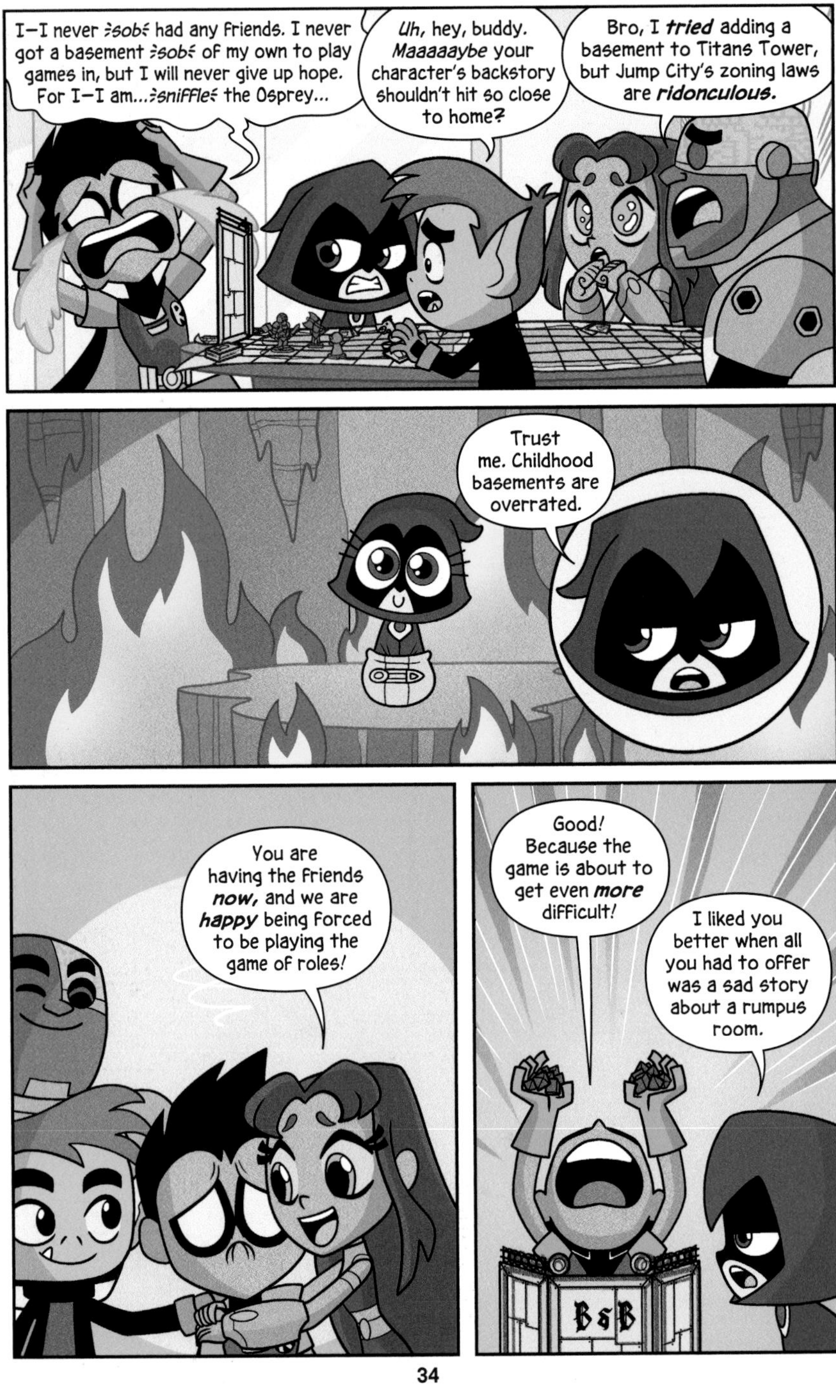

I—I never ⸮sob⸮ had any friends. I never got a basement ⸮sob⸮ of my own to play games in, but I will never give up hope. For I—I am...⸮sniffle⸮ the Osprey...
Uh, hey, buddy. Maaaaaybe your character's backstory shouldn't hit so close to home?
Bro, I tried adding a basement to Titans Tower, but Jump City's zoning laws are ridonculous.
Trust me. Childhood basements are overrated.
You are having the friends now, and we are happy being forced to be playing the game of roles!
Good! Because the game is about to get even more difficult!
I liked you better when all you had to offer was a sad story about a rumpus room.
B&B

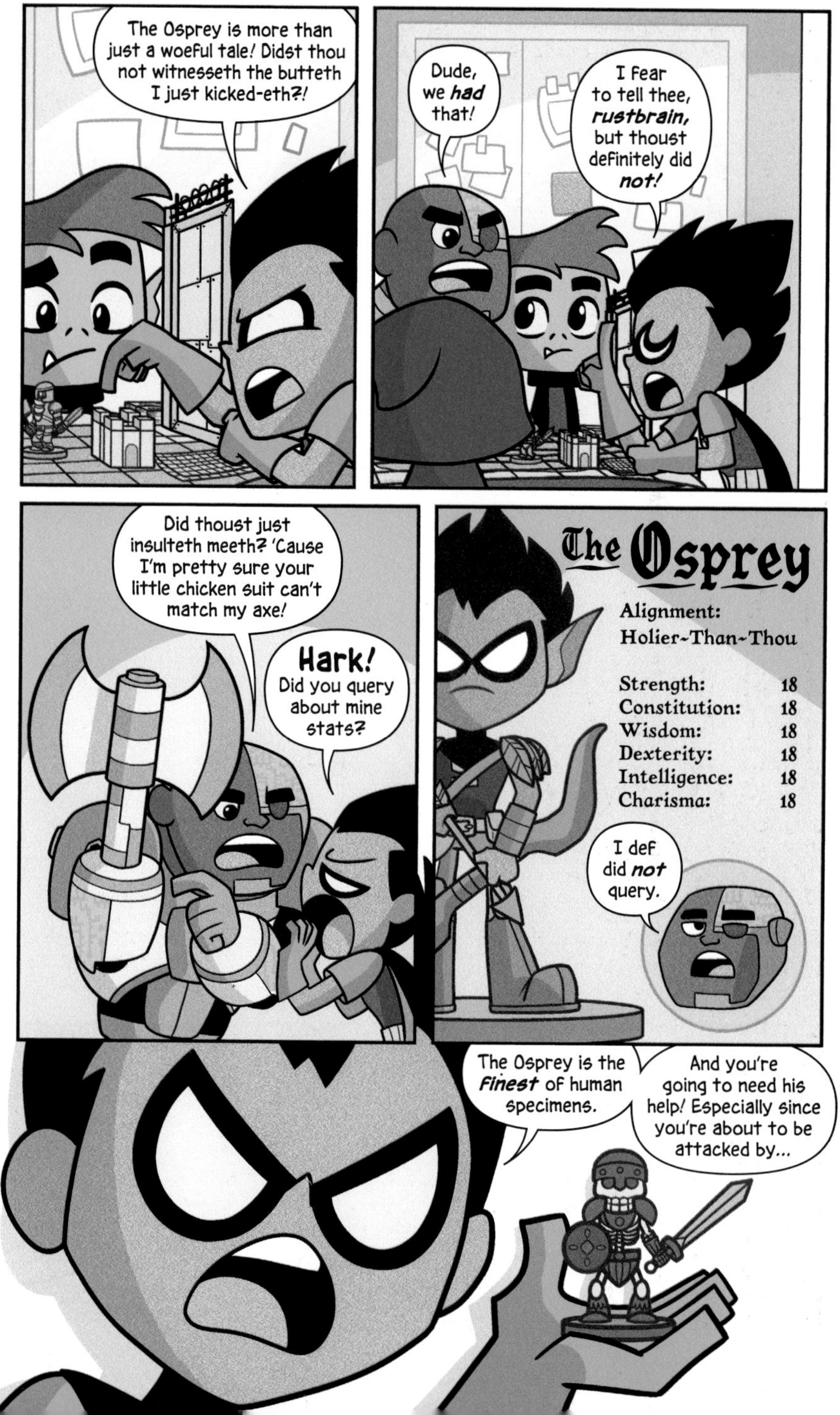

The Osprey is more than just a woeful tale! Didst thou not witnesseth the butteth I just kicked-eth?!
Dude, we *had* that!
I fear to tell thee, ***rustbrain,*** but thoust definitely did ***not!***
Did thoust just insulteth meeth? 'Cause I'm pretty sure your little chicken suit can't match my axe!
Hark! Did you query about mine stats?
The Osprey
Alignment: Holier-Than-Thou
Strength: 18
Constitution: 18
Wisdom: 18
Dexterity: 18
Intelligence: 18
Charisma: 18
I def did ***not*** query.
The Osprey is the ***finest*** of human specimens.
And you're going to need his help! Especially since you're about to be attacked by...

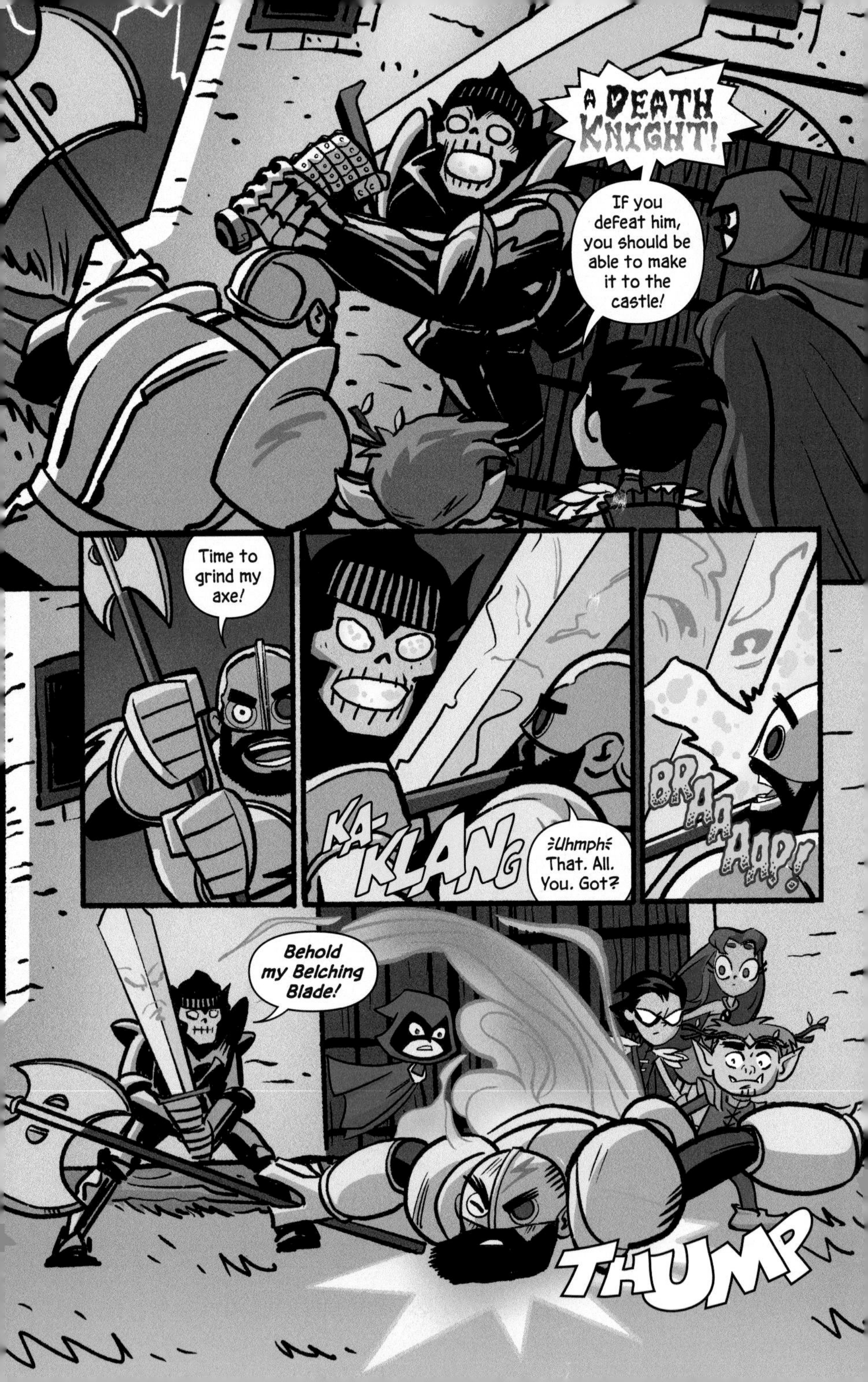
A DEATH KNIGHT!
If you defeat him, you should be able to make it to the castle!
Time to grind my axe!
KA-KLANG
Uhmph That. All. You. Got?
BRAAAAP!
Behold my Belching Blade!
THUMP

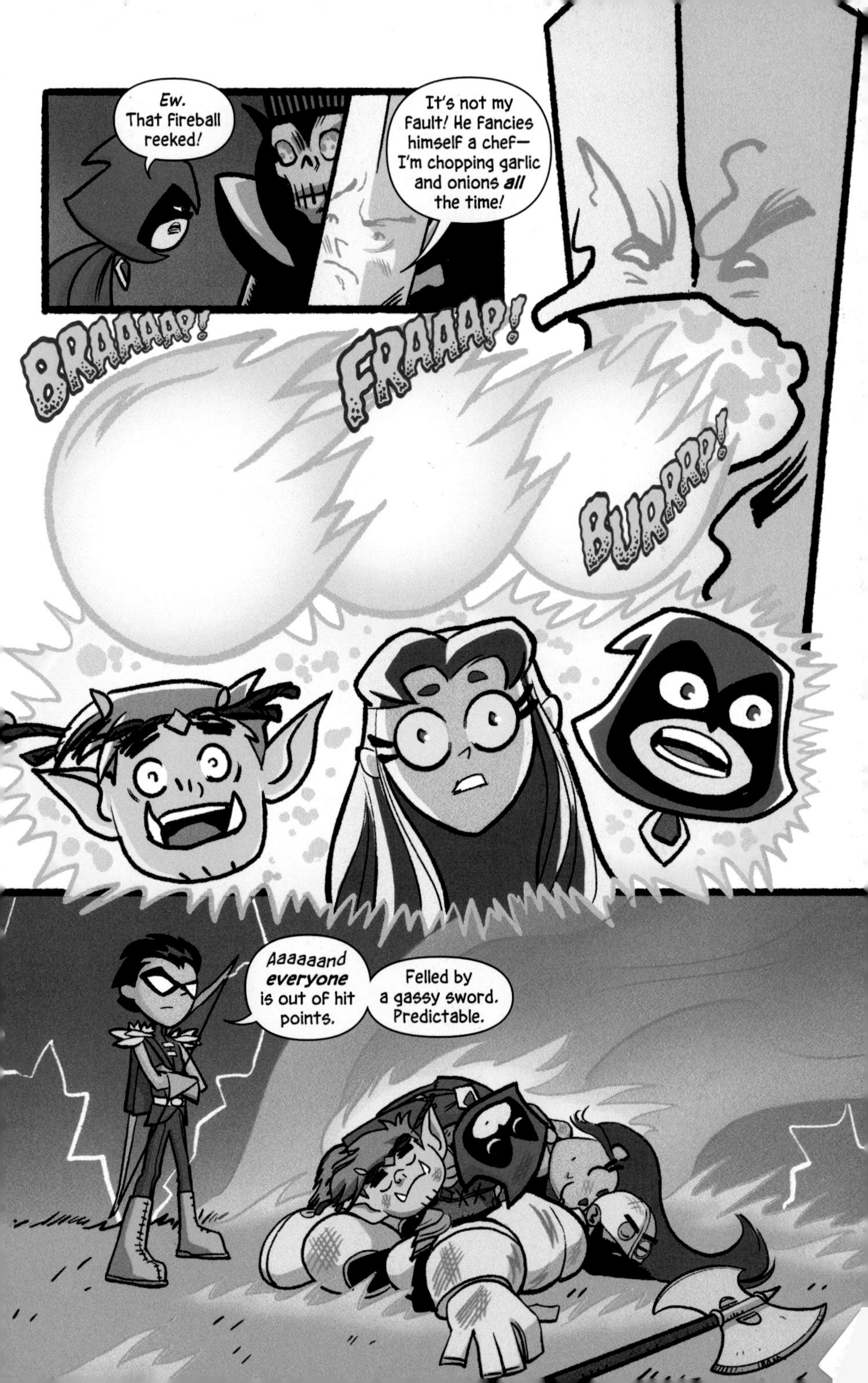
Ew. That fireball reeked!
It's not my fault! He fancies himself a chef— I'm chopping garlic and onions *all* the time!
BRAAAAAP!
FRAAAP!
BURRRP!
Aaaaaand *everyone* is out of hit points.
Felled by a gassy sword. Predictable.

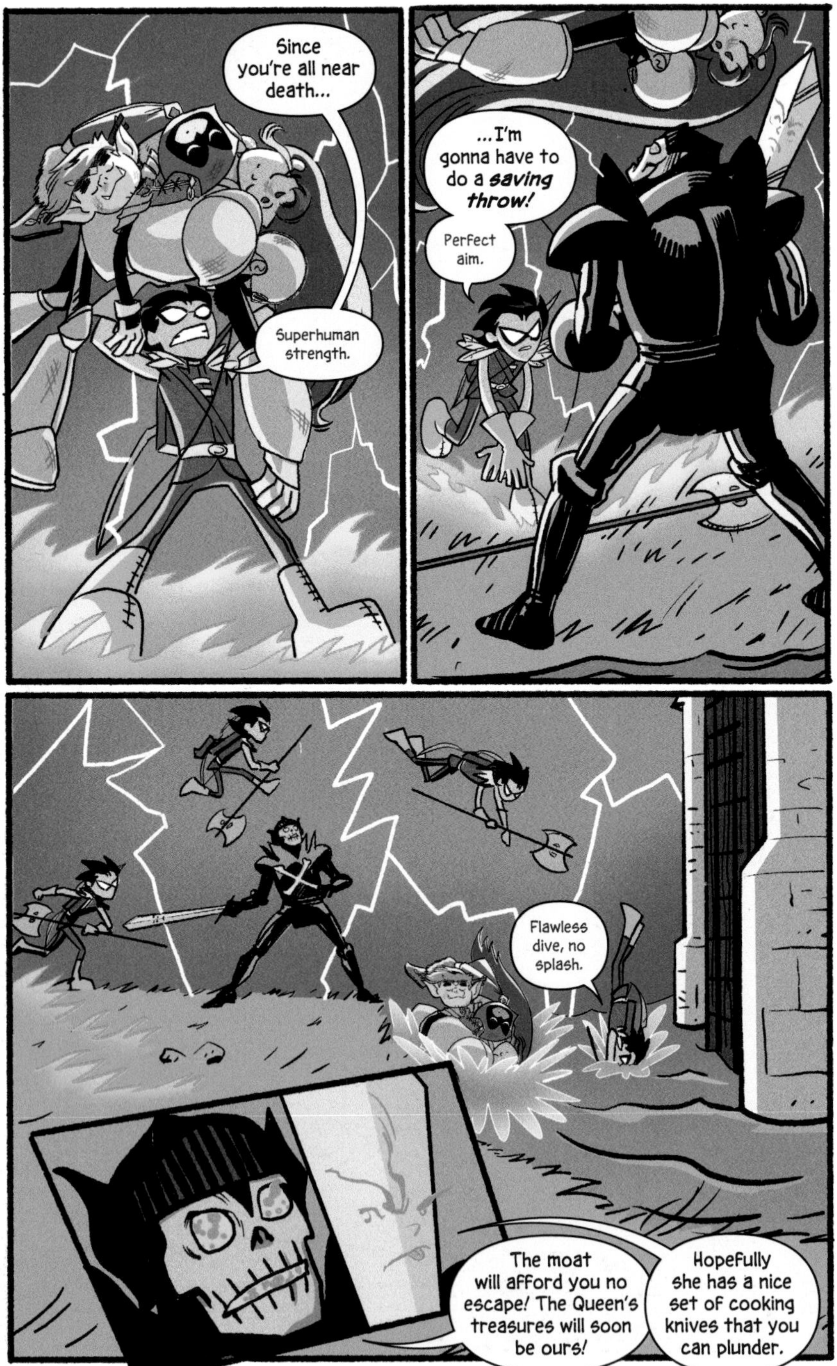
Since you're all near death...
Superhuman strength.
...I'm gonna have to do a *saving throw!*
Perfect aim.
Flawless dive, no splash.
The moat will afford you no escape! The Queen's treasures will soon be ours!
Hopefully she has a nice set of cooking knives that you can plunder.

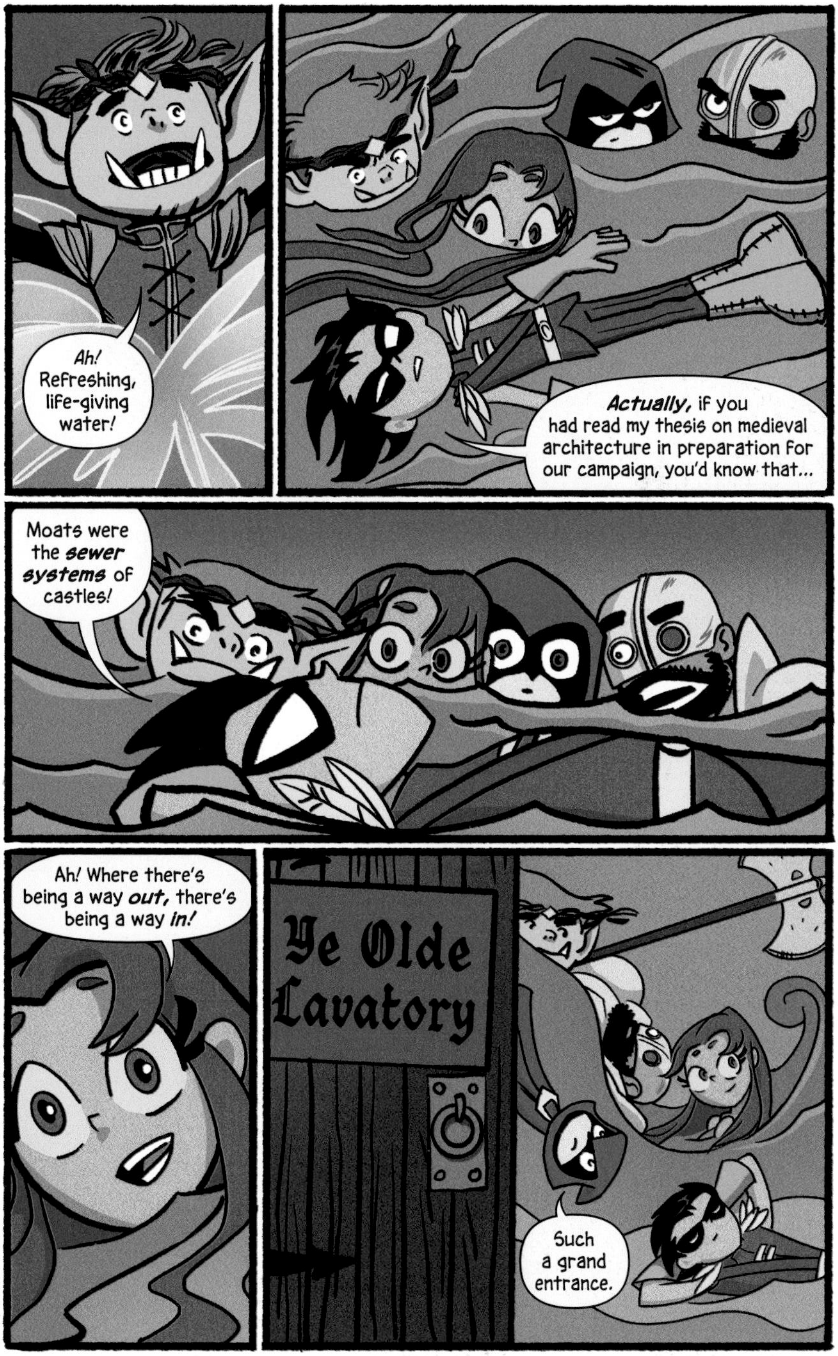
Ah! Refreshing, life-giving water!
Actually, if you had read my thesis on medieval architecture in preparation for our campaign, you'd know that...
Moats were the sewer systems of castles!
Ah! Where there's being a way out, there's being a way in!
Ye Olde Lavatory
Such a grand entrance.

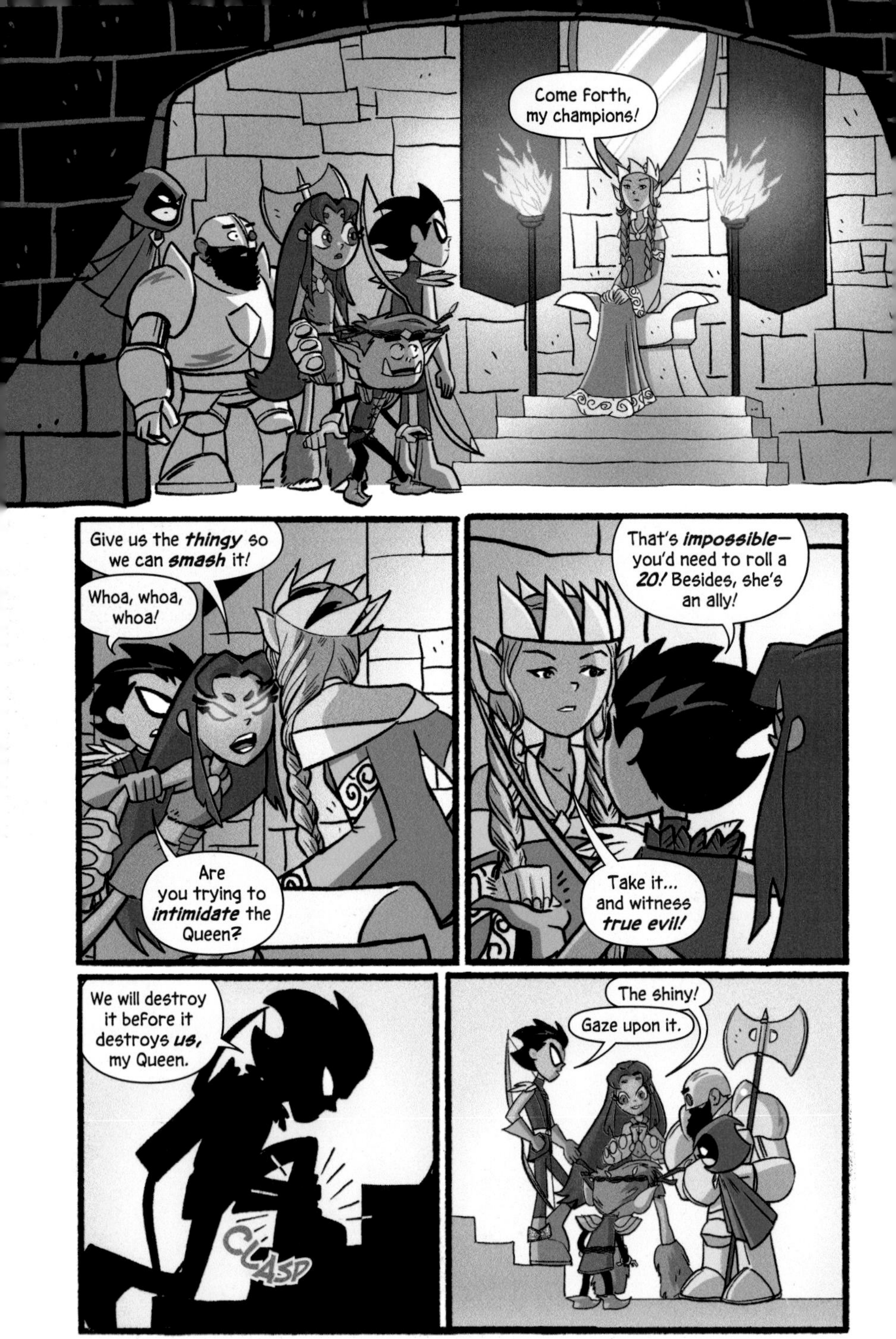
Come forth, my champions!
Give us the *thingy* so we can *smash* it!
Whoa, whoa, whoa!
Are you trying to *intimidate* the Queen?
That's *impossible*—you'd need to roll a *20!* Besides, she's an ally!
Take it... and witness *true evil!*
We will destroy it before it destroys *us,* my Queen.
CLASP
The shiny!
Gaze upon it.

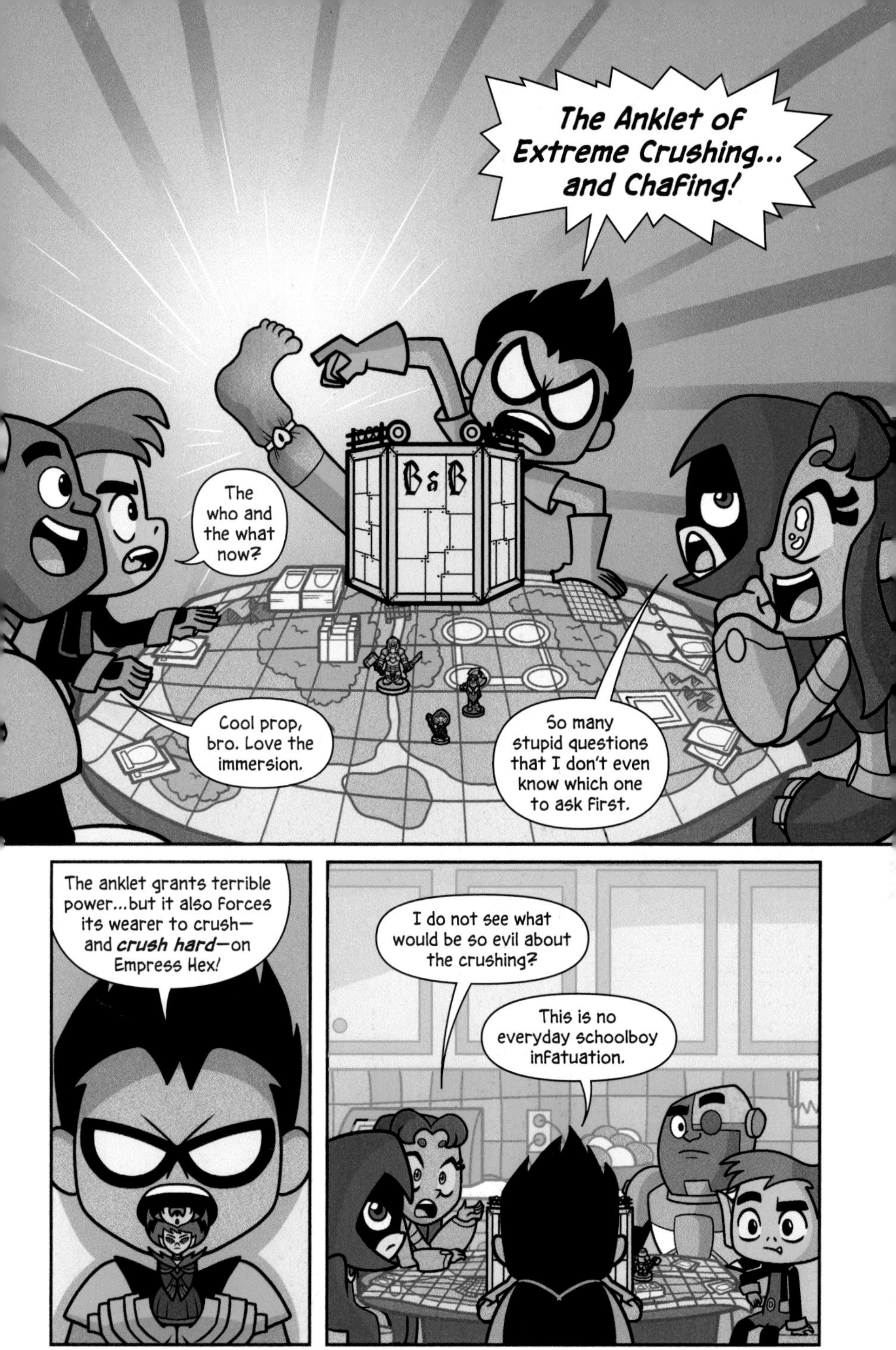
The Anklet of Extreme Crushing... and Chafing!
The who and the what now?
Cool prop, bro. Love the immersion.
So many stupid questions that I don't even know which one to ask first.
B&B
The anklet grants terrible power...but it also forces its wearer to crush—and *crush hard*—on Empress Hex!
I do not see what would be so evil about the crushing?
This is no everyday schoolboy infatuation.

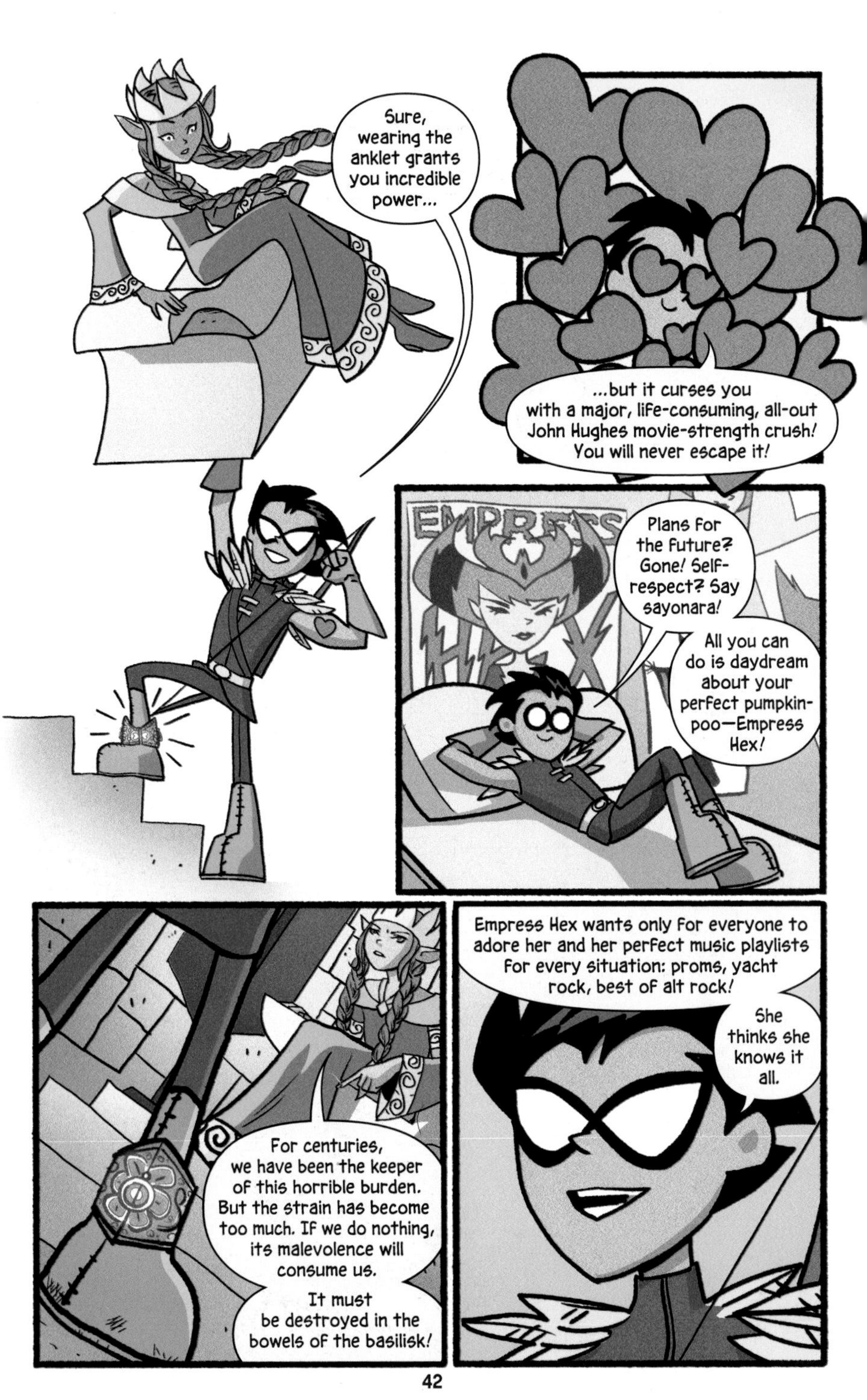

Sure, wearing the anklet grants you incredible power...
...but it curses you with a major, life-consuming, all-out John Hughes movie-strength crush! You will never escape it!
EMPRESS HEX
Plans for the future? Gone! Self-respect? Say sayonara!
All you can do is daydream about your perfect pumpkin-poo—Empress Hex!
For centuries, we have been the keeper of this horrible burden. But the strain has become too much. If we do nothing, its malevolence will consume us.
It must be destroyed in the bowels of the basilisk!
Empress Hex wants only for everyone to adore her and her perfect music playlists for every situation: proms, yacht rock, best of alt rock!
She thinks she knows it all.

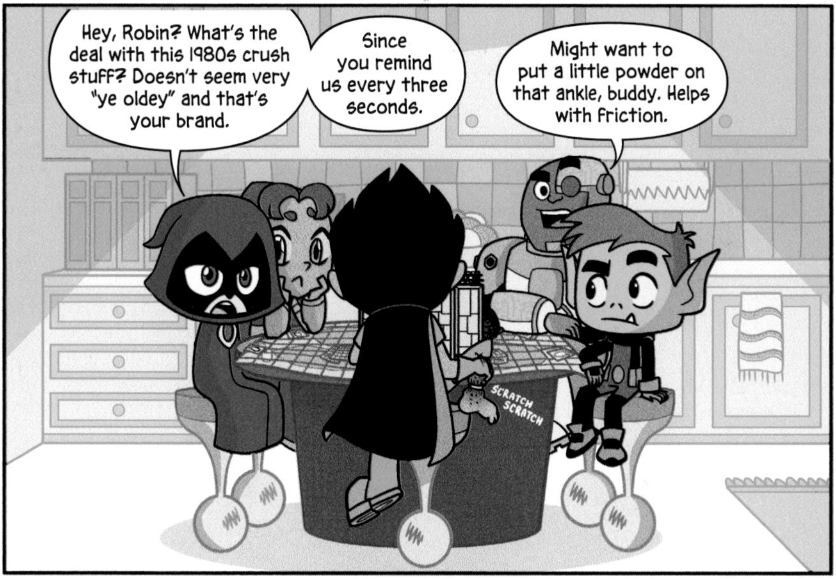
Hey, Robin? What's the deal with this 1980s crush stuff? Doesn't seem very "ye oldey" and that's your brand.
Since you remind us every three seconds.
Might want to put a little powder on that ankle, buddy. Helps with friction.
SCRATCH SCRATCH

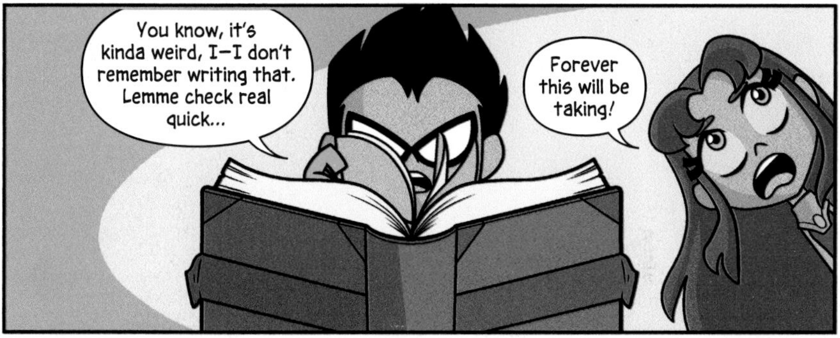
You know, it's kinda weird, I—I don't remember writing that. Lemme check real quick...
Forever this will be taking!

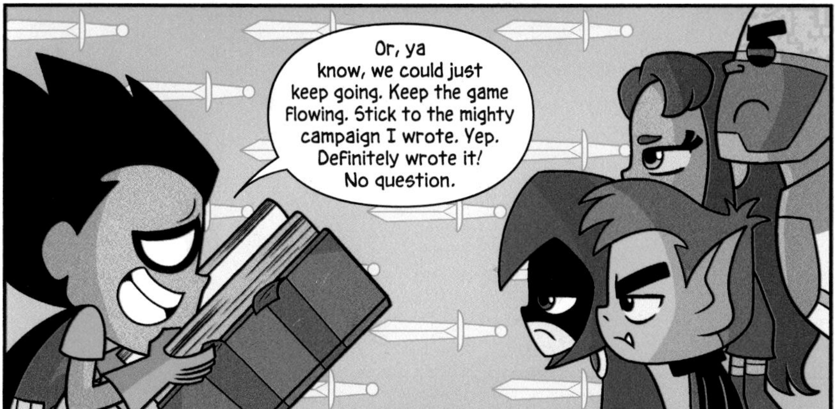
Or, ya know, we could just keep going. Keep the game flowing. Stick to the mighty campaign I wrote. Yep. Definitely wrote it! No question.

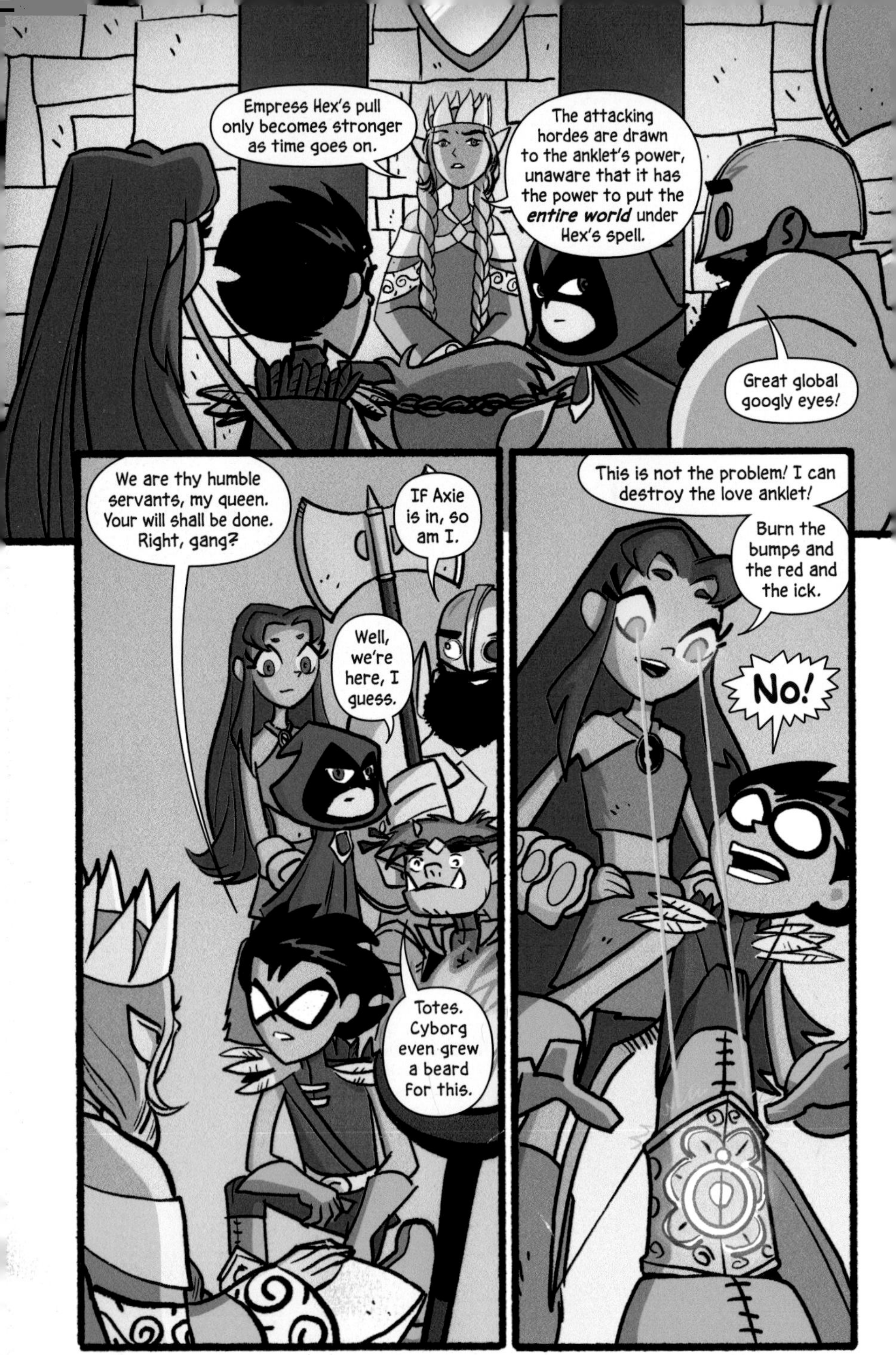

Empress Hex's pull only becomes stronger as time goes on.
The attacking hordes are drawn to the anklet's power, unaware that it has the power to put the *entire world* under Hex's spell.
Great global googly eyes!
We are thy humble servants, my queen. Your will shall be done. Right, gang?
If Axie is in, so am I.
Well, we're here, I guess.
Totes. Cyborg even grew a beard for this.
This is not the problem! I can destroy the love anklet!
Burn the bumps and the red and the ick.
No!

Chapter
Four

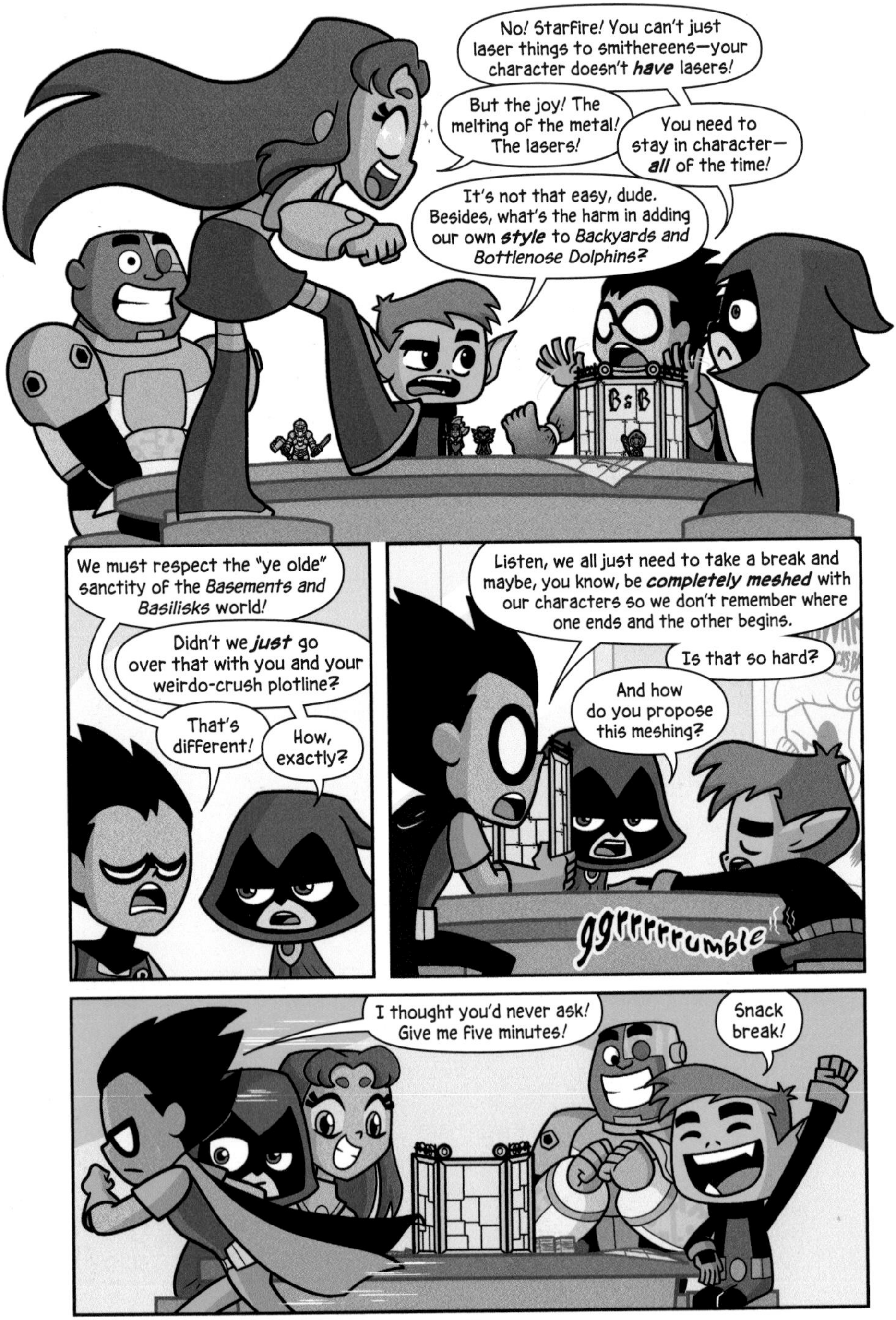
No! Starfire! You can't just laser things to smithereens—your character doesn't *have* lasers!
But the joy! The melting of the metal! The lasers!
You need to stay in character—*all* of the time!
It's not that easy, dude. Besides, what's the harm in adding our own *style* to *Backyards and Bottlenose Dolphins?*
B&B
We must respect the "ye olde" sanctity of the *Basements and Basilisks* world!
Didn't we *just* go over that with you and your weirdo-crush plotline?
That's different!
How, exactly?
Listen, we all just need to take a break and maybe, you know, be *completely meshed* with our characters so we don't remember where one ends and the other begins.
Is that so hard?
And how do you propose this meshing?
ggrrrrrrumble
I thought you'd never ask! Give me five minutes!
Snack break!

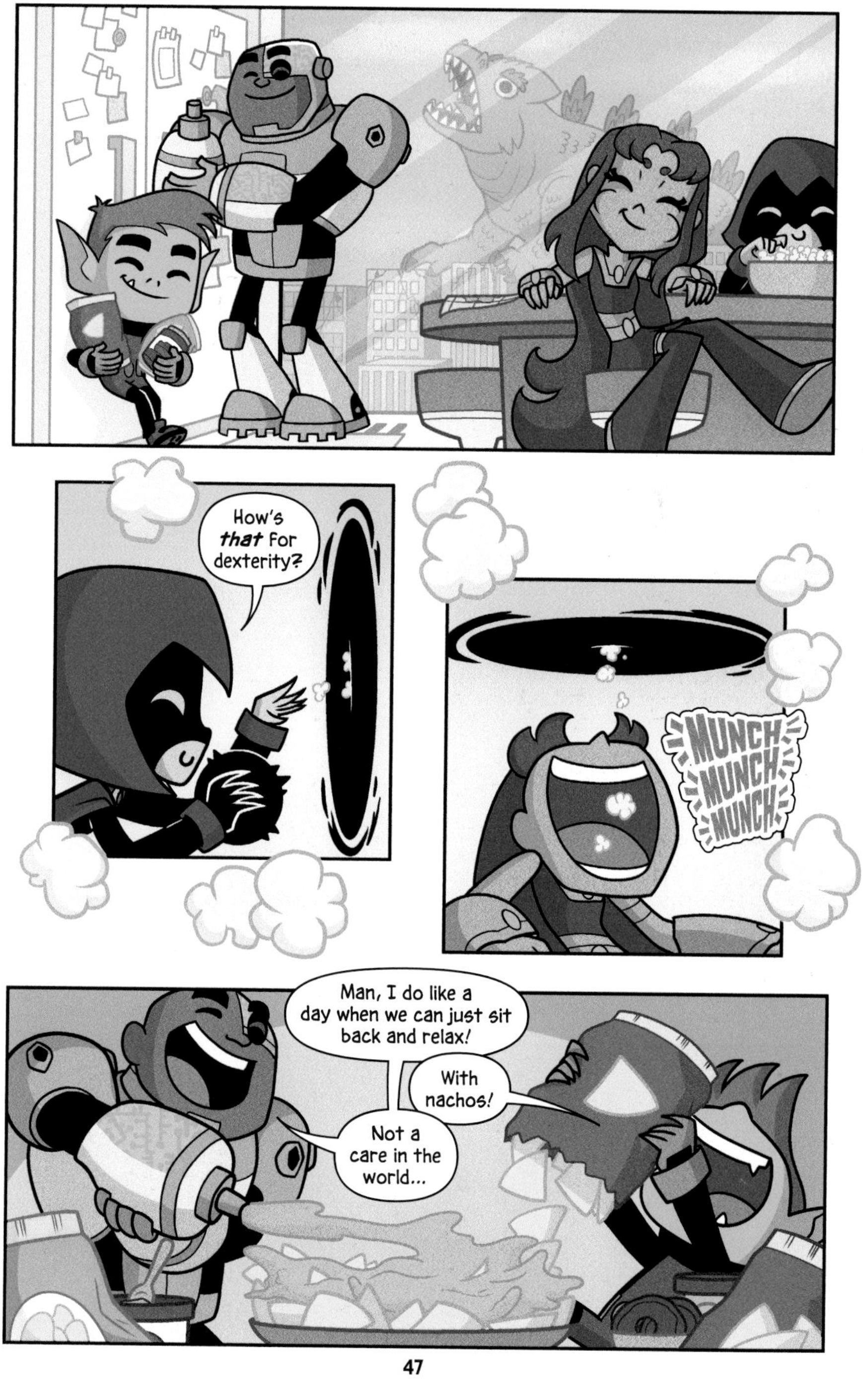

How's *that* for dexterity?
MUNCH MUNCH MUNCH
Man, I do like a day when we can just sit back and relax!
With nachos!
Not a care in the world...

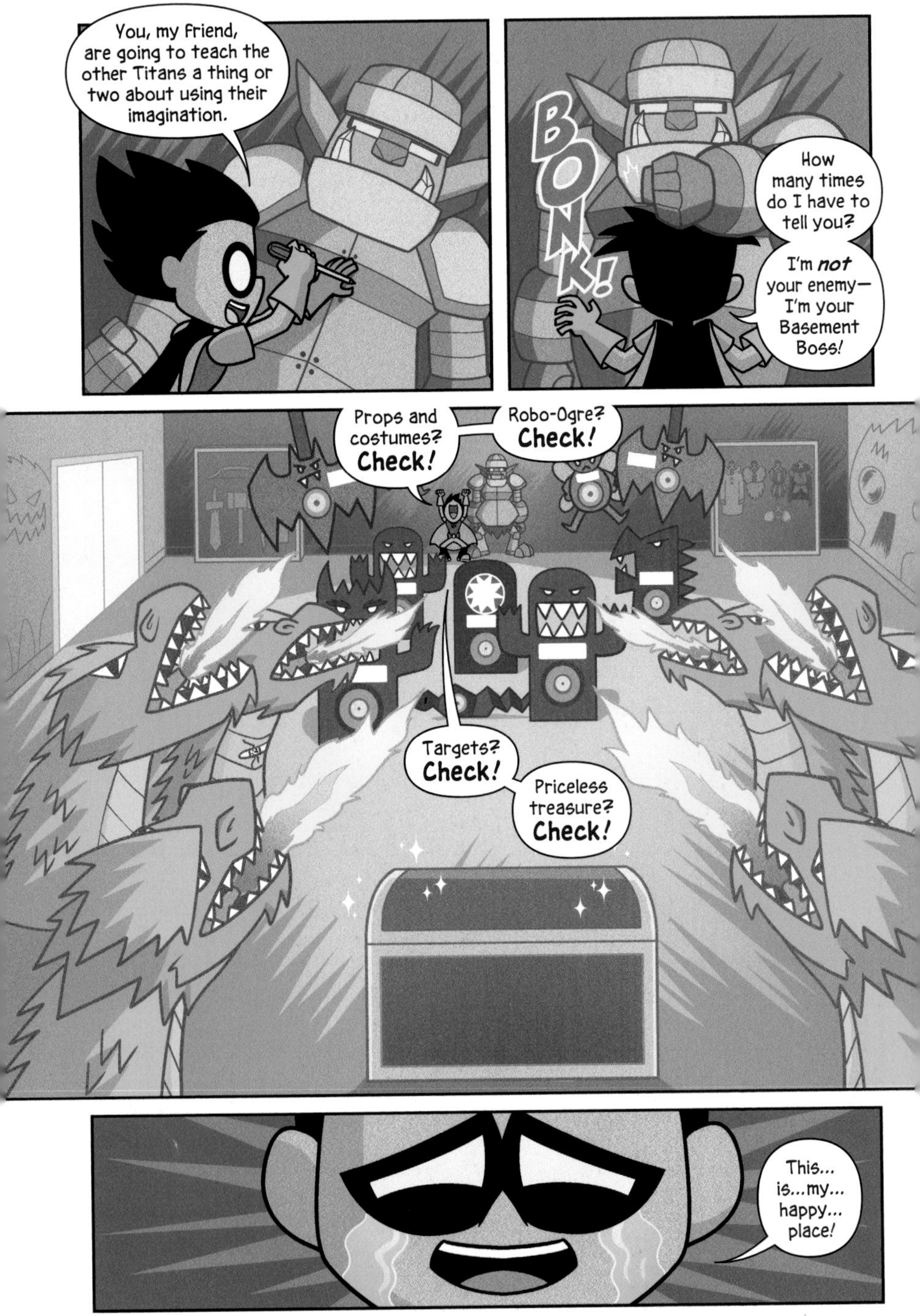
You, my friend, are going to teach the other Titans a thing or two about using their imagination.
BONK!
How many times do I have to tell you?
I'm *not* your enemy— I'm your Basement Boss!
Props and costumes? Check!
Robo-Ogre? Check!
Targets? Check!
Priceless treasure? Check!
This... is...my... happy... place!

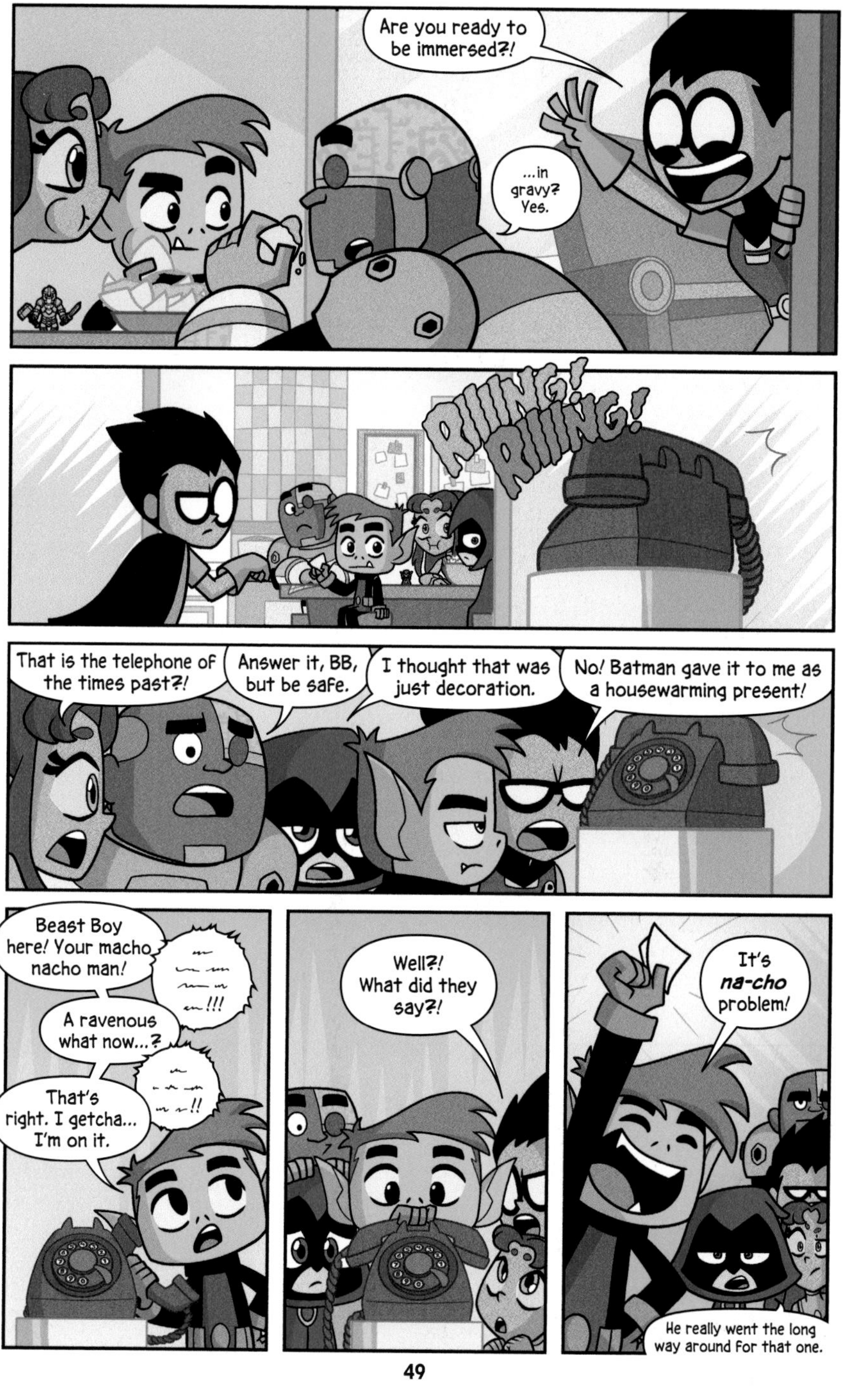
Are you ready to be immersed?!
...in gravy? Yes.
RIIING! RIIING!
That is the telephone of the times past?!
Answer it, BB, but be safe.
I thought that was just decoration.
No! Batman gave it to me as a housewarming present!
Beast Boy here! Your macho nacho man!
A ravenous what now...?
That's right. I getcha... I'm on it.
Well?! What did they say?!
It's *na-cho* problem!
He really went the long way around for that one.

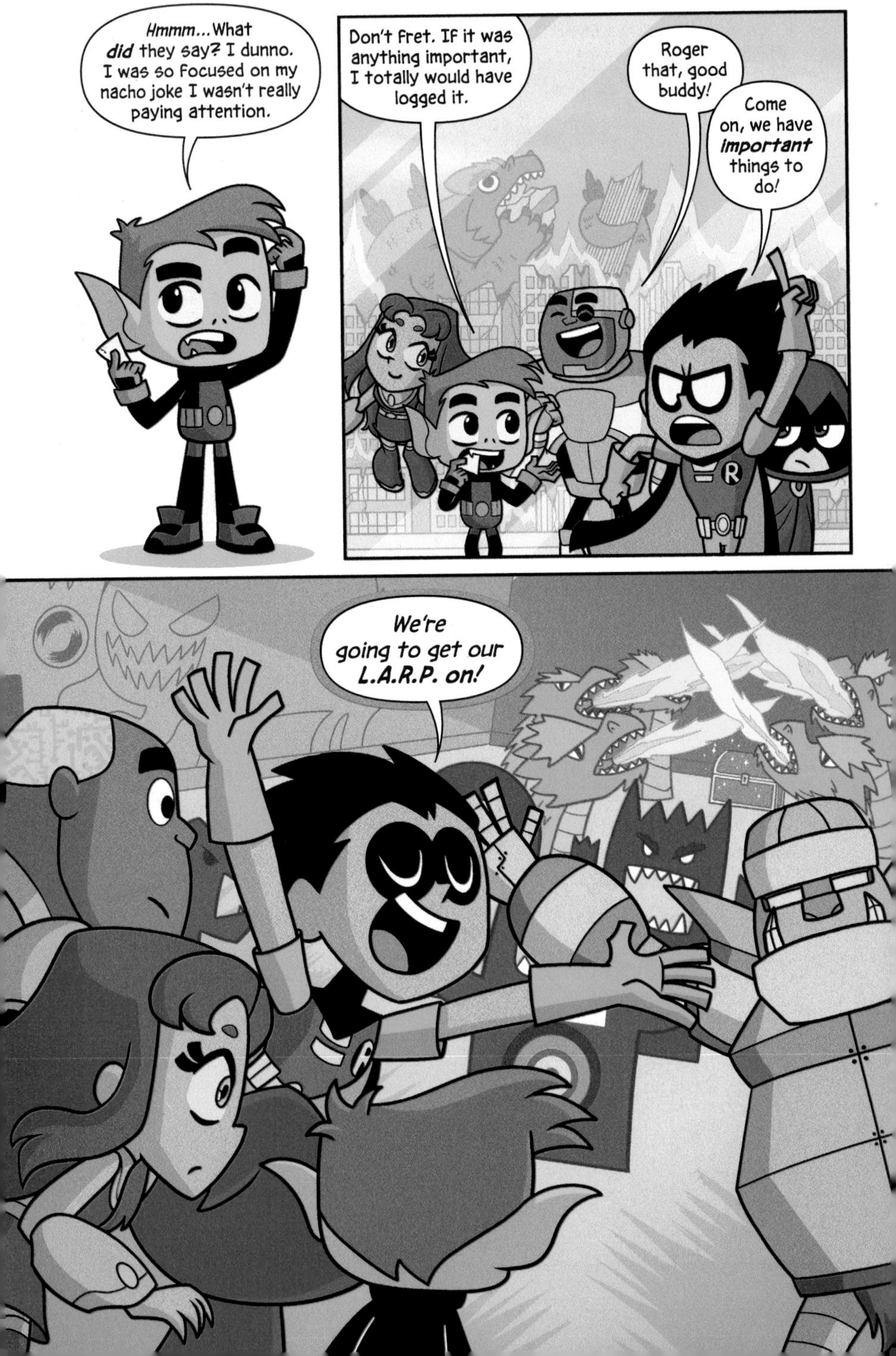
Hmmm...What *did* they say? I dunno. I was so focused on my nacho joke I wasn't really paying attention.
Don't fret. If it was anything important, I totally would have logged it.
Roger that, good buddy!
Come on, we have ***important*** things to do!
*We're going to get our **L.A.R.P. on!***

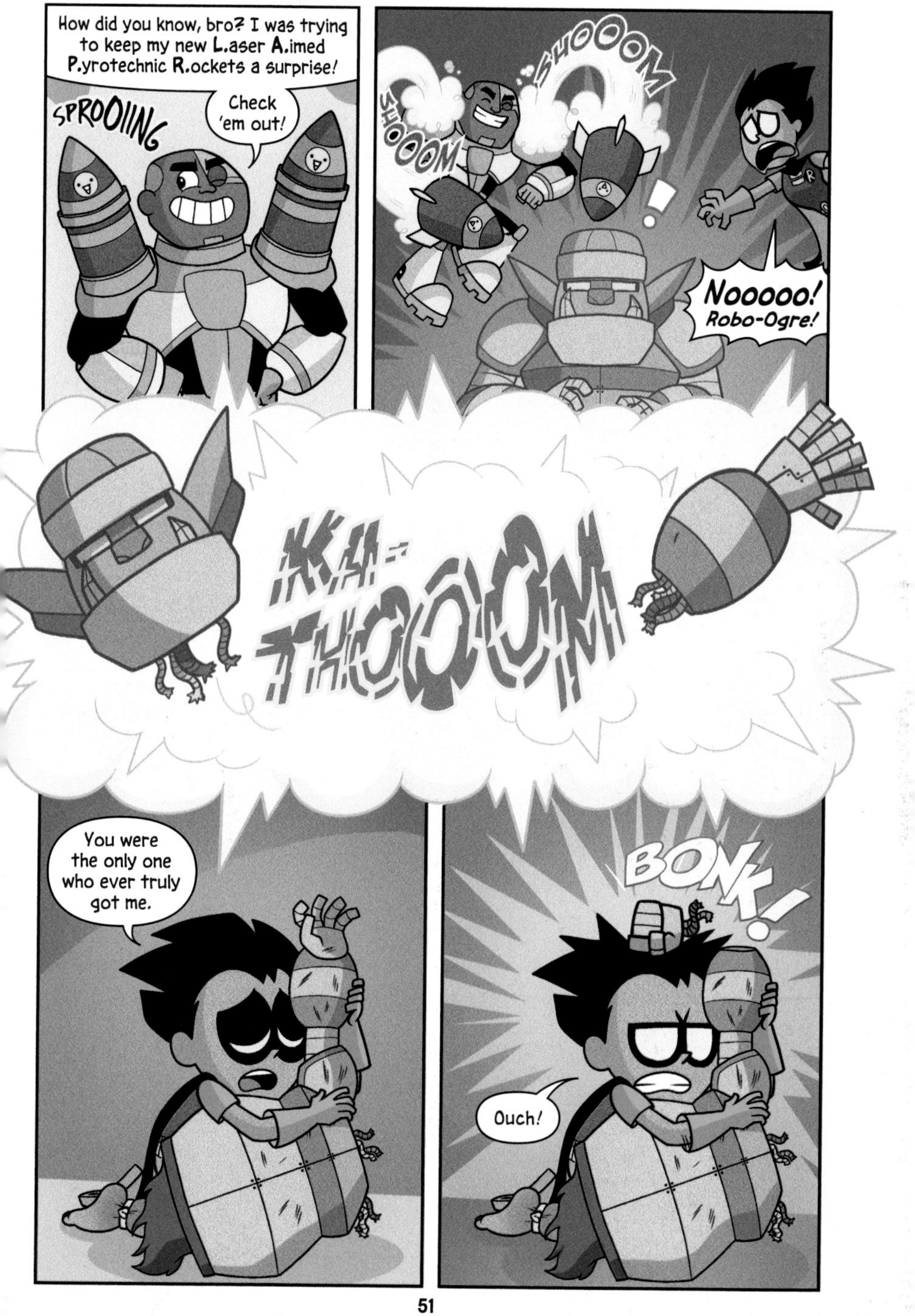
How did you know, bro? I was trying to keep my new L.aser A.imed P.yrotechnic R.ockets a surprise!
SPROOIING
Check 'em out!
SHOOOM
SHOOOM
!
Nooooo! Robo-Ogre!
KA-THOOOOM
You were the only one who ever truly got me.
BONK!
Ouch!

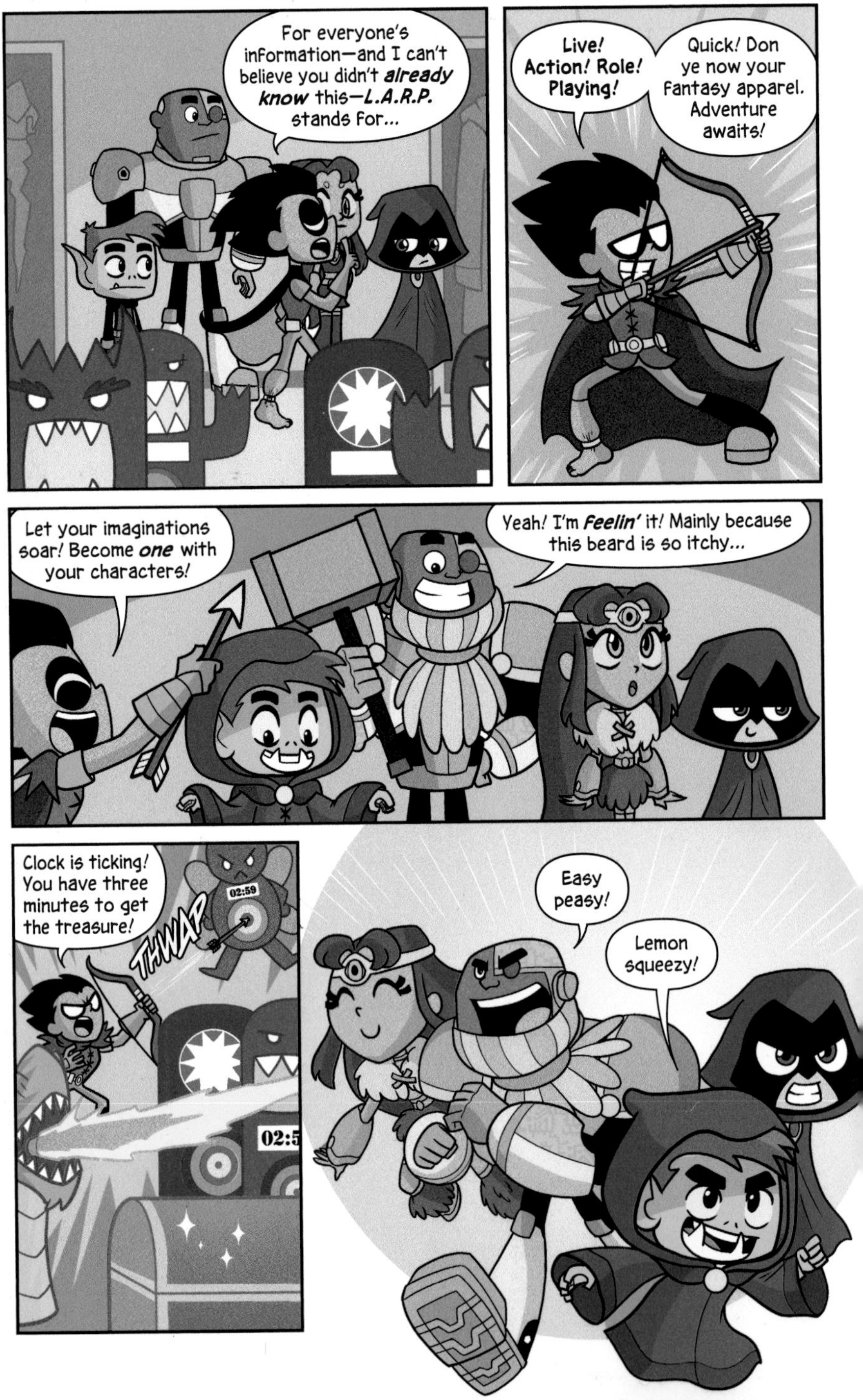
For everyone's information—and I can't believe you didn't *already know* this—*L.A.R.P.* stands for...
Live! Action! Role! Playing!
Quick! Don ye now your fantasy apparel. Adventure awaits!
Let your imaginations soar! Become *one* with your characters!
Yeah! I'm *Feelin'* it! Mainly because this beard is so itchy...
Clock is ticking! You have three minutes to get the treasure!
02:59
THWAP
02:5
Easy peasy!
Lemon squeezy!

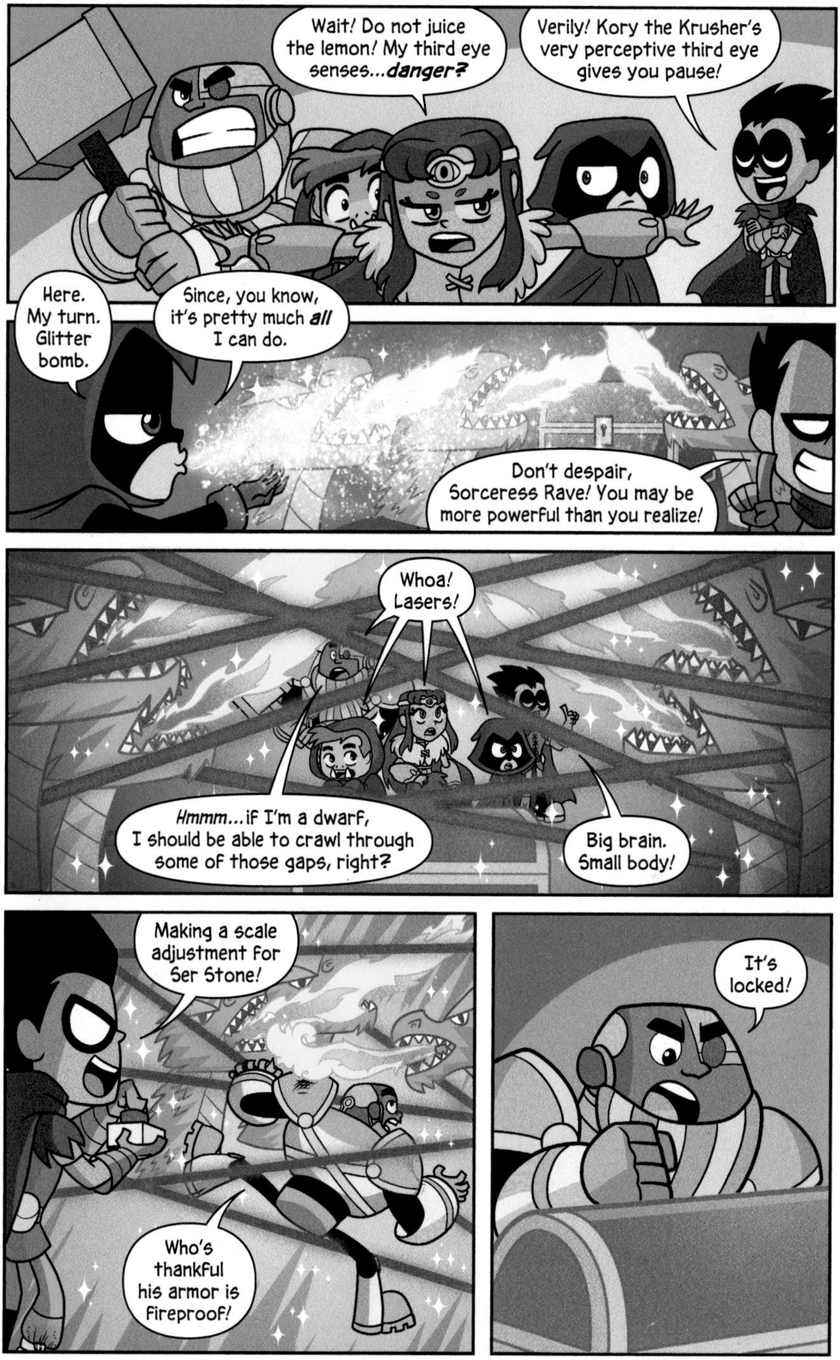

Wait! Do not juice the lemon! My third eye senses...**danger?**
Verily! Kory the Krusher's very perceptive third eye gives you pause!
Here. My turn. Glitter bomb.
Since, you know, it's pretty much *all* I can do.
Don't despair, Sorceress Rave! You may be more powerful than you realize!
Whoa! Lasers!
Hmmm... if I'm a dwarf, I should be able to crawl through some of those gaps, right?
Big brain. Small body!
Making a scale adjustment for Ser Stone!
Who's thankful his armor is fireproof!
It's locked!

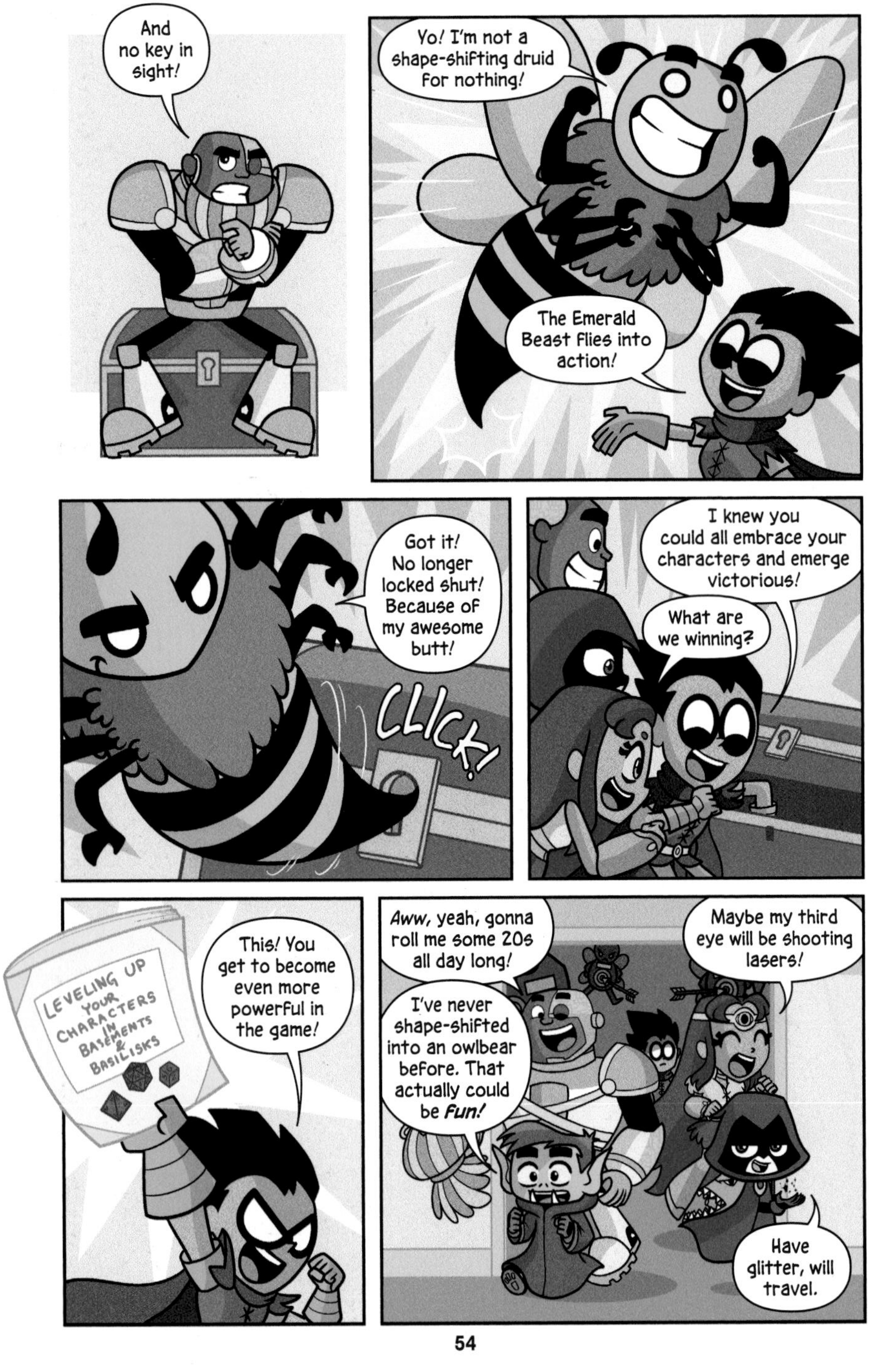
And no key in sight!
Yo! I'm not a shape-shifting druid for nothing!
The Emerald Beast flies into action!
Got it! No longer locked shut! Because of my awesome butt!
CLICK!
I knew you could all embrace your characters and emerge victorious!
What are we winning?
LEVELING UP YOUR CHARACTERS IN BASEMENTS & BASILISKS
This! You get to become even more powerful in the game!
Aww, yeah, gonna roll me some 20s all day long!
I've never shape-shifted into an owlbear before. That actually could be *fun!*
Maybe my third eye will be shooting lasers!
Have glitter, will travel.

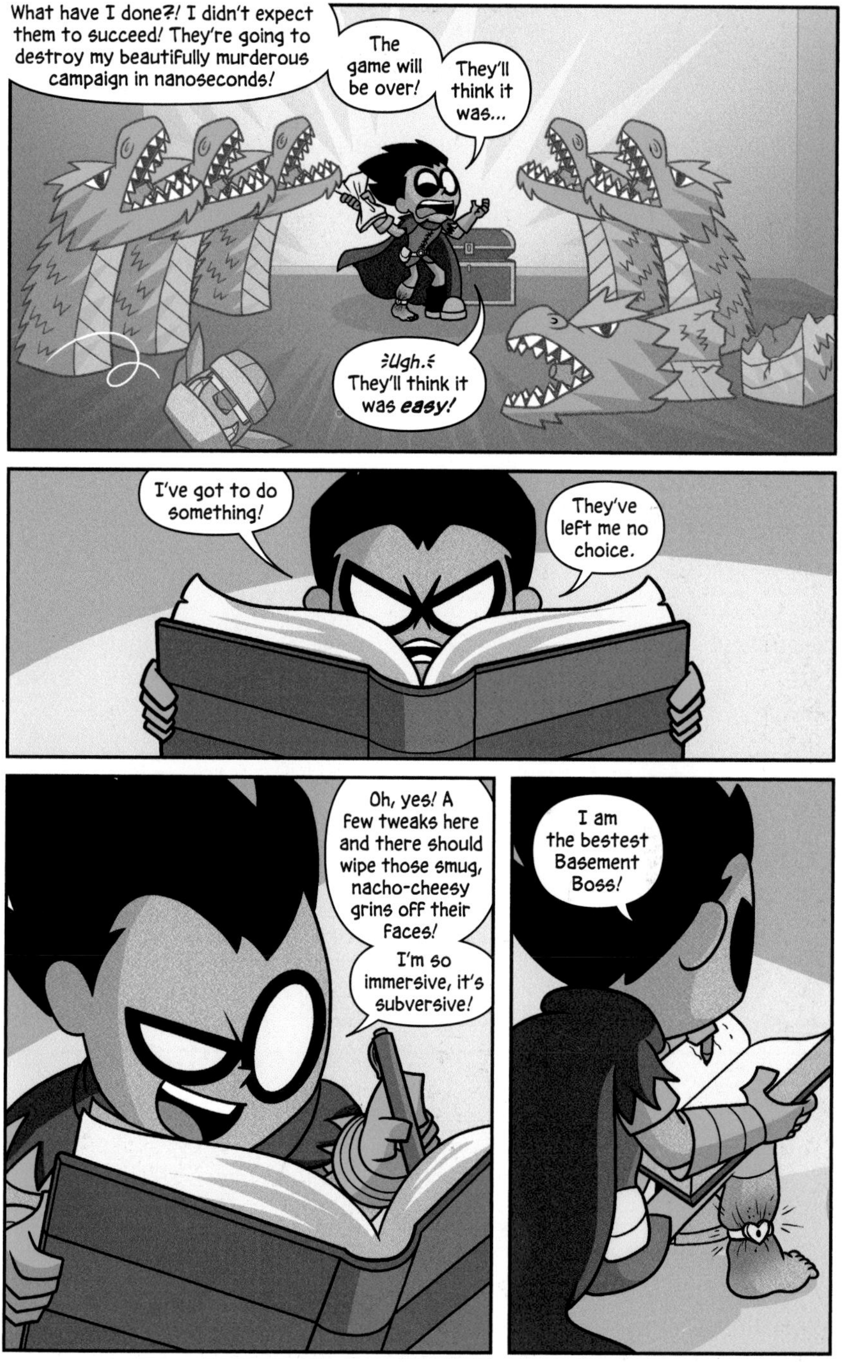
What have I done?! I didn't expect them to succeed! They're going to destroy my beautifully murderous campaign in nanoseconds!
The game will be over!
They'll think it was...
Ugh.
They'll think it was *easy*!
I've got to do something!
They've left me no choice.
Oh, yes! A few tweaks here and there should wipe those smug, nacho-cheesy grins off their faces!
I'm so immersive, it's subversive!
I am the bestest Basement Boss!

Chapter
Five

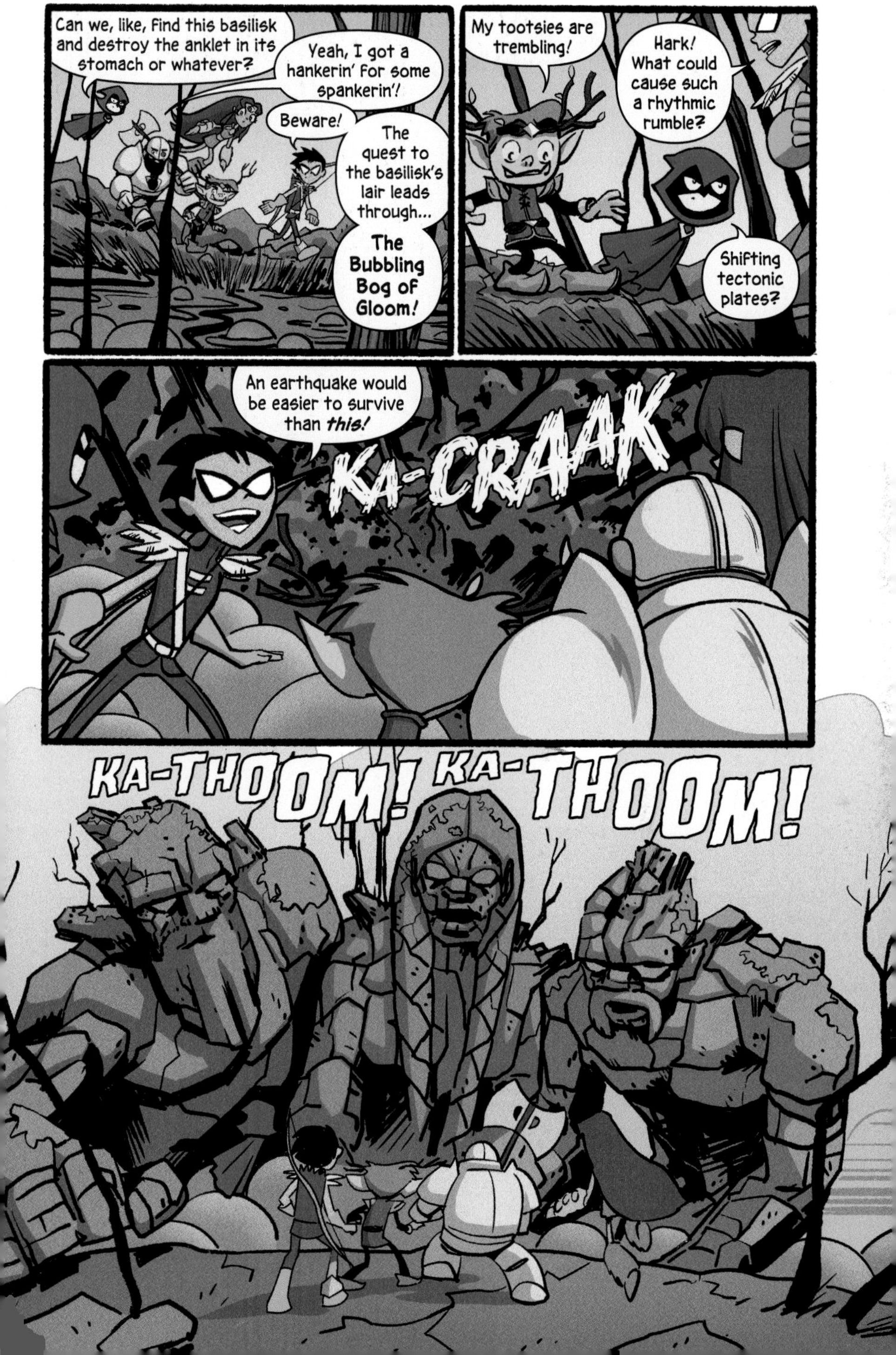
Can we, like, find this basilisk and destroy the anklet in its stomach or whatever?
Yeah, I got a hankerin' for some spankerin'!
Beware!
The quest to the basilisk's lair leads through...
The Bubbling Bog of Gloom!
My tootsies are trembling!
Hark! What could cause such a rhythmic rumble?
Shifting tectonic plates?
An earthquake would be easier to survive than this!
KA-CRAAK
KA-THOOM! KA-THOOM!

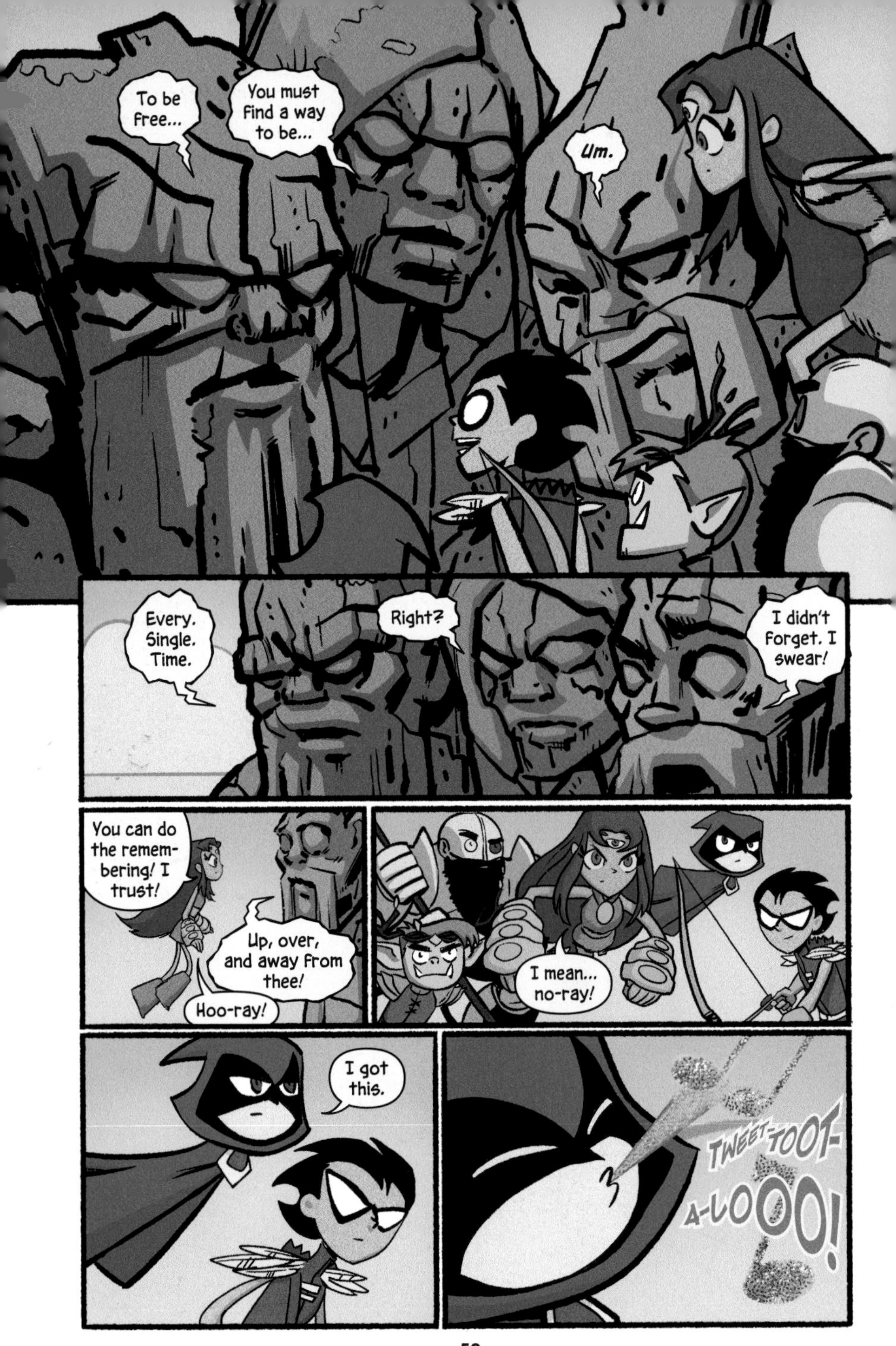
To be free...
You must find a way to be...
Um.
Every. Single. Time.
Right?
I didn't forget. I swear!
You can do the remembering! I trust!
Up, over, and away from thee!
Hoo-ray!
I mean... no-ray!
I got this.
TWEET-TOOT-A-LOOO!

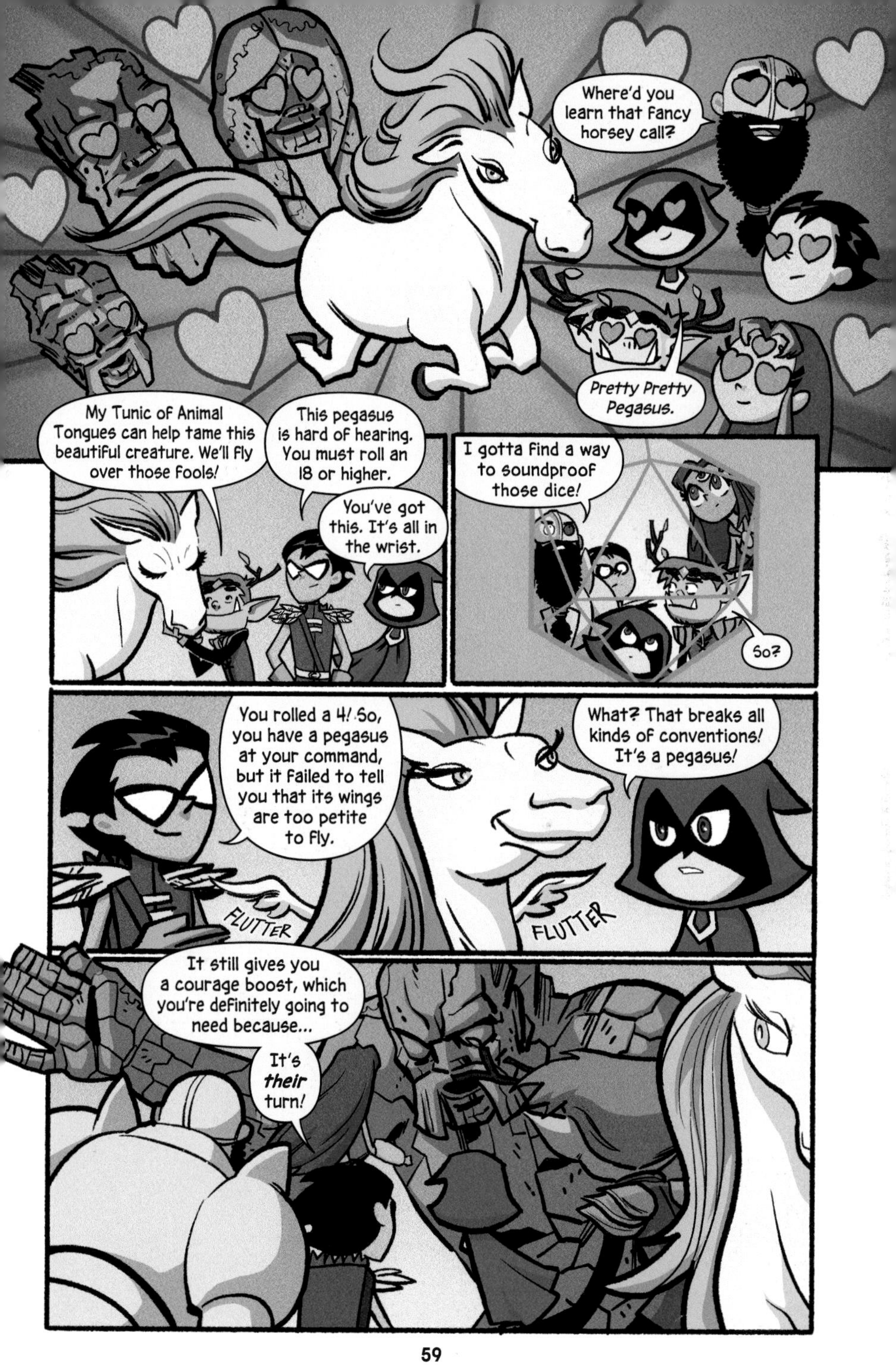
Where'd you learn that fancy horsey call?
Pretty Pretty Pegasus.
My Tunic of Animal Tongues can help tame this beautiful creature. We'll fly over those fools!
This pegasus is hard of hearing. You must roll an 18 or higher.
You've got this. It's all in the wrist.
I gotta find a way to soundproof those dice!
So?
You rolled a 4! So, you have a pegasus at your command, but it failed to tell you that its wings are too petite to fly.
What? That breaks all kinds of conventions! It's a pegasus!
FLUTTER
FLUTTER
It still gives you a courage boost, which you're definitely going to need because...
It's ***their*** turn!

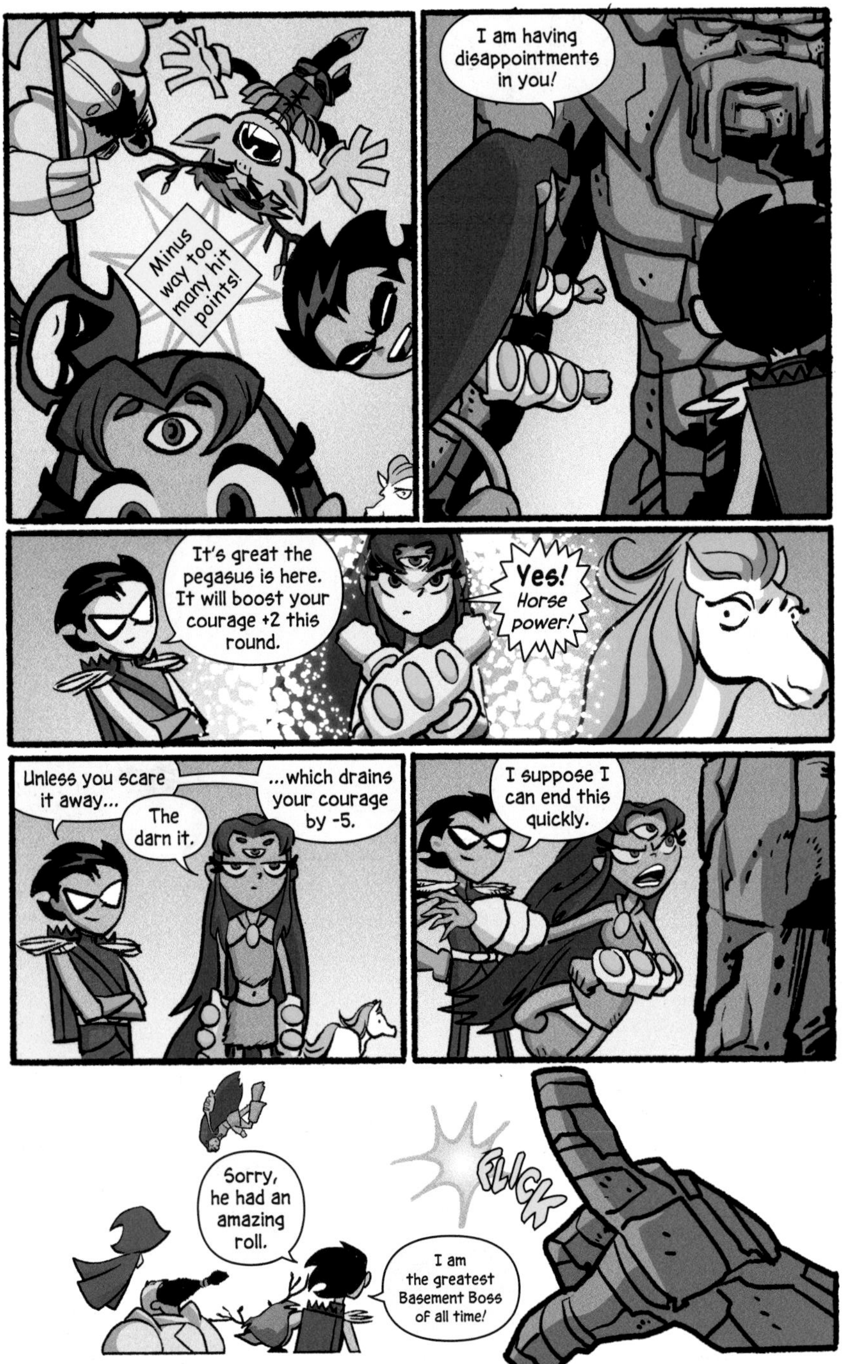
Minus way too many hit points!
I am having disappointments in you!
It's great the pegasus is here. It will boost your courage +2 this round.
Yes! Horse power!
Unless you scare it away...
The darn it.
...which drains your courage by -5.
I suppose I can end this quickly.
FLICK
Sorry, he had an amazing roll.
I am the greatest Basement Boss of all time!

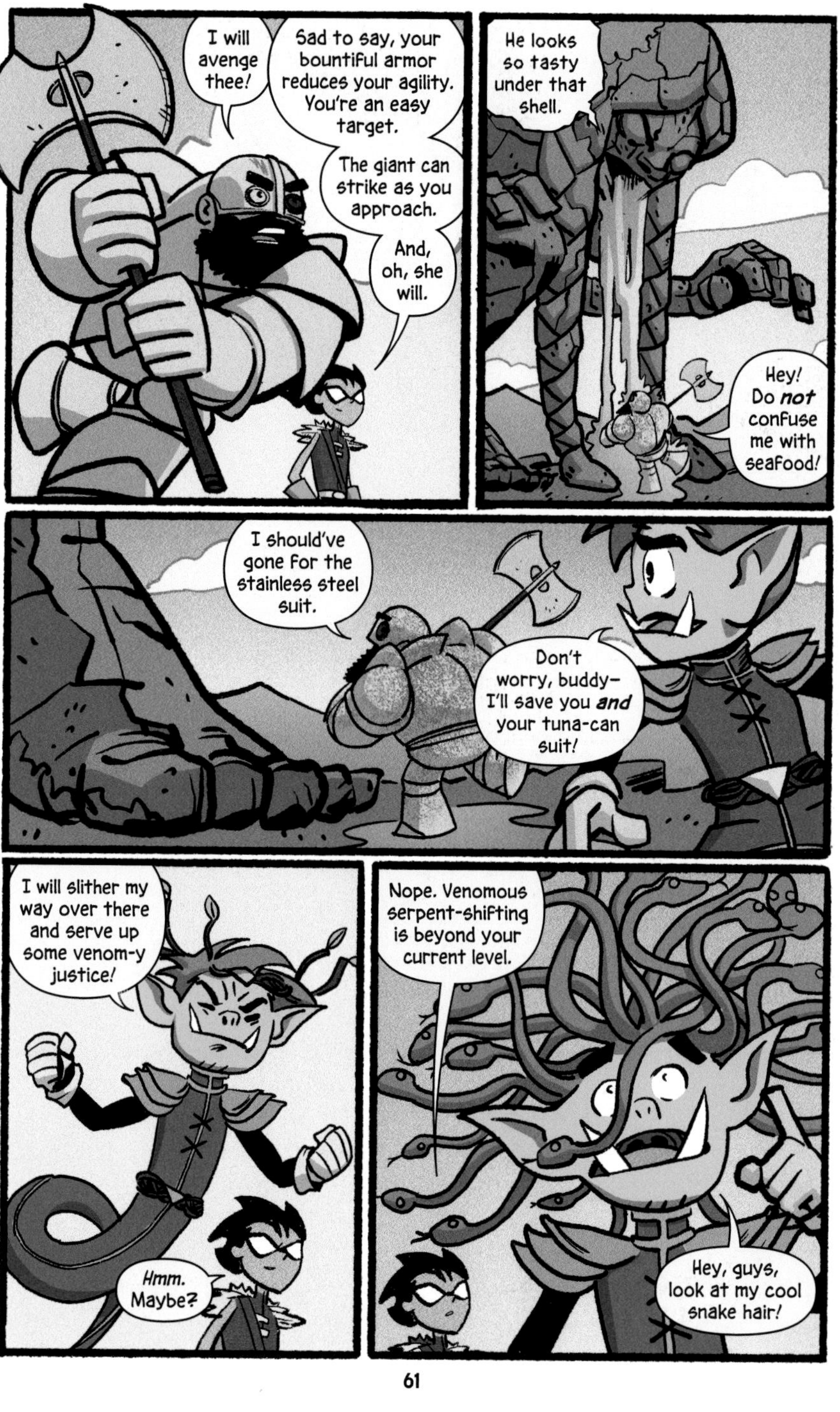
I will avenge thee!
Sad to say, your bountiful armor reduces your agility. You're an easy target.
The giant can strike as you approach.
And, oh, she will.
He looks so tasty under that shell.
Hey! Do *not* confuse me with seafood!
I should've gone for the stainless steel suit.
Don't worry, buddy— I'll save you *and* your tuna-can suit!
I will slither my way over there and serve up some venom-y justice!
Hmm. Maybe?
Nope. Venomous serpent-shifting is beyond your current level.
Hey, guys, look at my cool snake hair!

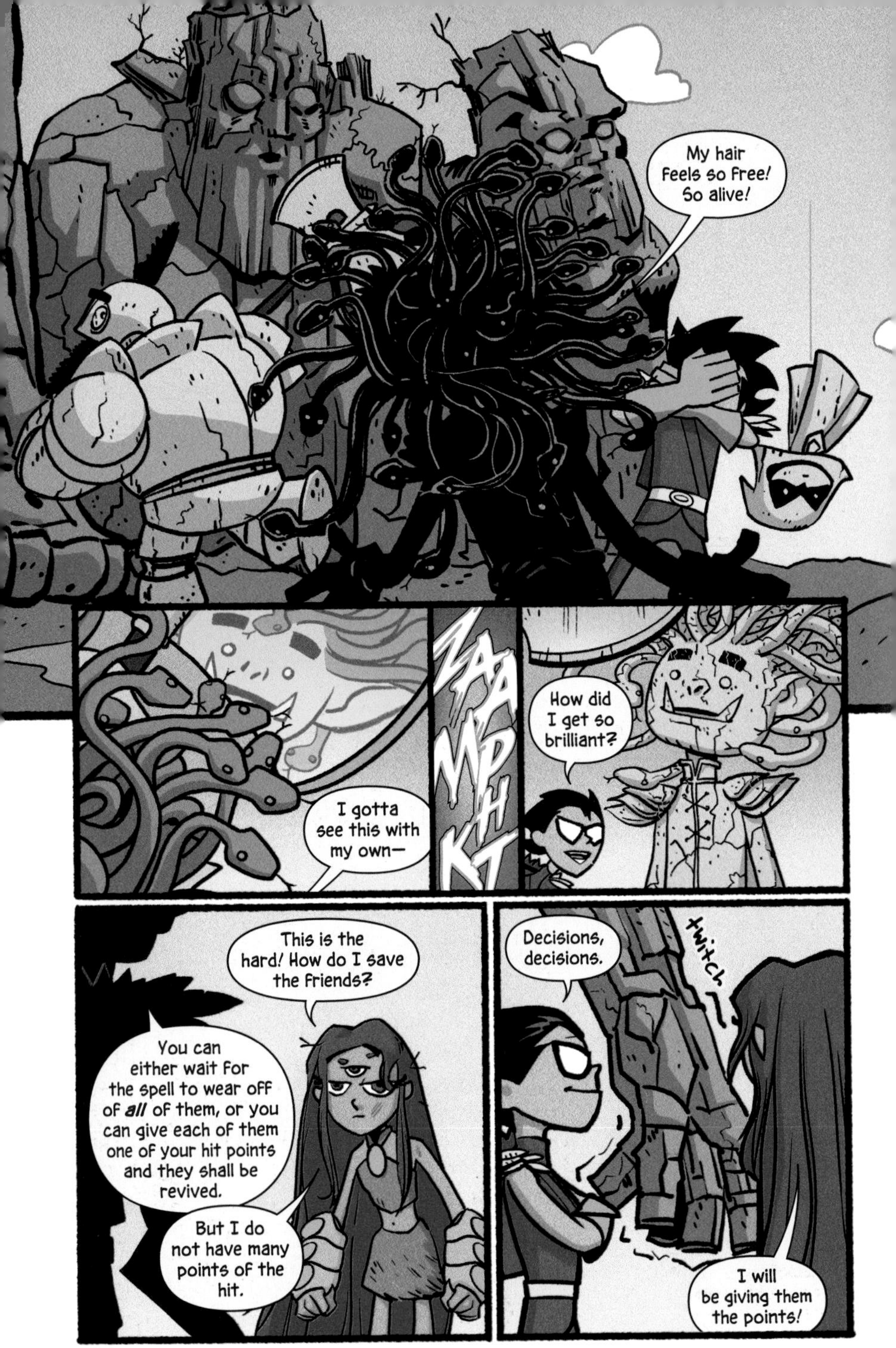
My hair feels so free! So alive!
I gotta see this with my own—
ZAAMPHKT
How did I get so brilliant?
This is the hard! How do I save the friends?
You can either wait for the spell to wear off of *all* of them, or you can give each of them one of your hit points and they shall be revived.
But I do not have many points of the hit.
Decisions, decisions.
twitch
I will be giving them the points!

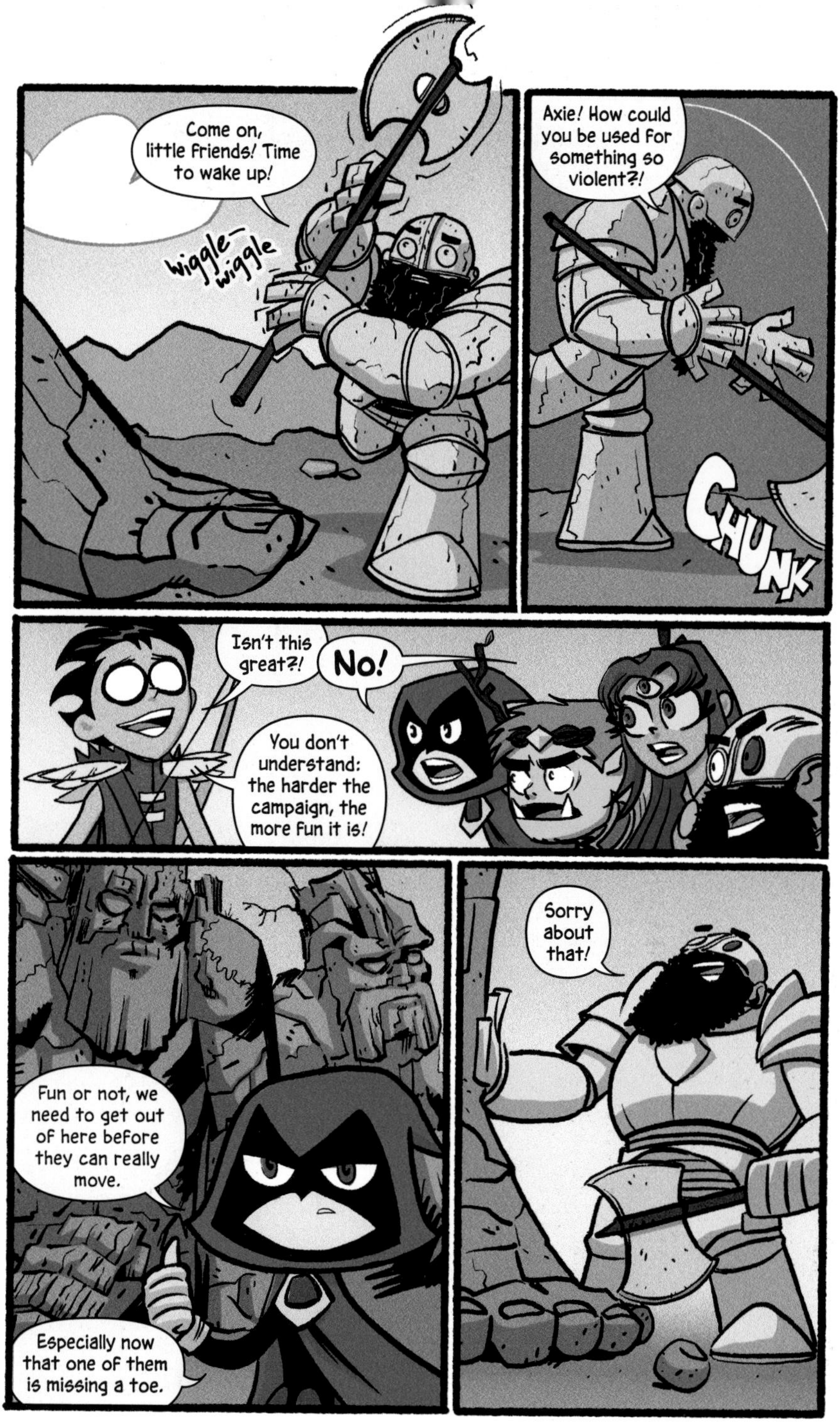
Come on, little friends! Time to wake up!
wiggle-wiggle
Axie! How could you be used for something so violent?!
CHUNK
Isn't this great?!
No!
You don't understand: the harder the campaign, the more fun it is!
Fun or not, we need to get out of here before they can really move.
Especially now that one of them is missing a toe.
Sorry about that!

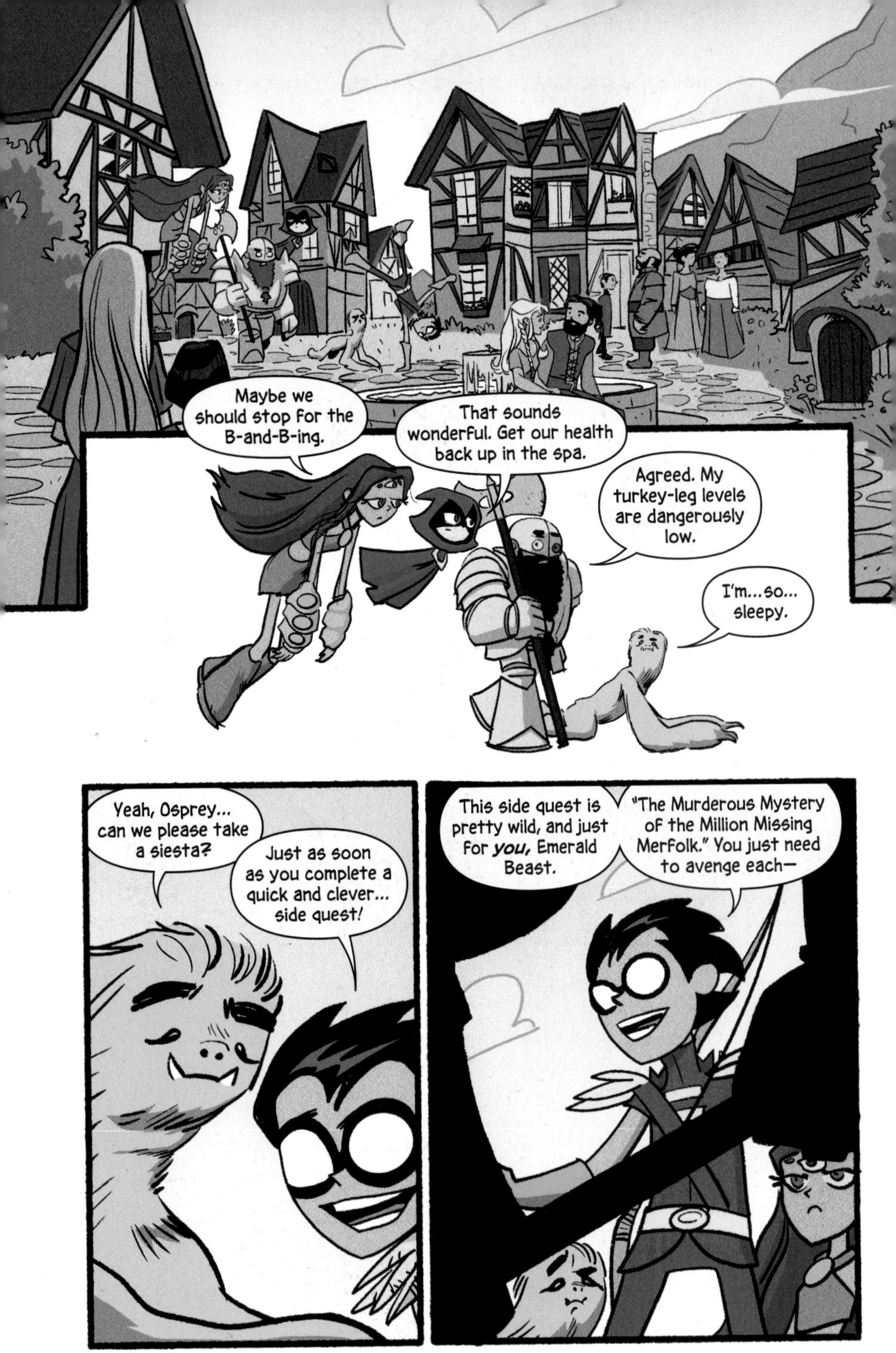
Maybe we should stop for the B-and-B-ing.
That sounds wonderful. Get our health back up in the spa.
Agreed. My turkey-leg levels are dangerously low.
I'm...so... sleepy.
Yeah, Osprey... can we please take a siesta?
Just as soon as you complete a quick and clever... side quest!
This side quest is pretty wild, and just for *you*, Emerald Beast.
"The Murderous Mystery of the Million Missing Merfolk." You just need to avenge each—

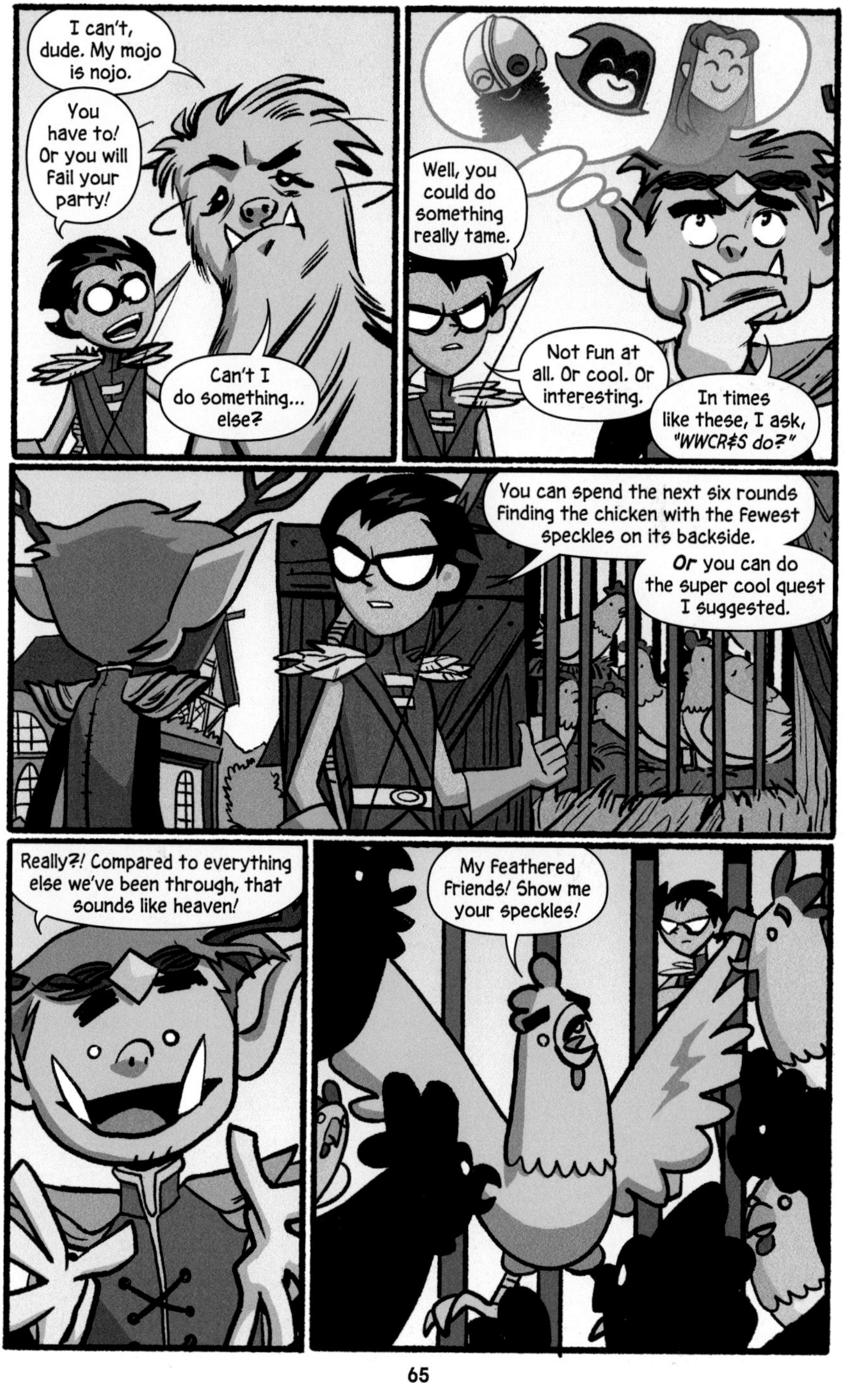
I can't, dude. My mojo is nojo.
You have to! Or you will fail your party!
Can't I do something... else?
Well, you could do something really tame.
Not fun at all. Or cool. Or interesting.
In times like these, I ask, "WWCR$S do?"
You can spend the next six rounds finding the chicken with the fewest speckles on its backside.
Or you can do the super cool quest I suggested.
Really?! Compared to everything else we've been through, that sounds like heaven!
My feathered friends! Show me your speckles!

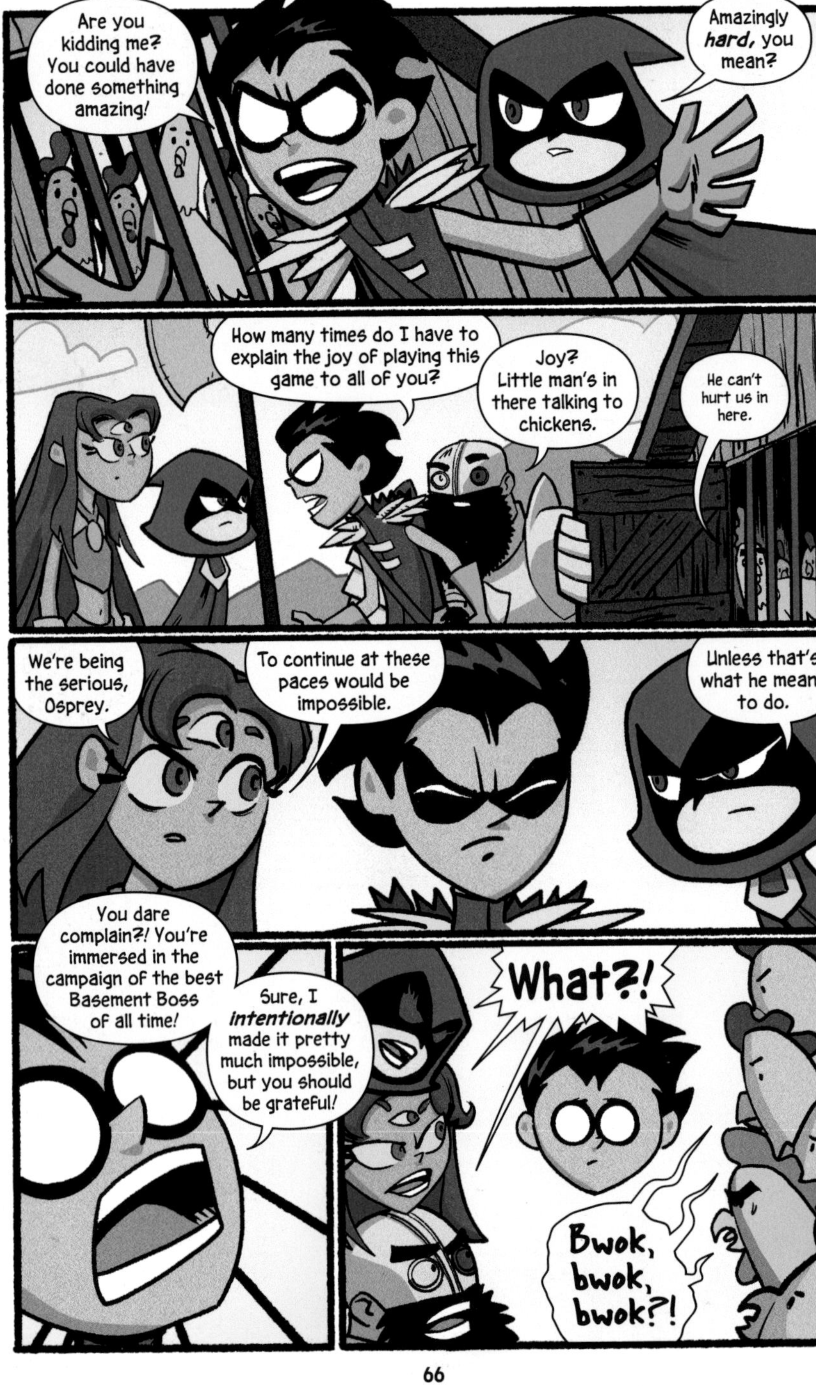

Are you kidding me? You could have done something amazing!
Amazingly *hard,* you mean?
How many times do I have to explain the joy of playing this game to all of you?
Joy? Little man's in there talking to chickens.
He can't hurt us in here.
We're being the serious, Osprey.
To continue at these paces would be impossible.
Unless that's what he meant to do.
You dare complain?! You're immersed in the campaign of the best Basement Boss of all time!
Sure, I *intentionally* made it pretty much impossible, but you should be grateful!
What?!
Bwok, bwok, bwok?!

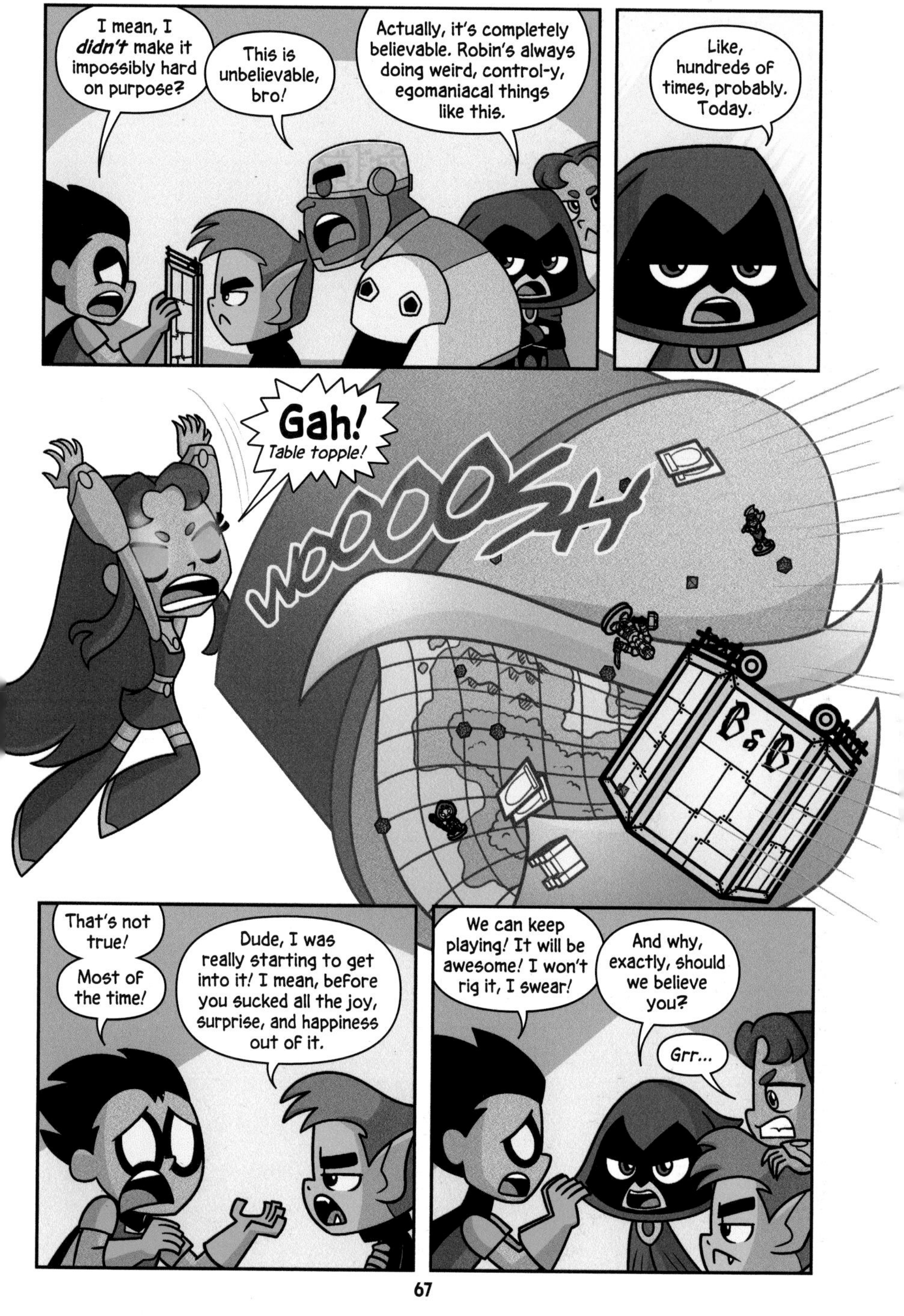

I mean, I *didn't* make it impossibly hard on purpose?
This is unbelievable, bro!
Actually, it's completely believable. Robin's always doing weird, control-y, egomaniacal things like this.
Like, hundreds of times, probably. Today.
Gah!
Table topple!
WOOOOSH
B&B
That's not true!
Most of the time!
Dude, I was really starting to get into it! I mean, before you sucked all the joy, surprise, and happiness out of it.
We can keep playing! It will be awesome! I won't rig it, I swear!
And why, exactly, should we believe you?
Grr...

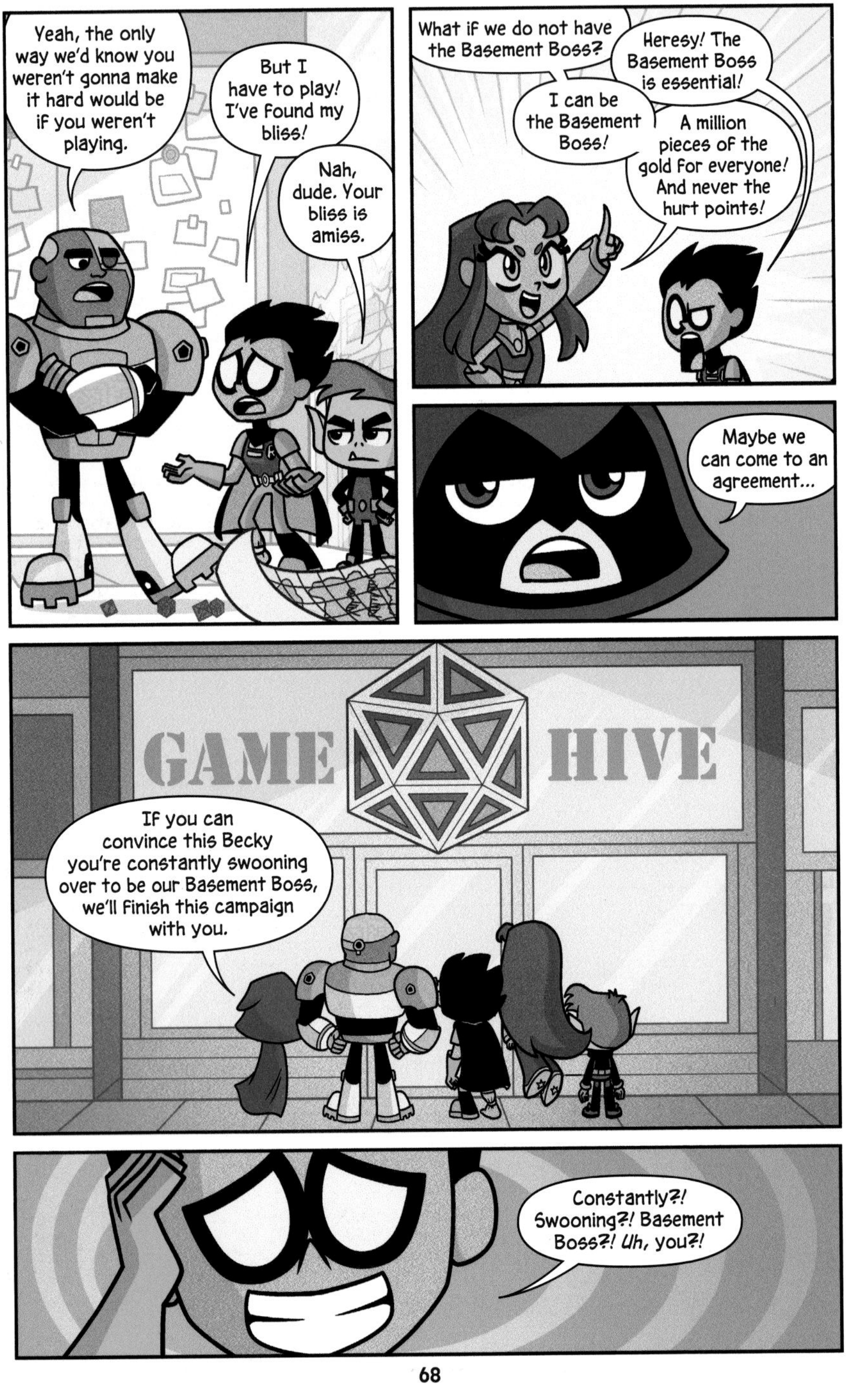
Yeah, the only way we'd know you weren't gonna make it hard would be if you weren't playing.
But I have to play! I've found my bliss!
Nah, dude. Your bliss is amiss.
What if we do not have the Basement Boss?
Heresy! The Basement Boss is essential!
I can be the Basement Boss!
A million pieces of the gold for everyone! And never the hurt points!
Maybe we can come to an agreement...
GAME HIVE
If you can convince this Becky you're constantly swooning over to be our Basement Boss, we'll finish this campaign with you.
Constantly?! Swooning?! Basement Boss?! Uh, you?!

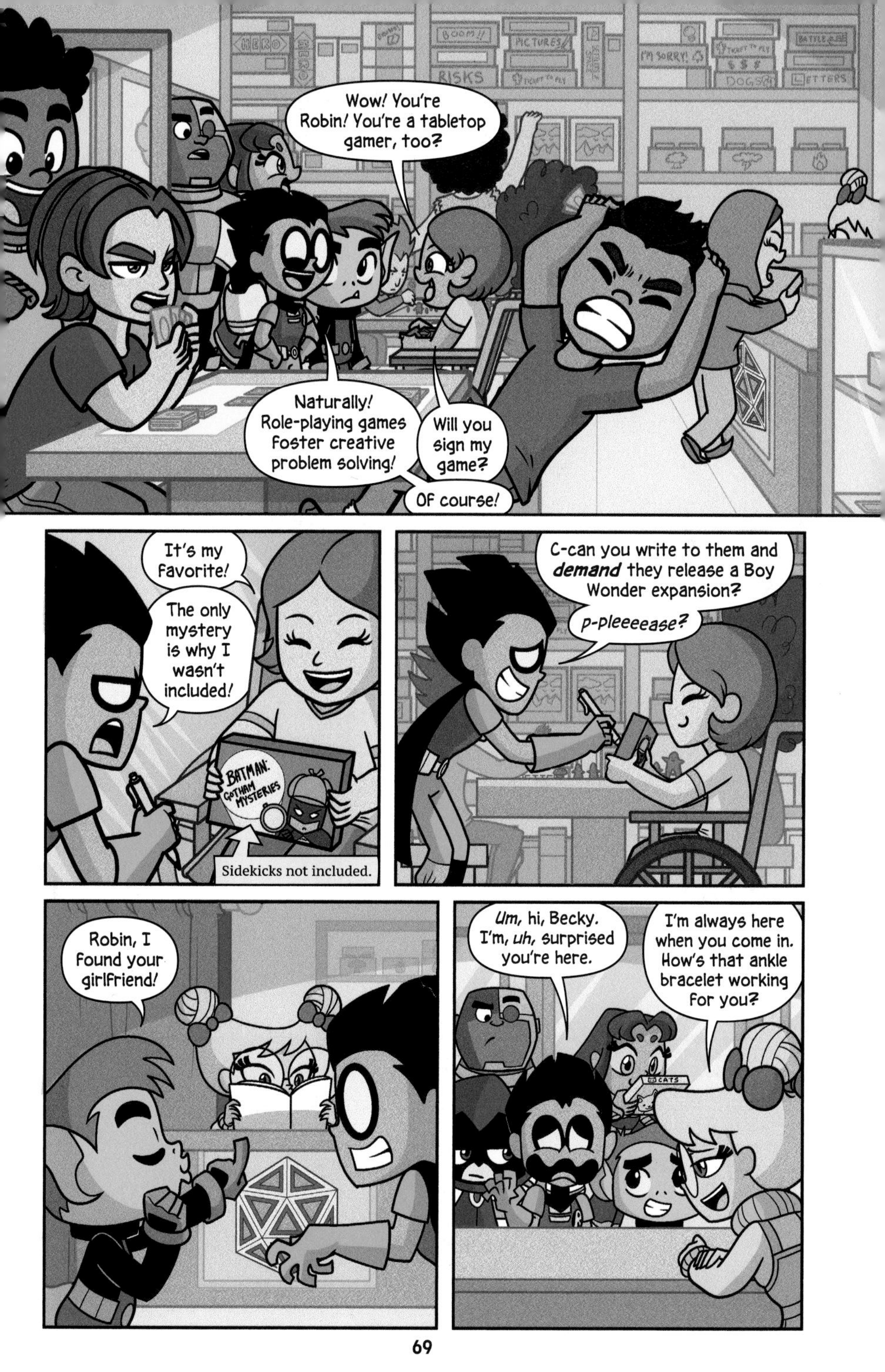
Wow! You're Robin! You're a tabletop gamer, too?
Naturally! Role-playing games foster creative problem solving!
Will you sign my game?
Of course!
It's my favorite!
The only mystery is why I wasn't included!
BATMAN: GOTHAM MYSTERIES
Sidekicks not included.
C-can you write to them and *demand* they release a Boy Wonder expansion?
p-pleeeease?
Robin, I found your girlfriend!
Um, hi, Becky. I'm, *uh*, surprised you're here.
I'm always here when you come in. How's that ankle bracelet working for you?

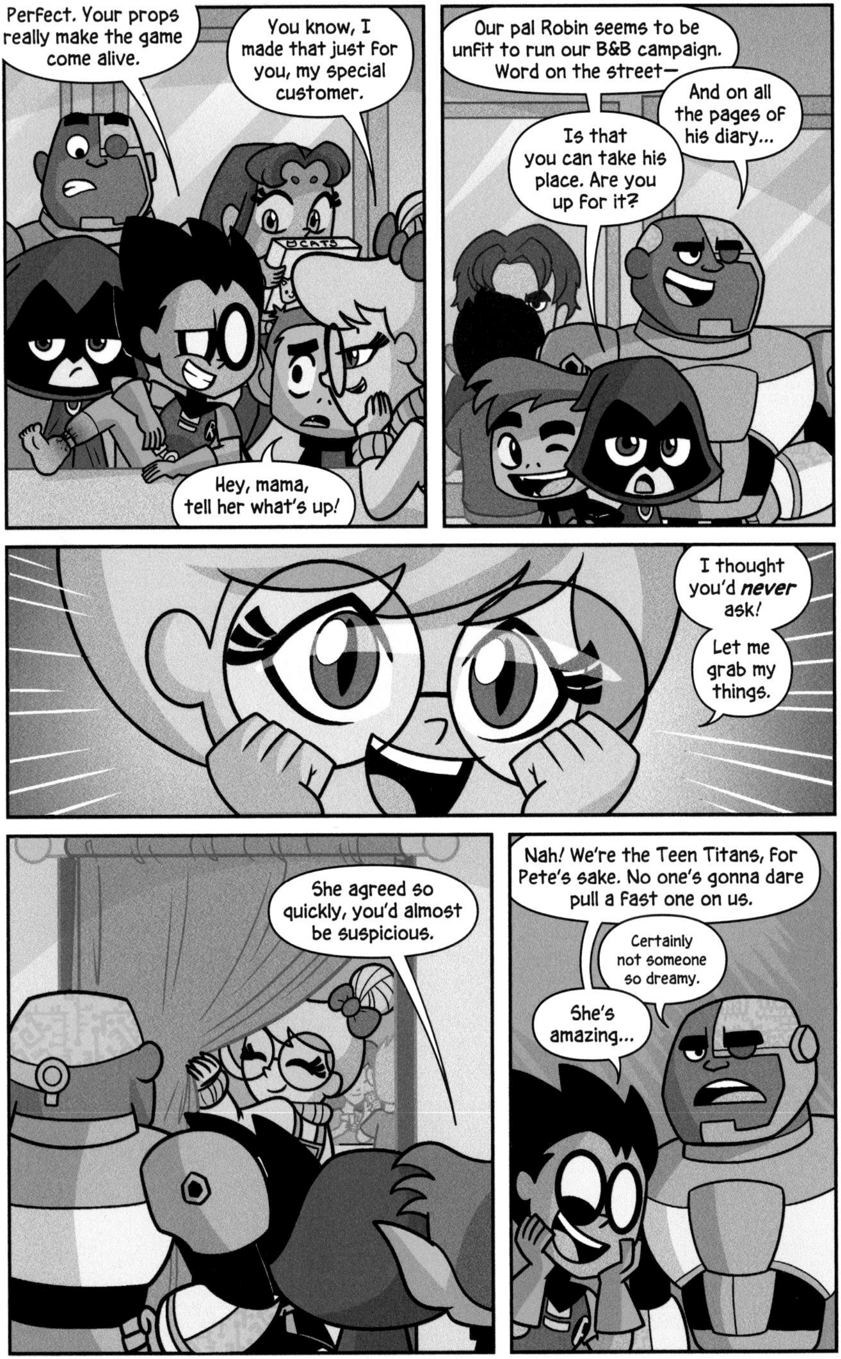

Perfect. Your props really make the game come alive.
You know, I made that just for you, my special customer.
Hey, mama, tell her what's up!
Our pal Robin seems to be unfit to run our B&B campaign. Word on the street—
Is that you can take his place. Are you up for it?
And on all the pages of his diary...
I thought you'd ***never*** ask!
Let me grab my things.
She agreed so quickly, you'd almost be suspicious.
Nah! We're the Teen Titans, for Pete's sake. No one's gonna dare pull a fast one on us.
She's amazing...
Certainly not someone so dreamy.

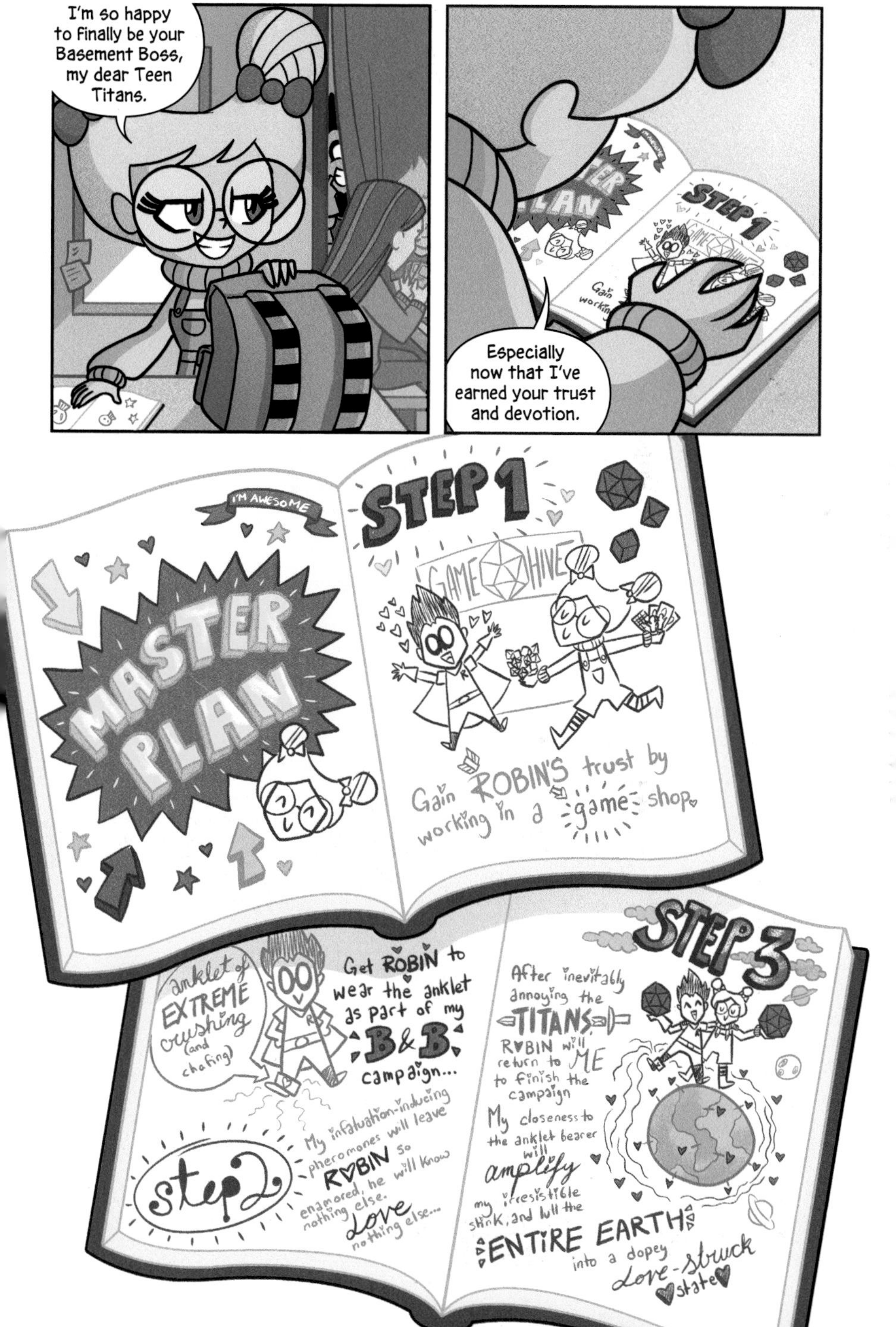
I'm so happy to finally be your Basement Boss, my dear Teen Titans.
Especially now that I've earned your trust and devotion.
I'M AWESOME
MASTER PLAN
STEP 1
GAME HIVE
Gain ROBIN'S trust by working in a game shop
anklet of EXTREME crushing (and chafing)
Get ROBIN to wear the anklet as part of my B&B campaign...
step 2
My infatuation-inducing pheromones will leave ROBIN so enamored, he will know nothing else.
Love nothing else...
STEP 3
After inevitably annoying the TITANS, ROBIN will return to ME to finish the campaign
My closeness to the anklet bearer will amplify my irresistible stink, and lull the ENTIRE EARTH into a dopey Love-struck state

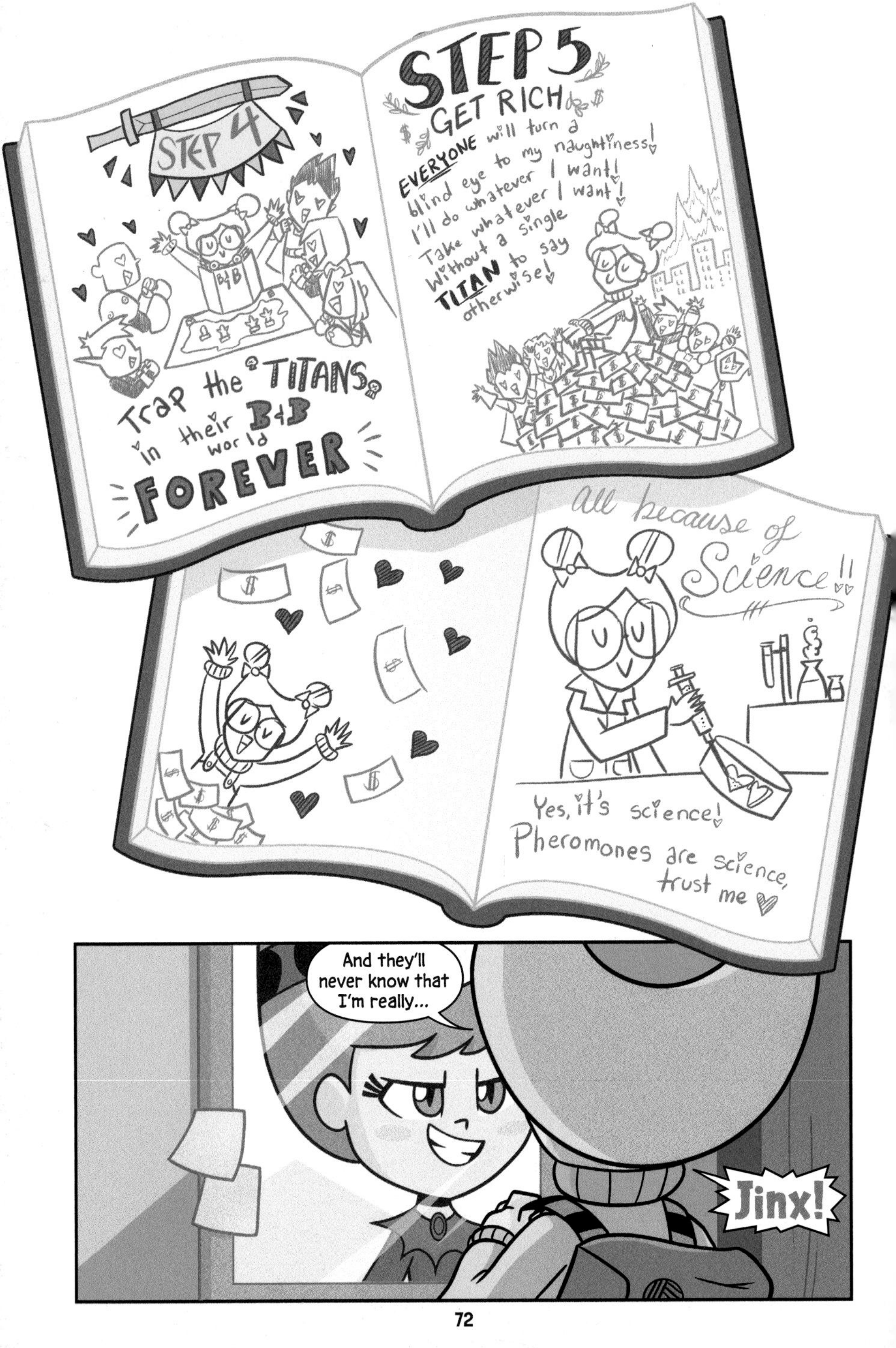
STEP 4
Trap the TITANS in their B+B world FOREVER
STEP 5
GET RICH
EVERYONE will turn a blind eye to my naughtiness!
I'll do whatever I want!
Take whatever I want!
Without a single TITAN to say otherwise!
all because of Science!!
Yes, it's science!
Pheromones are science, trust me
And they'll never know that I'm really...
Jinx!

Chapter
Six

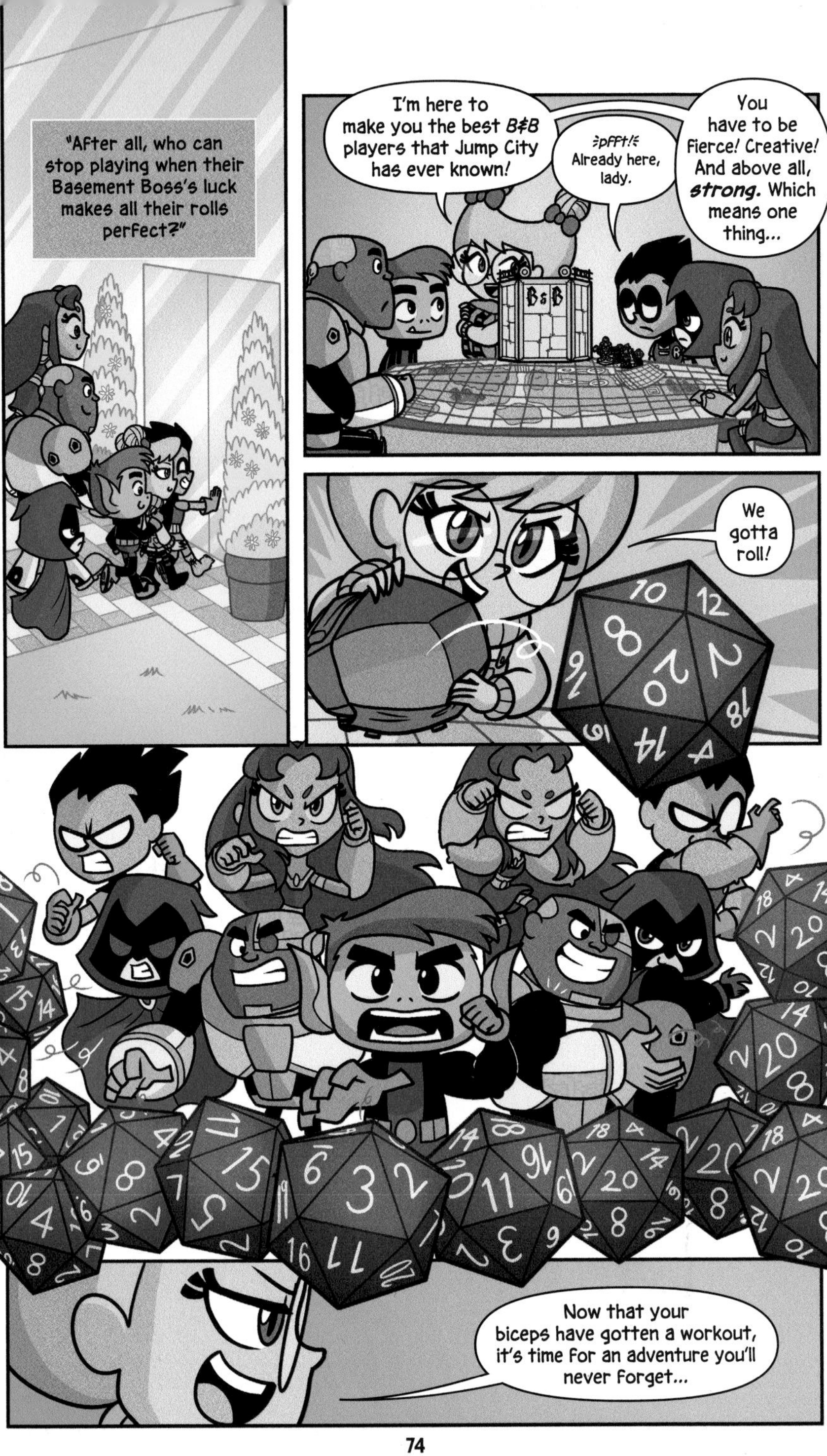
"After all, who can stop playing when their Basement Boss's luck makes all their rolls perfect?"
I'm here to make you the best B&B players that Jump City has ever known!
pfft! Already here, lady.
You have to be fierce! Creative! And above all, **strong.** Which means one thing...
We gotta roll!
Now that your biceps have gotten a workout, it's time for an adventure you'll never forget...

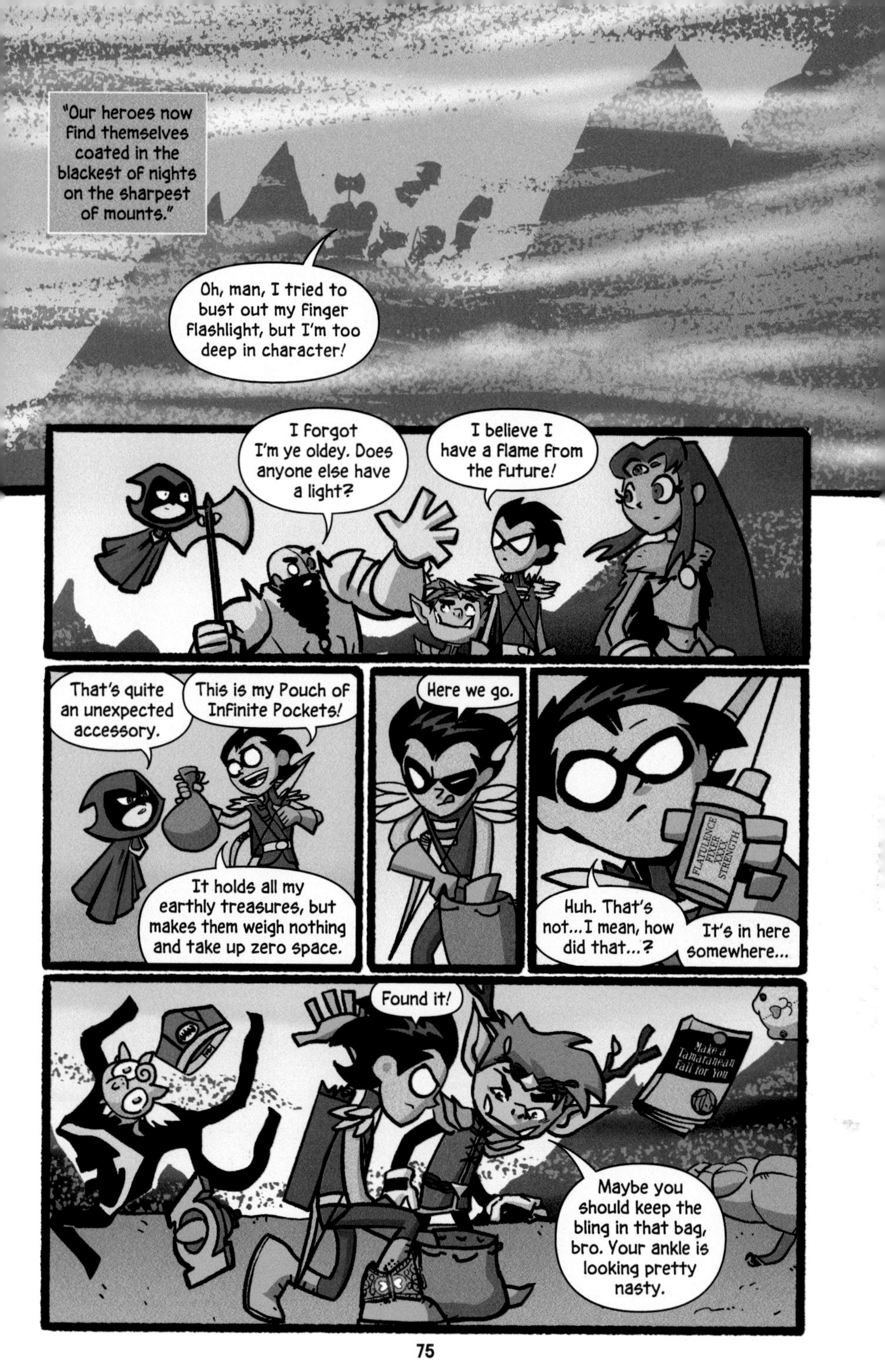
"Our heroes now find themselves coated in the blackest of nights on the sharpest of mounts."
Oh, man, I tried to bust out my finger flashlight, but I'm too deep in character!
I forgot I'm ye oldey. Does anyone else have a light?
I believe I have a flame from the future!
That's quite an unexpected accessory.
This is my Pouch of Infinite Pockets!
It holds all my earthly treasures, but makes them weigh nothing and take up zero space.
Here we go.
FLATULENCE FIXER XXXX STRENGTH
Huh. That's not...I mean, how did that...?
It's in here somewhere...
Found it!
Make a Tamaranean Fall for You
Maybe you should keep the bling in that bag, bro. Your ankle is looking pretty nasty.

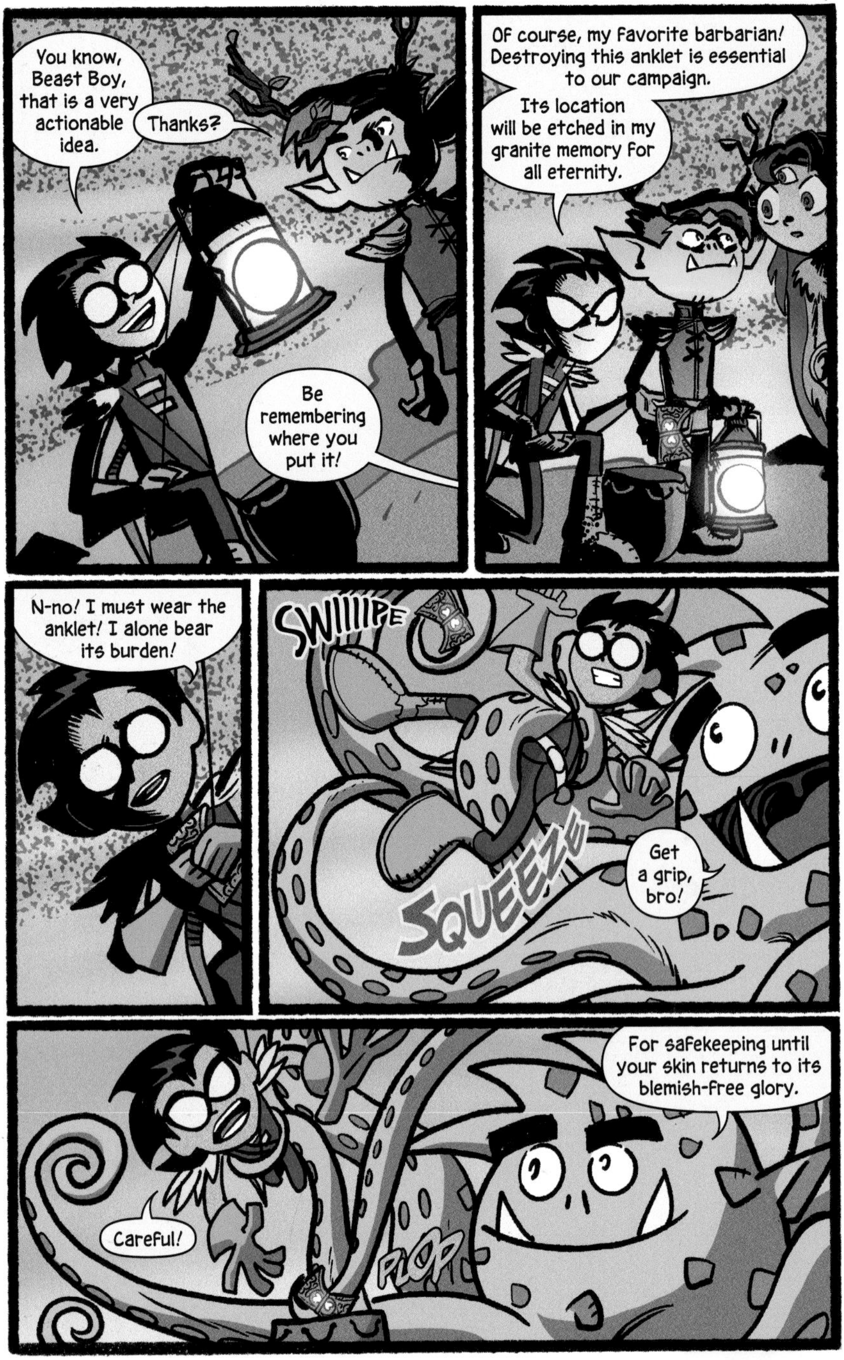
You know, Beast Boy, that is a very actionable idea.
Thanks?
Be remembering where you put it!
Of course, my favorite barbarian! Destroying this anklet is essential to our campaign.
Its location will be etched in my granite memory for all eternity.
N-no! I must wear the anklet! I alone bear its burden!
SWIIIIPE
SQUEEZE
Get a grip, bro!
For safekeeping until your skin returns to its blemish-free glory.
Careful!
PLOP

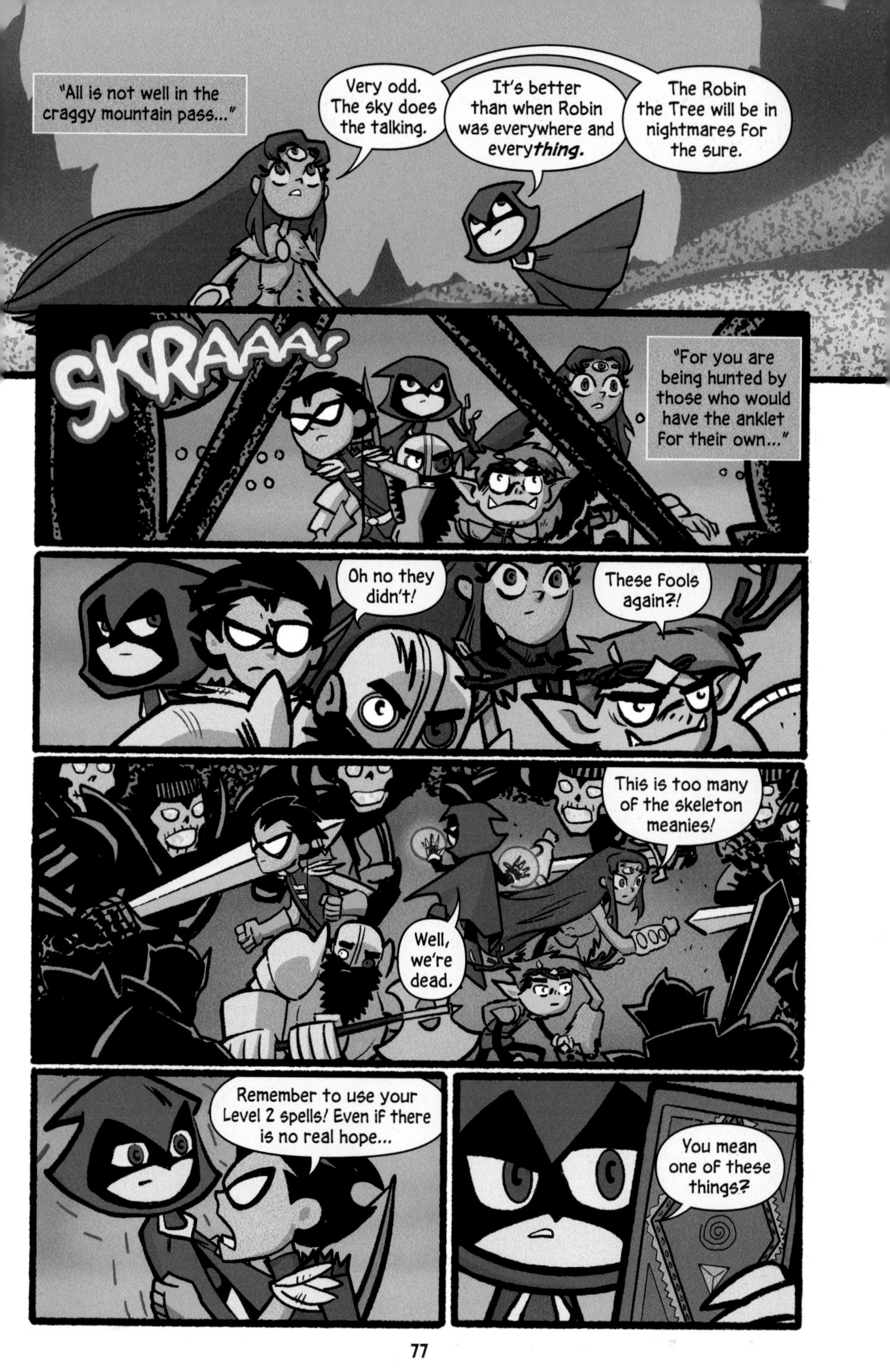
"All is not well in the craggy mountain pass..."
Very odd. The sky does the talking.
It's better than when Robin was everywhere and every*thing.*
The Robin the Tree will be in nightmares for the sure.
SKRAAA!
"For you are being hunted by those who would have the anklet for their own..."
Oh no they didn't!
These fools again?!
This is too many of the skeleton meanies!
Well, we're dead.
Remember to use your Level 2 spells! Even if there is no real hope...
You mean one of these things?

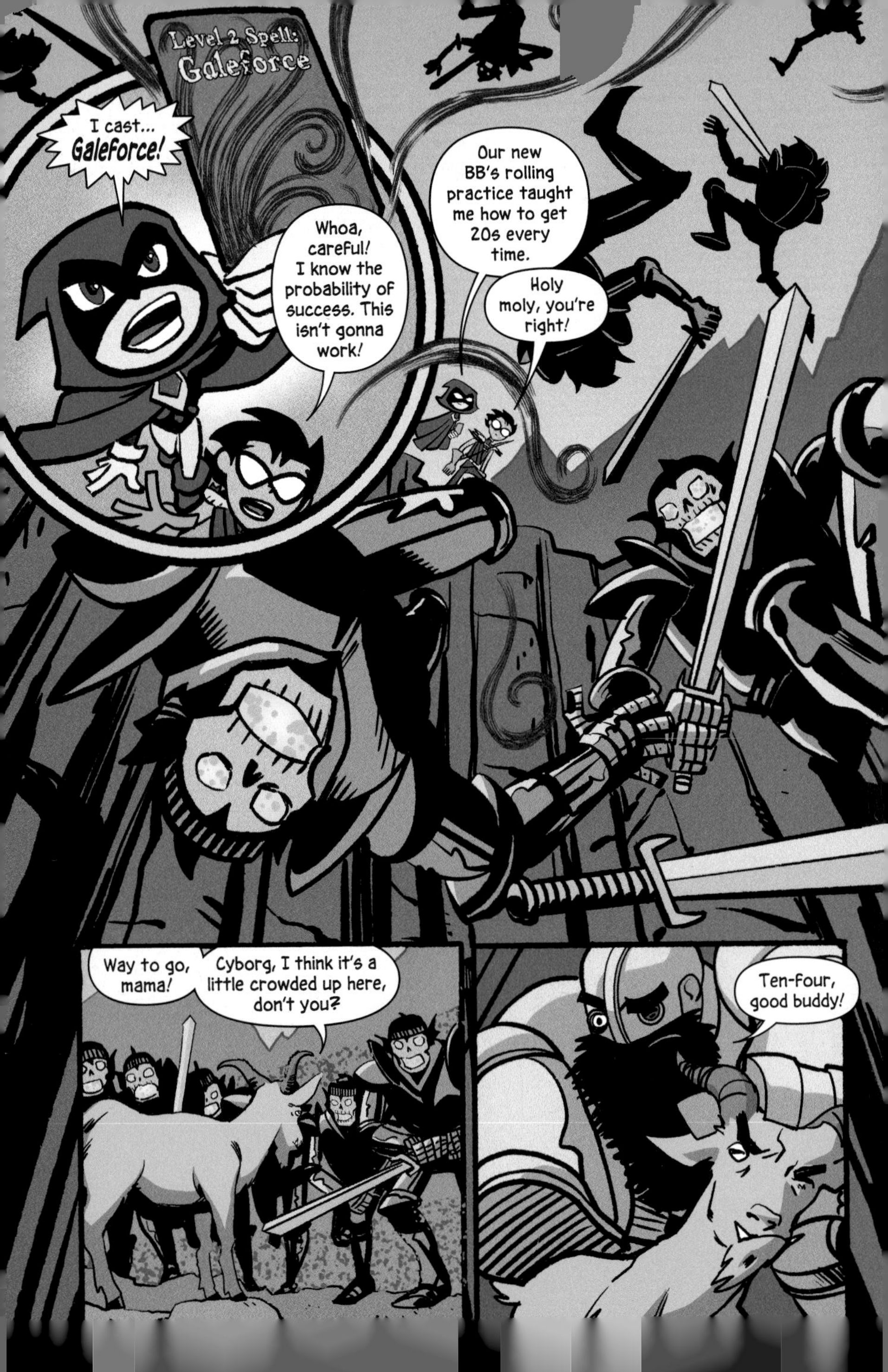
Level 2 Spell:
Galeforce
I cast... Galeforce!
Whoa, careful! I know the probability of success. This isn't gonna work!
Our new BB's rolling practice taught me how to get 20s every time.
Holy moly, you're right!
Way to go, mama!
Cyborg, I think it's a little crowded up here, don't you?
Ten-four, good buddy!

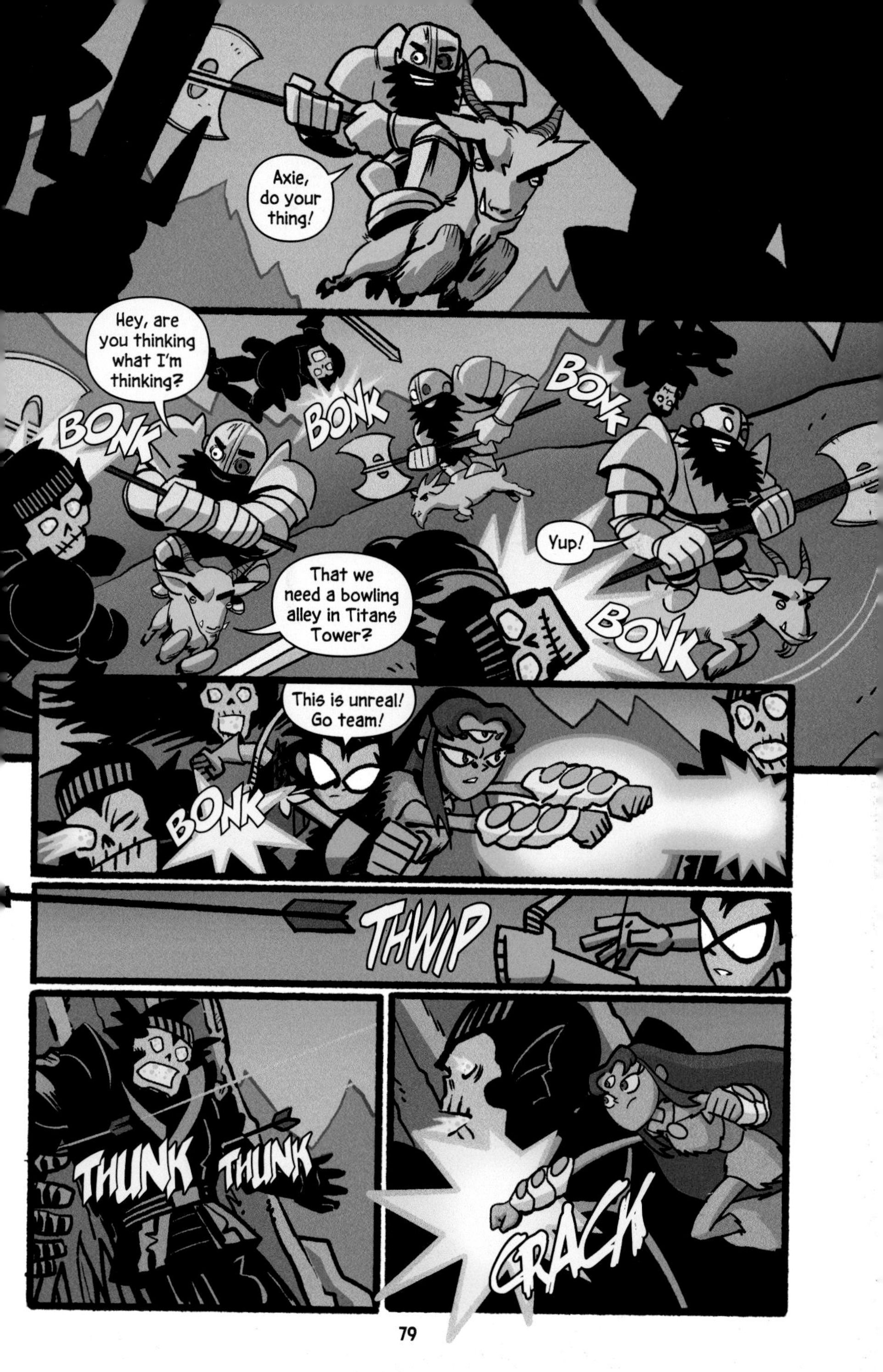
Axie, do your thing!
Hey, are you thinking what I'm thinking?
BONK
BONK
BONK
Yup!
That we need a bowling alley in Titans Tower?
BONK
This is unreal! Go team!
BONK
THWIP
THUNK THUNK
CRACK

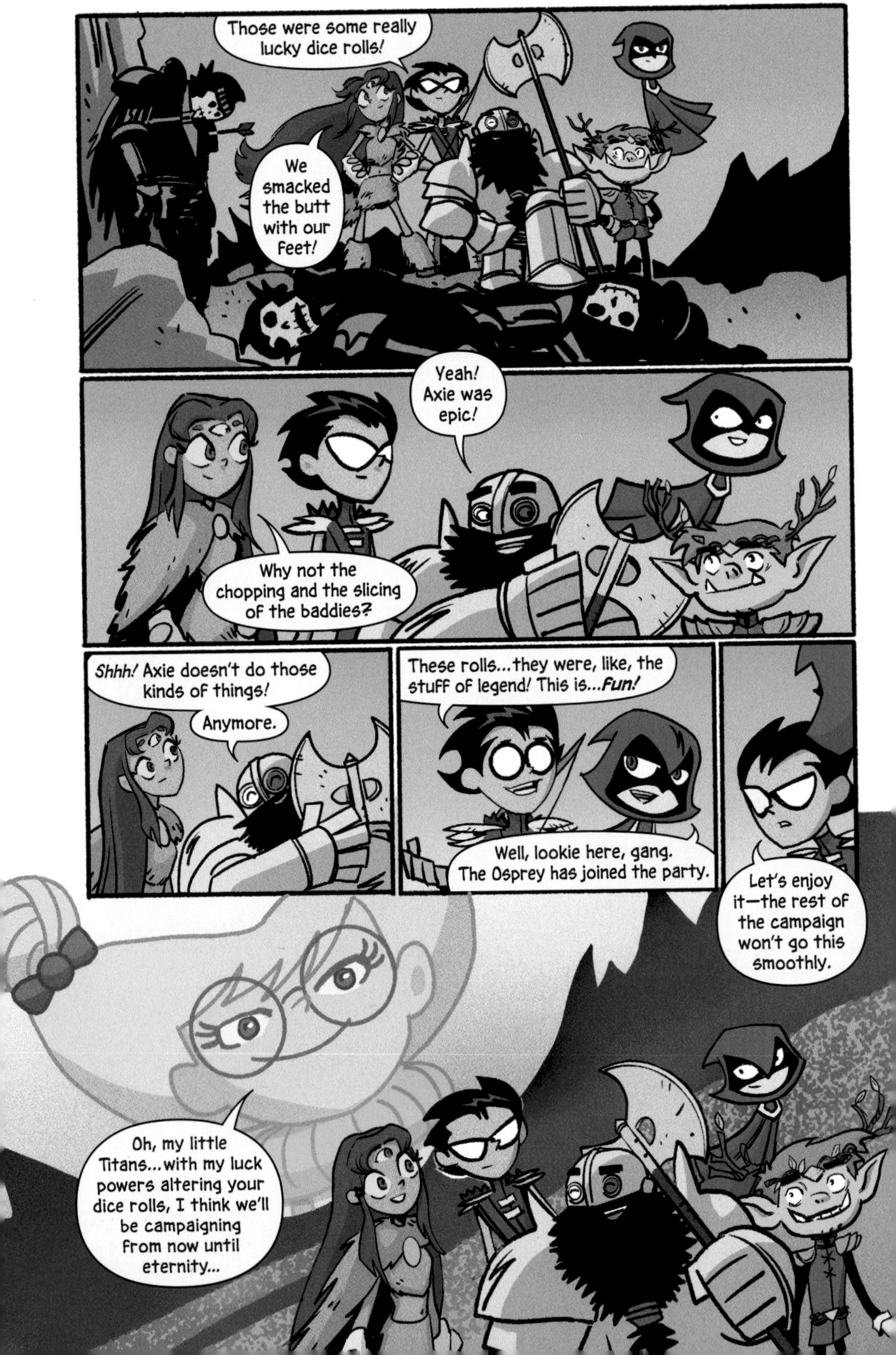

Those were some really lucky dice rolls!
We smacked the butt with our feet!
Yeah! Axie was epic!
Why not the chopping and the slicing of the baddies?
Shhh! Axie doesn't do those kinds of things!
Anymore.
These rolls...they were, like, the stuff of legend! This is...Fun!
Well, lookie here, gang. The Osprey has joined the party.
Let's enjoy it—the rest of the campaign won't go this smoothly.
Oh, my little Titans...with my luck powers altering your dice rolls, I think we'll be campaigning from now until eternity...

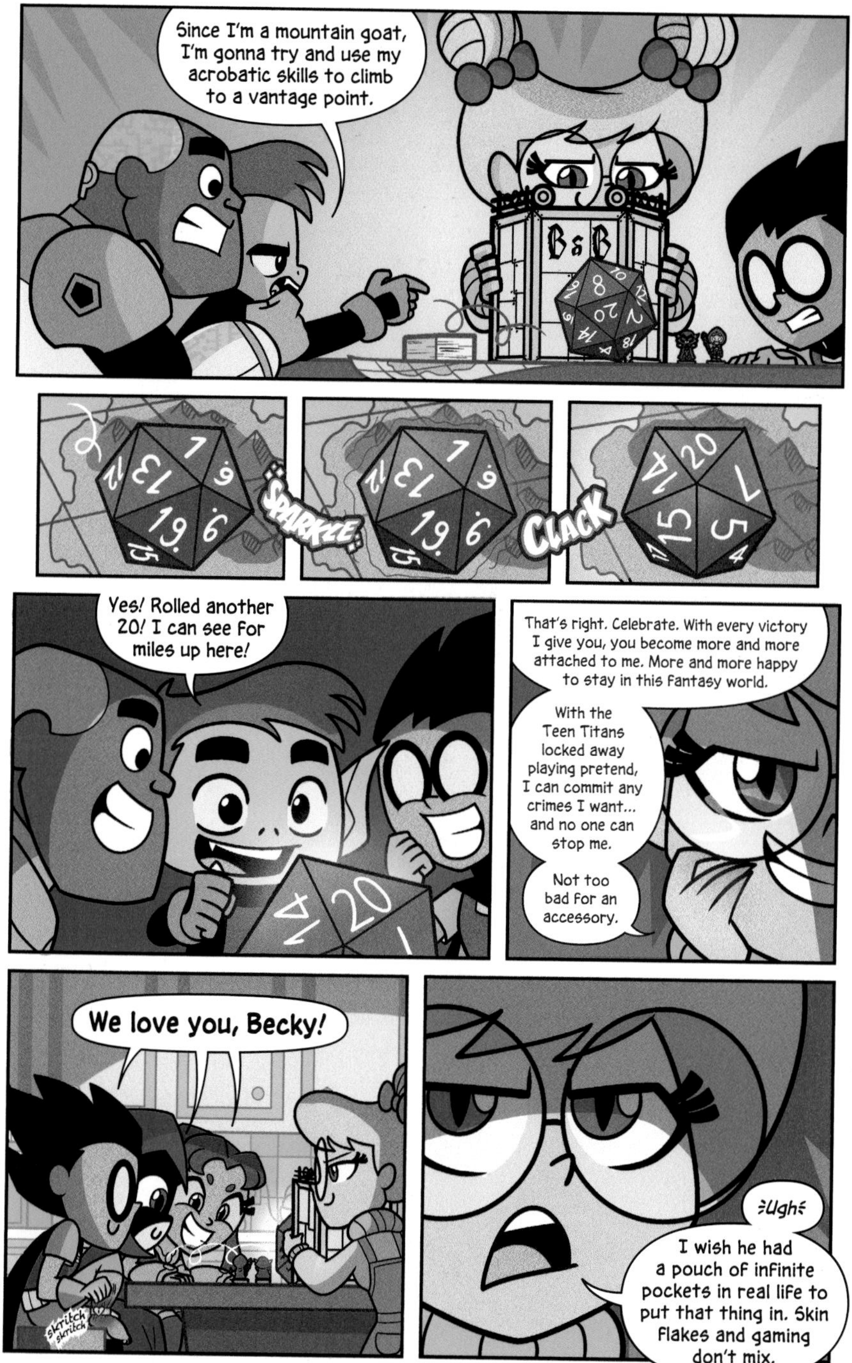
Since I'm a mountain goat, I'm gonna try and use my acrobatic skills to climb to a vantage point.
B&B
SPARKLE
CLACK
Yes! Rolled another 20! I can see for miles up here!
That's right. Celebrate. With every victory I give you, you become more and more attached to me. More and more happy to stay in this fantasy world.
With the Teen Titans locked away playing pretend, I can commit any crimes I want... and no one can stop me.
Not too bad for an accessory.
We love you, Becky!
skritch skritch
Ugh
I wish he had a pouch of infinite pockets in real life to put that thing in. Skin flakes and gaming don't mix.

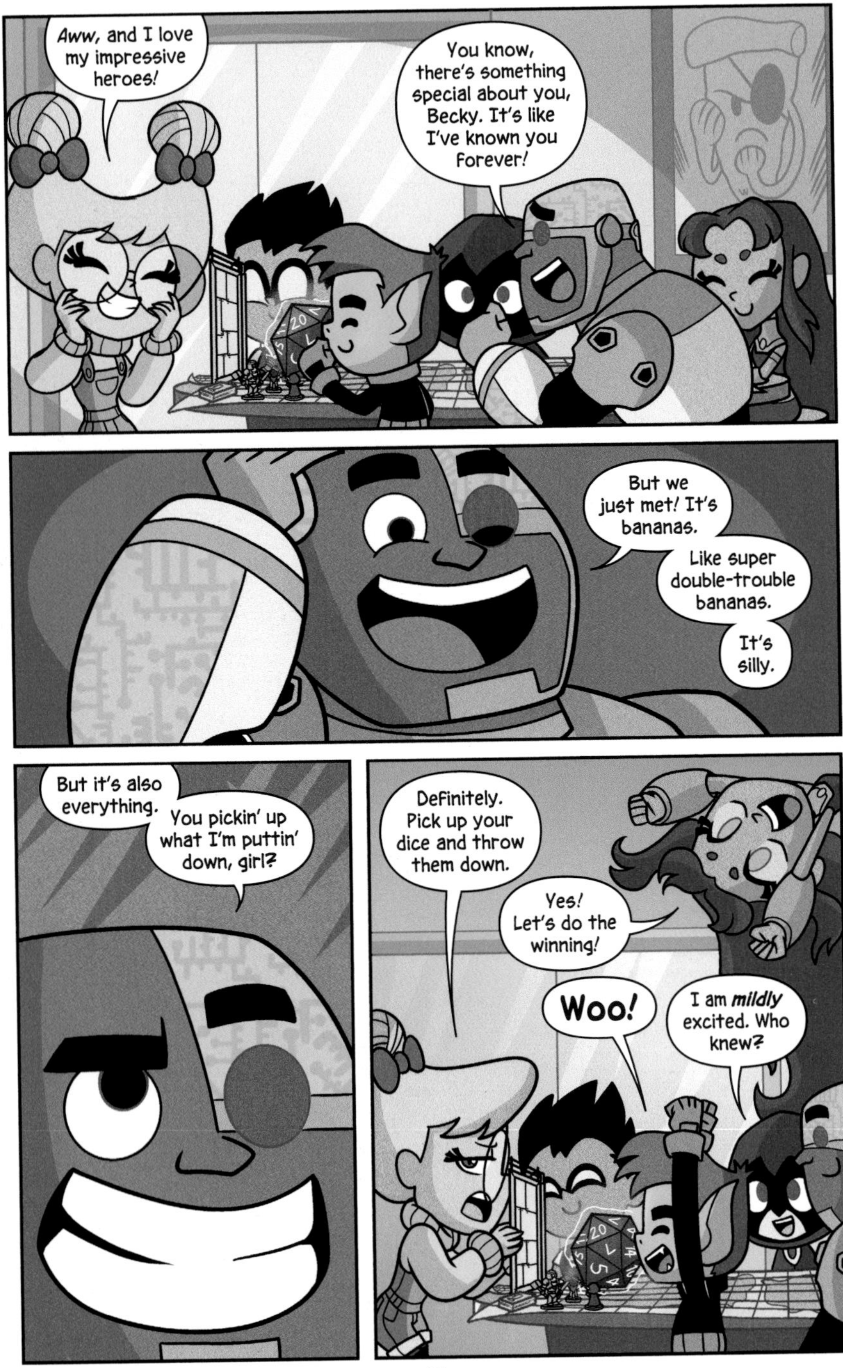
Aww, and I love my impressive heroes!
You know, there's something special about you, Becky. It's like I've known you forever!
But we just met! It's bananas.
Like super double-trouble bananas.
It's silly.
But it's also everything.
You pickin' up what I'm puttin' down, girl?
Definitely. Pick up your dice and throw them down.
Yes! Let's do the winning!
Woo!
I am *mildly* excited. Who knew?
20

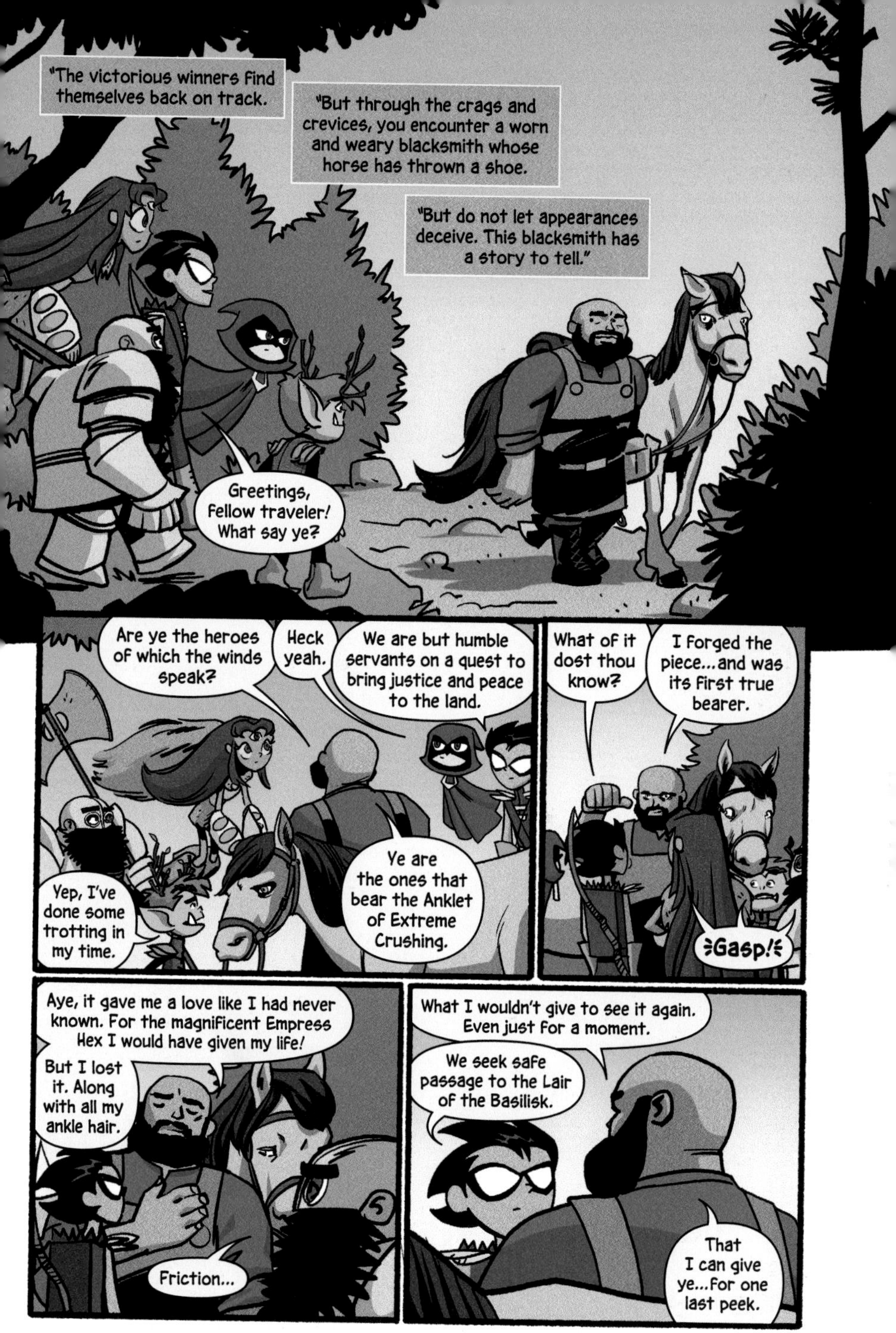
"The victorious winners find themselves back on track.
"But through the crags and crevices, you encounter a worn and weary blacksmith whose horse has thrown a shoe.
"But do not let appearances deceive. This blacksmith has a story to tell."
Greetings, fellow traveler! What say ye?
Are ye the heroes of which the winds speak?
Heck yeah.
We are but humble servants on a quest to bring justice and peace to the land.
Ye are the ones that bear the Anklet of Extreme Crushing.
Yep, I've done some trotting in my time.
What of it dost thou know?
I forged the piece...and was its first true bearer.
Gasp!
Aye, it gave me a love like I had never known. For the magnificent Empress Hex I would have given my life!
But I lost it. Along with all my ankle hair.
Friction...
What I wouldn't give to see it again. Even just for a moment.
We seek safe passage to the Lair of the Basilisk.
That I can give ye...For one last peek.

Chapter Seven

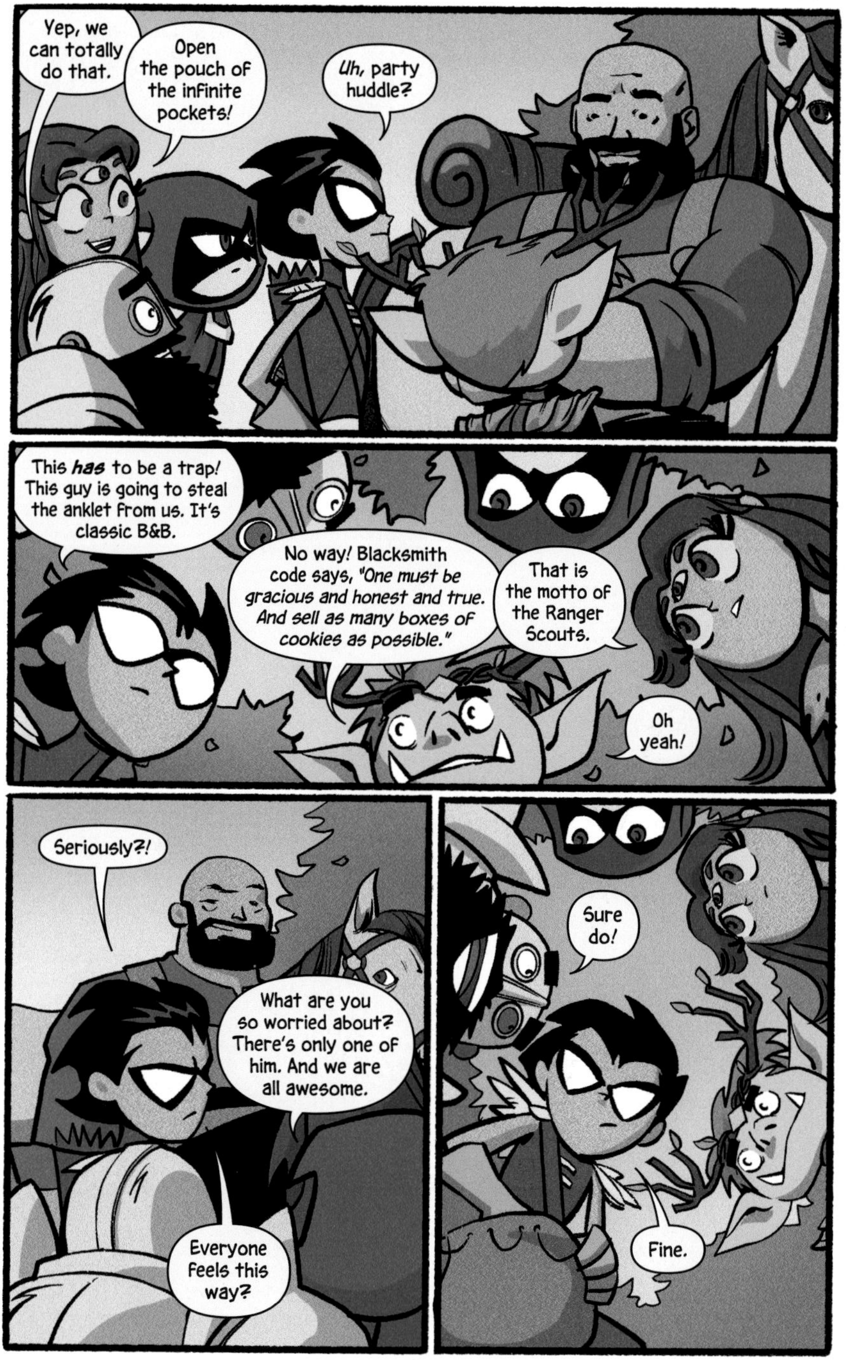
Yep, we can totally do that.
Open the pouch of the infinite pockets!
Uh, party huddle?
This *has* to be a trap! This guy is going to steal the anklet from us. It's classic B&B.
No way! Blacksmith code says, "One must be gracious and honest and true. And sell as many boxes of cookies as possible."
That is the motto of the Ranger Scouts.
Oh yeah!
Seriously?!
What are you so worried about? There's only one of him. And we are all awesome.
Everyone feels this way?
Sure do!
Fine.

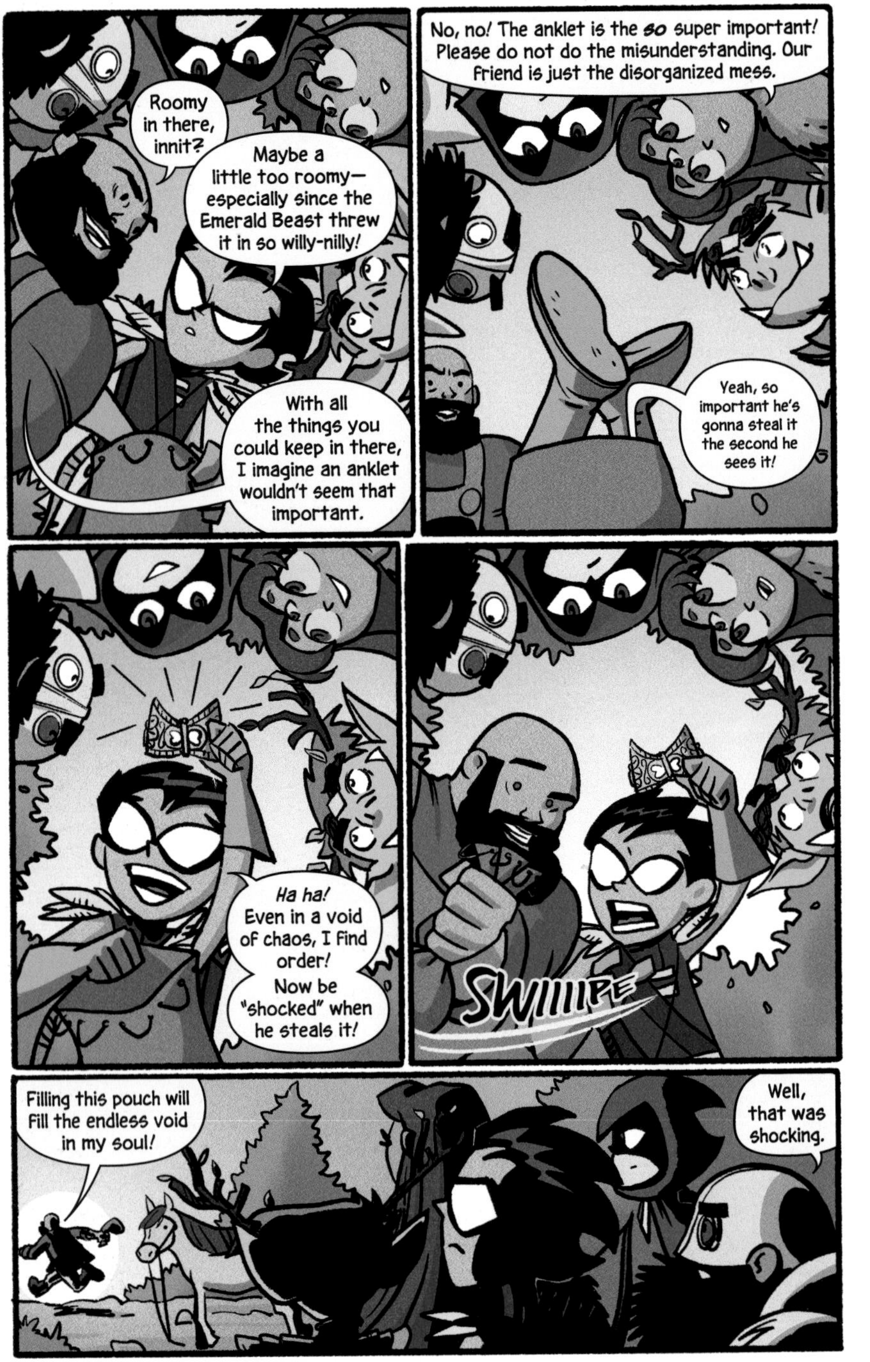
Roomy in there, innit?
Maybe a little too roomy—especially since the Emerald Beast threw it in so willy-nilly!
With all the things you could keep in there, I imagine an anklet wouldn't seem that important.
No, no! The anklet is the *so* super important! Please do not do the misunderstanding. Our friend is just the disorganized mess.
Yeah, so important he's gonna steal it the second he sees it!
Ha ha! Even in a void of chaos, I find order!
Now be "shocked" when he steals it!
SWIIIIPE
Filling this pouch will fill the endless void in my soul!
Well, that was shocking.

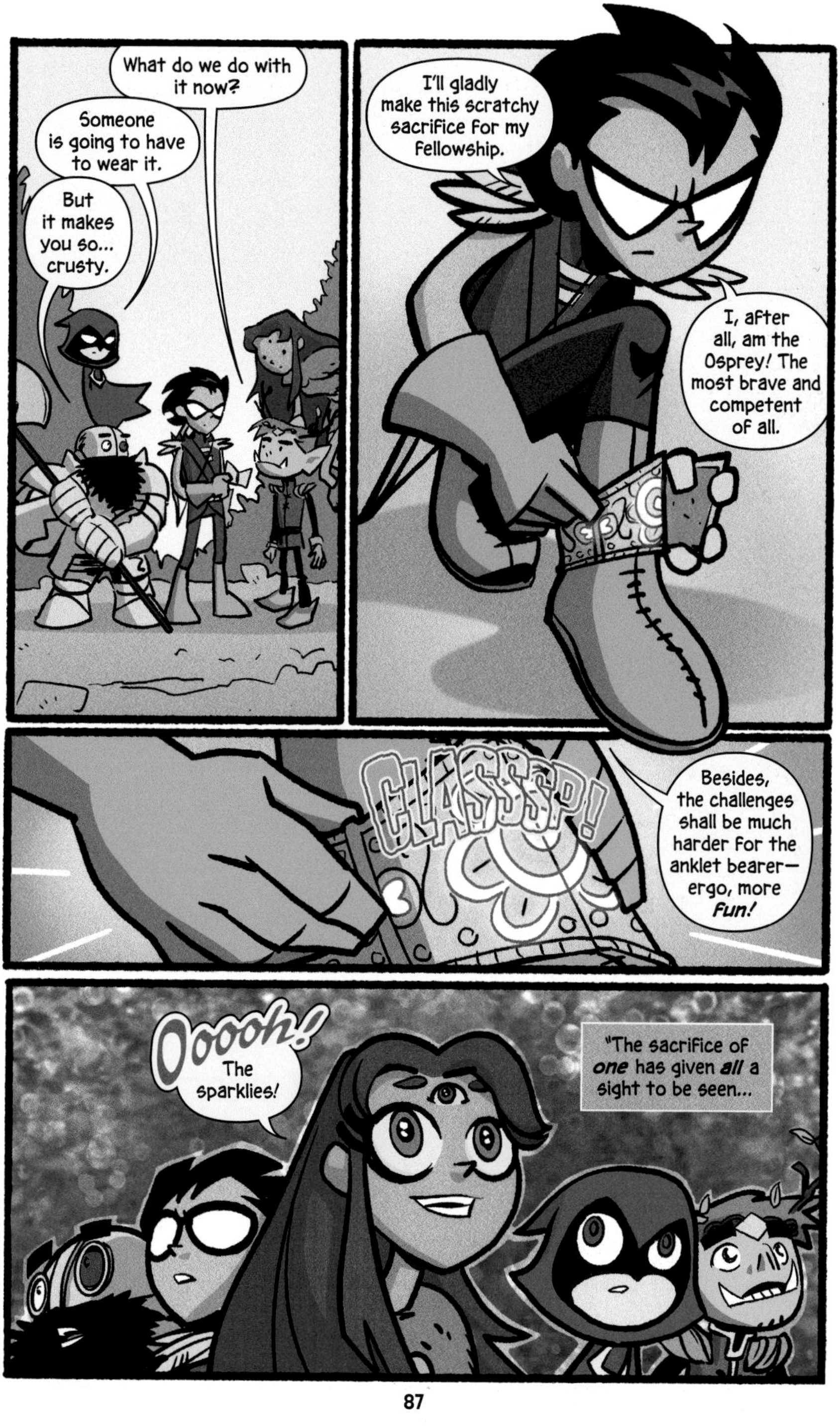
What do we do with it now?
Someone is going to have to wear it.
But it makes you so... crusty.
I'll gladly make this scratchy sacrifice for my fellowship.
I, after all, am the Osprey! The most brave and competent of all.
CLASSSP!
Besides, the challenges shall be much harder for the anklet bearer—ergo, more *fun!*
Ooooh! The sparklies!
"The sacrifice of *one* has given *all* a sight to be seen...

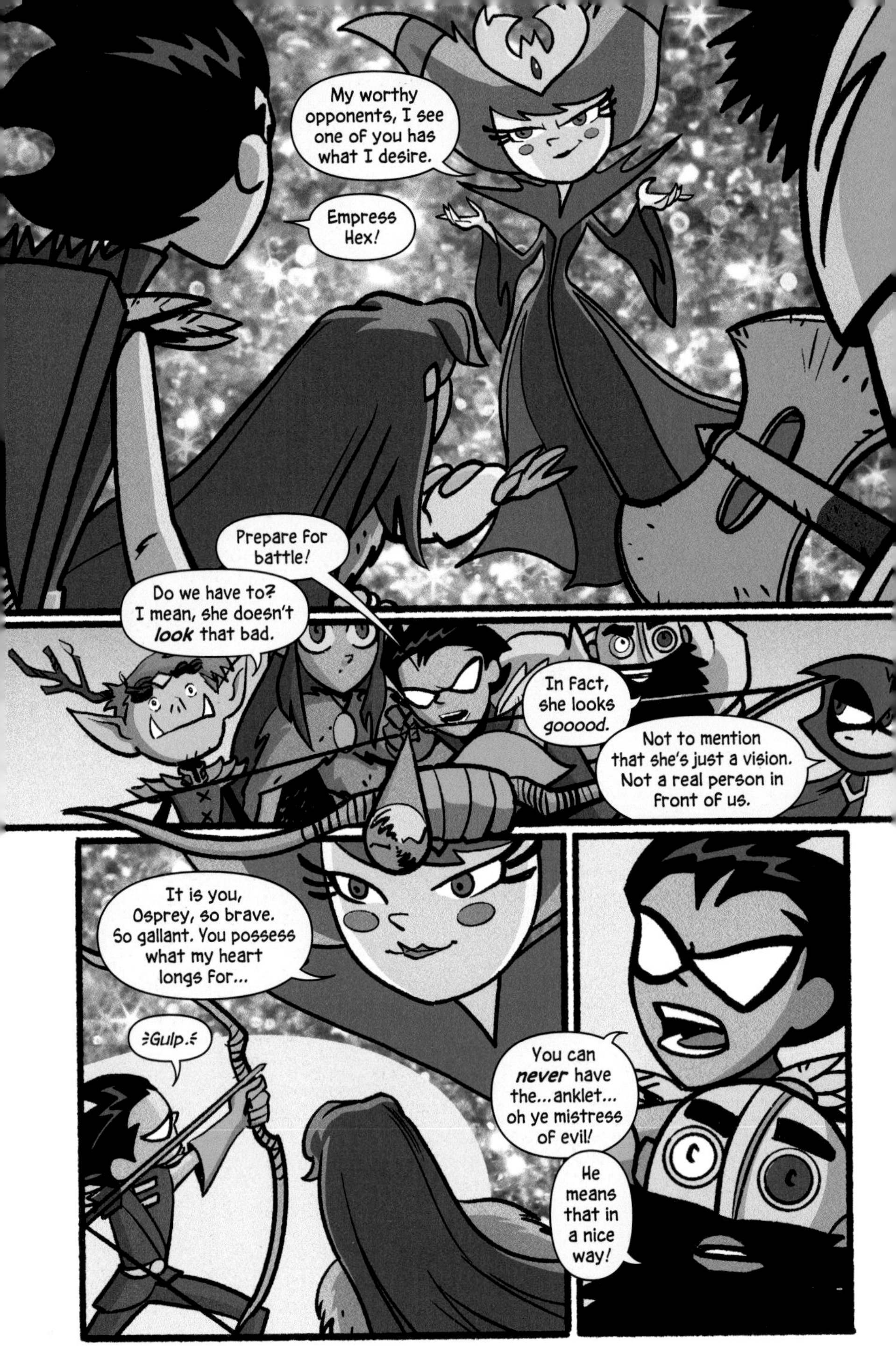
My worthy opponents, I see one of you has what I desire.
Empress Hex!
Prepare for battle!
Do we have to? I mean, she doesn't *look* that bad.
In fact, she looks *gooood.*
Not to mention that she's just a vision. Not a real person in front of us.
It is you, Osprey, so brave. So gallant. You possess what my heart longs for...
Gulp.
You can *never* have the...anklet... oh ye mistress of evil!
He means that in a nice way!

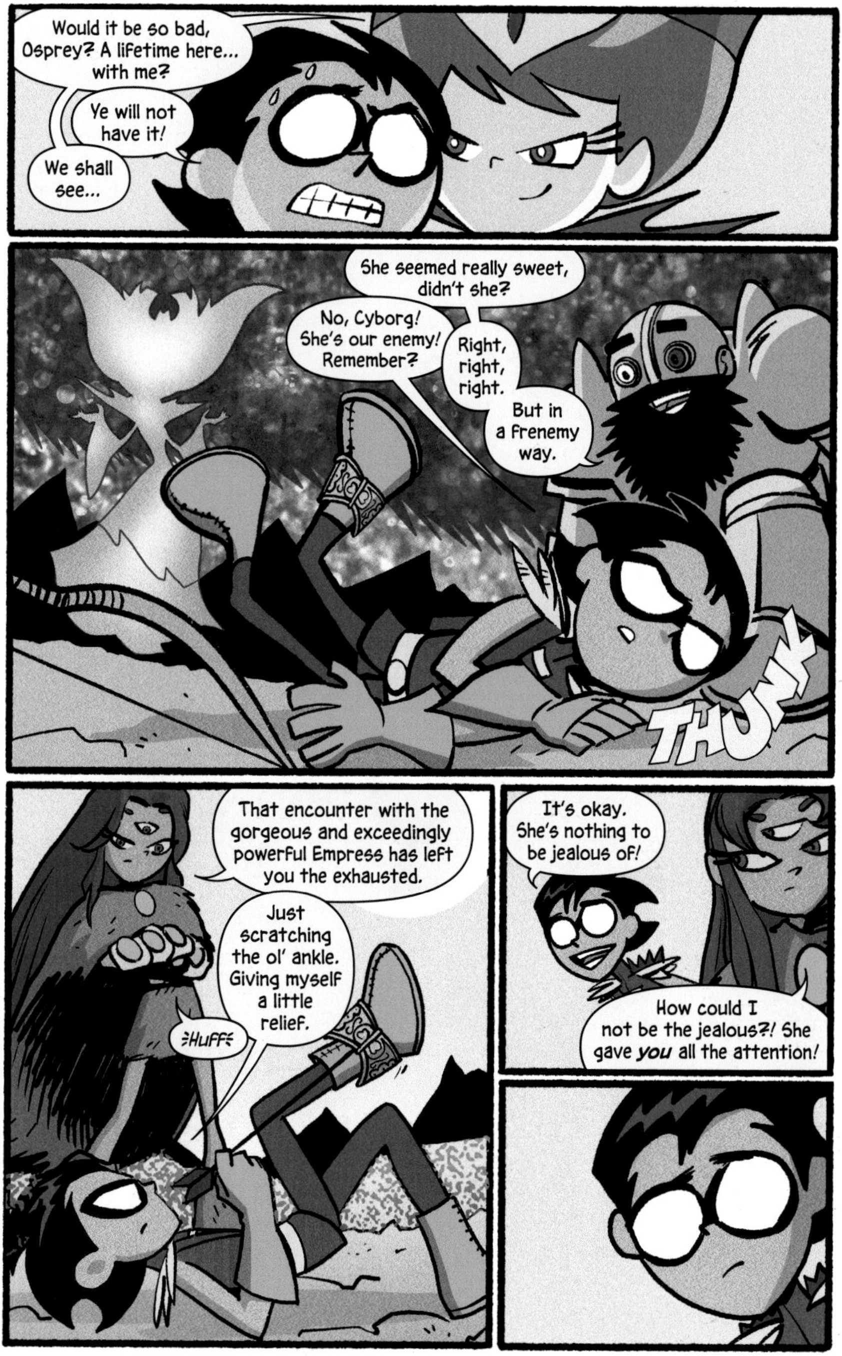

Would it be so bad, Osprey? A lifetime here... with me?
Ye will not have it!
We shall see...
She seemed really sweet, didn't she?
No, Cyborg! She's our enemy! Remember?
Right, right, right.
But in a frenemy way.
THUNK
That encounter with the gorgeous and exceedingly powerful Empress has left you the exhausted.
Just scratching the ol' ankle. Giving myself a little relief.
HUFF
It's okay. She's nothing to be jealous of!
How could I not be the jealous?! She gave *you* all the attention!

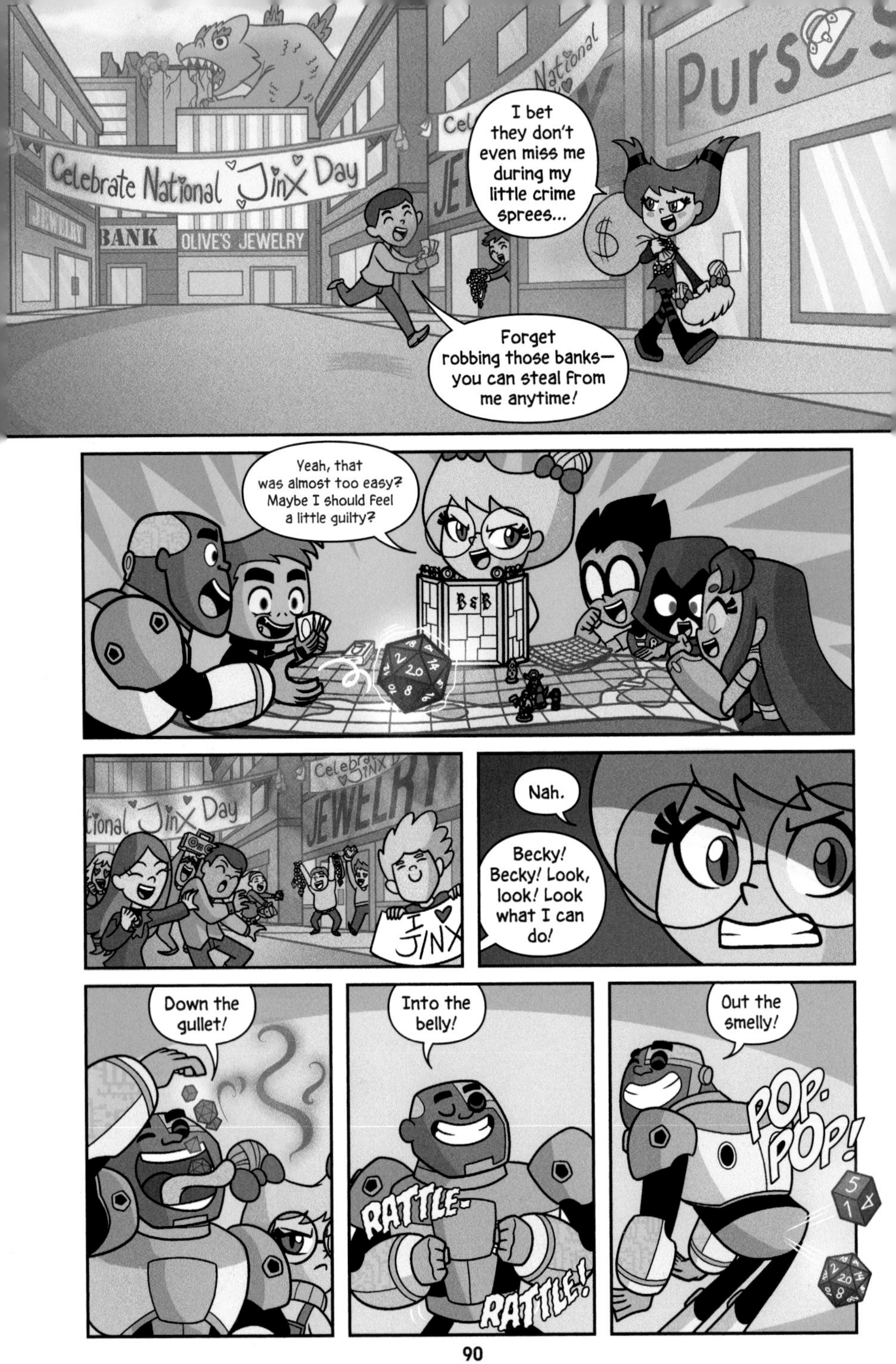
Celebrate National Jinx Day
BANK
OLIVE'S JEWELRY
Purses
I bet they don't even miss me during my little crime sprees...
Forget robbing those banks—you can steal from me anytime!
Yeah, that was almost too easy? Maybe I should feel a little guilty?
B&B
Celebrate Jinx
JEWELRY
Nah.
Becky! Becky! Look, look! Look what I can do!
I ♥ JINX
Down the gullet!
Into the belly!
RATTLE-RATTLE!
Out the smelly!
POP-POP!

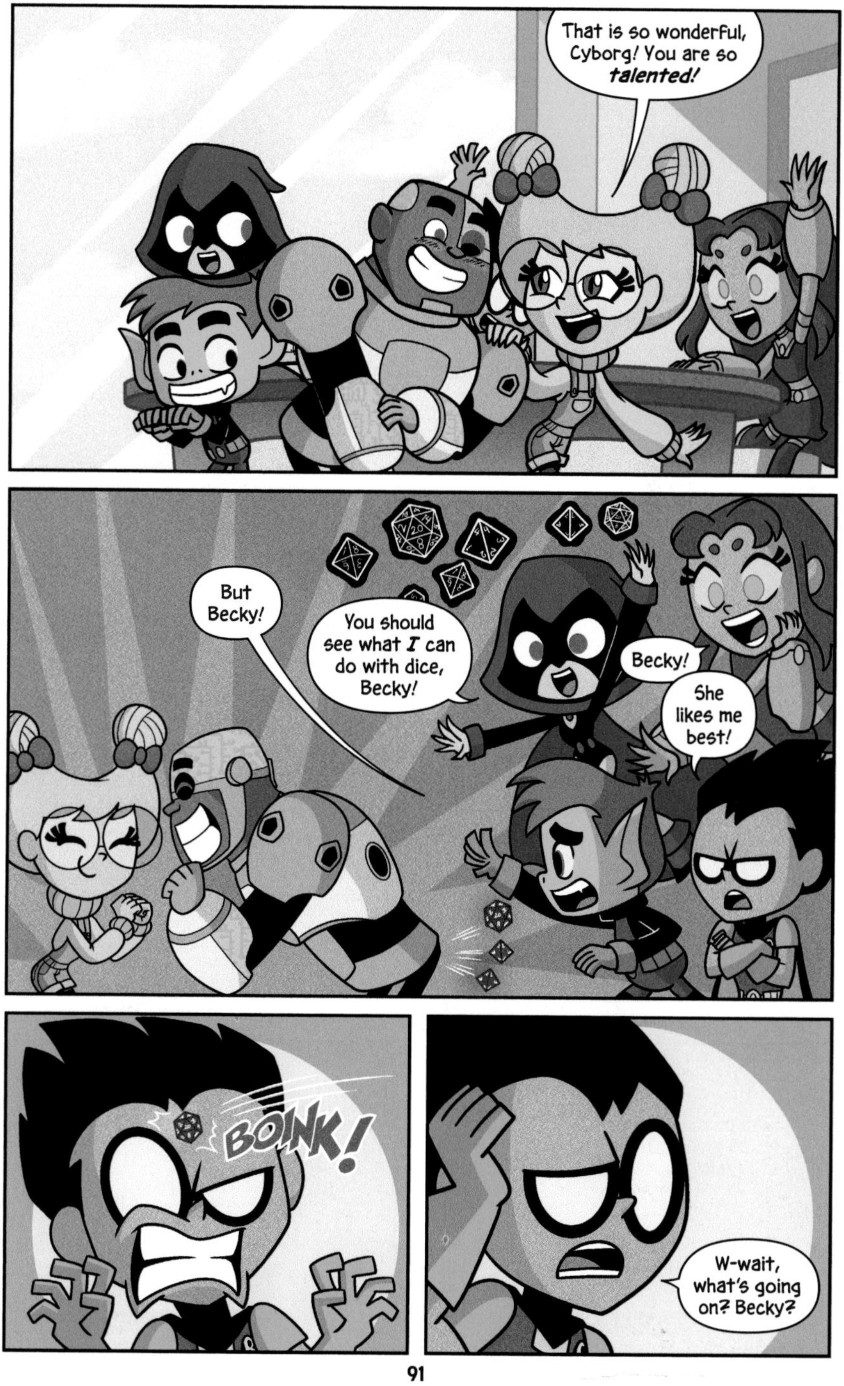

That is so wonderful, Cyborg! You are so *talented!*
But Becky!
You should see what *I* can do with dice, Becky!
Becky!
She likes me best!
BOINK!
W-wait, what's going on? Becky?

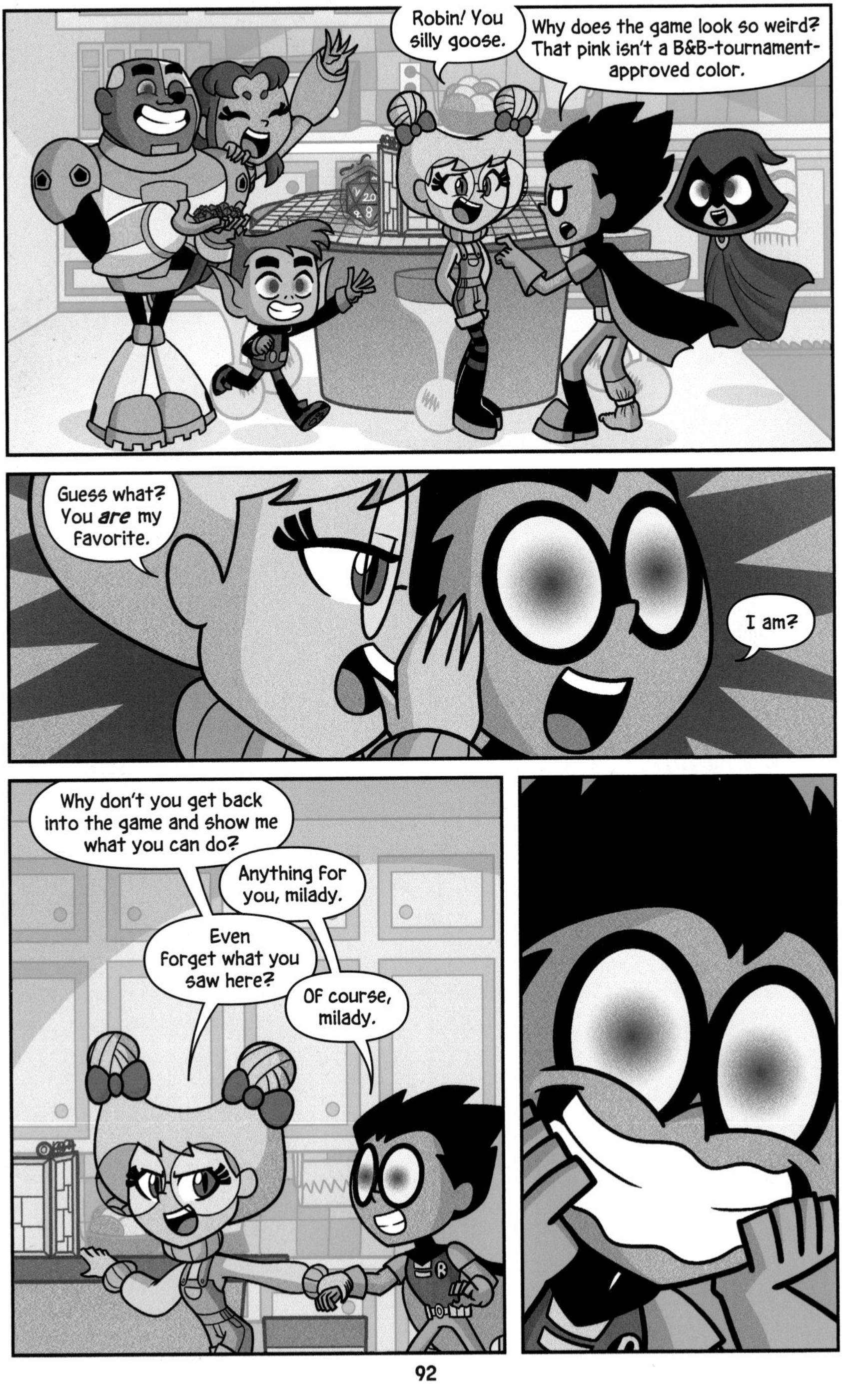
Robin! You silly goose.
Why does the game look so weird? That pink isn't a B&B-tournament-approved color.
Guess what? You *are* my favorite.
I am?
Why don't you get back into the game and show me what you can do?
Anything for you, milady.
Even forget what you saw here?
Of course, milady.

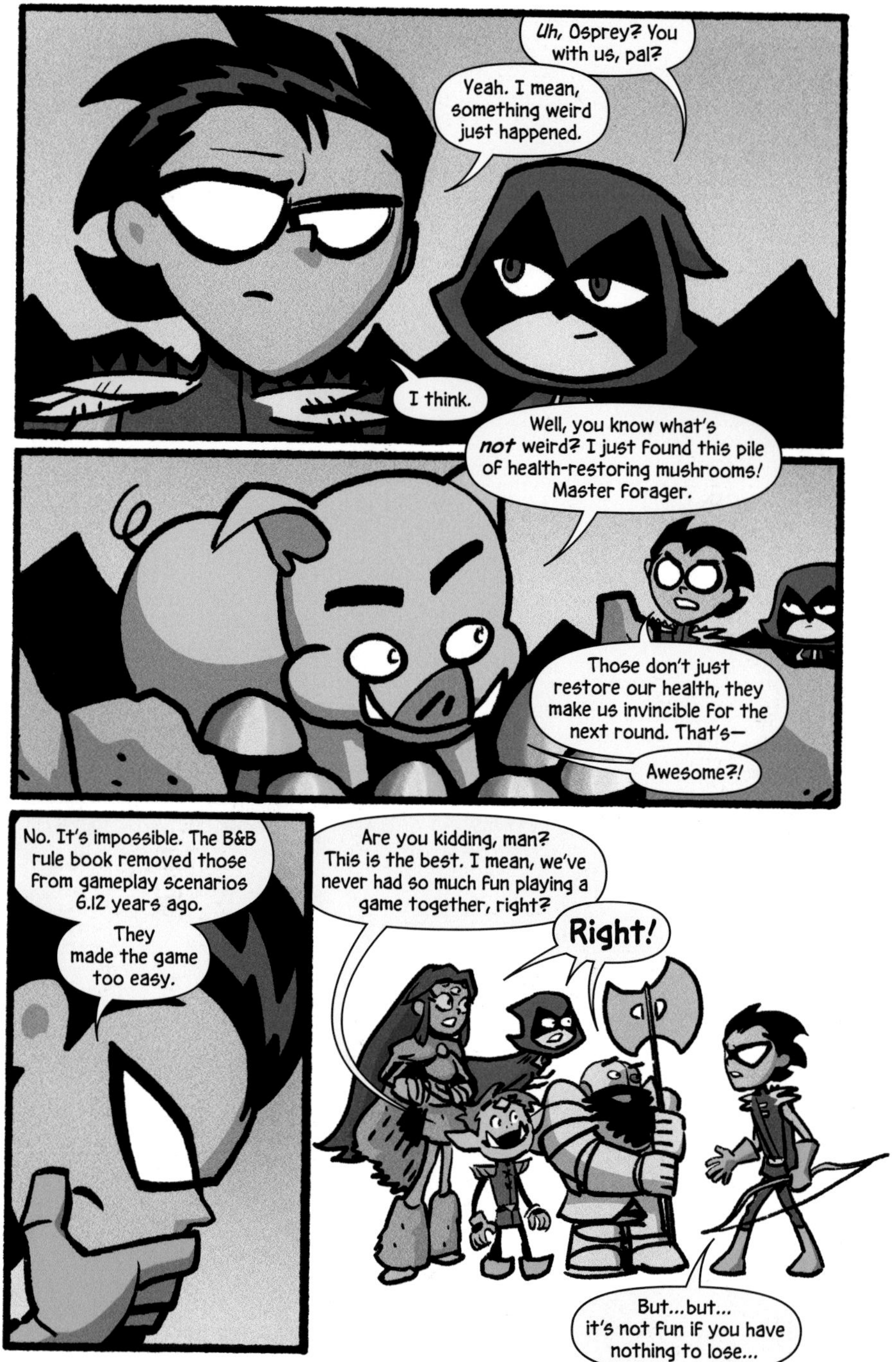
Uh, Osprey? You with us, pal?
Yeah. I mean, something weird just happened.
I think.
Well, you know what's *not* weird? I just found this pile of health-restoring mushrooms! Master forager.
Those don't just restore our health, they make us invincible for the next round. That's—
Awesome?!
No. It's impossible. The B&B rule book removed those from gameplay scenarios 6.12 years ago.
They made the game too easy.
Are you kidding, man? This is the best. I mean, we've never had so much fun playing a game together, right?
Right!
But...but... it's not fun if you have nothing to lose...

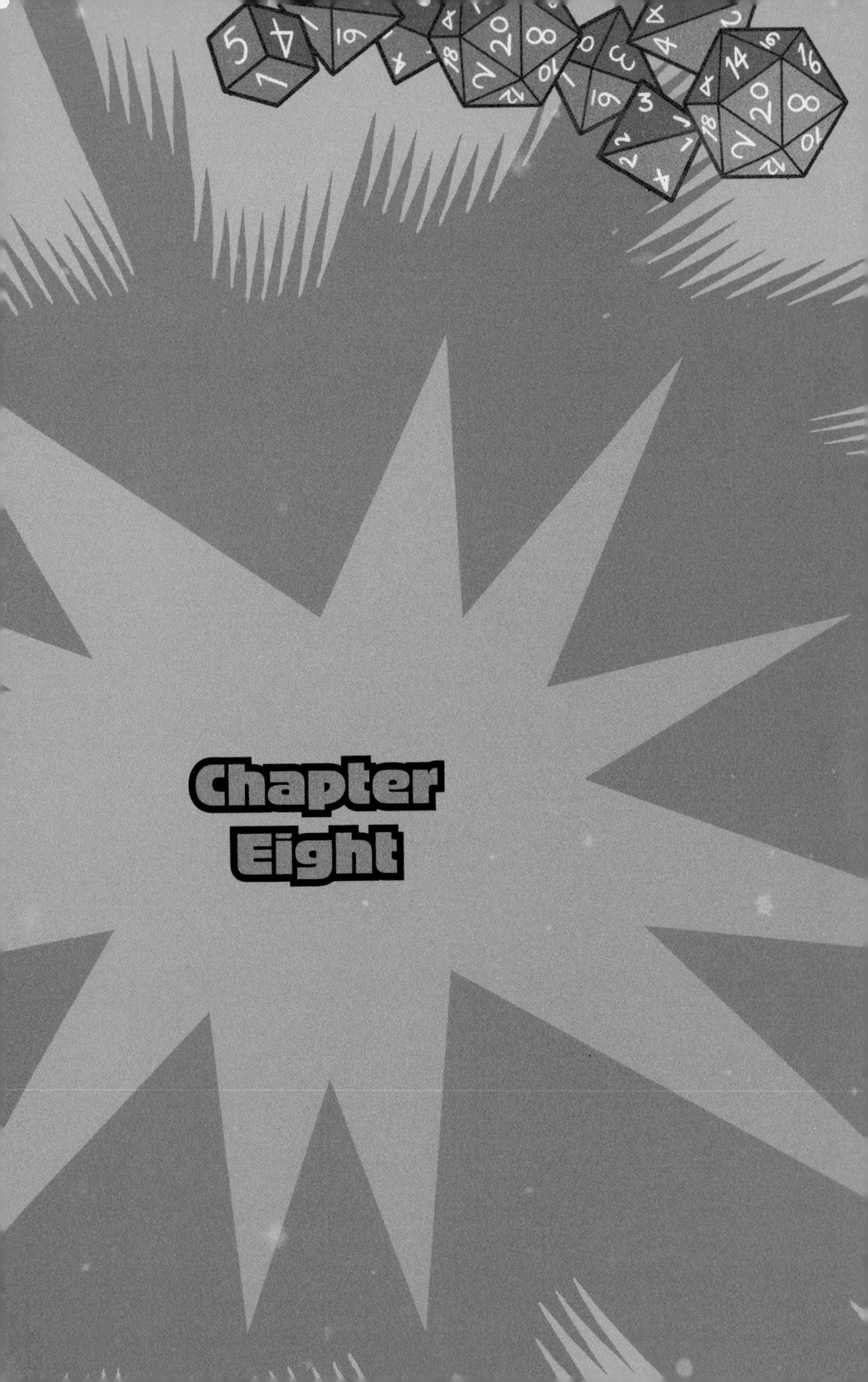

Chapter Eight

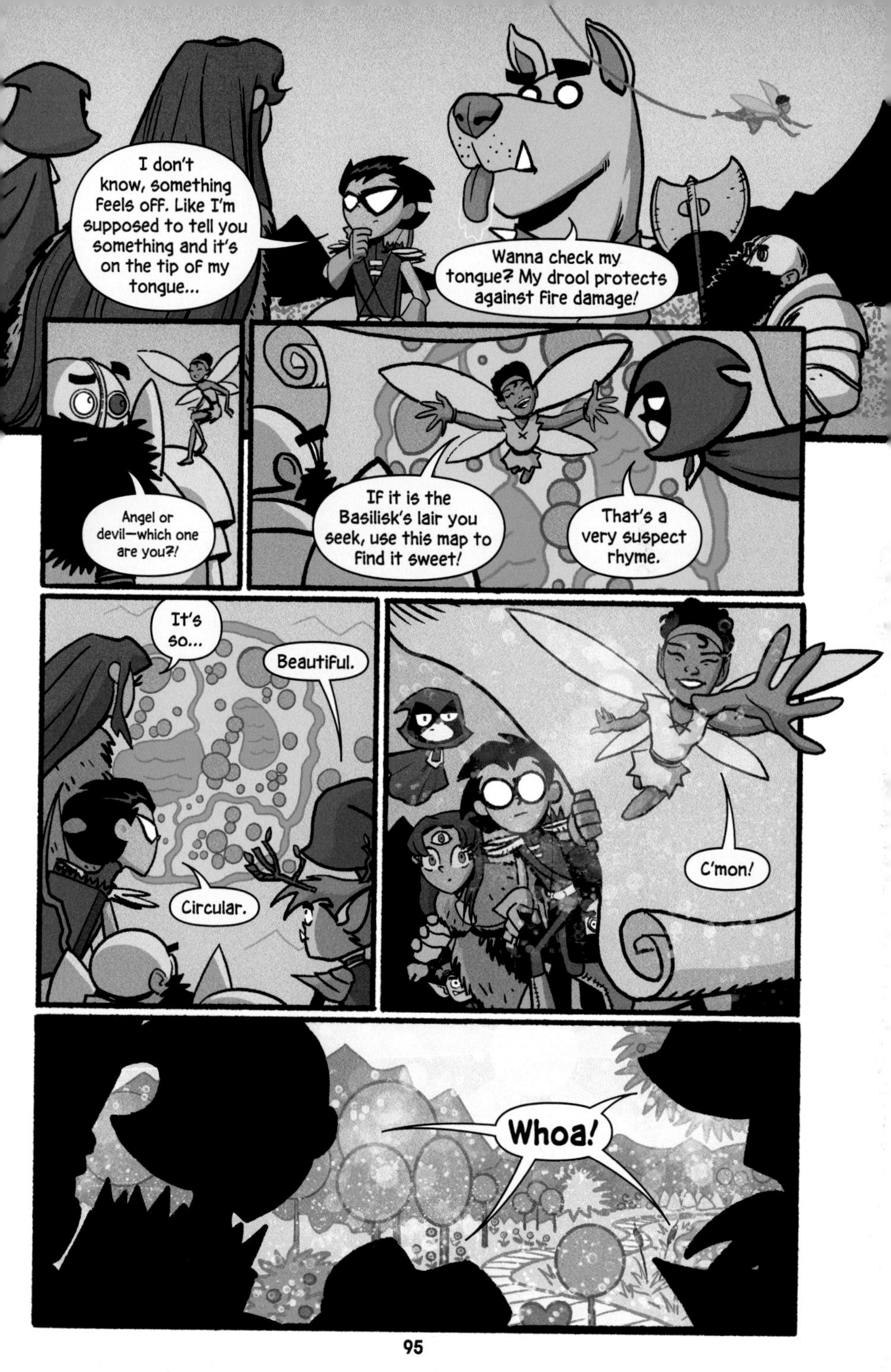
I don't know, something feels off. Like I'm supposed to tell you something and it's on the tip of my tongue...
Wanna check my tongue? My drool protects against fire damage!
Angel or devil—which one are you?!
If it is the Basilisk's lair you seek, use this map to find it sweet!
That's a very suspect rhyme.
It's so...
Beautiful.
Circular.
C'mon!
Whoa!

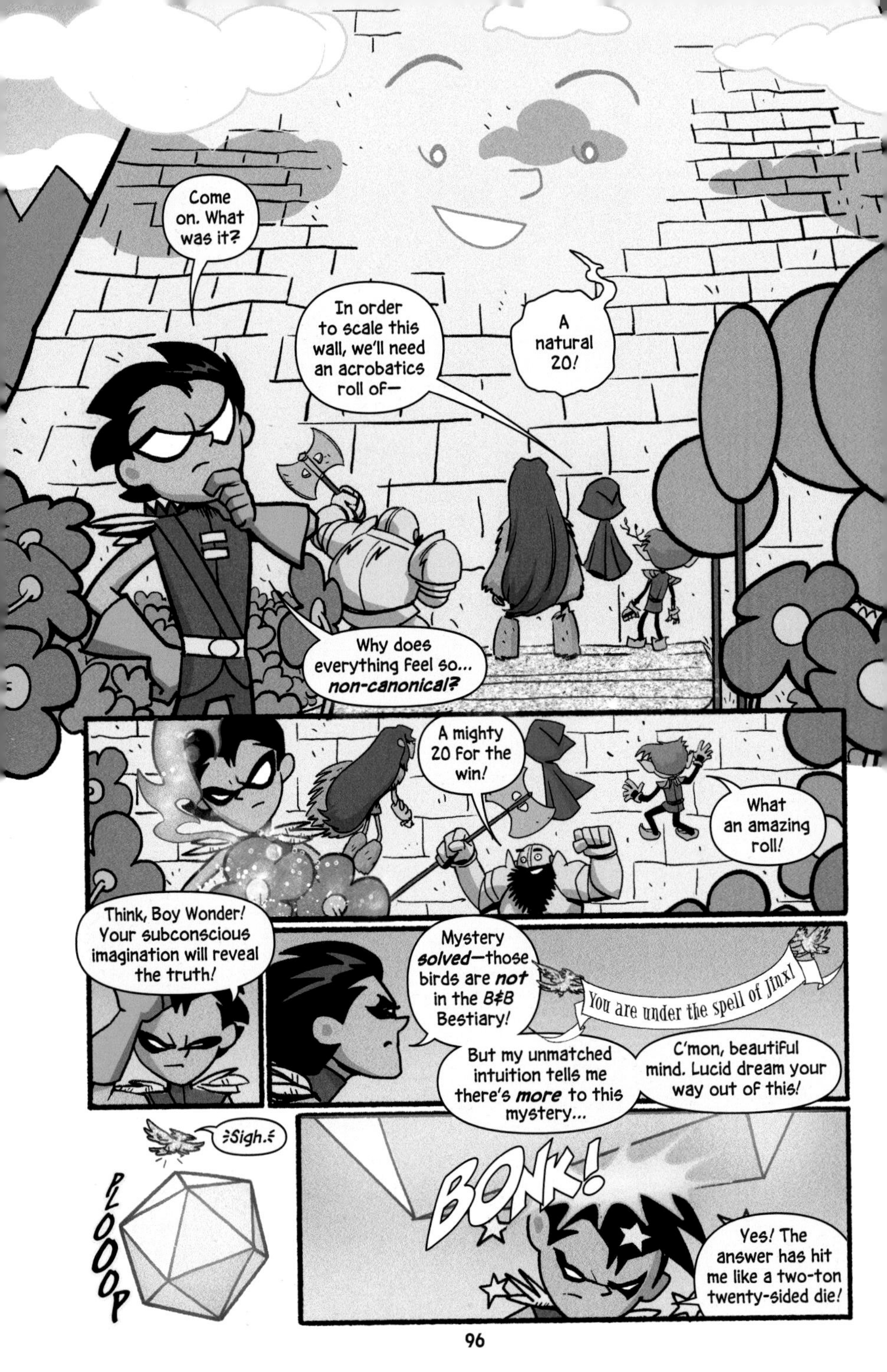

Come on. What was it?
In order to scale this wall, we'll need an acrobatics roll of—
A natural 20!
Why does everything feel so... *non-canonical?*
A mighty 20 for the win!
What an amazing roll!
Think, Boy Wonder! Your subconscious imagination will reveal the truth!
Mystery *solved*—those birds are *not* in the B&B Bestiary!
You are under the spell of Jinx!
But my unmatched intuition tells me there's *more* to this mystery...
C'mon, beautiful mind. Lucid dream your way out of this!
Sigh.
PLOOOP
BONK!
Yes! The answer has hit me like a two-ton twenty-sided die!

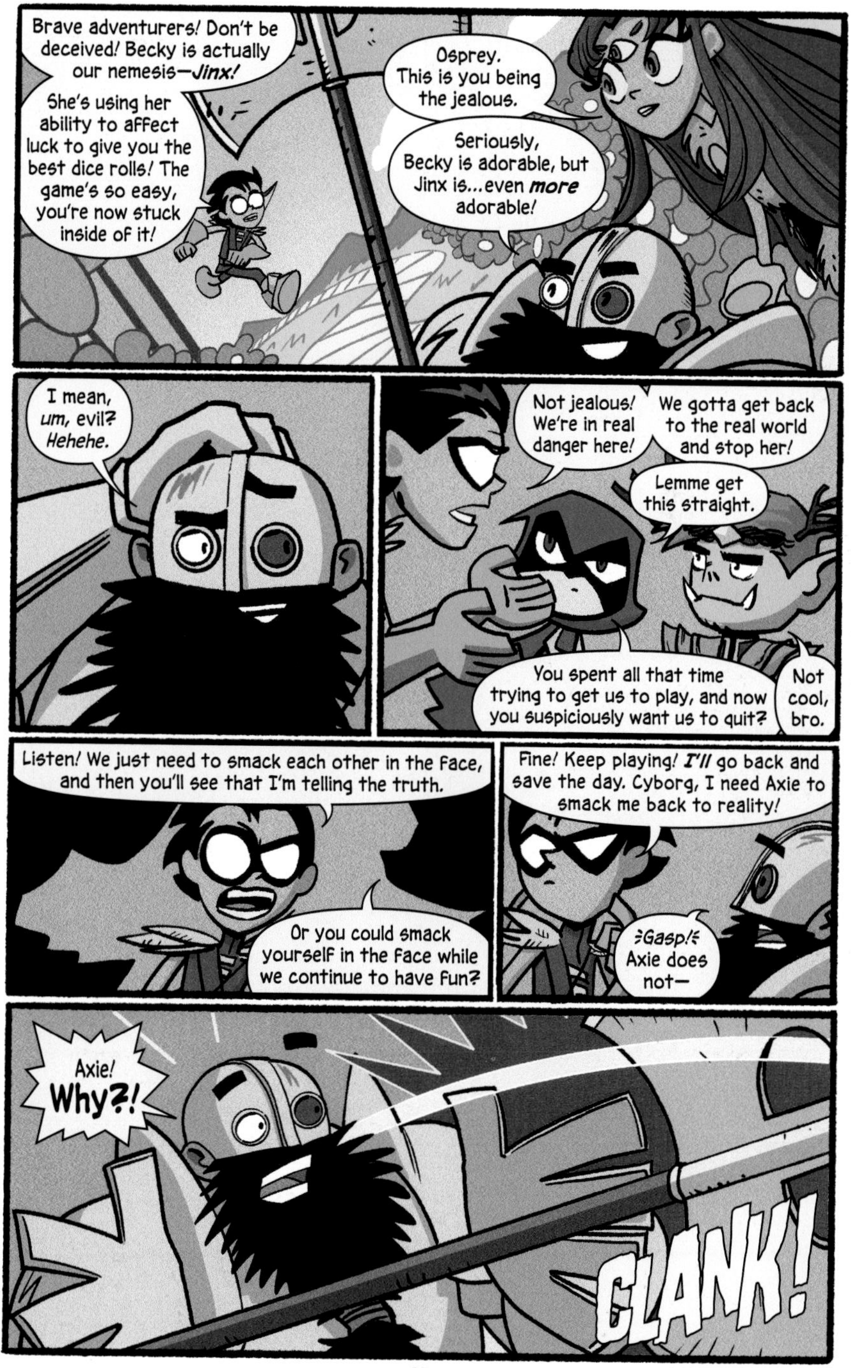
Brave adventurers! Don't be deceived! Becky is actually our nemesis—*Jinx!*
She's using her ability to affect luck to give you the best dice rolls! The game's so easy, you're now stuck inside of it!
Osprey. This is you being the jealous.
Seriously, Becky is adorable, but Jinx is...even *more* adorable!
I mean, *um, evil? Hehehe.*
Not jealous! We're in real danger here!
We gotta get back to the real world and stop her!
Lemme get this straight.
You spent all that time trying to get us to play, and now you suspiciously want us to quit?
Not cool, bro.
Listen! We just need to smack each other in the face, and then you'll see that I'm telling the truth.
Or you could smack yourself in the face while we continue to have fun?
Fine! Keep playing! *I'll* go back and save the day. Cyborg, I need Axie to smack me back to reality!
Gasp! Axie does not—
Axie! Why?!
CLANK!

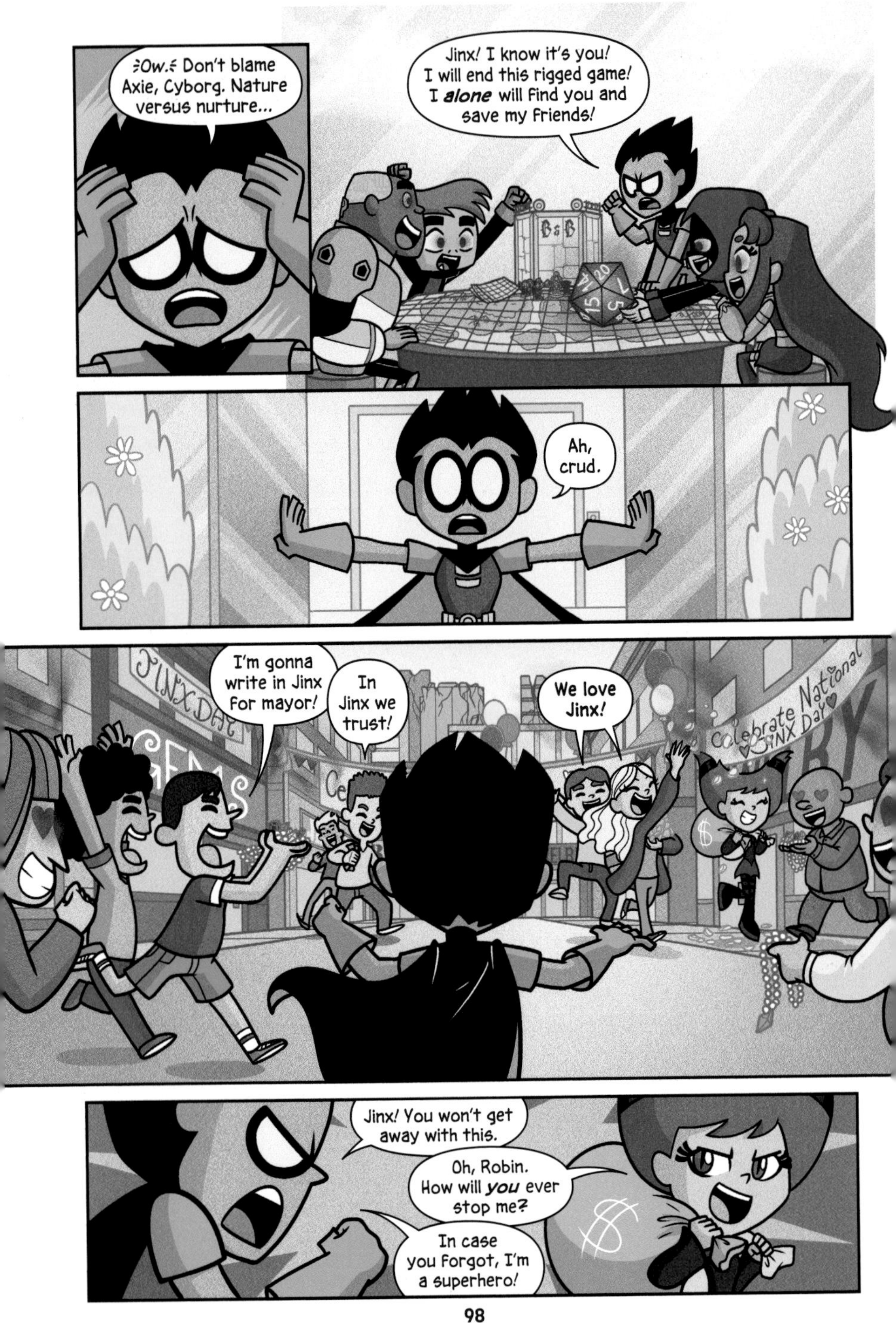
Ow. Don't blame Axie, Cyborg. Nature versus nurture...
Jinx! I know it's you! I will end this rigged game! I *alone* will find you and save my friends!
B&B
Ah, crud.
JINX DAY
GEMS
I'm gonna write in Jinx for mayor!
In Jinx we trust!
We love Jinx!
Celebrate National JINX Day
Jinx! You won't get away with this.
Oh, Robin. How will *you* ever stop me?
In case you forgot, I'm a superhero!

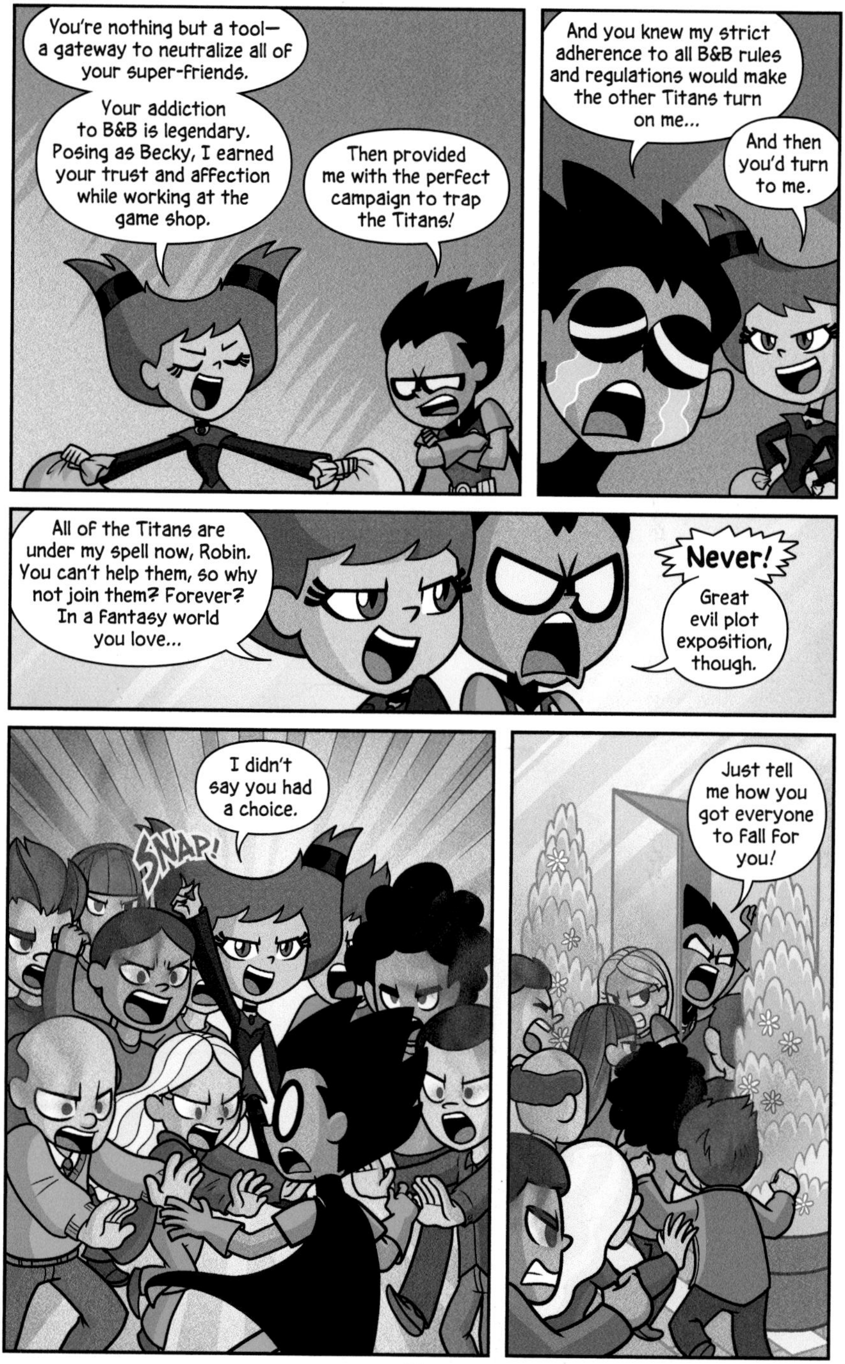
You're nothing but a tool— a gateway to neutralize all of your super-friends.
Your addiction to B&B is legendary. Posing as Becky, I earned your trust and affection while working at the game shop.
Then provided me with the perfect campaign to trap the Titans!
And you knew my strict adherence to all B&B rules and regulations would make the other Titans turn on me...
And then you'd turn to me.
All of the Titans are under my spell now, Robin. You can't help them, so why not join them? Forever? In a fantasy world you love...
Never!
Great evil plot exposition, though.
I didn't say you had a choice.
SNAP!
Just tell me how you got everyone to fall for you!

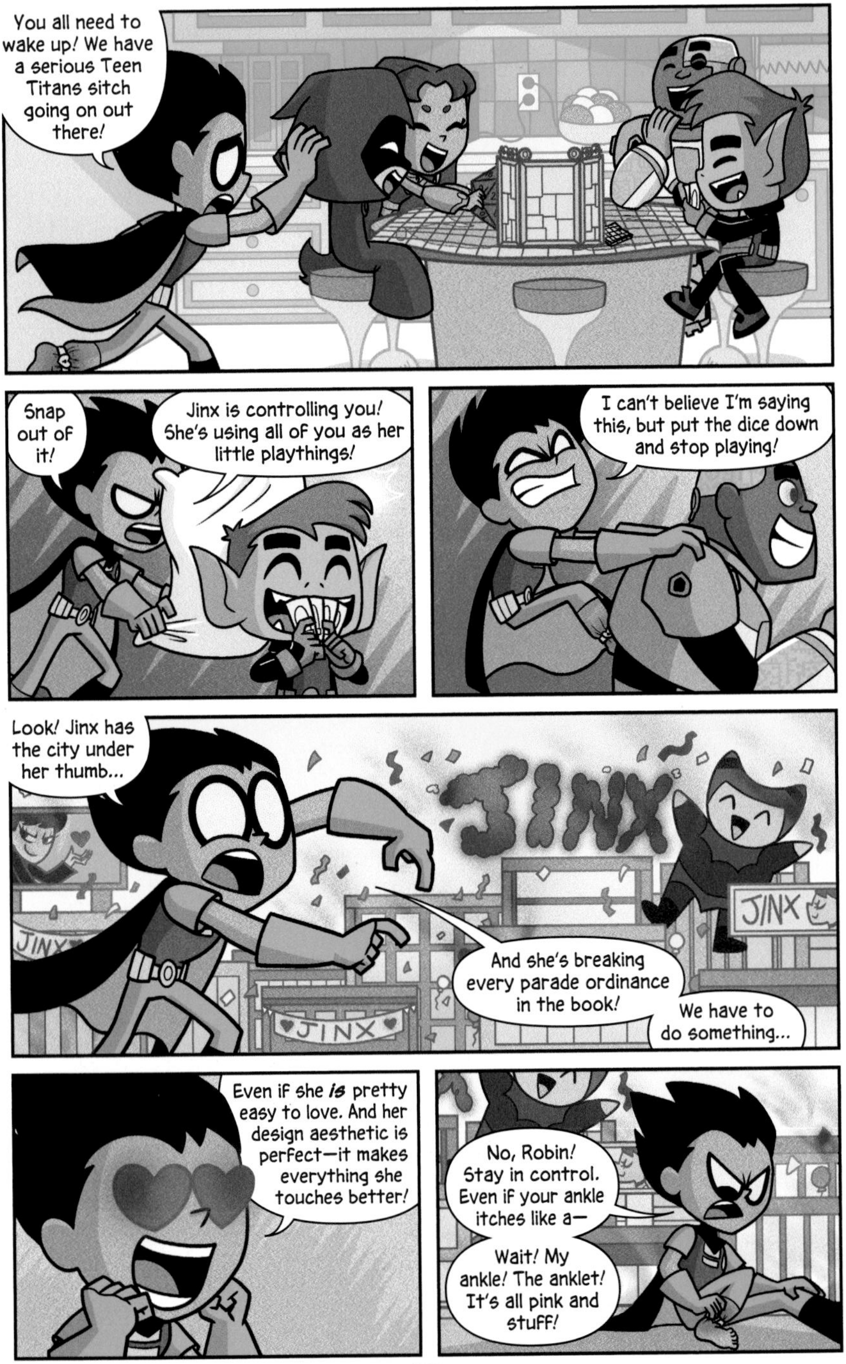
You all need to wake up! We have a serious Teen Titans sitch going on out there!
Snap out of it!
Jinx is controlling you! She's using all of you as her little playthings!
I can't believe I'm saying this, but put the dice down and stop playing!
Look! Jinx has the city under her thumb...
JINX
JINX
JINX
♥JINX♥
And she's breaking every parade ordinance in the book!
We have to do something...
Even if she *is* pretty easy to love. And her design aesthetic is perfect—it makes everything she touches better!
No, Robin! Stay in control. Even if your ankle itches like a—
Wait! My ankle! The anklet! It's all pink and stuff!

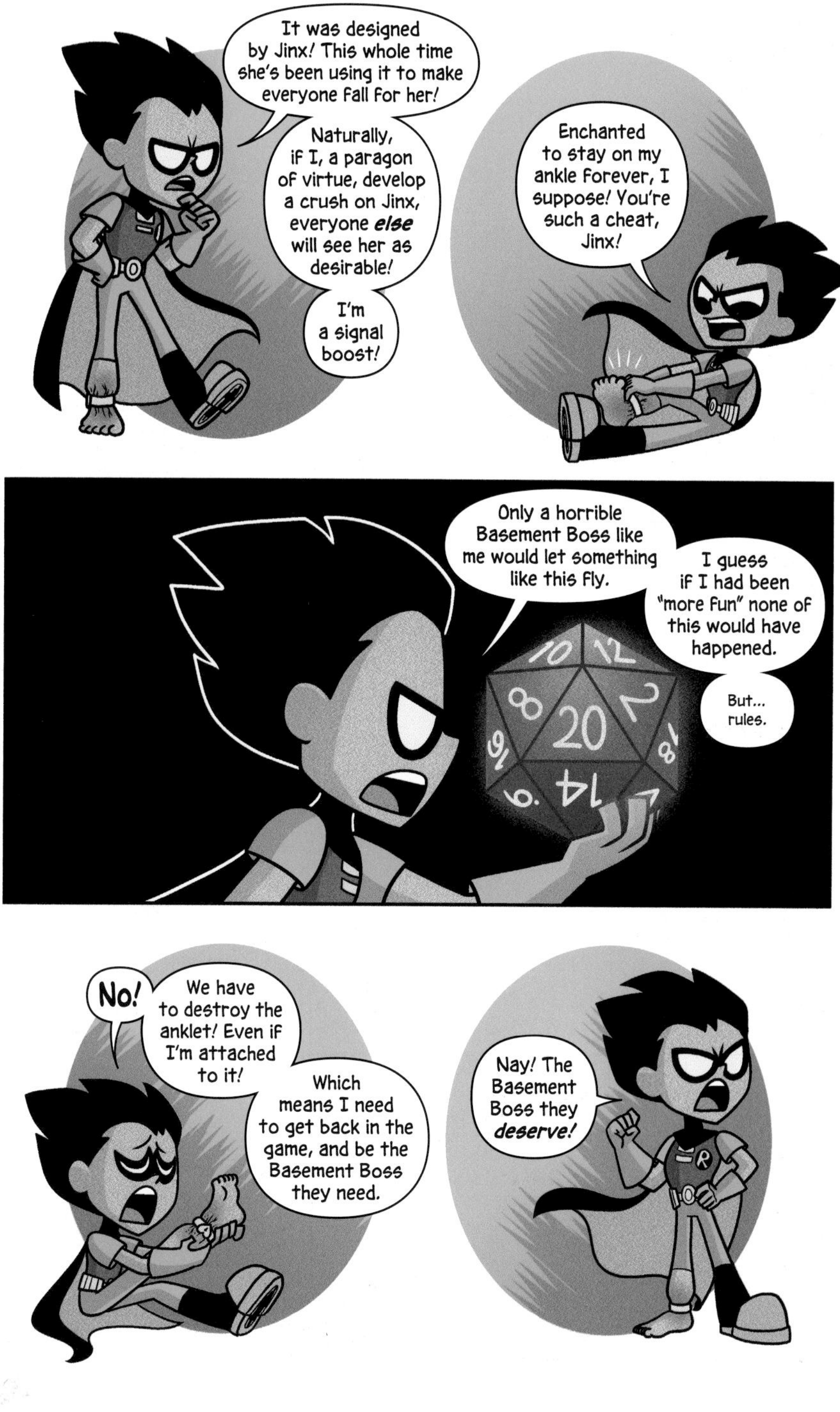

It was designed by Jinx! This whole time she's been using it to make everyone fall for her!
Naturally, if I, a paragon of virtue, develop a crush on Jinx, everyone *else* will see her as desirable!
I'm a signal boost!
Enchanted to stay on my ankle forever, I suppose! You're such a cheat, Jinx!
Only a horrible Basement Boss like me would let something like this fly.
I guess if I had been "more fun" none of this would have happened.
But... rules.
No!
We have to destroy the anklet! Even if I'm attached to it!
Which means I need to get back in the game, and be the Basement Boss they need.
Nay! The Basement Boss they *deserve!*

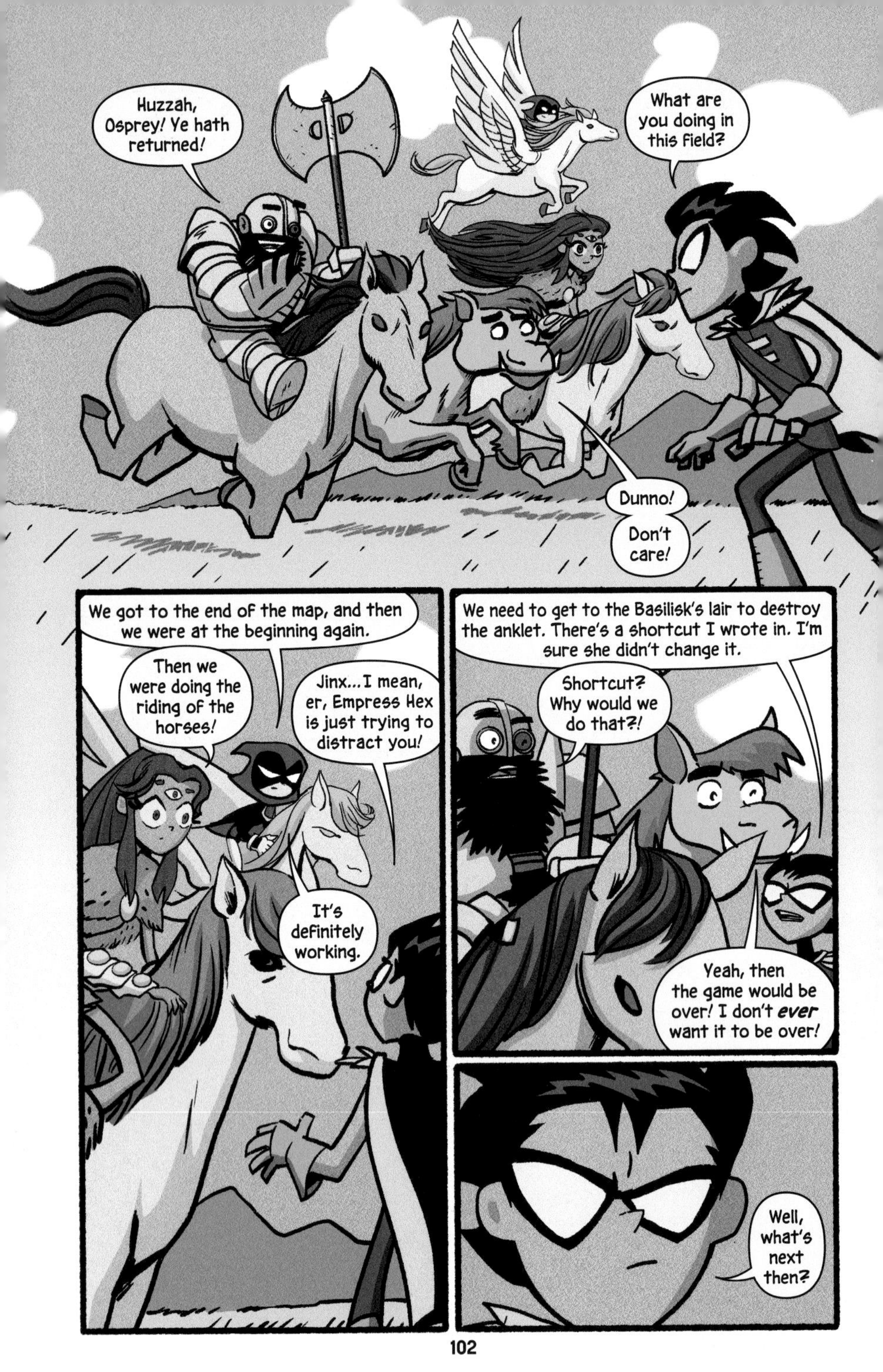
Huzzah, Osprey! Ye hath returned!
What are you doing in this field?
Dunno!
Don't care!
We got to the end of the map, and then we were at the beginning again.
Then we were doing the riding of the horses!
Jinx... I mean, er, Empress Hex is just trying to distract you!
It's definitely working.
We need to get to the Basilisk's lair to destroy the anklet. There's a shortcut I wrote in. I'm sure she didn't change it.
Shortcut? Why would we do that?!
Yeah, then the game would be over! I don't *ever* want it to be over!
Well, what's next then?

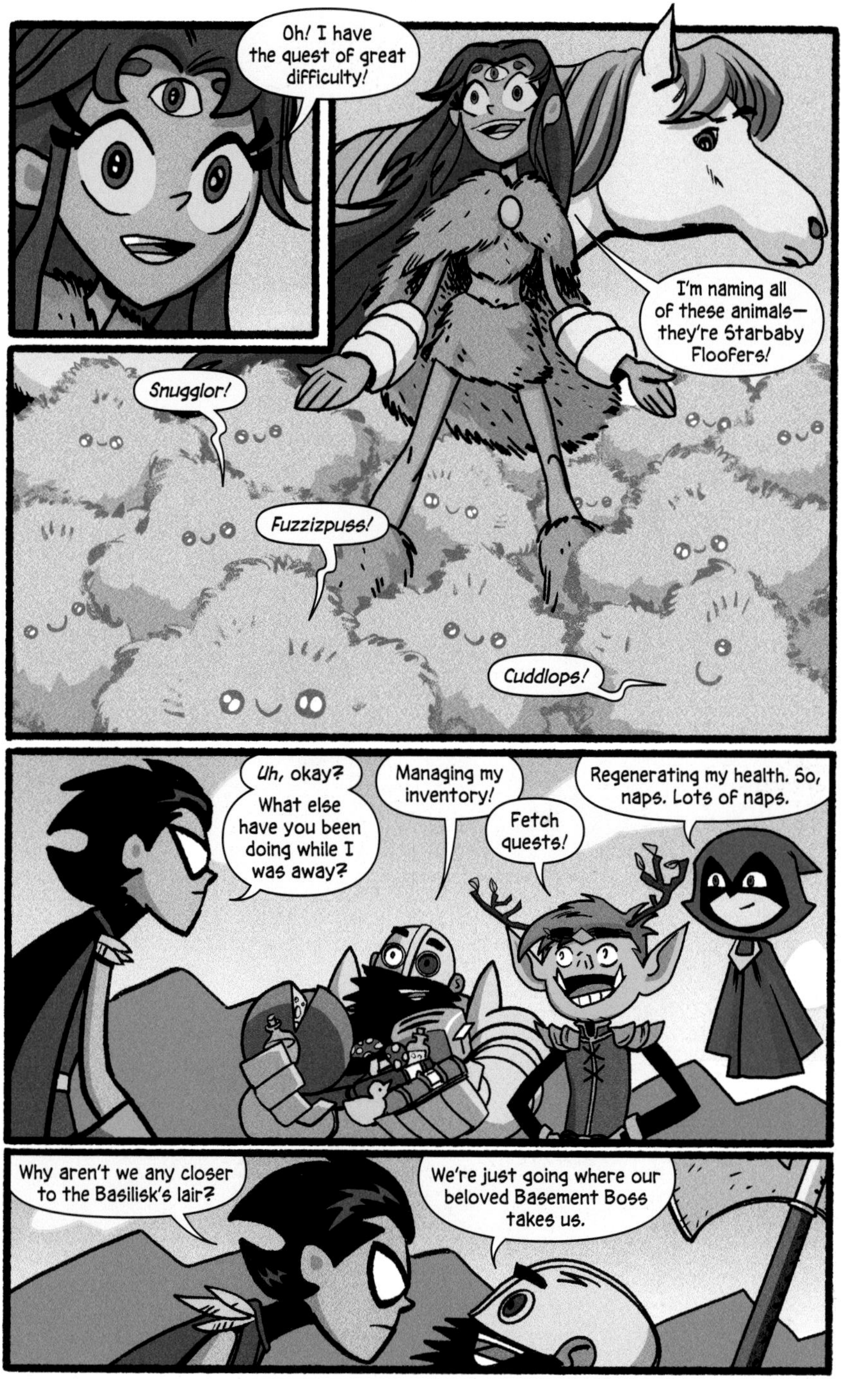
Oh! I have the quest of great difficulty!
I'm naming all of these animals—they're Starbaby Floofers!
Snugglor!
Fuzzizpuss!
Cuddlops!
Uh, okay?
What else have you been doing while I was away?
Managing my inventory!
Fetch quests!
Regenerating my health. So, naps. Lots of naps.
Why aren't we any closer to the Basilisk's lair?
We're just going where our beloved Basement Boss takes us.

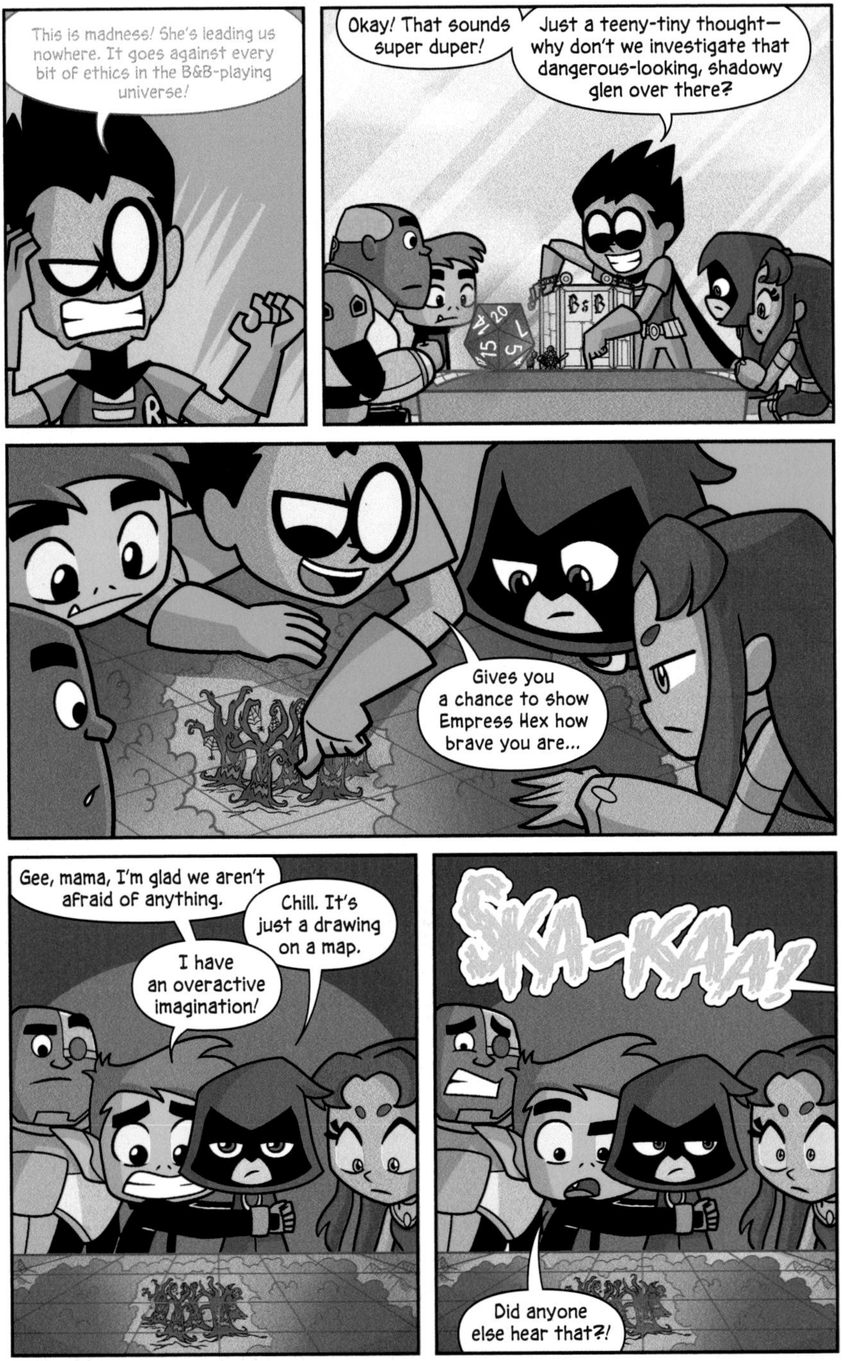
This is madness! She's leading us nowhere. It goes against every bit of ethics in the B&B-playing universe!
Okay! That sounds super duper!
Just a teeny-tiny thought—why don't we investigate that dangerous-looking, shadowy glen over there?
B&B
15
14
20
7
5
Gives you a chance to show Empress Hex how brave you are...
Gee, mama, I'm glad we aren't afraid of anything.
Chill. It's just a drawing on a map.
I have an overactive imagination!
SKA-KAA!
Did anyone else hear that?!

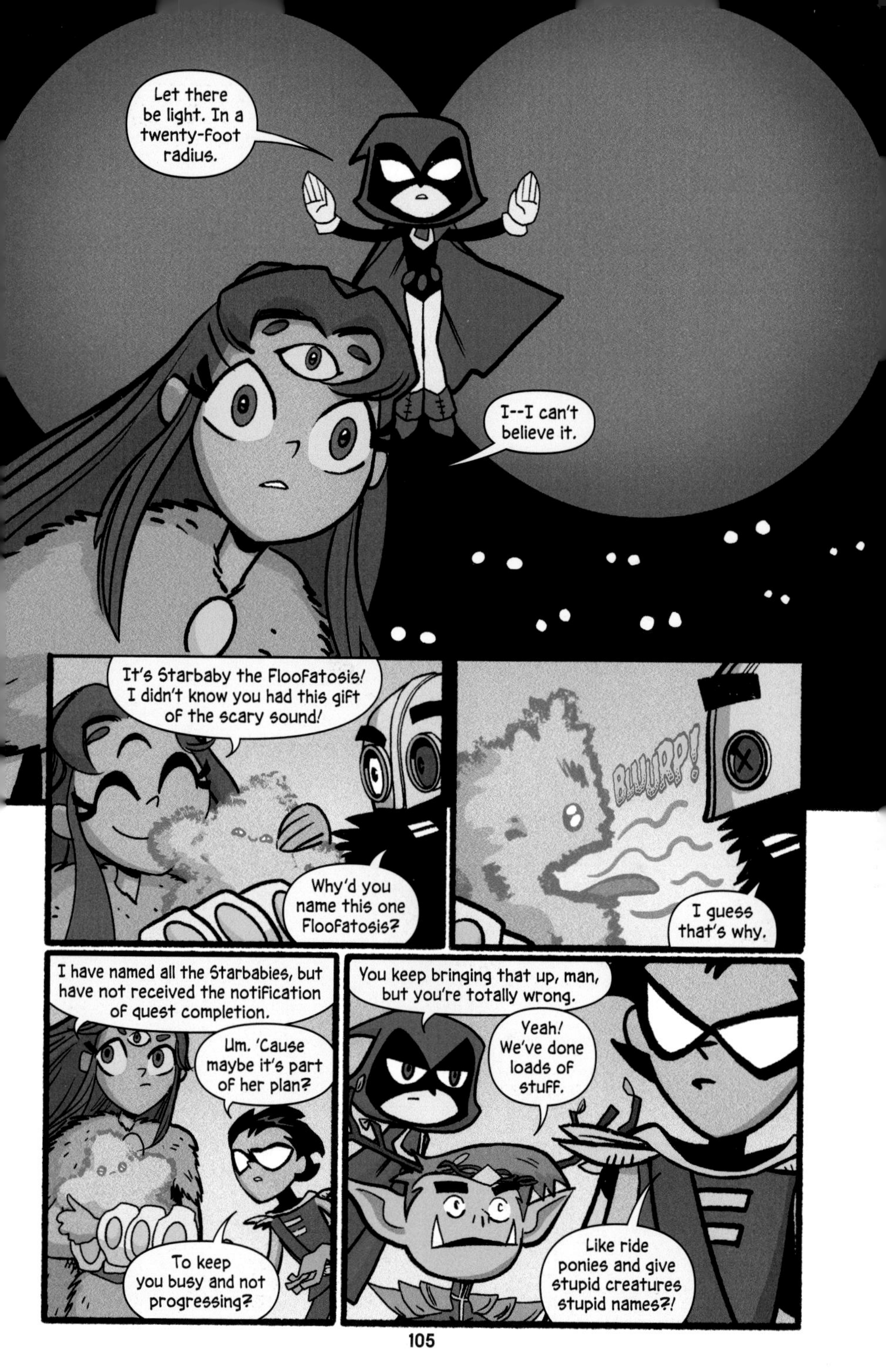
Let there be light. In a twenty-foot radius.
I--I can't believe it.
It's Starbaby the Floofatosis! I didn't know you had this gift of the scary sound!
Why'd you name this one Floofatosis?
BLUURP!
I guess that's why.
I have named all the Starbabies, but have not received the notification of quest completion.
Um. 'Cause maybe it's part of her plan?
To keep you busy and not progressing?
You keep bringing that up, man, but you're totally wrong.
Yeah! We've done loads of stuff.
Like ride ponies and give stupid creatures stupid names?!

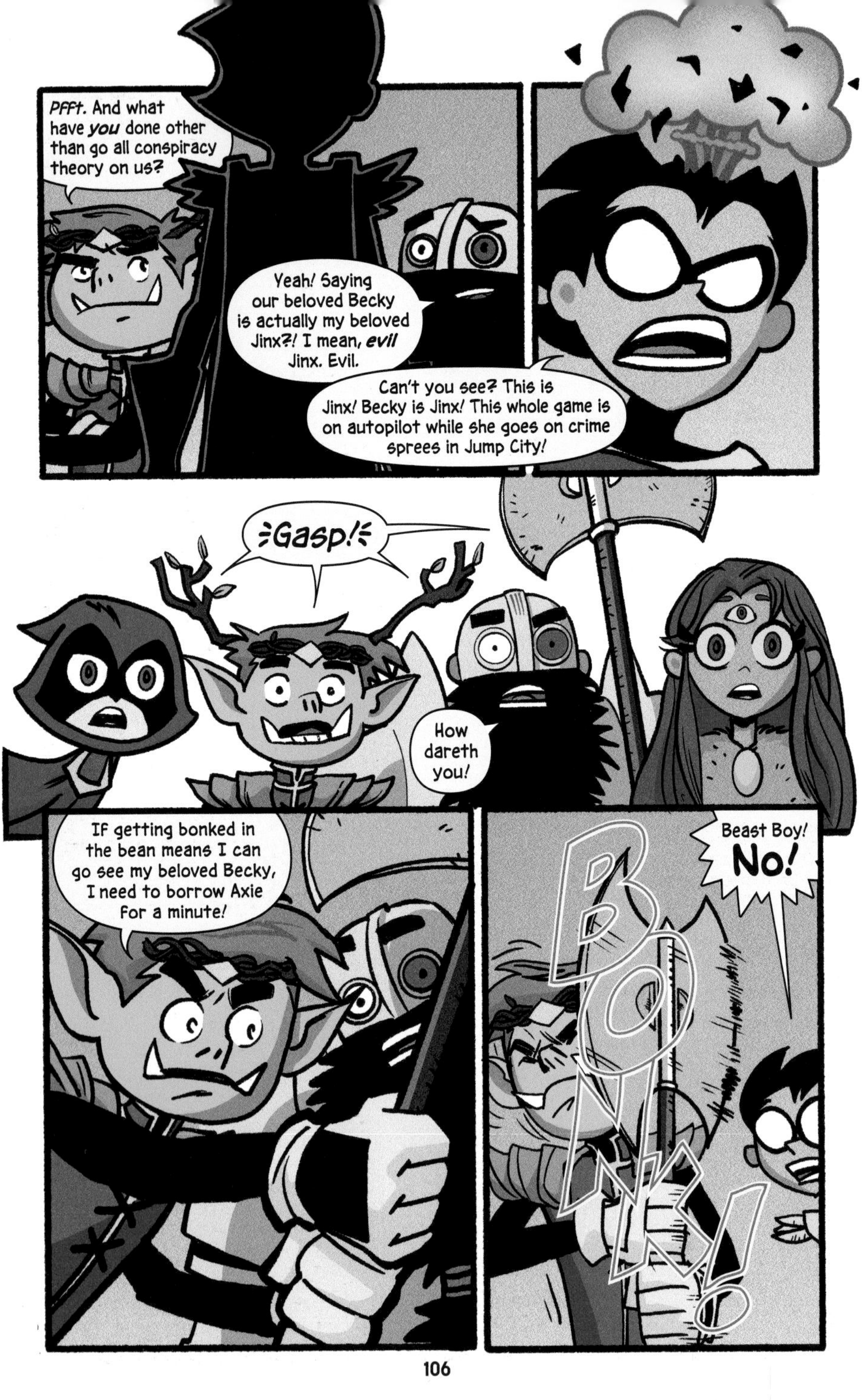
PFFt. And what have you done other than go all conspiracy theory on us?
Yeah! Saying our beloved Becky is actually my beloved Jinx?! I mean, evil Jinx. Evil.
Can't you see? This is Jinx! Becky is Jinx! This whole game is on autopilot while she goes on crime sprees in Jump City!
Gasp!
How dareth you!
If getting bonked in the bean means I can go see my beloved Becky, I need to borrow Axie for a minute!
Beast Boy! No!
BONK!

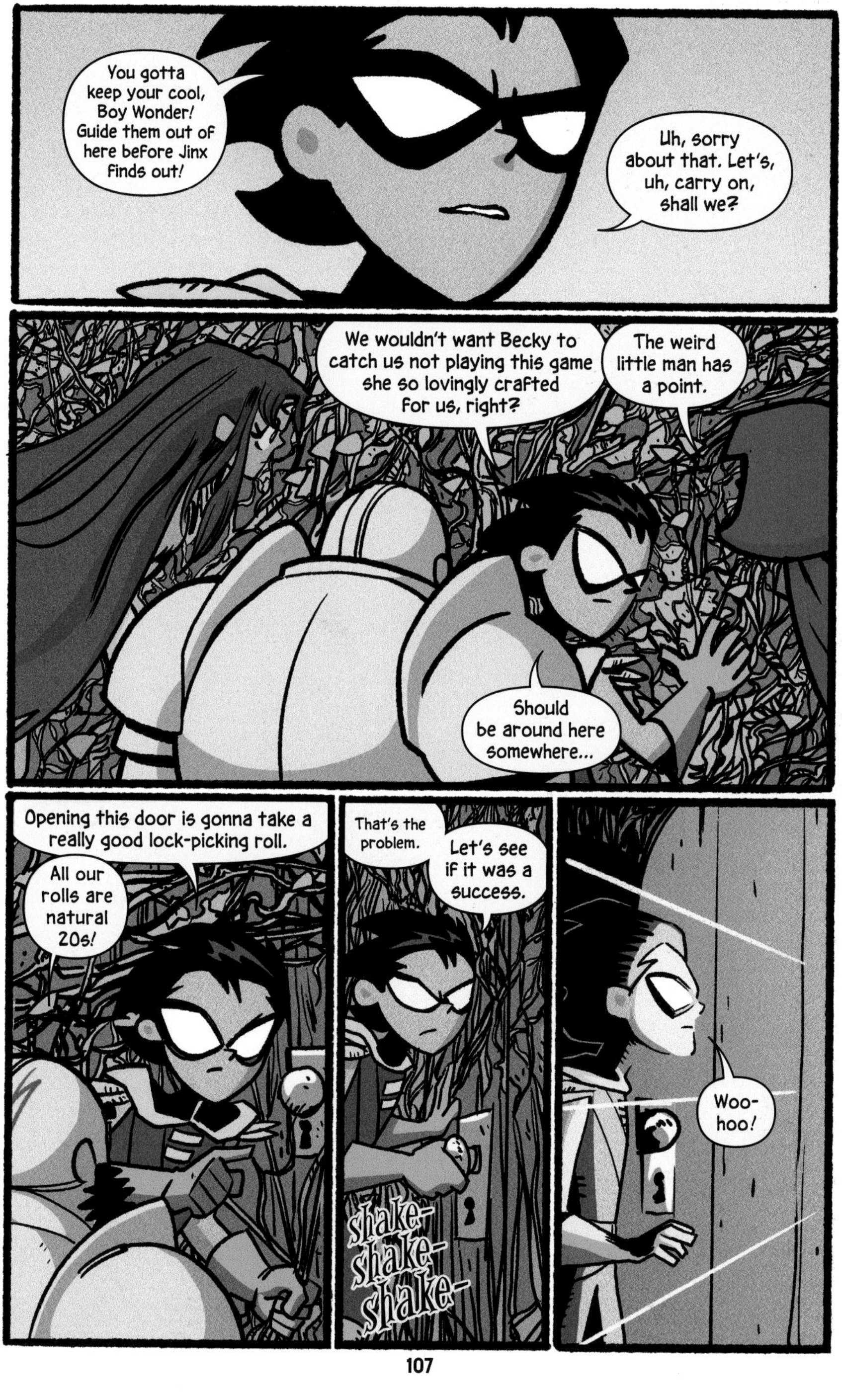
You gotta keep your cool, Boy Wonder! Guide them out of here before Jinx finds out!
Uh, sorry about that. Let's, uh, carry on, shall we?
We wouldn't want Becky to catch us not playing this game she so lovingly crafted for us, right?
The weird little man has a point.
Should be around here somewhere...
Opening this door is gonna take a really good lock-picking roll.
All our rolls are natural 20s!
That's the problem.
Let's see if it was a success.
shake-shake-shake-
Woo-hoo!

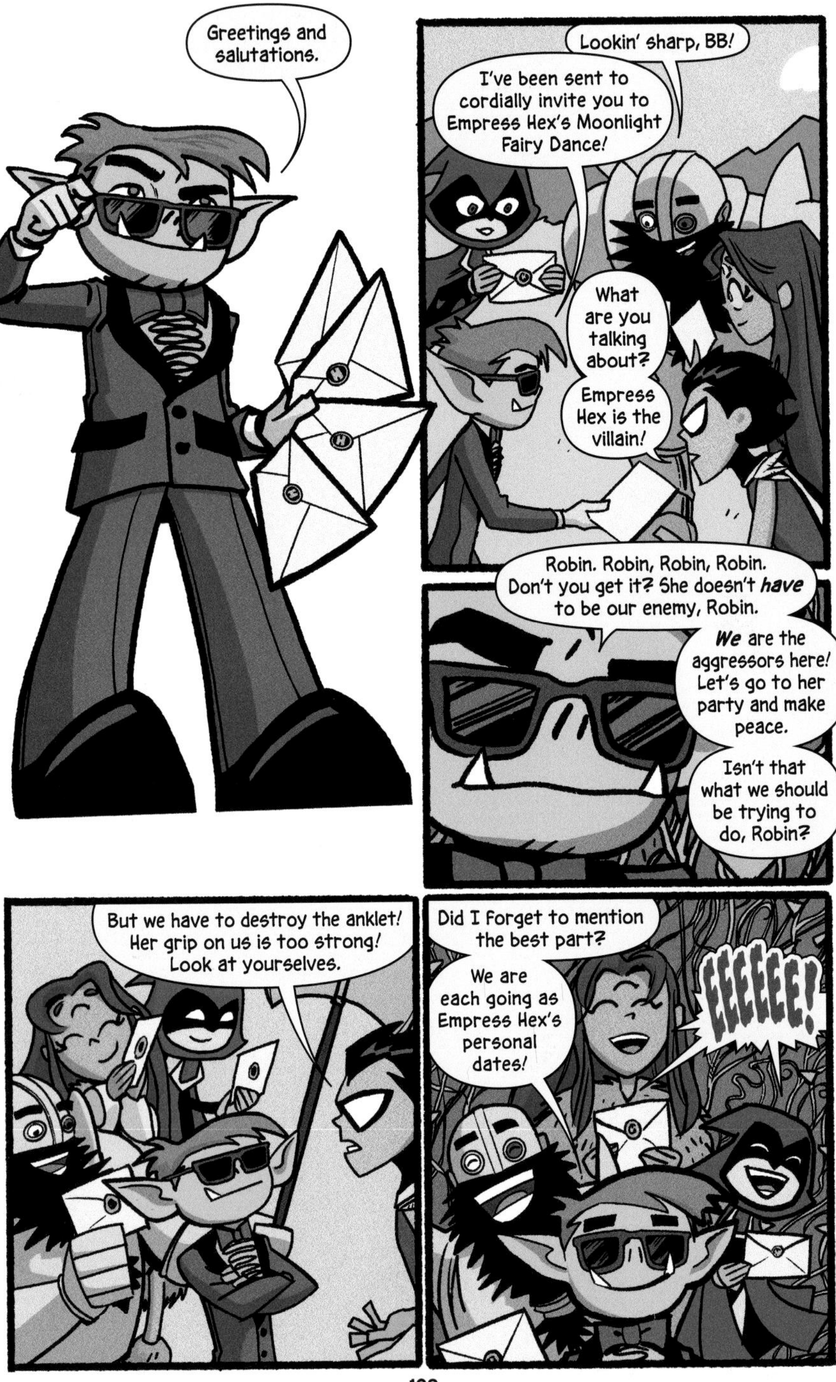

Greetings and salutations.
Lookin' sharp, BB!
I've been sent to cordially invite you to Empress Hex's Moonlight Fairy Dance!
What are you talking about?
Empress Hex is the villain!
Robin. Robin, Robin, Robin. Don't you get it? She doesn't *have* to be our enemy, Robin.
We are the aggressors here! Let's go to her party and make peace.
Isn't that what we should be trying to do, Robin?
But we have to destroy the anklet! Her grip on us is too strong! Look at yourselves.
Did I forget to mention the best part?
We are each going as Empress Hex's personal dates!
EEEEEE!

Chapter
Nine

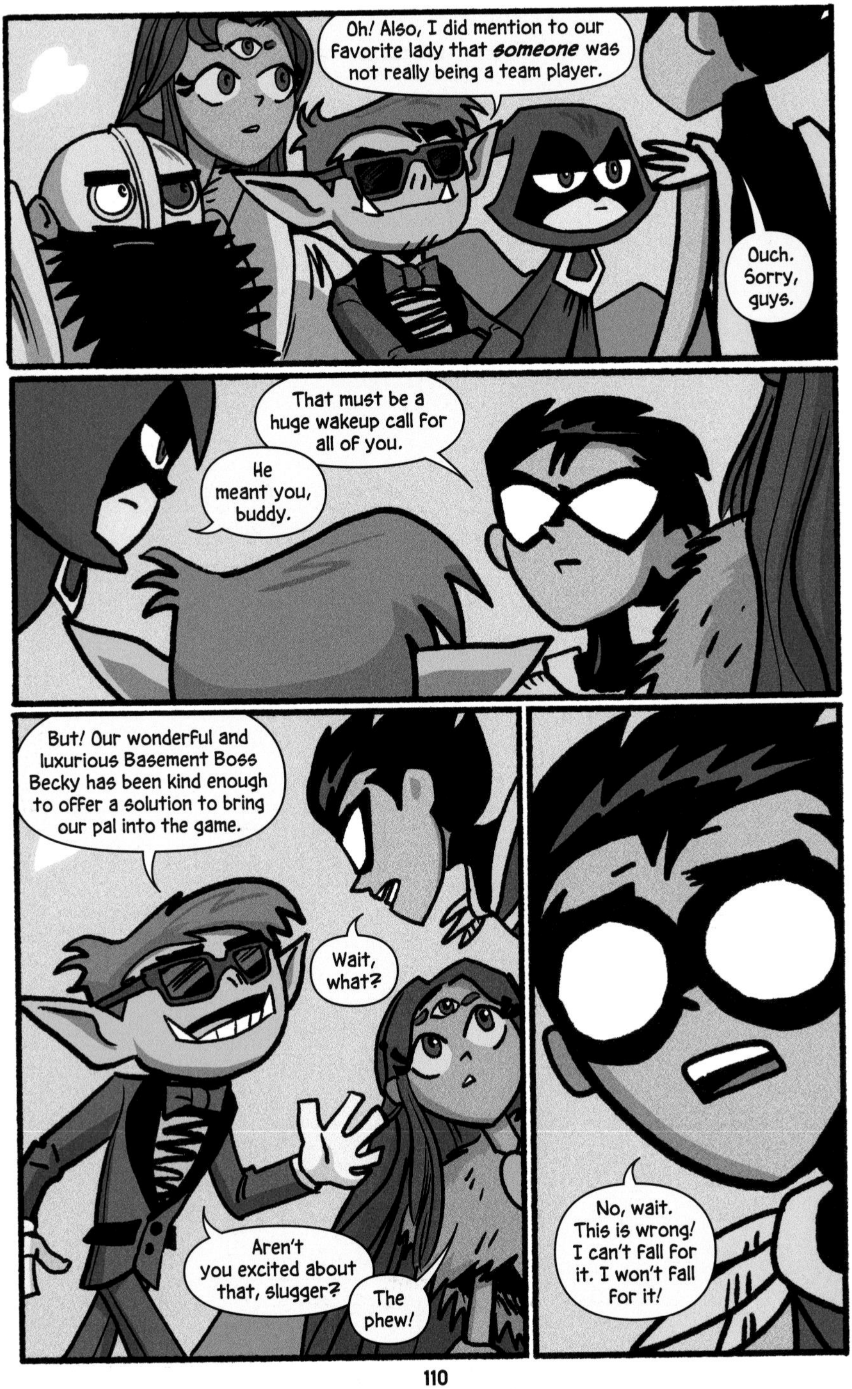
Oh! Also, I did mention to our favorite lady that *someone* was not really being a team player.
Ouch. Sorry, guys.
That must be a huge wakeup call for all of you.
He meant you, buddy.
But! Our wonderful and luxurious Basement Boss Becky has been kind enough to offer a solution to bring our pal into the game.
Wait, what?
Aren't you excited about that, slugger?
The phew!
No, wait. This is wrong! I can't fall for it. I won't fall for it!

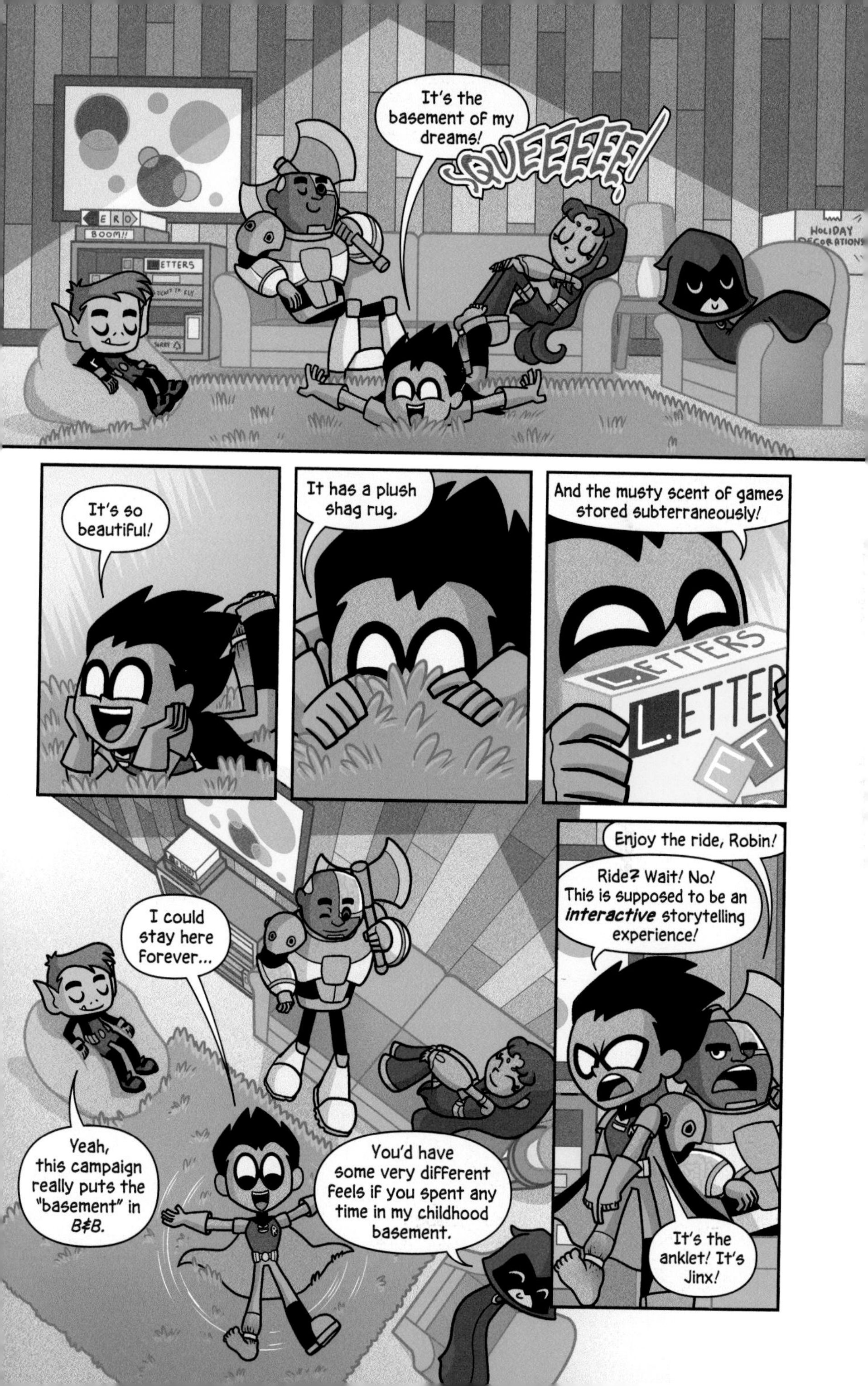

It's the basement of my dreams!
SQUEEEEEE!
ERO
BOOM!!
LETTERS
HOLIDAY DECORATIONS
It's so beautiful!
It has a plush shag rug.
And the musty scent of games stored subterraneously!
LETTERS
LETTER
ET
I could stay here forever...
Yeah, this campaign really puts the "basement" in B&B.
You'd have some very different feels if you spent any time in my childhood basement.
Enjoy the ride, Robin!
Ride? Wait! No! This is supposed to be an *interactive* storytelling experience!
It's the anklet! It's Jinx!

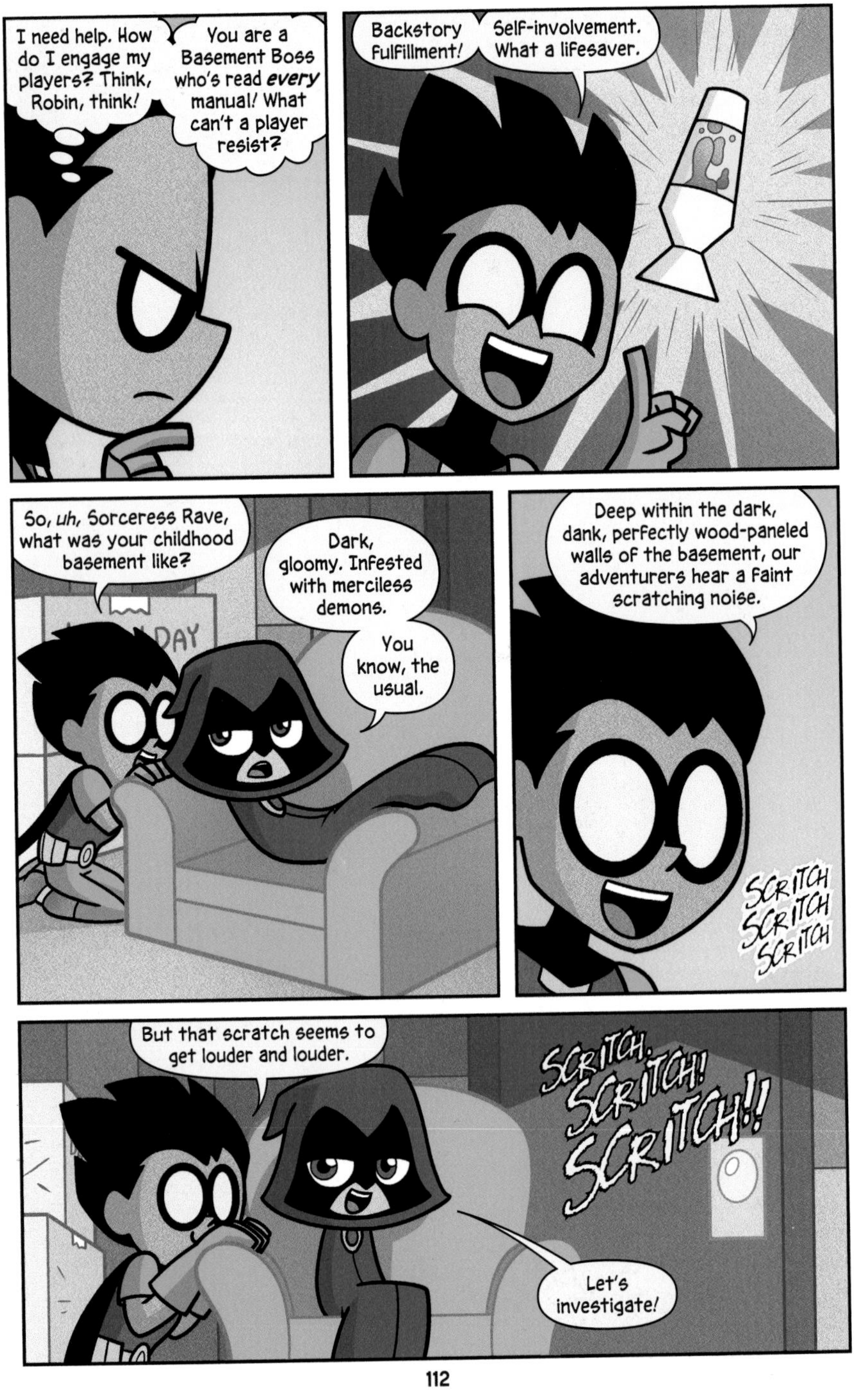
I need help. How do I engage my players? Think, Robin, think!
You are a Basement Boss who's read *every* manual! What can't a player resist?
Backstory fulfillment!
Self-involvement. What a lifesaver.
So, *uh*, Sorceress Rave, what was your childhood basement like?
Dark, gloomy. Infested with merciless demons.
You know, the usual.
Deep within the dark, dank, perfectly wood-paneled walls of the basement, our adventurers hear a faint scratching noise.
SCRITCH SCRITCH SCRITCH
But that scratch seems to get louder and louder.
SCRITCH. SCRITCH! SCRITCH!!
Let's investigate!

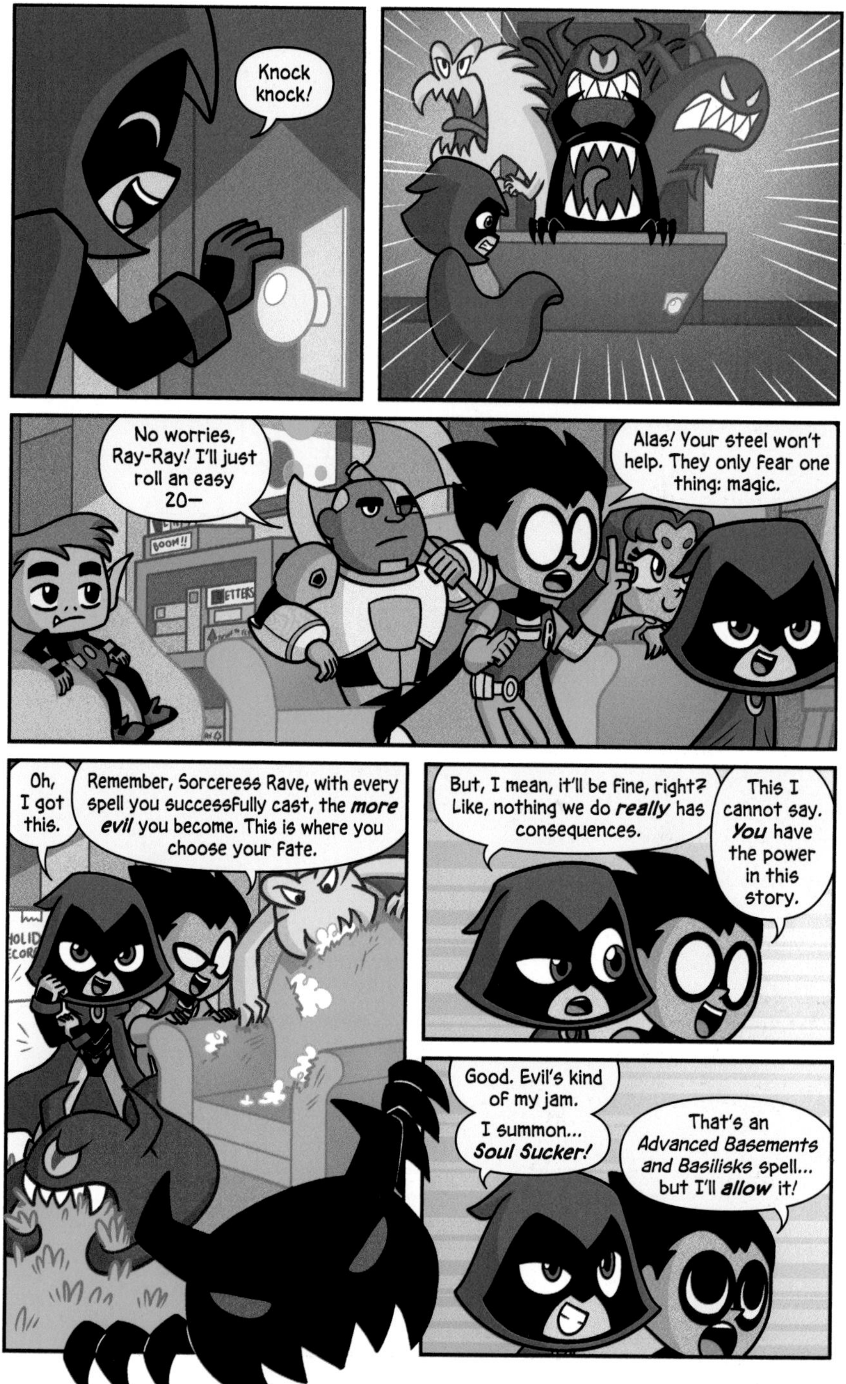
Knock knock!
No worries, Ray-Ray! I'll just roll an easy 20—
BOOM!!
Alas! Your steel won't help. They only fear one thing: magic.
Oh, I got this.
Remember, Sorceress Rave, with every spell you successfully cast, the *more evil* you become. This is where you choose your fate.
But, I mean, it'll be fine, right? Like, nothing we do *really* has consequences.
This I cannot say. *You* have the power in this story.
Good. Evil's kind of my jam.
I summon... *Soul Sucker!*
That's an *Advanced Basements and Basilisks* spell... but I'll *allow* it!

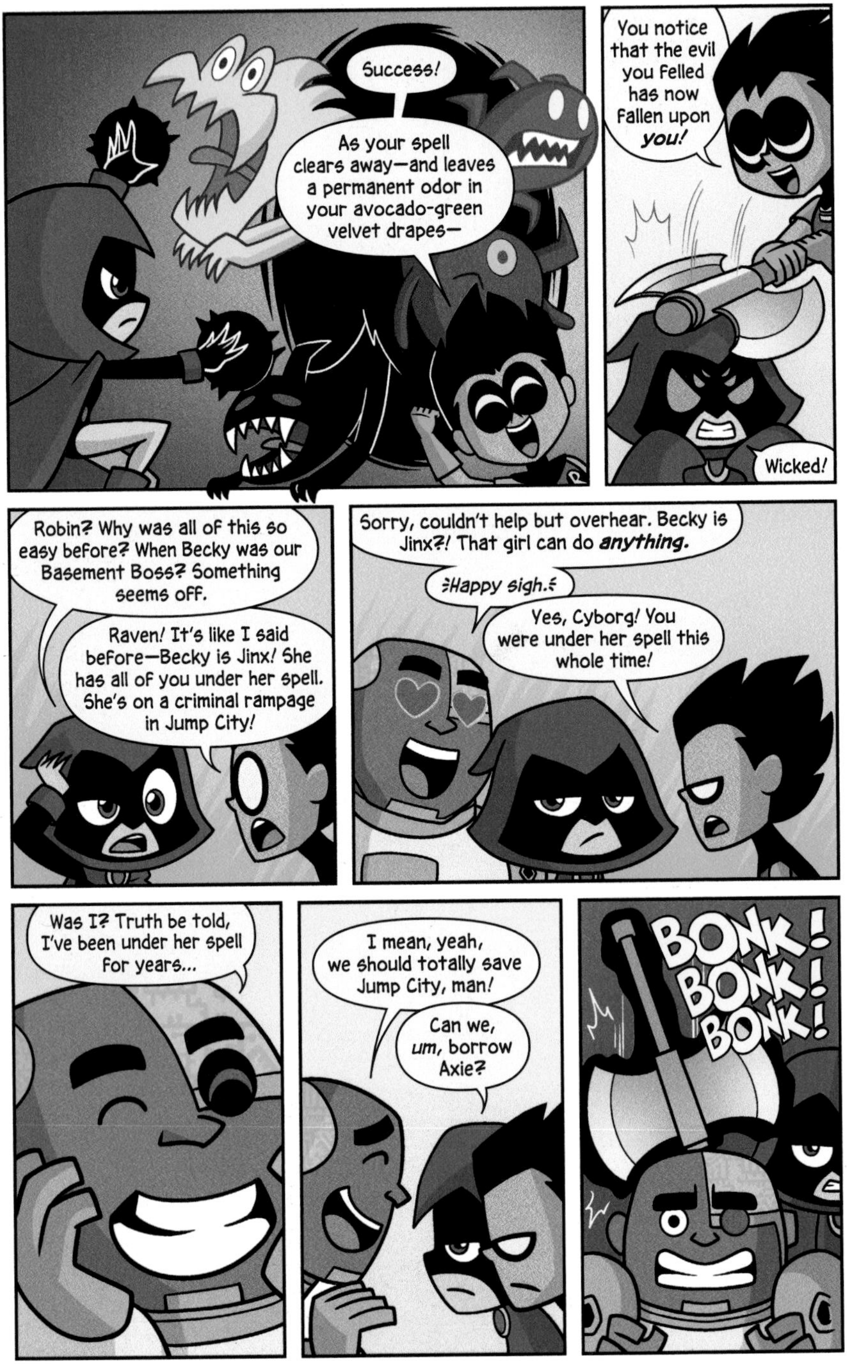
Success!
As your spell clears away—and leaves a permanent odor in your avocado-green velvet drapes—
You notice that the evil you felled has now fallen upon *you!*
Wicked!
Robin? Why was all of this so easy before? When Becky was our Basement Boss? Something seems off.
Raven! It's like I said before—Becky is Jinx! She has all of you under her spell. She's on a criminal rampage in Jump City!
Sorry, couldn't help but overhear. Becky is Jinx?! That girl can do *anything.*
Happy sigh.
Yes, Cyborg! You were under her spell this whole time!
Was I? Truth be told, I've been under her spell for years...
I mean, yeah, we should totally save Jump City, man!
Can we, *um,* borrow Axie?
BONK! BONK! BONK!

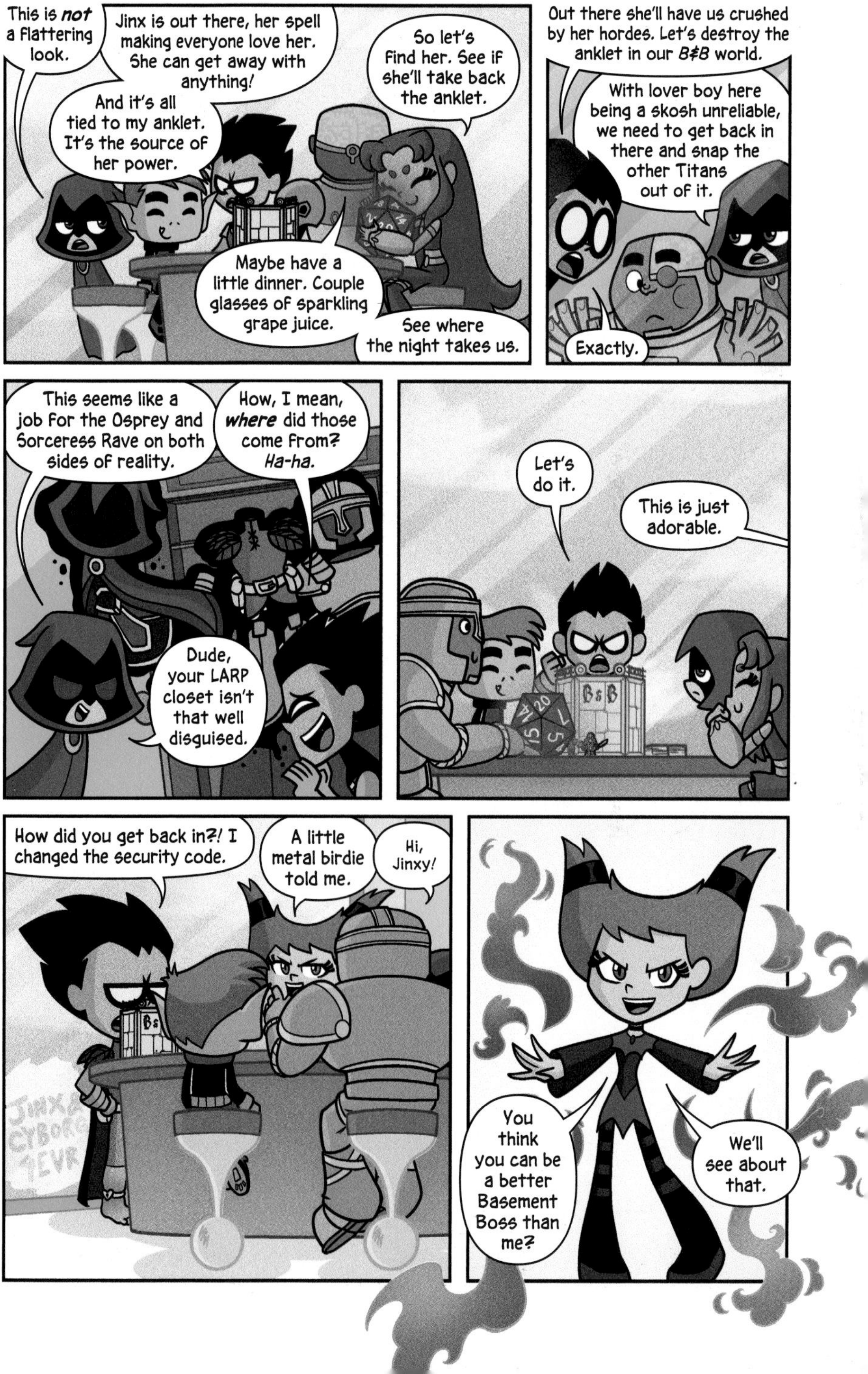
This is *not* a flattering look.
Jinx is out there, her spell making everyone love her. She can get away with anything!
And it's all tied to my anklet. It's the source of her power.
So let's find her. See if she'll take back the anklet.
Maybe have a little dinner. Couple glasses of sparkling grape juice.
See where the night takes us.
Out there she'll have us crushed by her hordes. Let's destroy the anklet in our *B&B* world.
With lover boy here being a skosh unreliable, we need to get back in there and snap the other Titans out of it.
Exactly.
This seems like a job for the Osprey and Sorceress Rave on both sides of reality.
How, I mean, ***where*** did those come from? *Ha-ha.*
Dude, your LARP closet isn't that well disguised.
Let's do it.
This is just adorable.
B&B
How did you get back in?! I changed the security code.
A little metal birdie told me.
Hi, Jinxy!
JINX & CYBORG 4EVR
You think you can be a better Basement Boss than me?
We'll see about that.

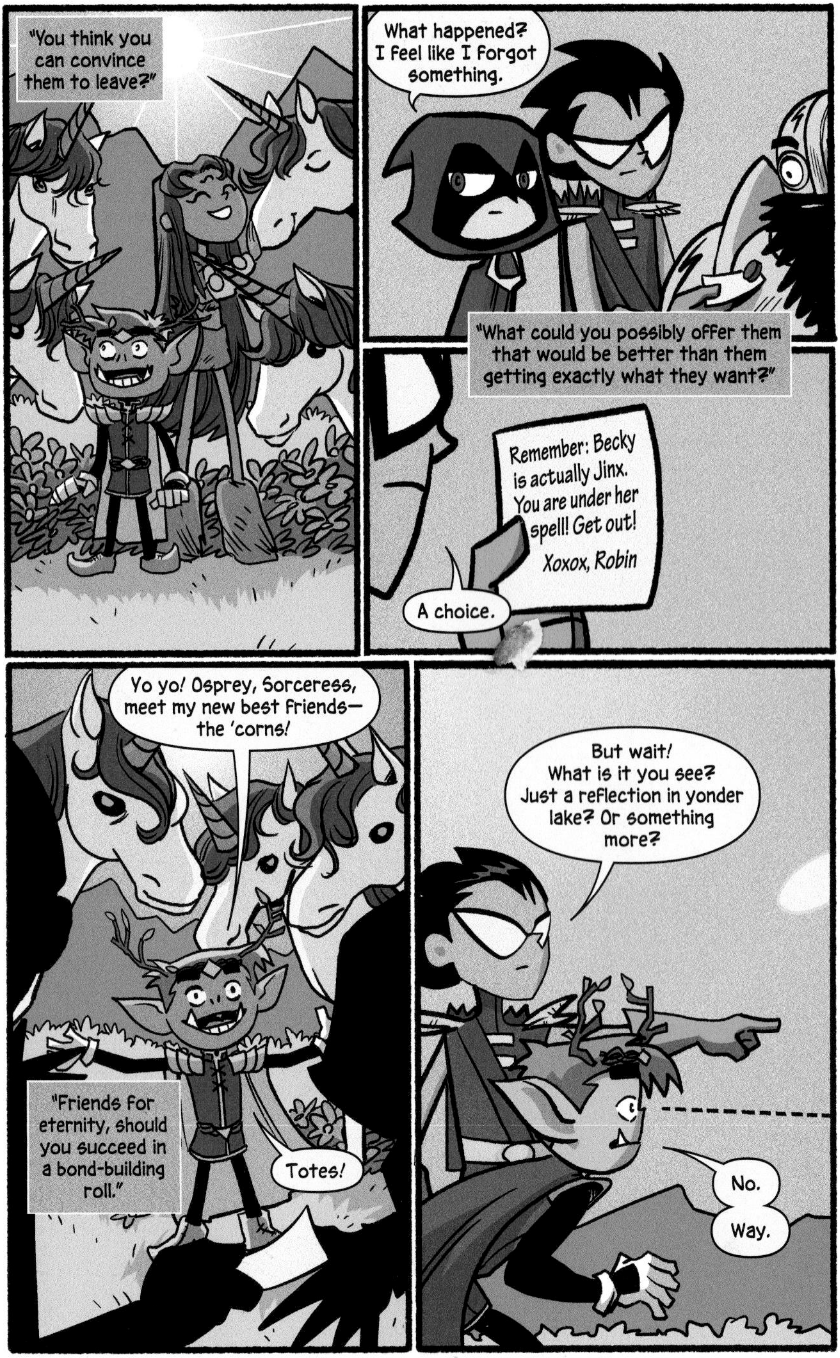
"You think you can convince them to leave?"
What happened? I feel like I forgot something.
"What could you possibly offer them that would be better than them getting exactly what they want?"
Remember: Becky is actually Jinx. You are under her spell! Get out! Xoxox, Robin
A choice.
Yo yo! Osprey, Sorceress, meet my new best friends—the 'corns!
"Friends for eternity, should you succeed in a bond-building roll."
Totes!
But wait! What is it you see? Just a reflection in yonder lake? Or something more?
No.
Way.

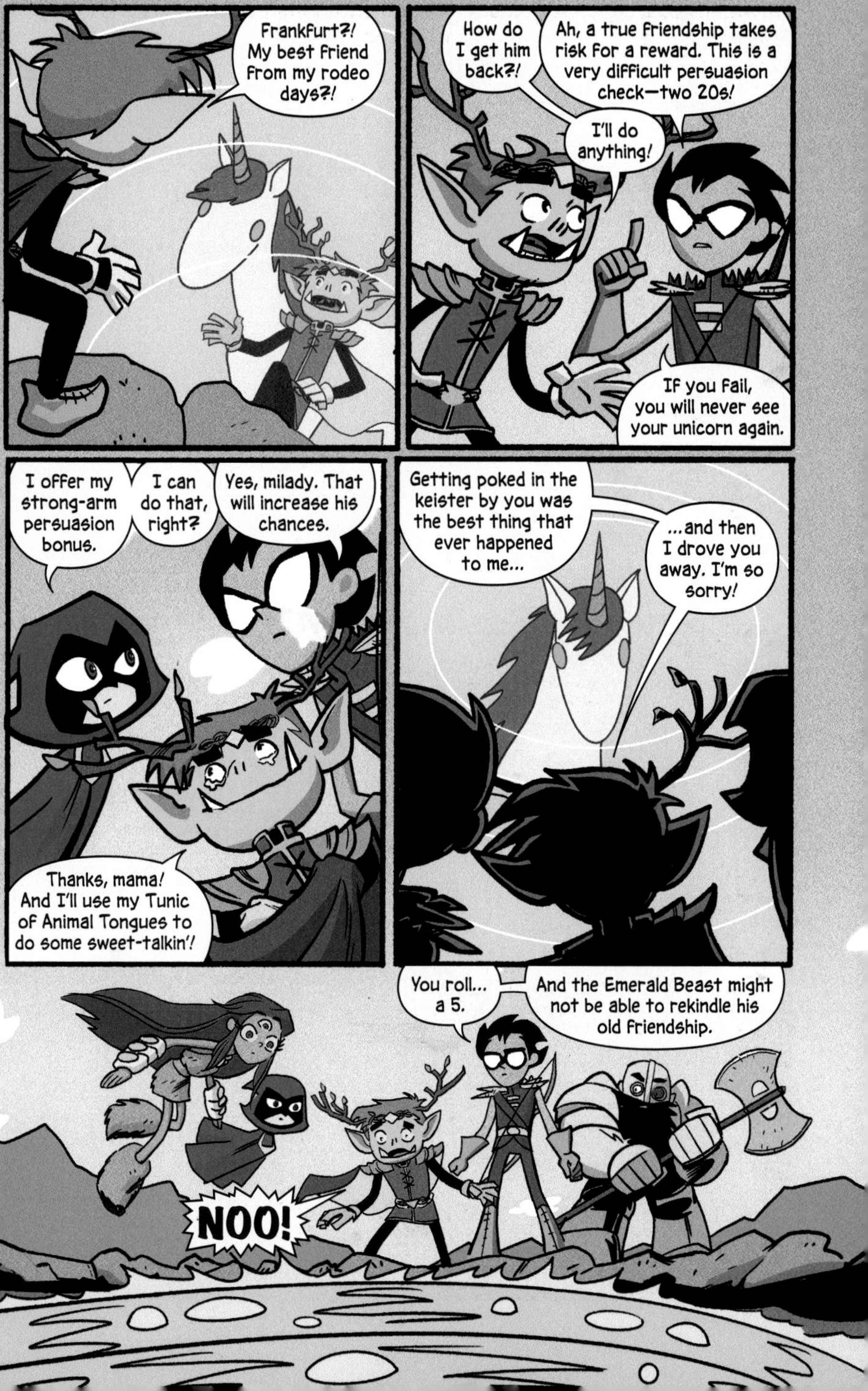
Frankfurt?! My best friend from my rodeo days?!
How do I get him back?!
Ah, a true friendship takes risk for a reward. This is a very difficult persuasion check—two 20s!
I'll do anything!
If you fail, you will never see your unicorn again.
I offer my strong-arm persuasion bonus.
I can do that, right?
Yes, milady. That will increase his chances.
Thanks, mama! And I'll use my Tunic of Animal Tongues to do some sweet-talkin'!
Getting poked in the keister by you was the best thing that ever happened to me...
...and then I drove you away. I'm so sorry!
You roll... a 5.
And the Emerald Beast might not be able to rekindle his old friendship.
NOO!

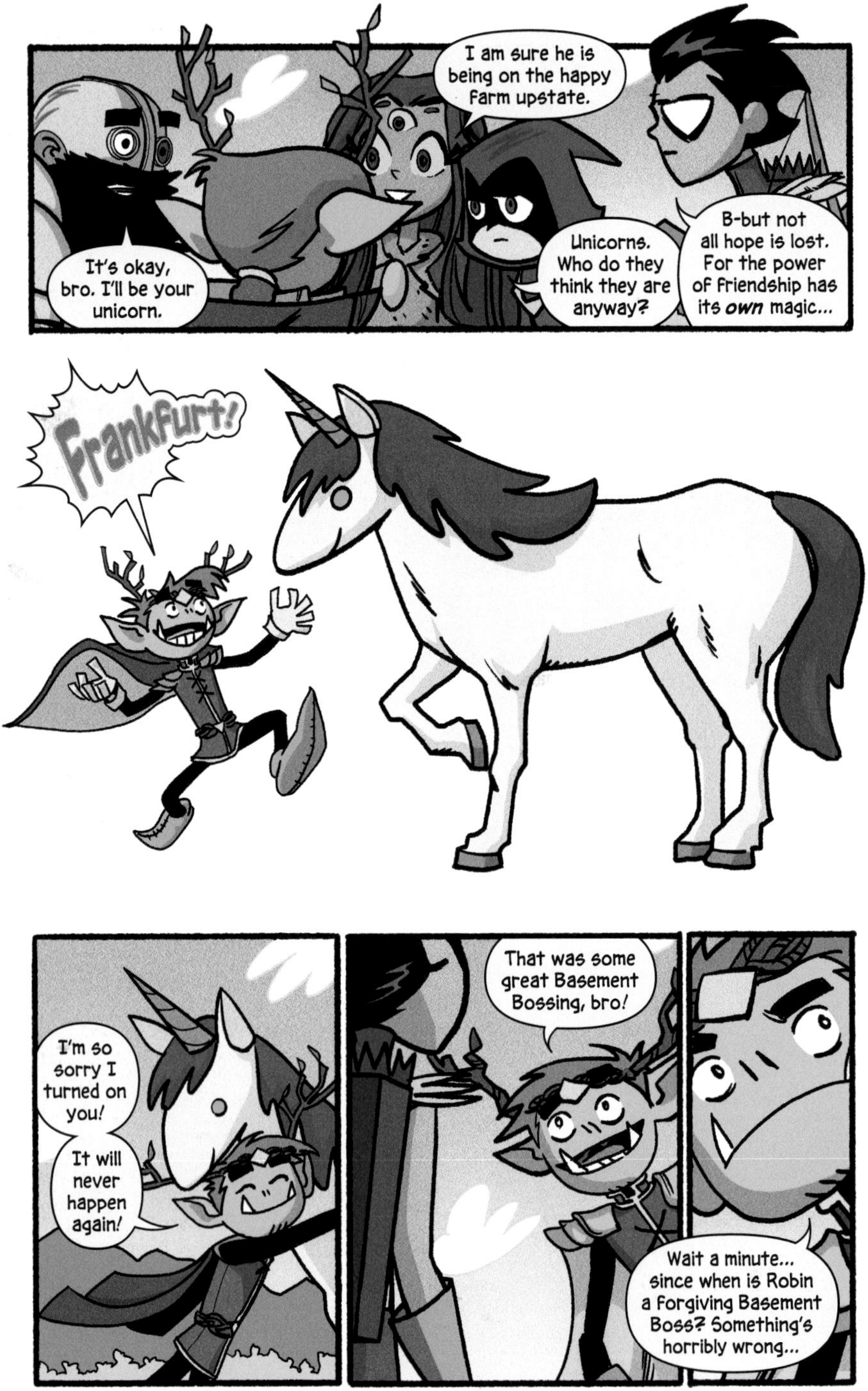
I am sure he is being on the happy farm upstate.
It's okay, bro. I'll be your unicorn.
Unicorns. Who do they think they are anyway?
B-but not all hope is lost. For the power of friendship has its *own* magic...
Frankfurt!
I'm so sorry I turned on you!
It will never happen again!
That was some great Basement Bossing, bro!
Wait a minute... since when is Robin a forgiving Basement Boss? Something's horribly wrong...

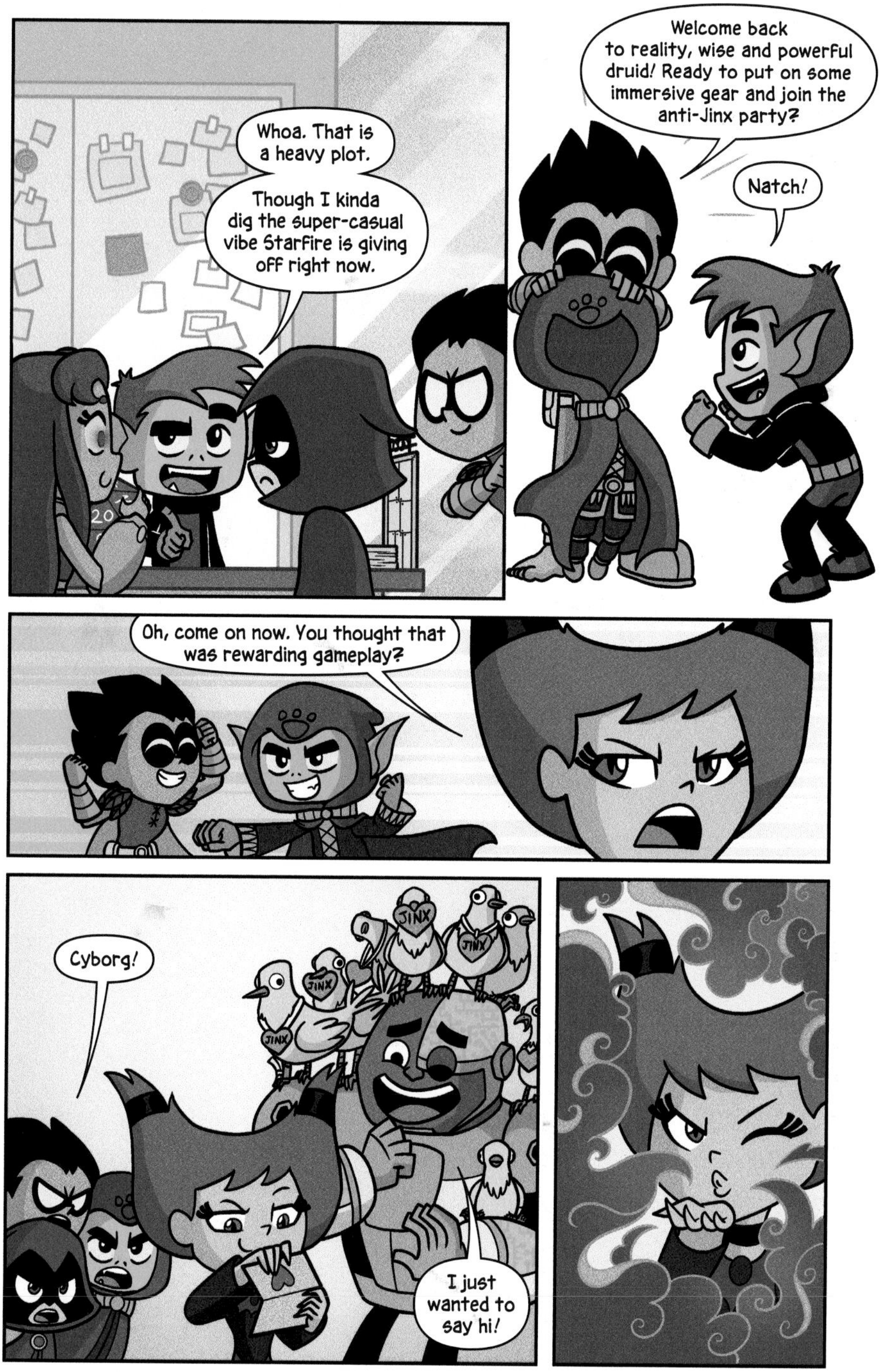
Whoa. That is a heavy plot.
Though I kinda dig the super-casual vibe Starfire is giving off right now.
Welcome back to reality, wise and powerful druid! Ready to put on some immersive gear and join the anti-Jinx party?
Natch!
Oh, come on now. You thought that was rewarding gameplay?
Cyborg!
JINX
JINX
JINX
JINX
I just wanted to say hi!

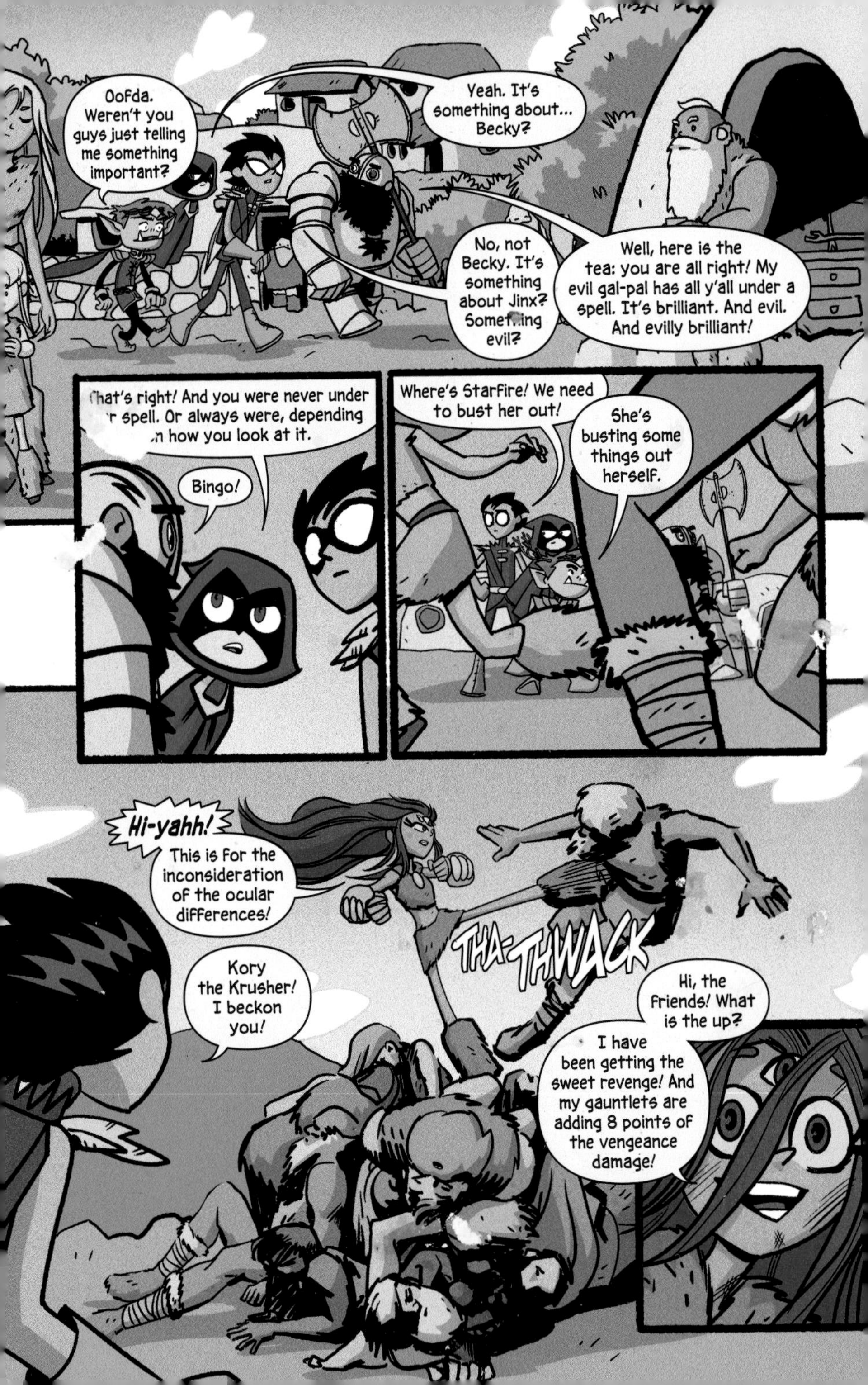
Oofda. Weren't you guys just telling me something important?
Yeah. It's something about... Becky?
No, not Becky. It's something about Jinx? Somet ing evil?
Well, here is the tea: you are all right! My evil gal-pal has all y'all under a spell. It's brilliant. And evil. And evilly brilliant!
hat's right! And you were never under r spell. Or always were, depending n how you look at it.
Bingo!
Where's Starfire! We need to bust her out!
She's busting some things out herself.
Hi-yahh!
This is for the inconsideration of the ocular differences!
THA-THWACK
Kory the Krusher! I beckon you!
Hi, the friends! What is the up?
I have been getting the sweet revenge! And my gauntlets are adding 8 points of the vengeance damage!

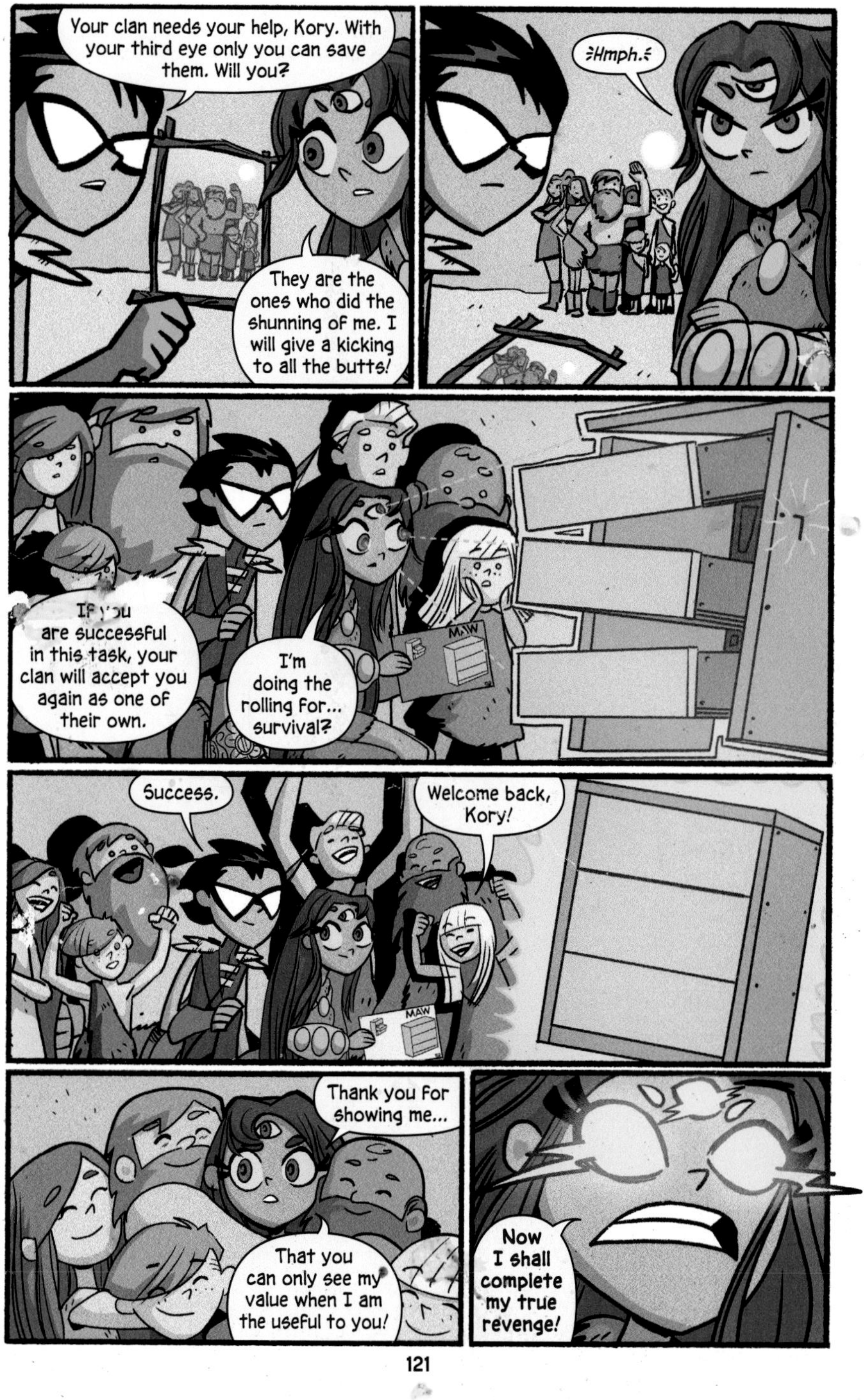
Your clan needs your help, Kory. With your third eye only you can save them. Will you?
They are the ones who did the shunning of me. I will give a kicking to all the butts!
Hmph.
If you are successful in this task, your clan will accept you again as one of their own.
I'm doing the rolling for... survival?
MAW
Success.
Welcome back, Kory!
MAW
Thank you for showing me...
That you can only see my value when I am the useful to you!
Now I shall complete my true revenge!

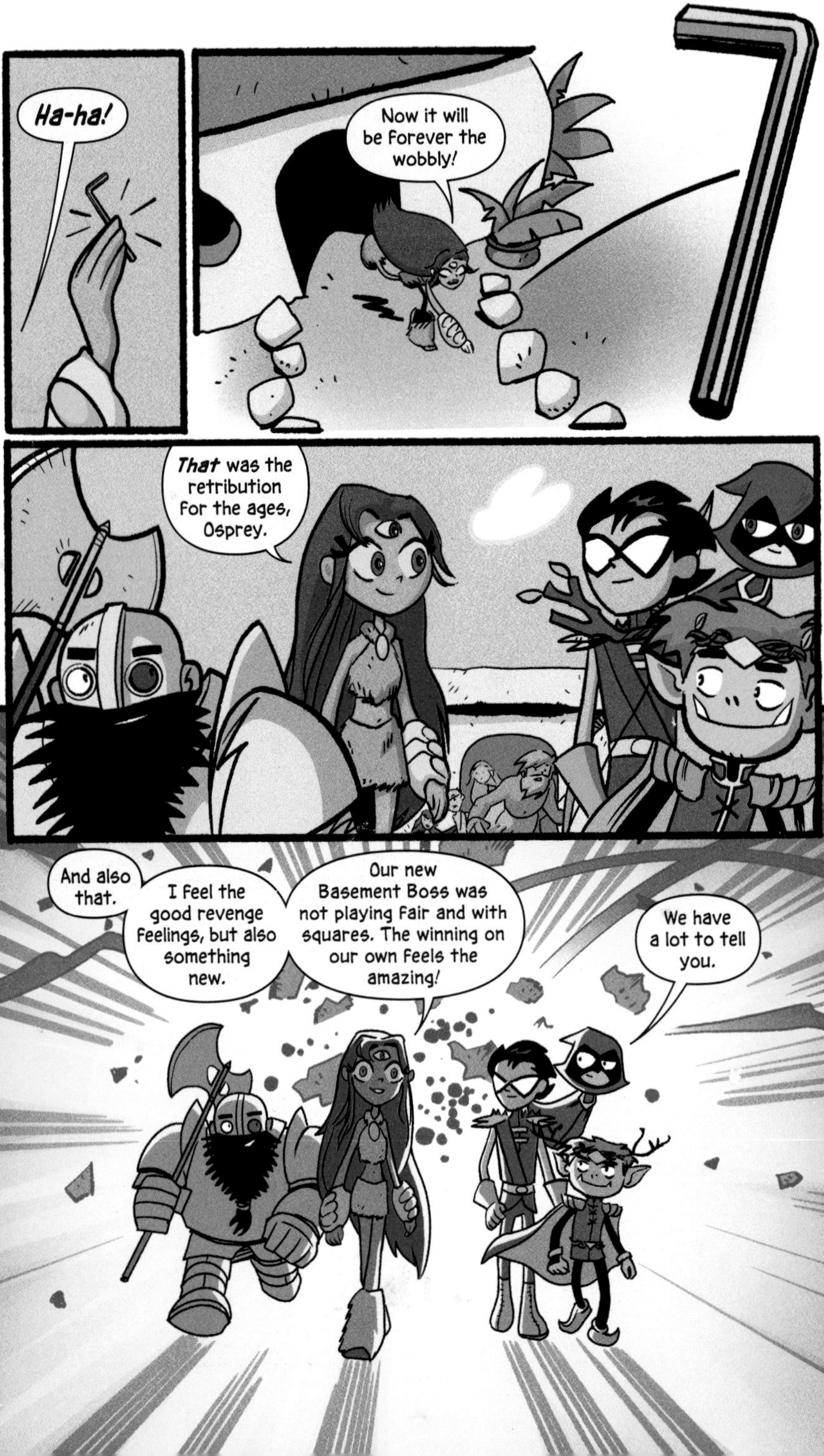
Ha-ha!
Now it will be forever the wobbly!
That was the retribution for the ages, Osprey.
And also that.
I feel the good revenge feelings, but also something new.
Our new Basement Boss was not playing fair and with squares. The winning on our own feels the amazing!
We have a lot to tell you.

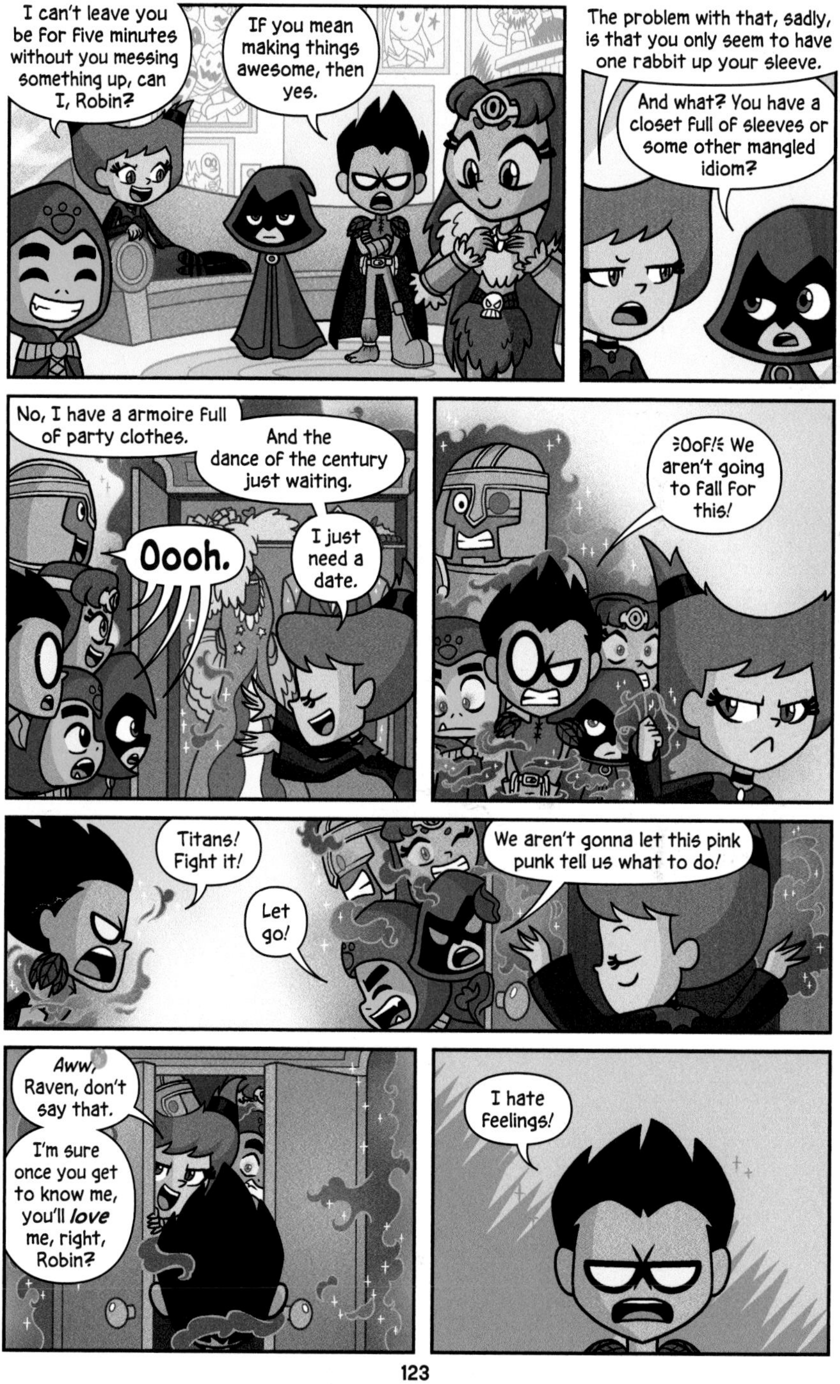

I can't leave you be for five minutes without you messing something up, can I, Robin?
If you mean making things awesome, then yes.
The problem with that, sadly, is that you only seem to have one rabbit up your sleeve.
And what? You have a closet full of sleeves or some other mangled idiom?
No, I have a armoire full of party clothes.
And the dance of the century just waiting.
Oooh.
I just need a date.
Oof! We aren't going to fall for this!
Titans! Fight it!
Let go!
We aren't gonna let this pink punk tell us what to do!
Aww, Raven, don't say that.
I'm sure once you get to know me, you'll *love* me, right, Robin?
I hate Feelings!

Chapter
Ten

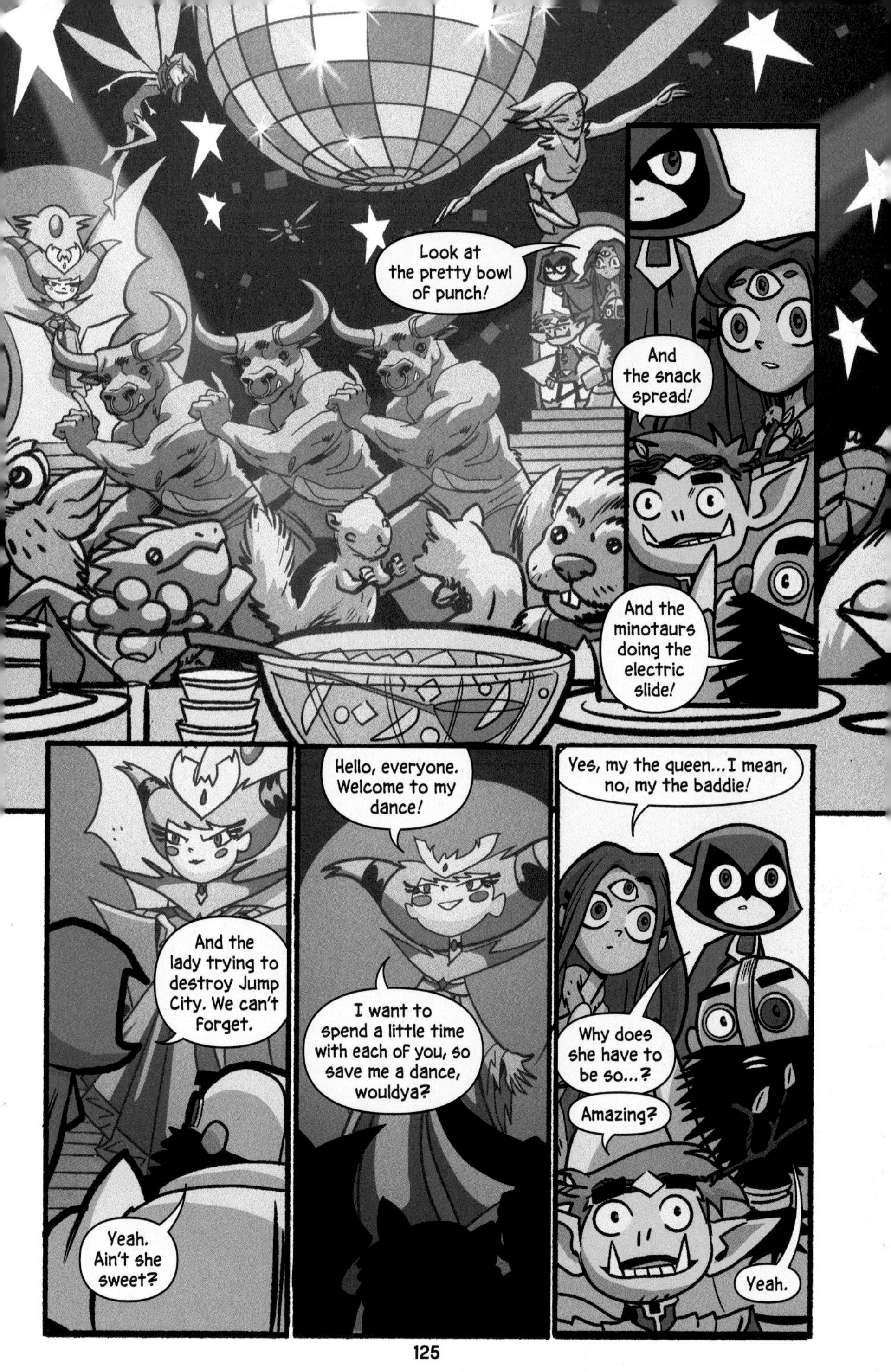
Look at the pretty bowl of punch!
And the snack spread!
And the minotaurs doing the electric slide!
And the lady trying to destroy Jump City. We can't forget.
Yeah. Ain't she sweet?
Hello, everyone. Welcome to my dance!
I want to spend a little time with each of you, so save me a dance, wouldya?
Yes, my the queen... I mean, no, my the baddie!
Why does she have to be so...?
Amazing?
Yeah.

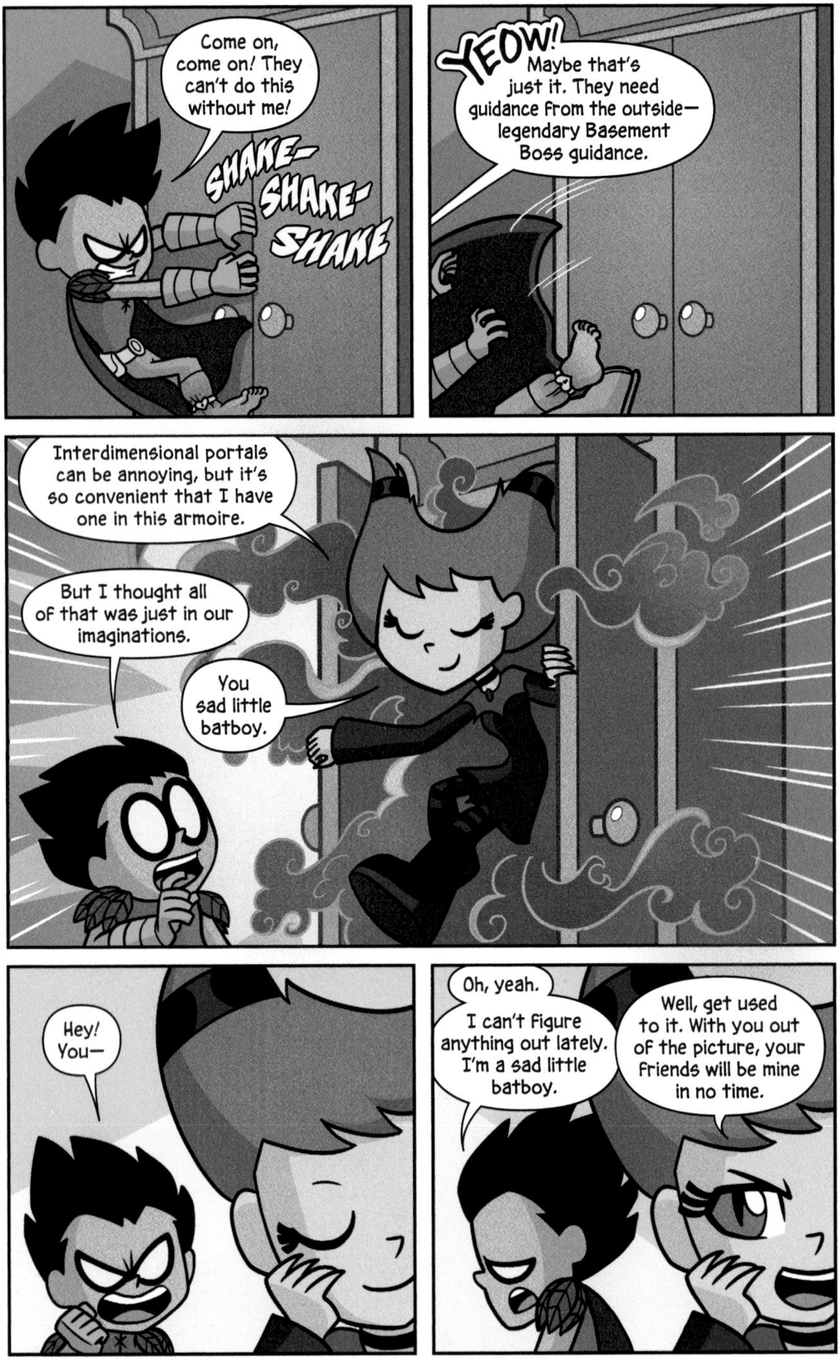
Come on, come on! They can't do this without me!
SHAKE-SHAKE-SHAKE
YEOW!
Maybe that's just it. They need guidance from the outside—legendary Basement Boss guidance.
Interdimensional portals can be annoying, but it's so convenient that I have one in this armoire.
But I thought all of that was just in our imaginations.
You sad little batboy.
Hey! You—
Oh, yeah.
I can't figure anything out lately. I'm a sad little batboy.
Well, get used to it. With you out of the picture, your friends will be mine in no time.

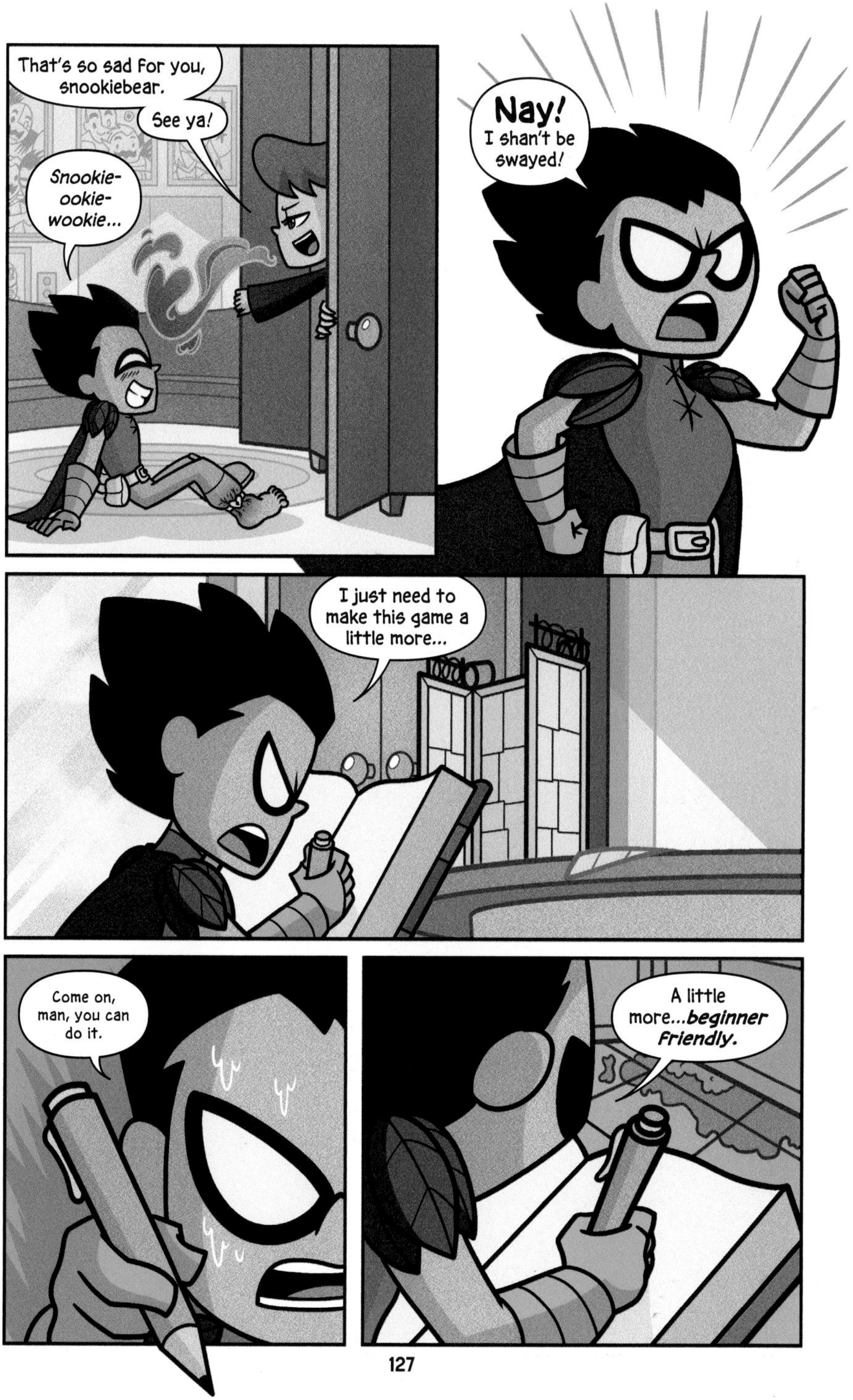

That's so sad for you, snookiebear.
See ya!
Snookie-ookie-wookie...
Nay! I shan't be swayed!
I just need to make this game a little more...
Come on, man, you can do it.
A little more...*beginner friendly.*

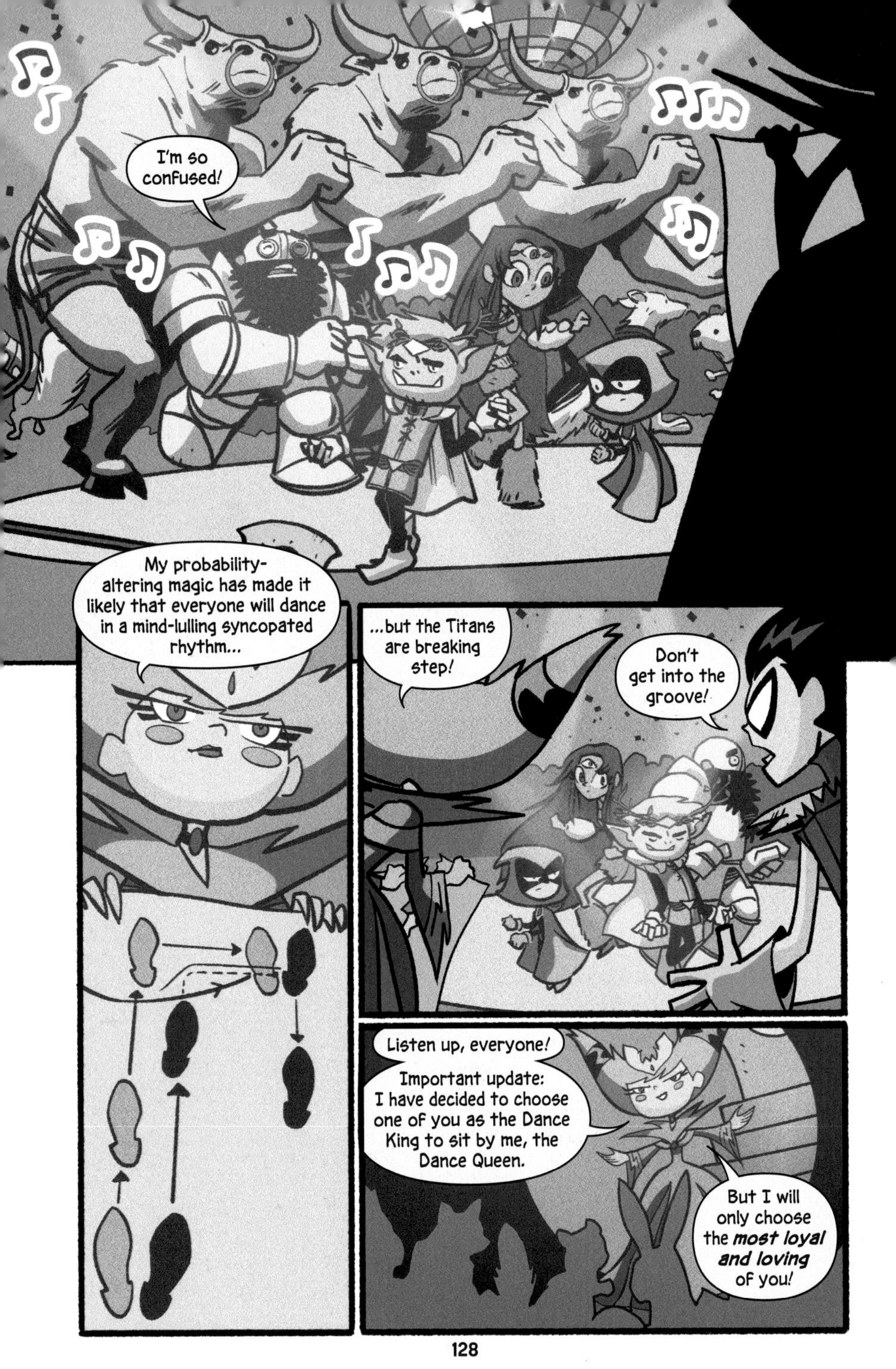
I'm so confused!
My probability-altering magic has made it likely that everyone will dance in a mind-lulling syncopated rhythm...
...but the Titans are breaking step!
Don't get into the groove!
Listen up, everyone!
Important update: I have decided to choose one of you as the Dance King to sit by me, the Dance Queen.
But I will only choose the ***most loyal and loving*** of you!

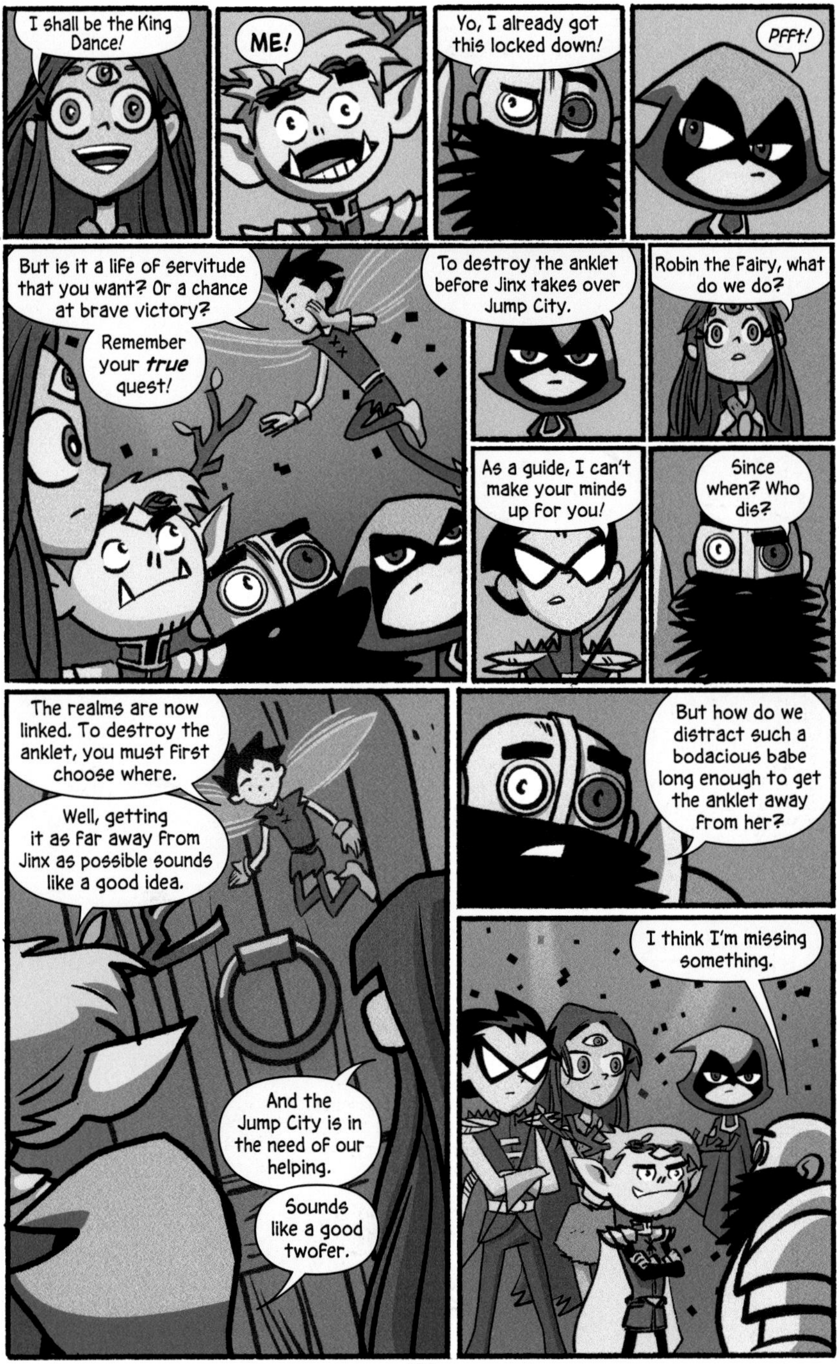

I shall be the King Dance!
ME!
Yo, I already got this locked down!
Pfft!
But is it a life of servitude that you want? Or a chance at brave victory?
Remember your *true* quest!
To destroy the anklet before Jinx takes over Jump City.
Robin the Fairy, what do we do?
As a guide, I can't make your minds up for you!
Since when? Who dis?
The realms are now linked. To destroy the anklet, you must first choose where.
Well, getting it as far away from Jinx as possible sounds like a good idea.
And the Jump City is in the need of our helping.
Sounds like a good twofer.
But how do we distract such a bodacious babe long enough to get the anklet away from her?
I think I'm missing something.

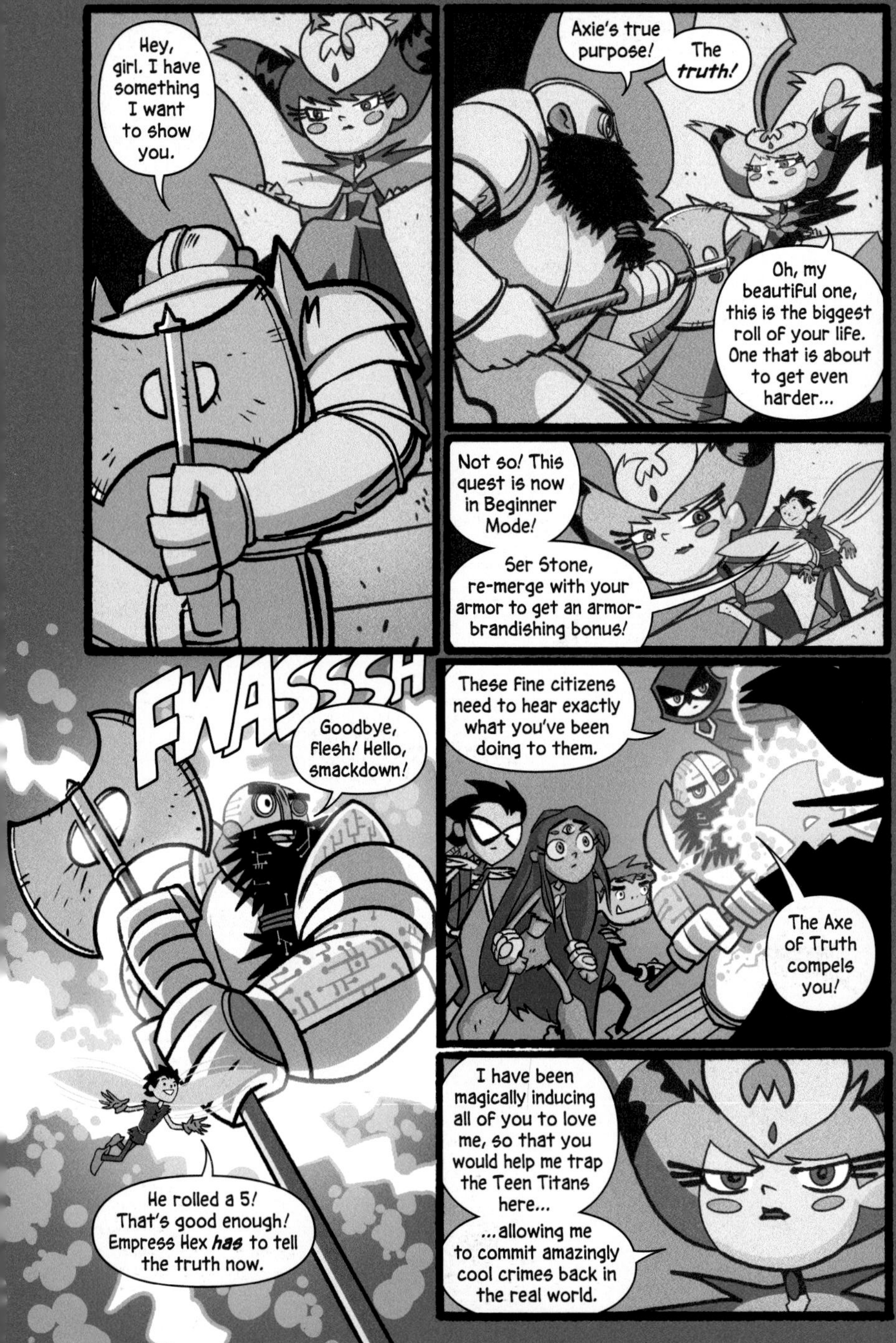
Hey, girl. I have something I want to show you.
Axie's true purpose!
The *truth!*
Oh, my beautiful one, this is the biggest roll of your life. One that is about to get even harder...
Not so! This quest is now in Beginner Mode!
Ser Stone, re-merge with your armor to get an armor-brandishing bonus!
FWASSSH
Goodbye, Flesh! Hello, smackdown!
He rolled a 5! That's good enough! Empress Hex *has* to tell the truth now.
These fine citizens need to hear exactly what you've been doing to them.
The Axe of Truth compels you!
I have been magically inducing all of you to love me, so that you would help me trap the Teen Titans here...
...allowing me to commit amazingly cool crimes back in the real world.

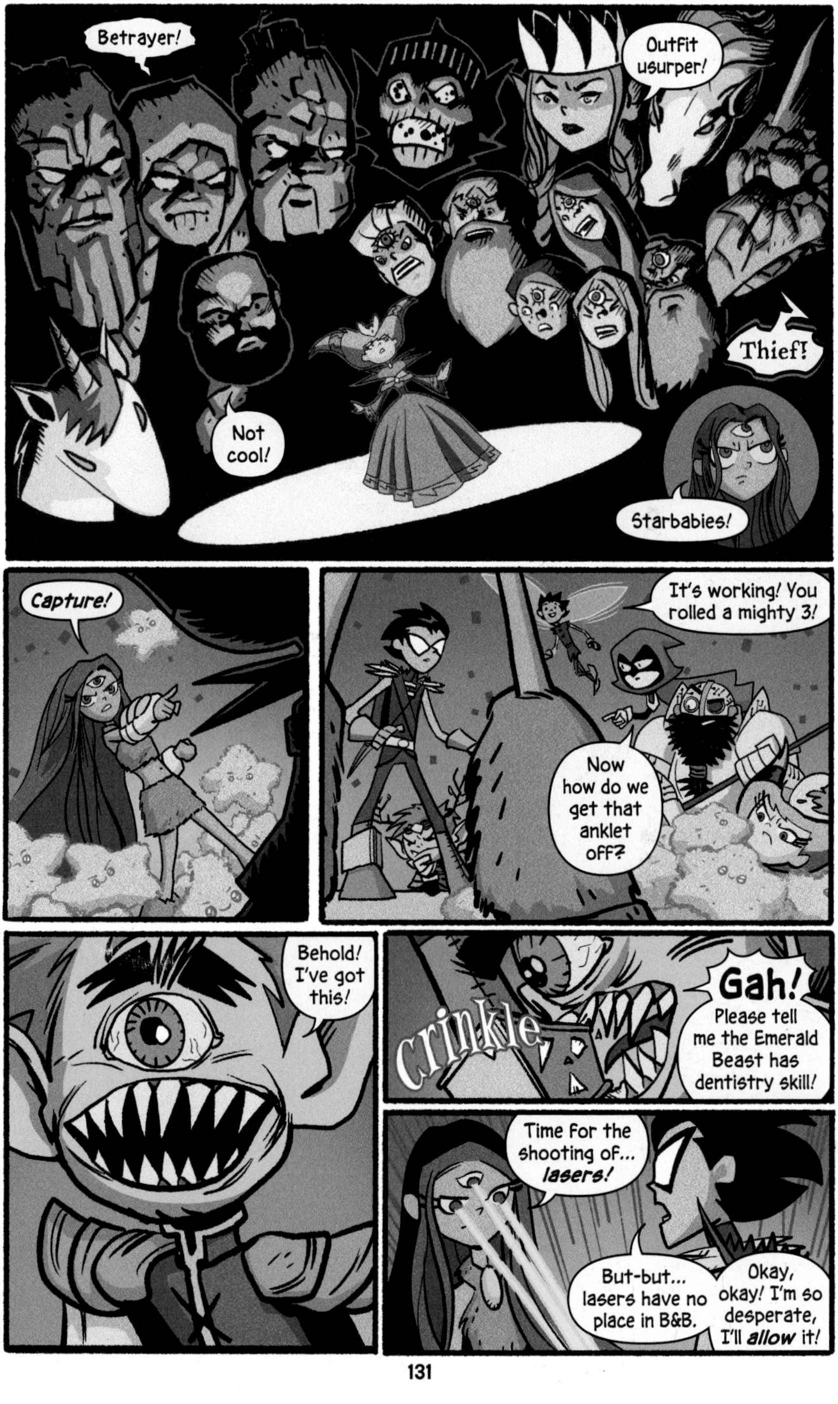
Betrayer!
Outfit usurper!
Thief!
Not cool!
Starbabies!
Capture!
It's working! You rolled a mighty 3!
Now how do we get that anklet off?
Behold! I've got this!
CRINKLE
Gah! Please tell me the Emerald Beast has dentistry skill!
Time for the shooting of... *lasers!*
But-but... lasers have no place in B&B.
Okay, okay! I'm so desperate, I'll *allow* it!

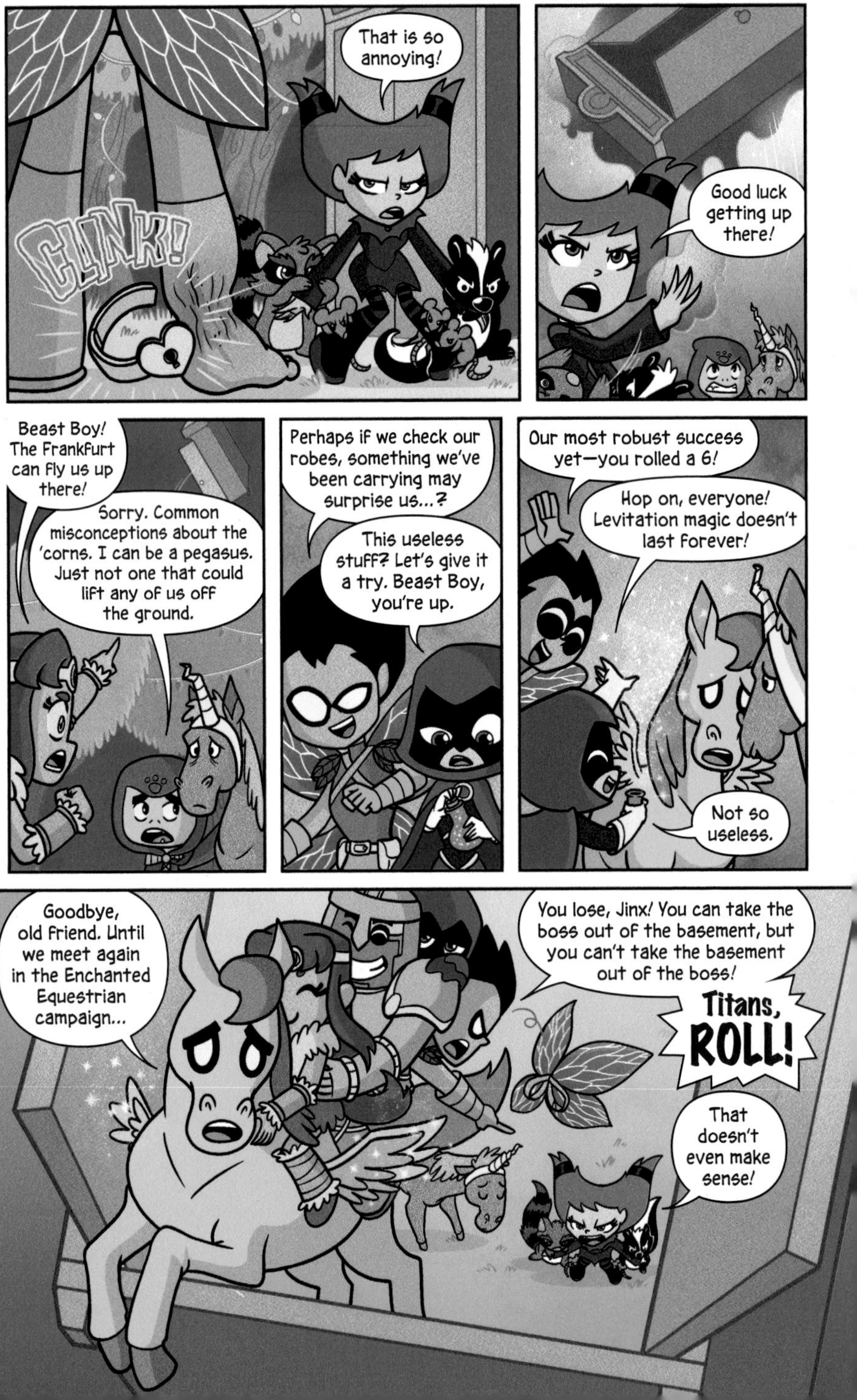

CLINK!
That is so annoying!
Good luck getting up there!
Beast Boy! The Frankfurt can fly us up there!
Sorry. Common misconceptions about the 'corns. I can be a pegasus. Just not one that could lift any of us off the ground.
Perhaps if we check our robes, something we've been carrying may surprise us...?
This useless stuff? Let's give it a try. Beast Boy, you're up.
Our most robust success yet—you rolled a 6!
Hop on, everyone! Levitation magic doesn't last forever!
Not so useless.
Goodbye, old friend. Until we meet again in the Enchanted Equestrian campaign...
You lose, Jinx! You can take the boss out of the basement, but you can't take the basement out of the boss!
Titans, ROLL!
That doesn't even make sense!

Chapter
Eleven

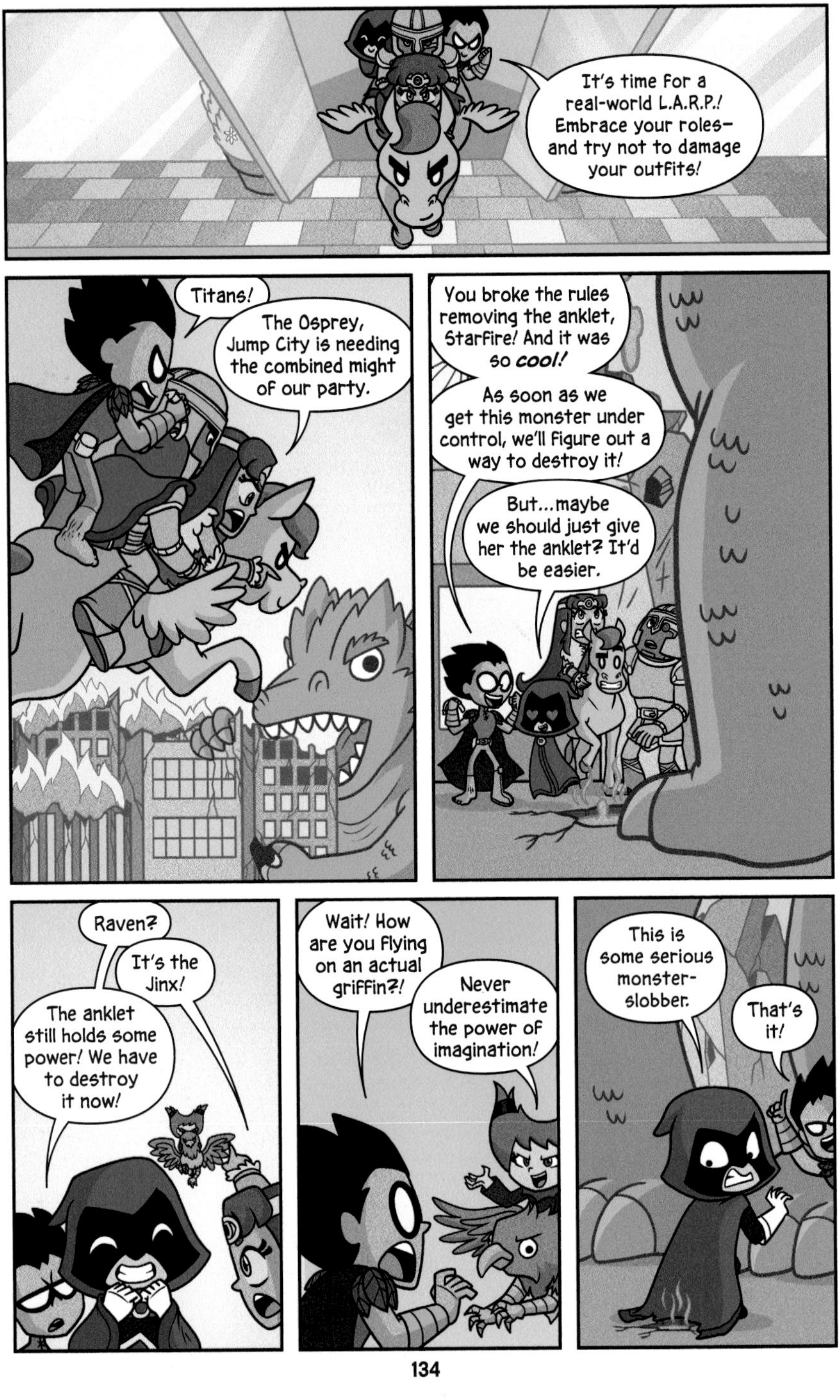
It's time for a real-world L.A.R.P.! Embrace your roles— and try not to damage your outfits!
Titans!
The Osprey, Jump City is needing the combined might of our party.
You broke the rules removing the anklet, Starfire! And it was so *cool!*
As soon as we get this monster under control, we'll figure out a way to destroy it!
But...maybe we should just give her the anklet? It'd be easier.
Raven?
It's the Jinx!
The anklet still holds some power! We have to destroy it now!
Wait! How are you flying on an actual griffin?!
Never underestimate the power of imagination!
This is some serious monster-slobber.
That's it!

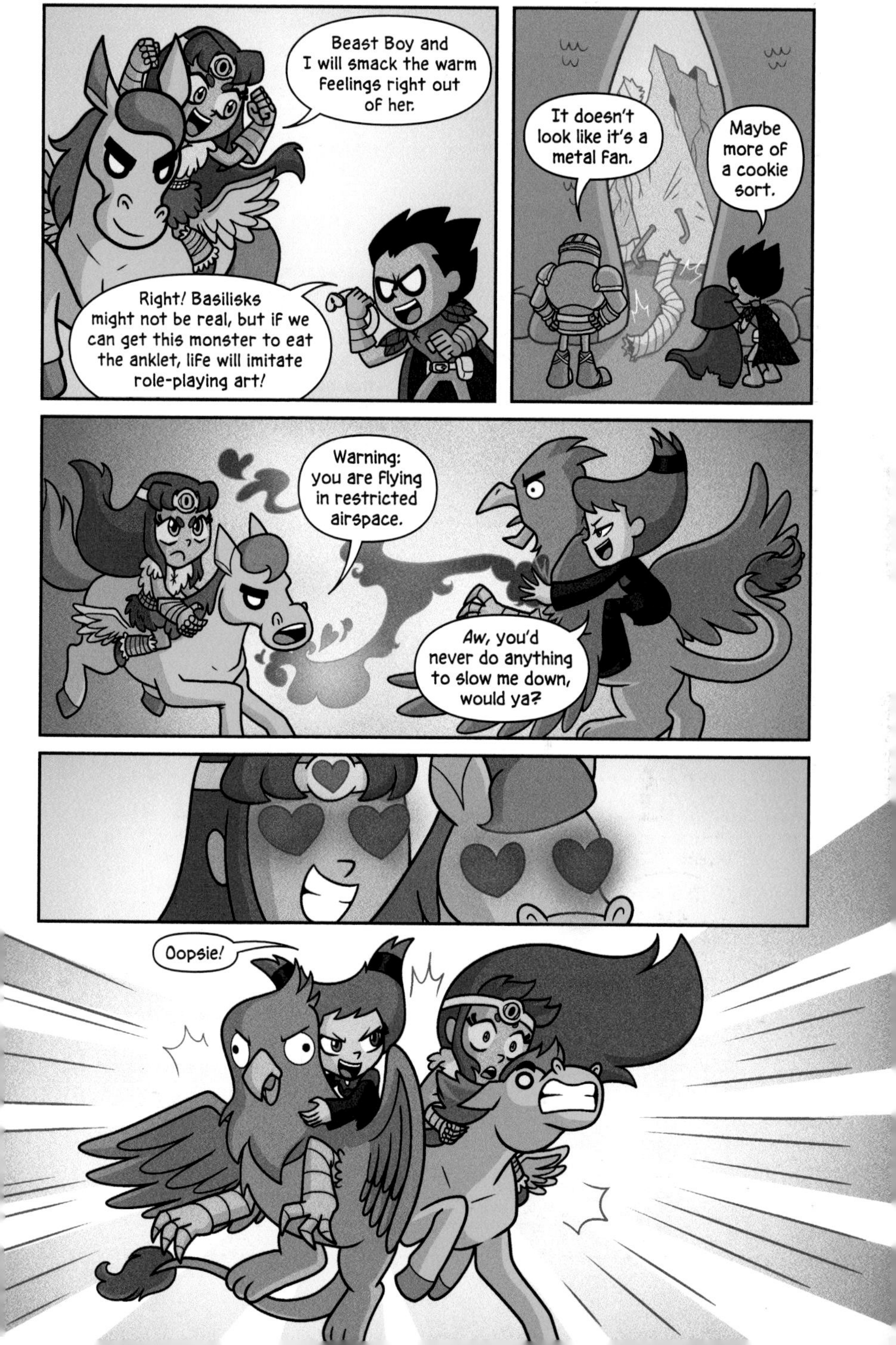

Beast Boy and I will smack the warm feelings right out of her.
Right! Basilisks might not be real, but if we can get this monster to eat the anklet, life will imitate role-playing art!
It doesn't look like it's a metal fan.
Maybe more of a cookie sort.
Warning: you are flying in restricted airspace.
Aw, you'd never do anything to slow me down, would ya?
Oopsie!

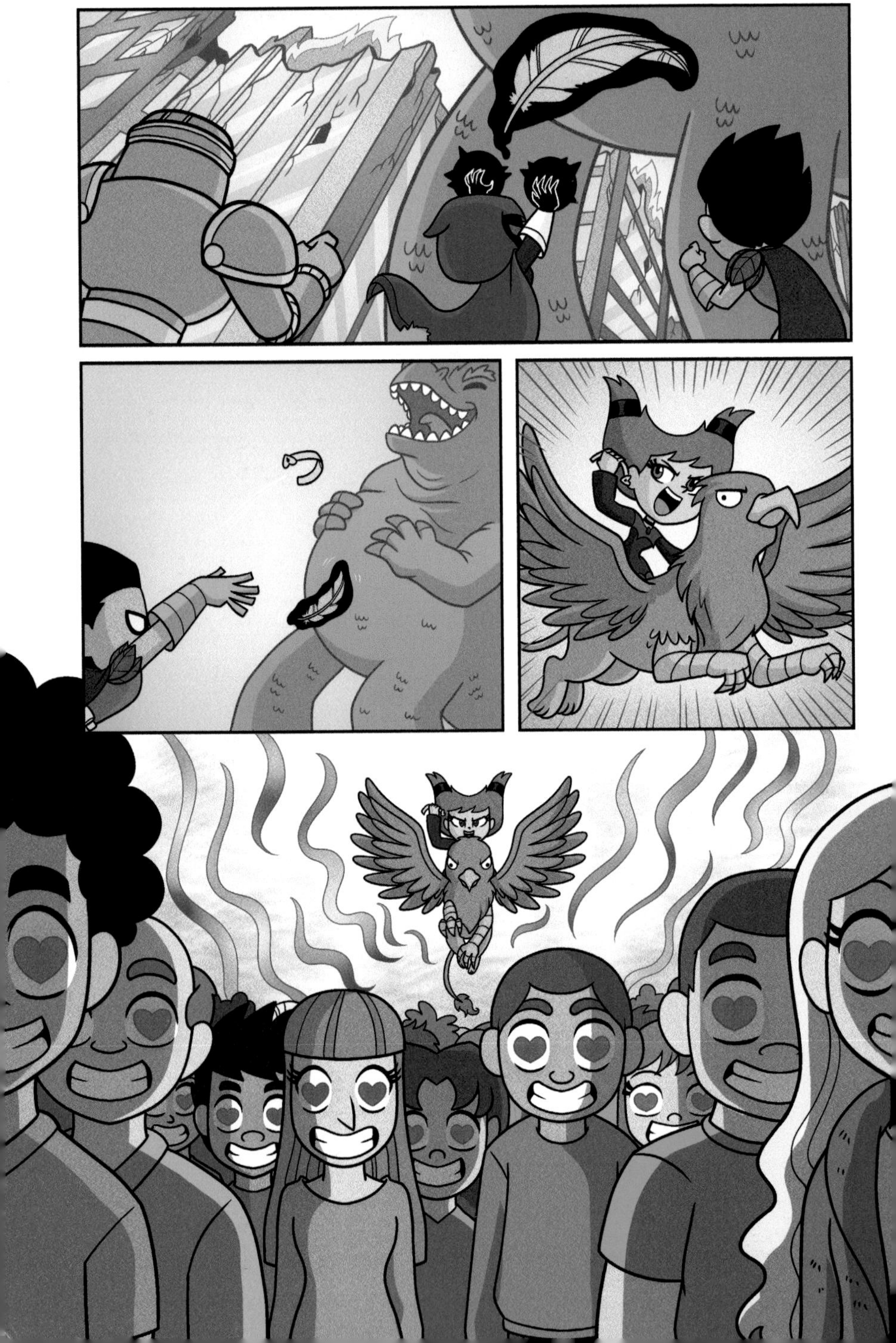

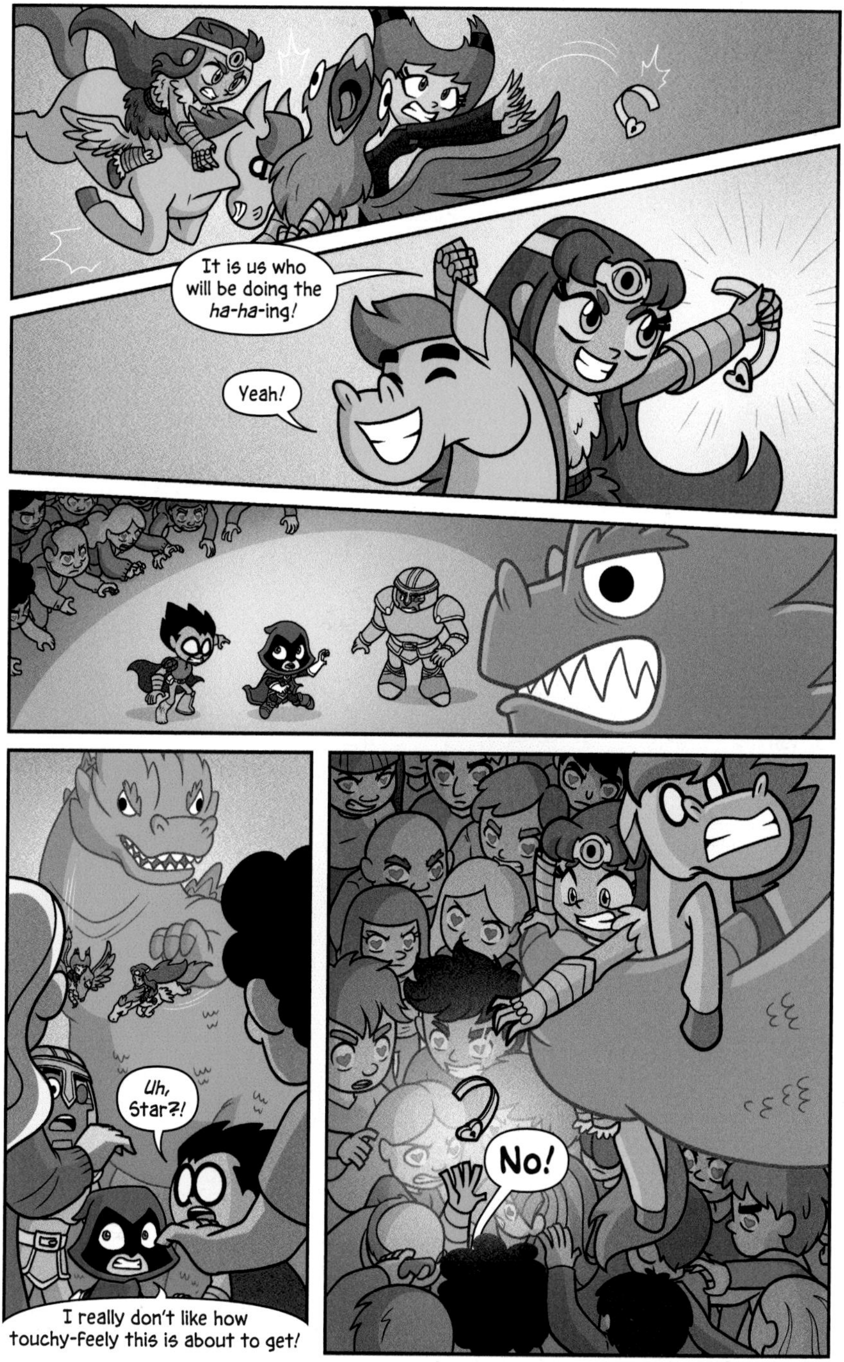

It is us who will be doing the *ha-ha*-ing!
Yeah!
Uh, Star?!
I really don't like how touchy-feely this is about to get!
No!

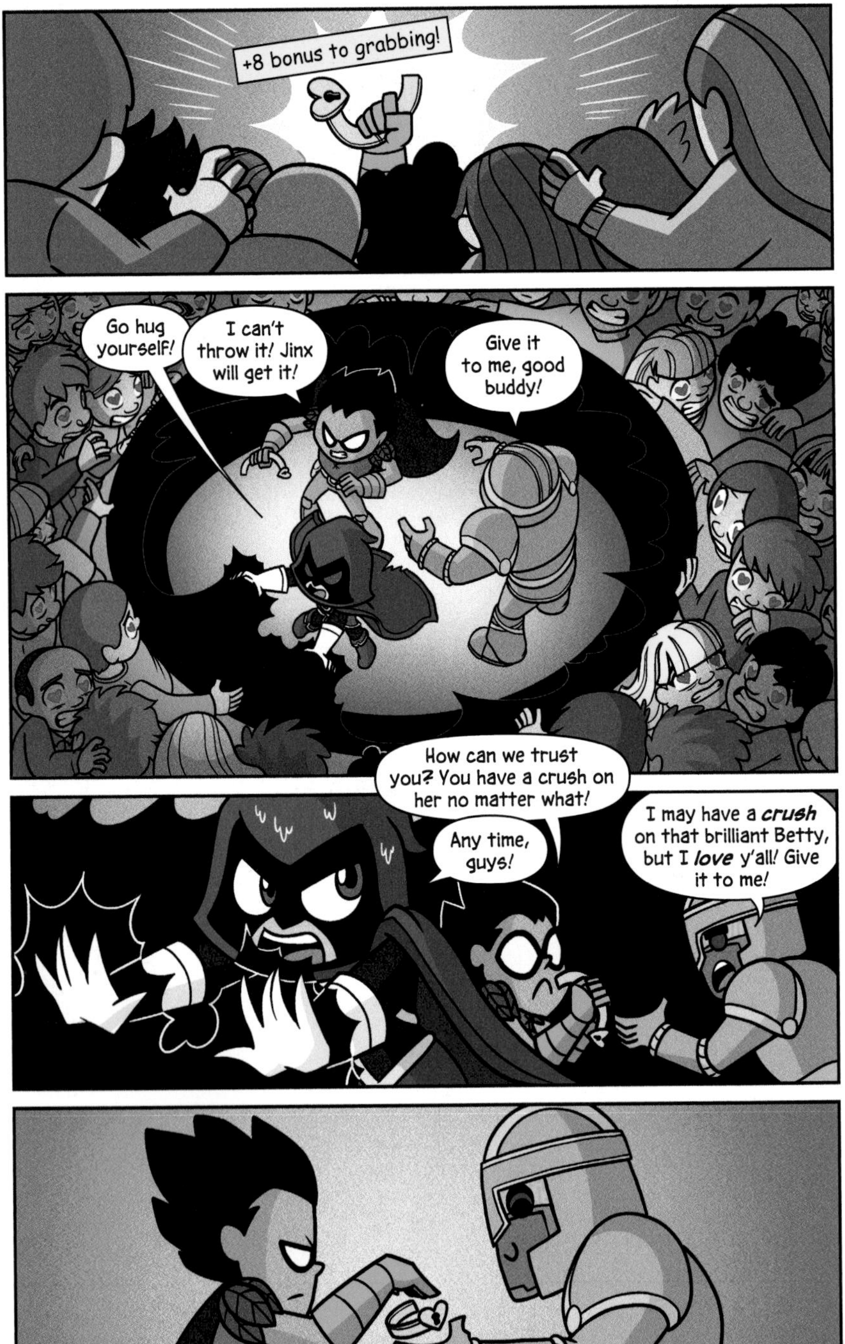
+8 bonus to grabbing!
Go hug yourself!
I can't throw it! Jinx will get it!
Give it to me, good buddy!
How can we trust you? You have a crush on her no matter what!
Any time, guys!
I may have a *crush* on that brilliant Betty, but I *love* y'all! Give it to me!

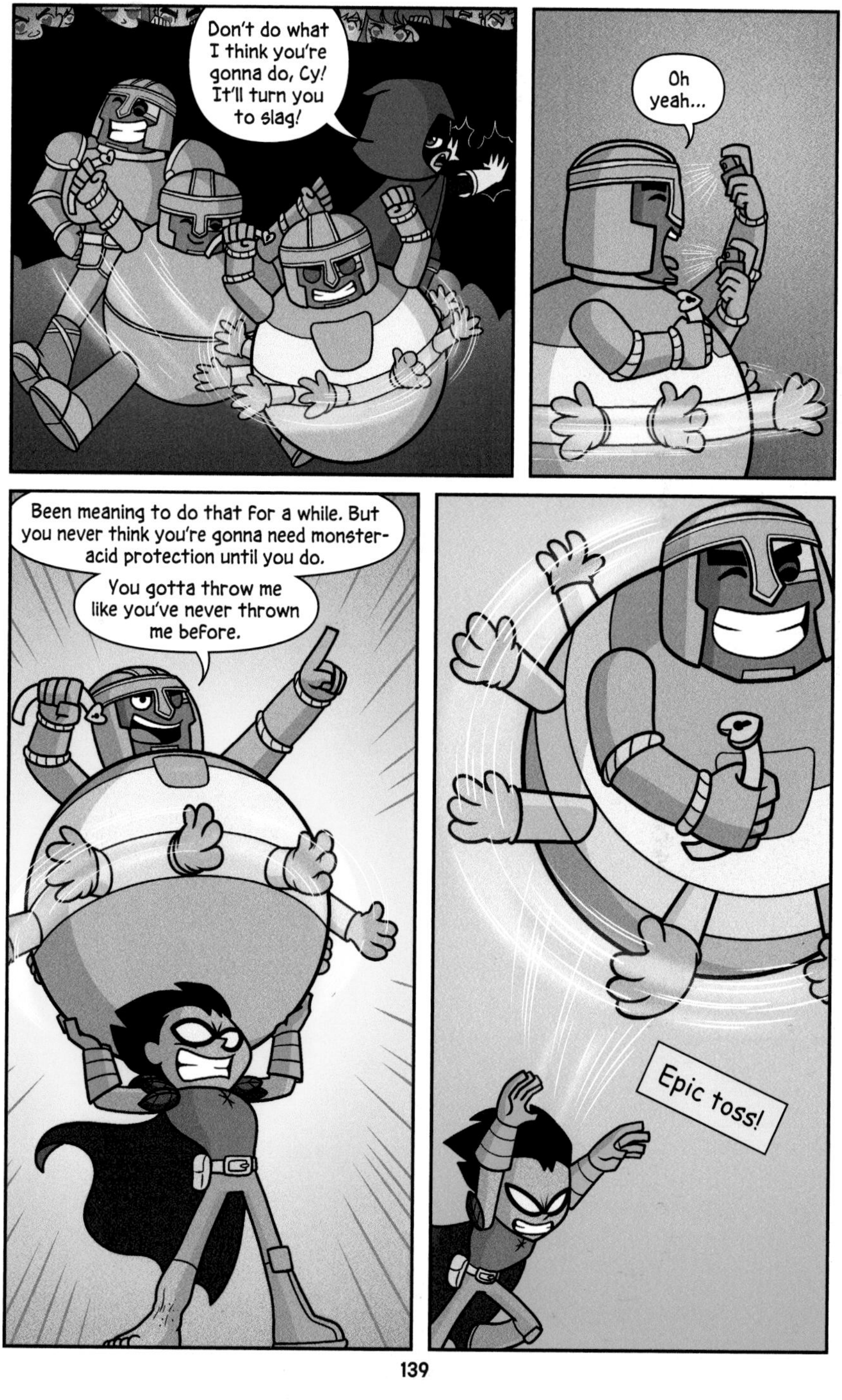
Don't do what I think you're gonna do, Cy! It'll turn you to slag!
Oh yeah...
Been meaning to do that for a while. But you never think you're gonna need monster-acid protection until you do.
You gotta throw me like you've never thrown me before.
Epic toss!

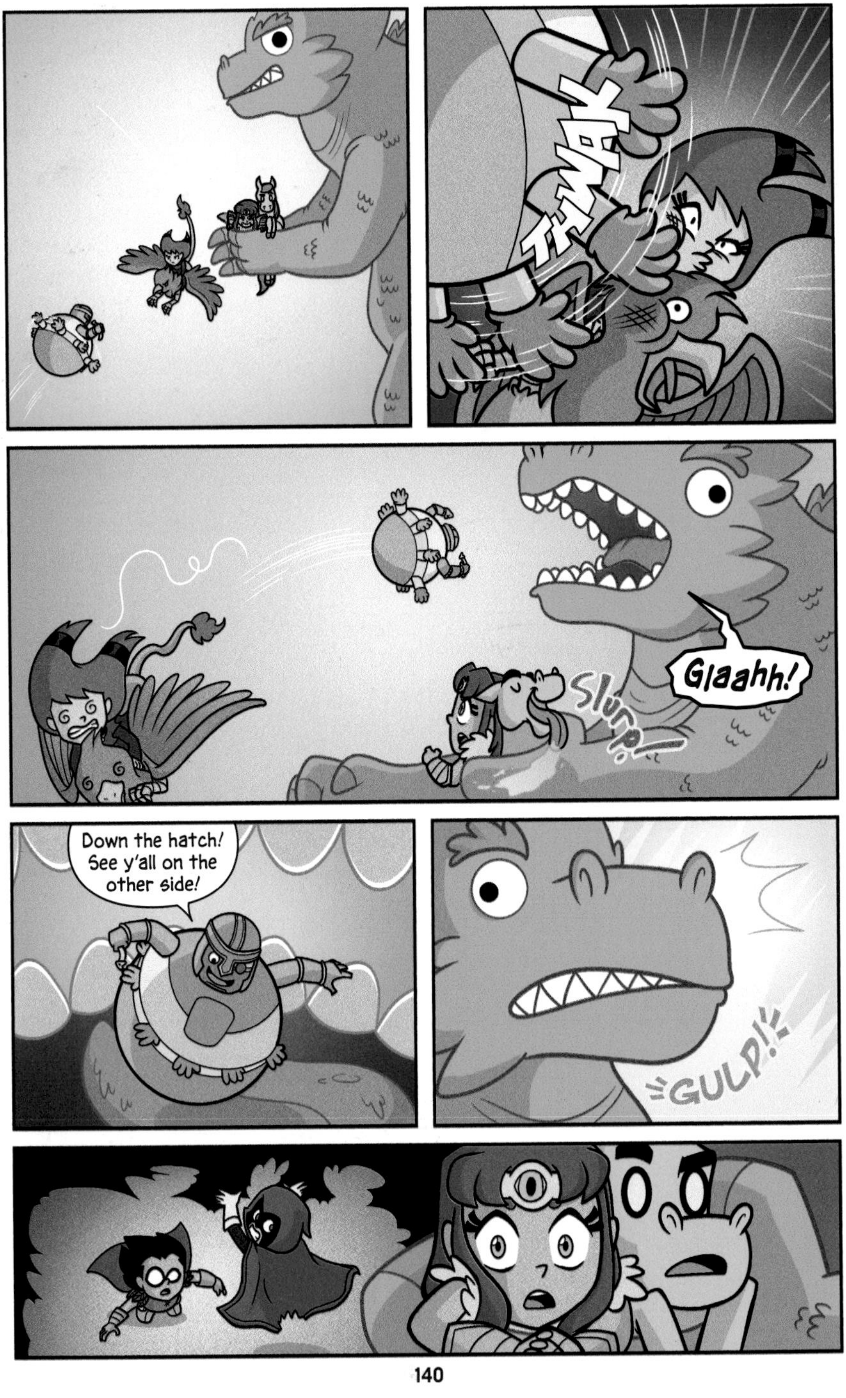
THWAK
Glaahh!
Slurp!
Down the hatch! See y'all on the other side!
GULP!

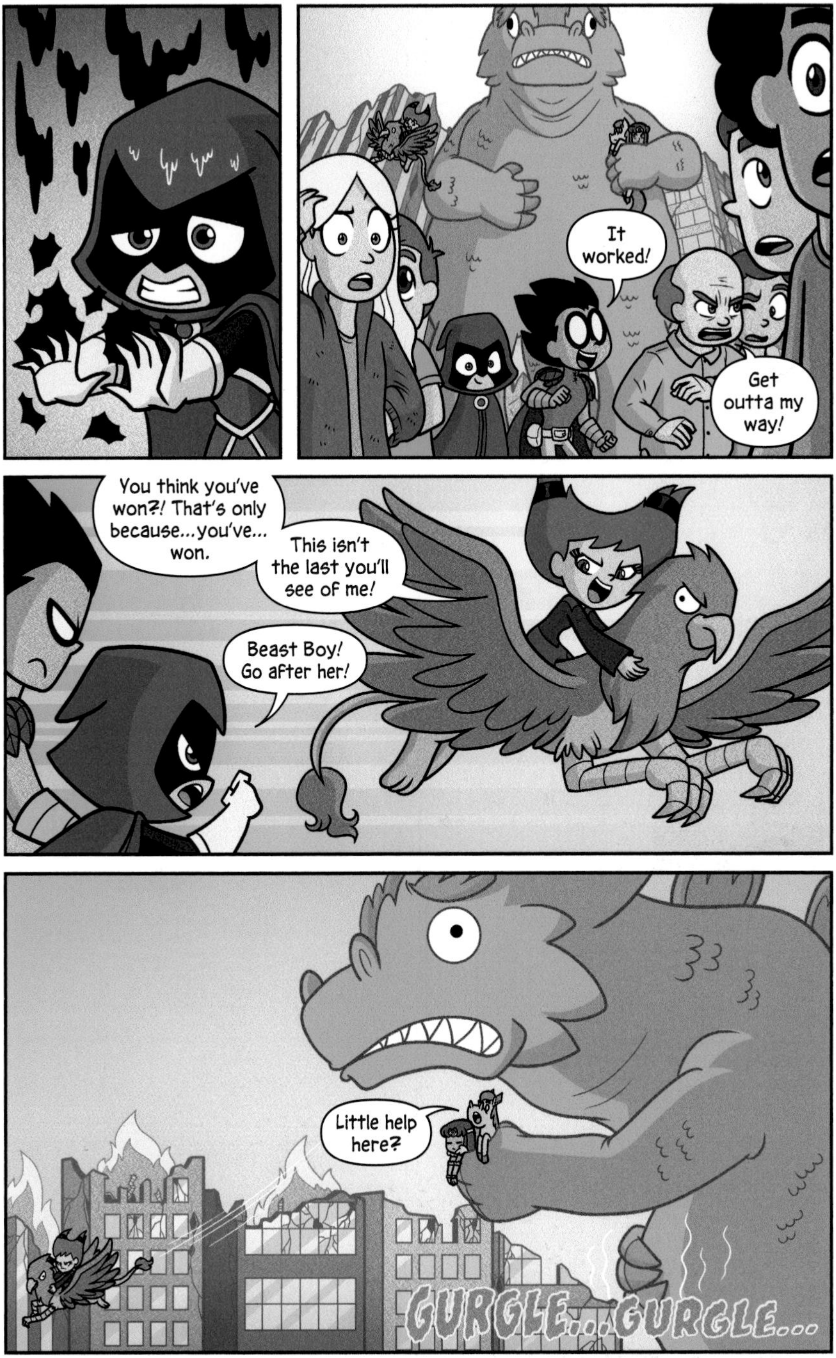
It worked!
Get outta my way!
You think you've won?! That's only because...you've... won.
This isn't the last you'll see of me!
Beast Boy! Go after her!
Little help here?
GURGLE...GURGLE...

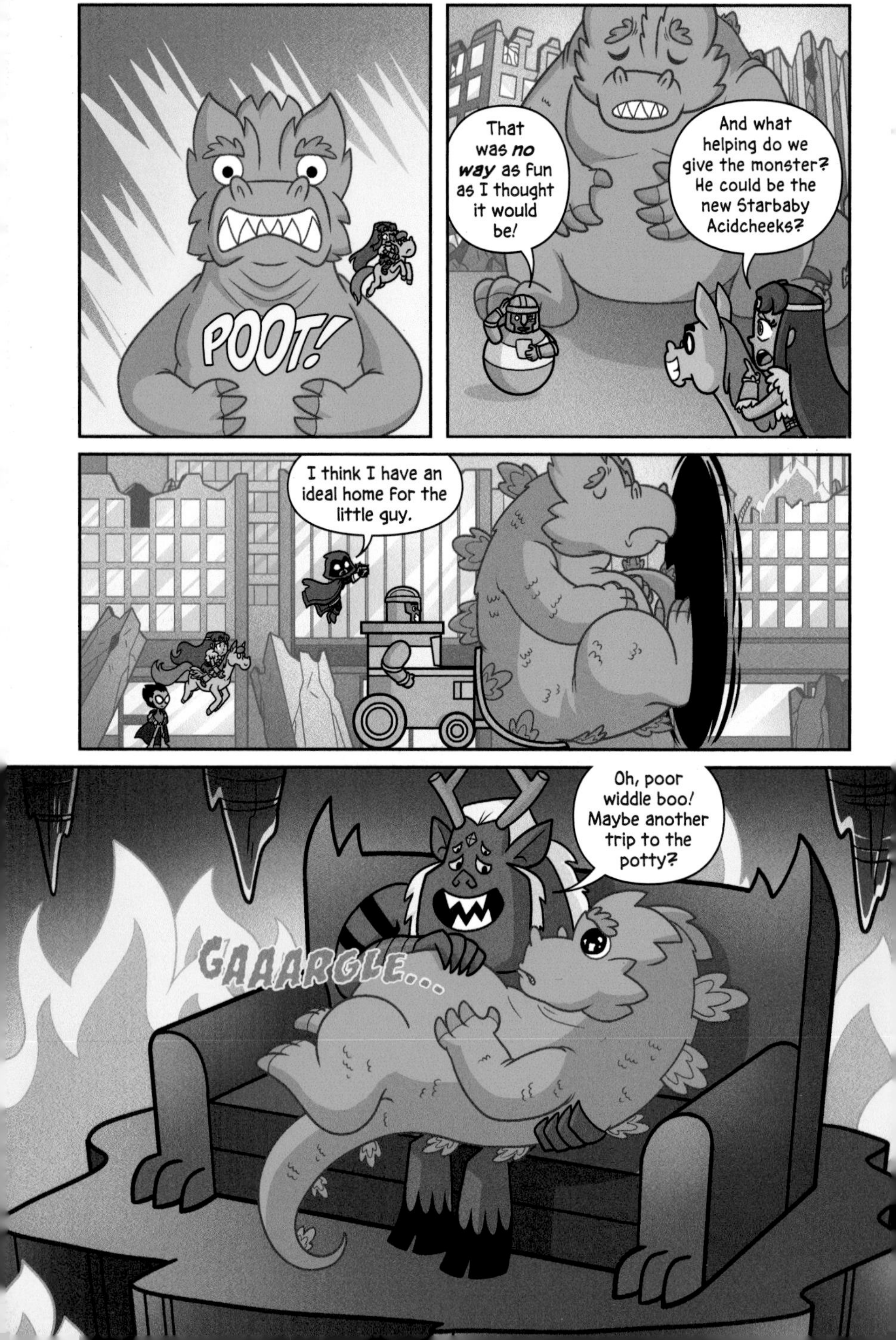
POOT!
That was no way as fun as I thought it would be!
And what helping do we give the monster? He could be the new Starbaby Acidcheeks?
I think I have an ideal home for the little guy.
Oh, poor widdle boo! Maybe another trip to the potty?
GAAARGLE...

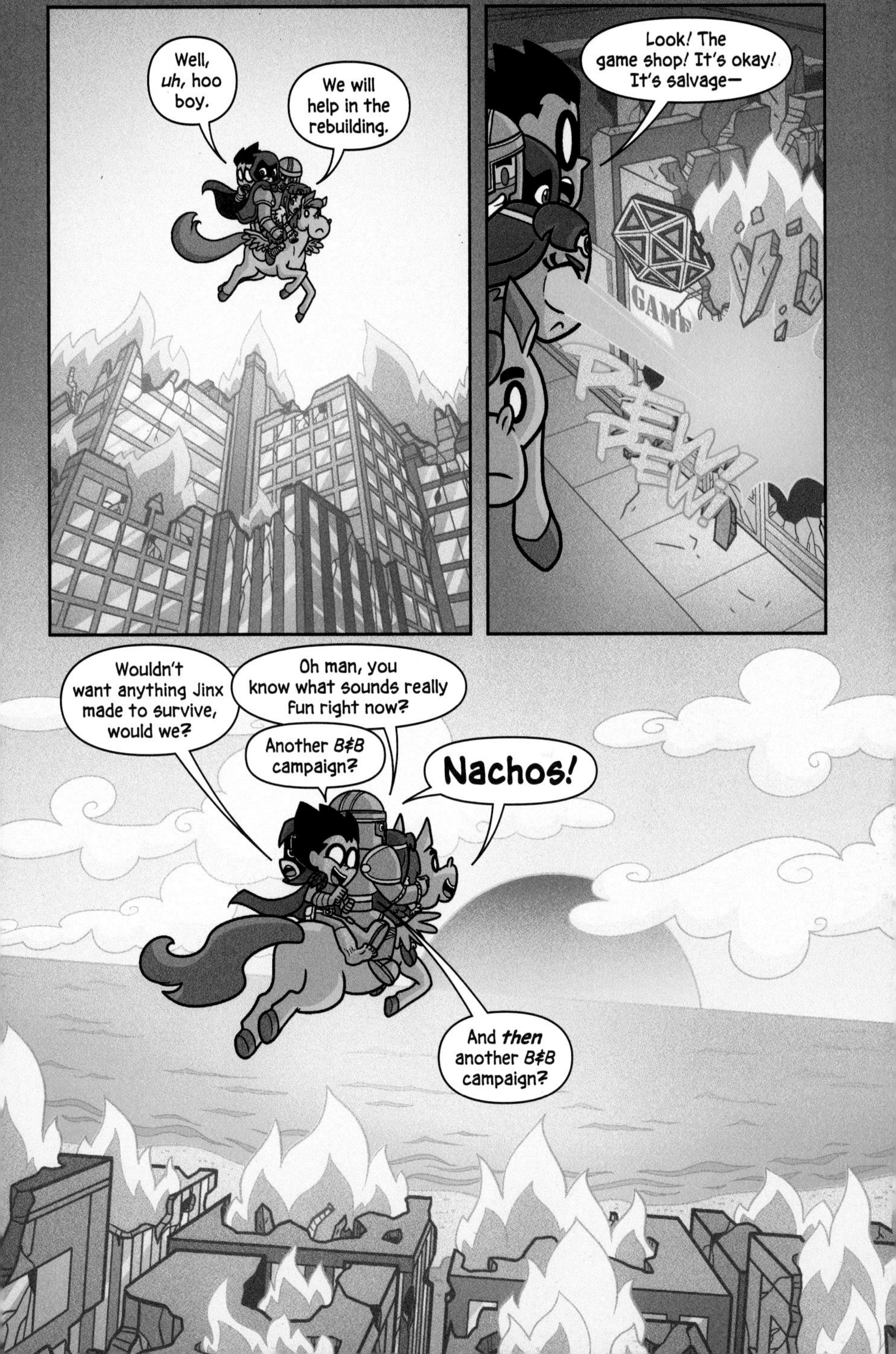
Well, *uh,* hoo boy.
We will help in the rebuilding.
Look! The game shop! It's okay! It's salvage—
GAME
PEEW!
Wouldn't want anything Jinx made to survive, would we?
Oh man, you know what sounds really fun right now?
Another *B&B* campaign?
Nachos!
And *then* another *B&B* campaign?

HEATHER NUHFER has written a lot of things—most of them intentionally. Her comics include *Wonder Woman, Teen Titans Go!, Scooby Doo,* and *Fraggle Rock.* Her *My Little Pony: Friendship Is Magic* comics have sold millions of copies worldwide. Her tween novel series, *My So-Called Superpowers,* is available now. She has also scripted episodes of the animated TV series *Littlest Pet Shop: A World of Our Own.* Heather lives with her very odd dog, Einstein, and her slightly less odd husband, Paul.

P.C. MORRISSEY is an Eisner Award-winning graphic novel editor and writer. His editing credits include *The Muppet Show Comic Book* and the graphic novel anthology *Mouse Guard: Legends of the Guard.* As a writer, Paul has penned several all-ages comics, most notably *Teen Titans Go!, Sesame Street,* and *Fraggle Rock.* In addition to being occasional co-writers, Paul and Heather Nuhfer are happily married nerds.

AGNES GARBOWSKA has made her name in comics illustrating such titles as the *New York Times* bestselling and award-winning *DC Super Hero Girls* for DC Comics. In addition, her portfolio includes a long run on *My Little Pony* for IDW, *Teen Titans Go!* for DC Comics, *Grumpy Cat* for Dynamite Entertainment, and Sonic Universe "Off Panel" strips for Archie Comics. When she's not illustrating comics, she is giving snuggles to her two little dogs, Olive and Otis.

SANDY JARRELL has spent the last ten years drawing comics for DC (*Teen Titans Go!, DC Comics Bombshells, Black Canary,* and *Batman '66*), Archie (*Reggie and Me, Archie*), and Oni Press (the Eisner-nominated *Meteor Men*). Next he'll be working on Dark Horse Comics' adaptation of Neil Gaiman's *Norse Mythology.* He lives in North Carolina with his wife, two kids, and two dogs.

SILVANA BRYS is a colorist and graphic designer who has colored *Scooby-Doo, Where Are You?, Teen Titans Go!, Scooby-Doo Team-Up,* and *Looney Tunes* for DC Comics, plus *Tom and Jerry* and many other comics and books. She lives in a small village in Argentina. Her home is also her office and she loves to create there, surrounded by forests and mountains.

WENDY BROOME, colorist extraordinaire, has been coloring comics since the dawn of time...well the dawn of Photoshop anyway. Over the years she has worked on everything from *DV8* to *Astro City* and *DC Comics Bombshells,* but she's having fun with the *DC Super Hero Girls* and *Teen Titans Go!* stories in her current workload. Her children, Jaedon and Camryn, only wish she'd started coloring comics like these years ago so they would have been allowed to read them in elementary school.

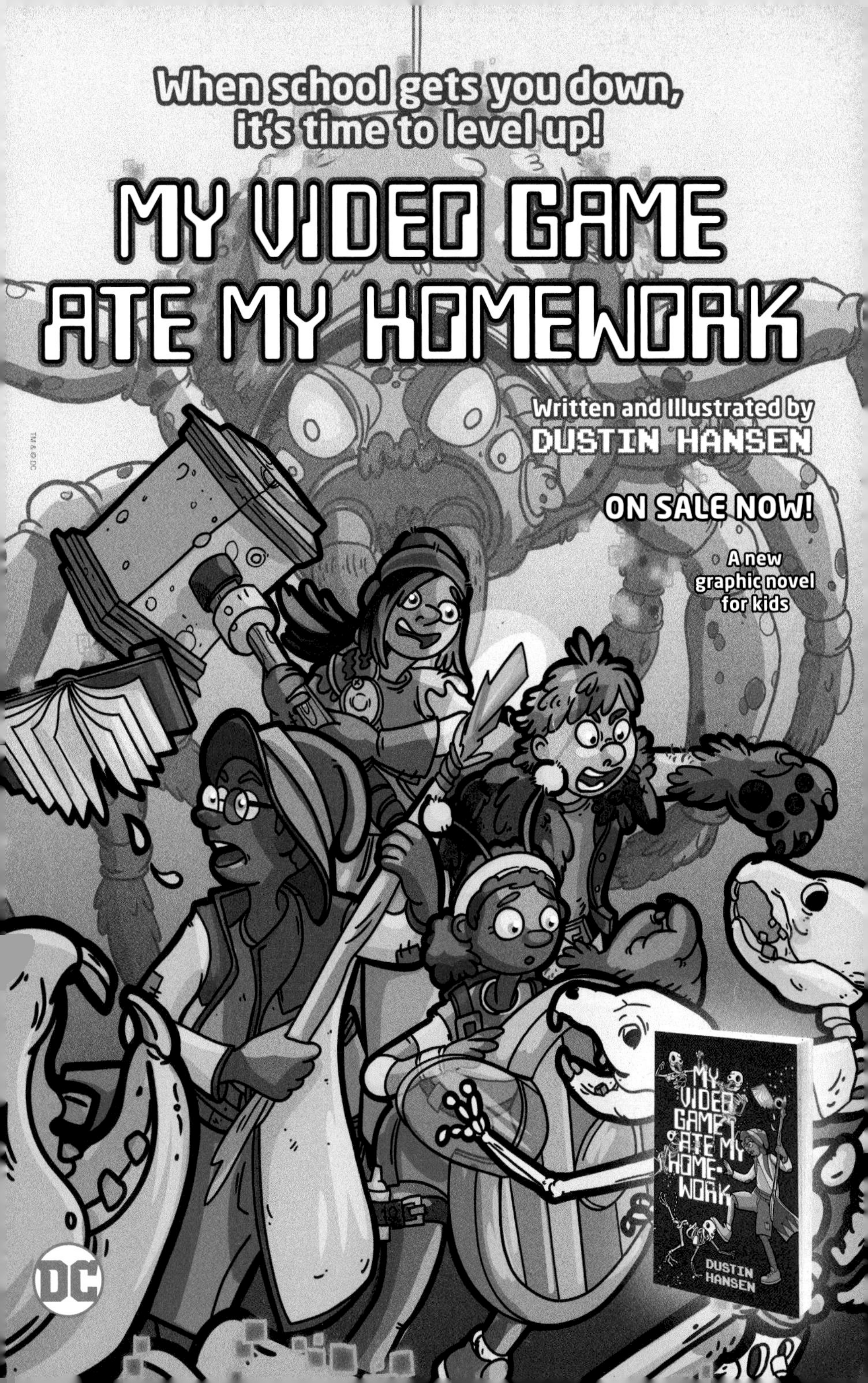
When school gets you down, it's time to level up!
MY VIDEO GAME ATE MY HOMEWORK
Written and Illustrated by
DUSTIN HANSEN
ON SALE NOW!
A new graphic novel for kids
TM & © DC
MY VIDEO GAME ATE MY HOME-WORK
DUSTIN HANSEN
DC

Casey Clive loves Halloween, scary movies, and

Of course, it's a little complicated when the monsters you love need a place to stay, something to eat, and lots of attention. Sixth grade math is stressful enough—will protecting his monsters from townspeople and a new threat be the last straw for Casey?

This winter, acclaimed "monsterologist" Kirk Scroggs brings his hilariously scary pen to the page in an all-new graphic novel showing that friendship and trust go so much deeper than scaly, slimy, or squishy skin.

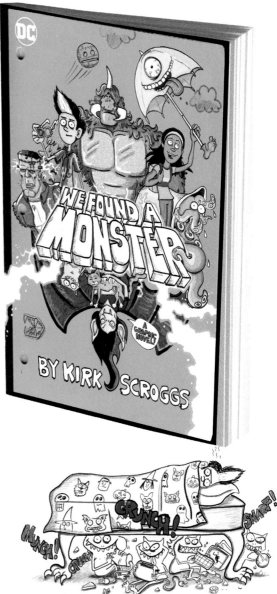

Zandra was interrupted by Ms. Kindle, who had an interesting proposition for me...

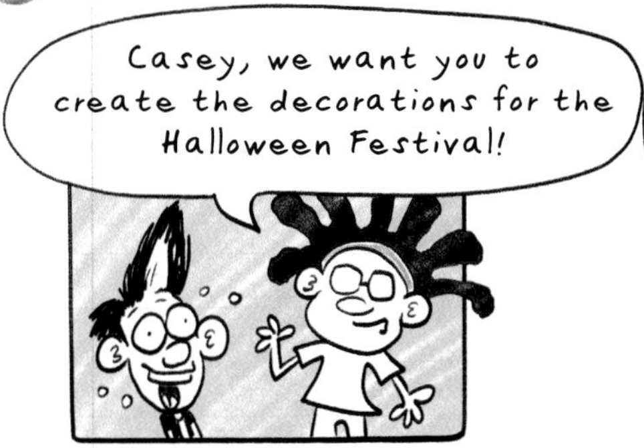
Casey, we want you to create the decorations for the Halloween Festival!

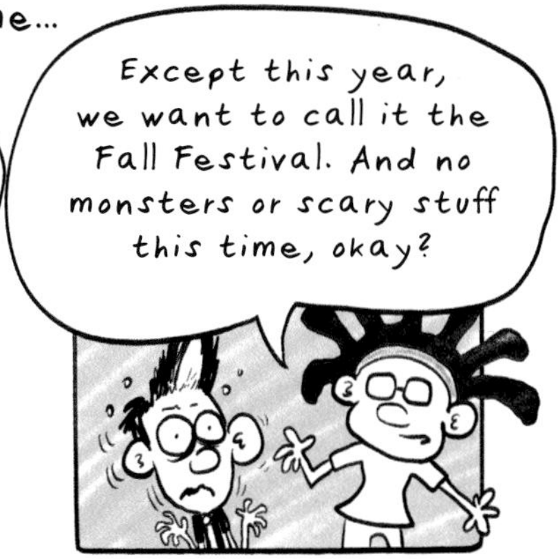
Except this year, we want to call it the Fall Festival. And no monsters or scary stuff this time, okay?

No monsters or scary stuff?! I calmly explained to Ms. K what Halloween is all about...

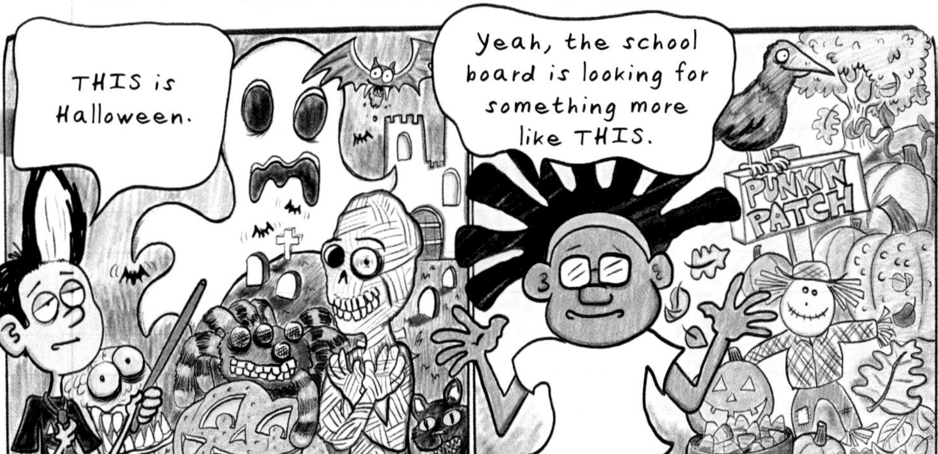
THIS is Halloween.
Yeah, the school board is looking for something more like THIS.
PUNKIN PATCH

I had to get out of there.

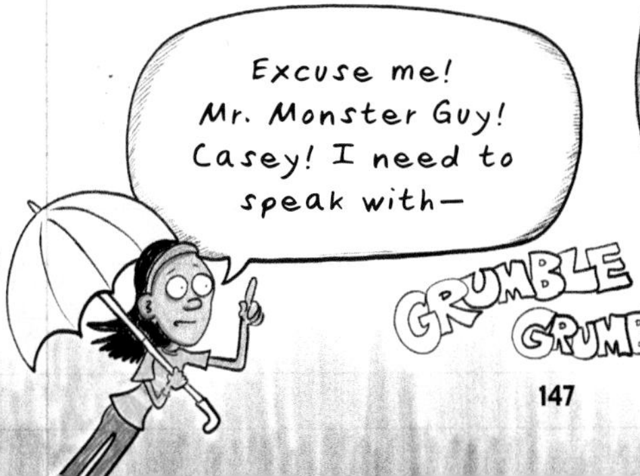
Excuse me! Mr. Monster Guy! Casey! I need to speak with—
GRUMBLE
GRUMBLE

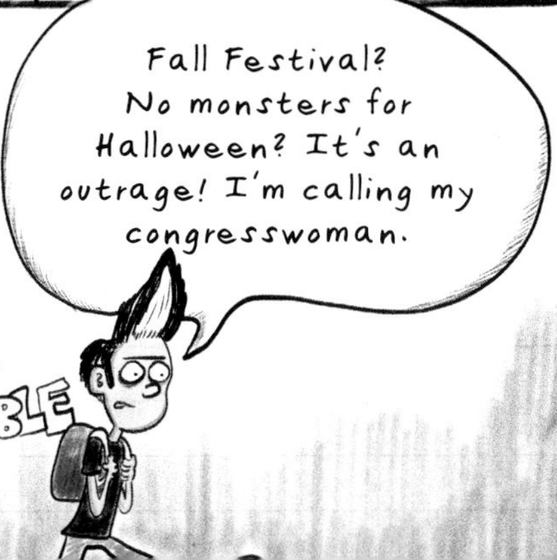
Fall Festival? No monsters for Halloween? It's an outrage! I'm calling my congresswoman.

What's the big deal lately with making everything safe and "un-scary"? Seems like folks used to love monsters and spooky stuff. Now, it gets everyone all panicked.

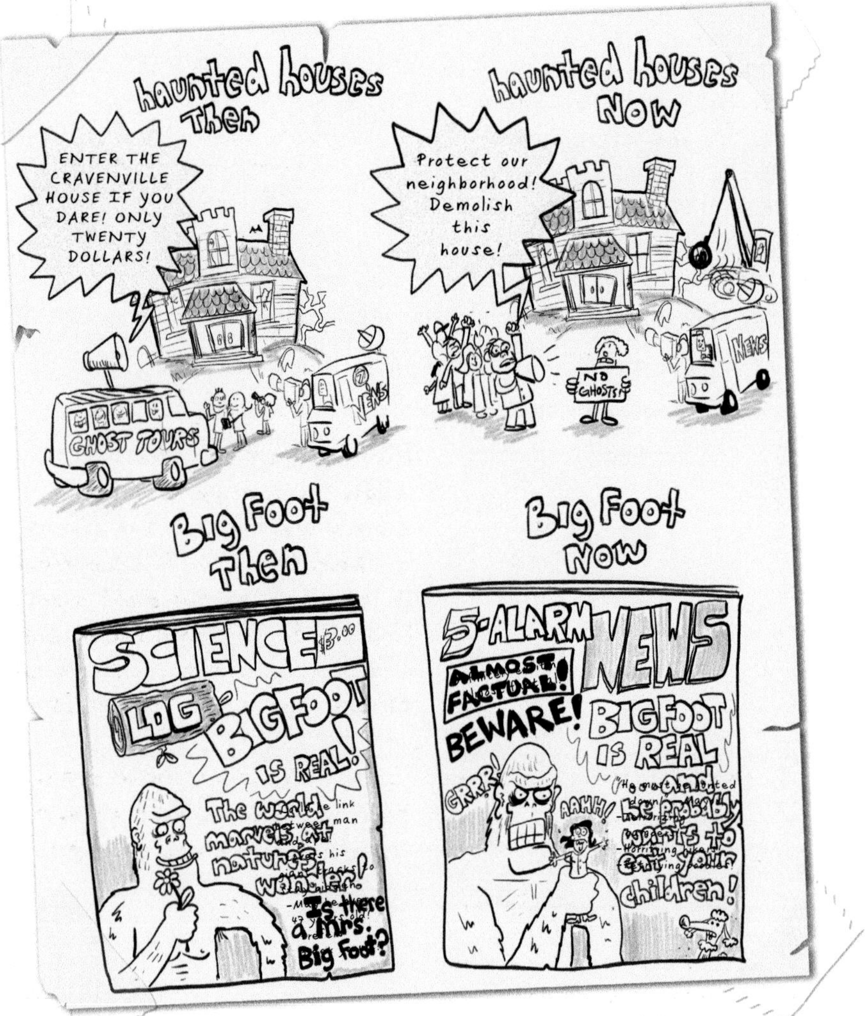
haunted houses Then
ENTER THE CRAVENVILLE HOUSE IF YOU DARE! ONLY TWENTY DOLLARS!
GHOST TOURS
NEWS
haunted houses NOW
Protect our neighborhood! Demolish this house!
NO GHOSTS!
NEWS
Big Foot Then
SCIENCE LOG $3.00
BIGFOOT IS REAL!
The world marvels at nature's wonder!
Is there a Mrs. Big Foot?
Big Foot NOW
5-ALARM NEWS
ALMOST FACTUAL!
BEWARE!
BIGFOOT IS REAL
and he probably wants to eat your children!
GRRR!
AAHH!

Calm down, people! Not all monsters are bad. I should know. I live with Frankenstein. The scariest thing about him is his snoring.

Dad thinks it's me. He even bought me some nasal anti-snoring strips!

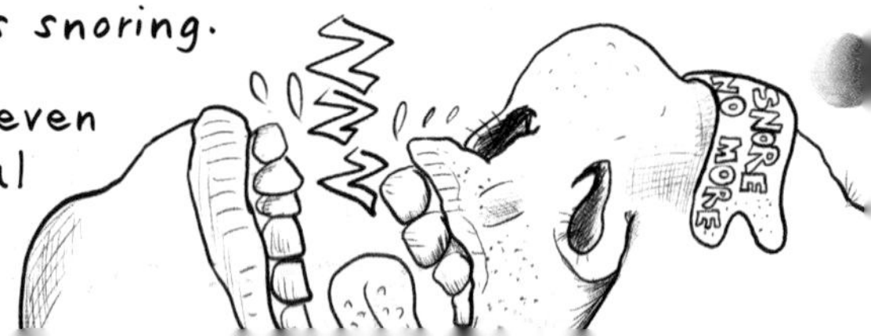
SNORE NO MORE

HOME

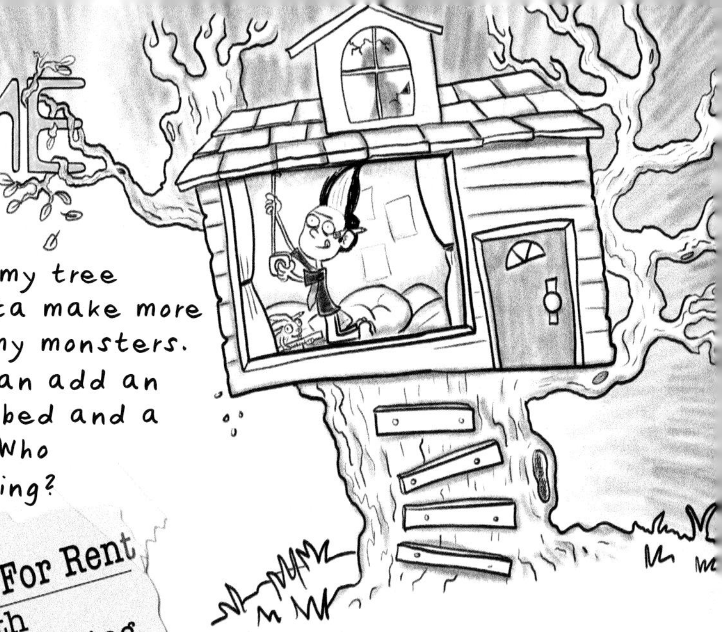

It's after school now. Measuring my tree house. Gotta make more space for my monsters. Maybe I can add an additional bed and a bathroom? Who am I kidding?

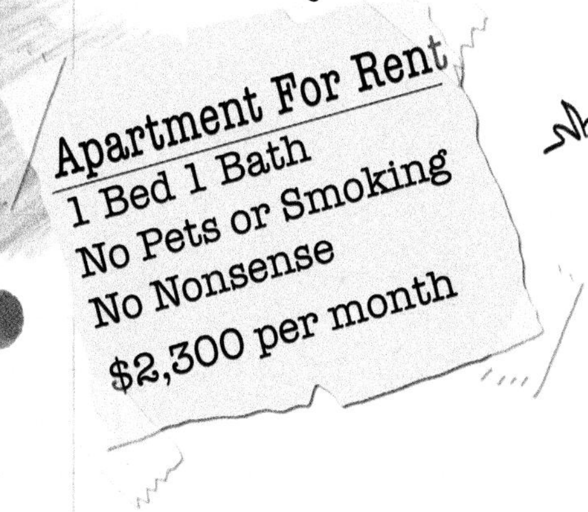

Apartment For Rent
1 Bed 1 Bath
No Pets or Smoking
No Nonsense
$2,300 per month

Don't think my measly allowance can afford a new apartment for them either. Maybe I can find a very open-minded person looking for a roommate...or eight roommates, some of them hungry for humans.

I vented to Dad about the school board's plan to ruin the Halloween Festival with fall colors and decorative gourds.

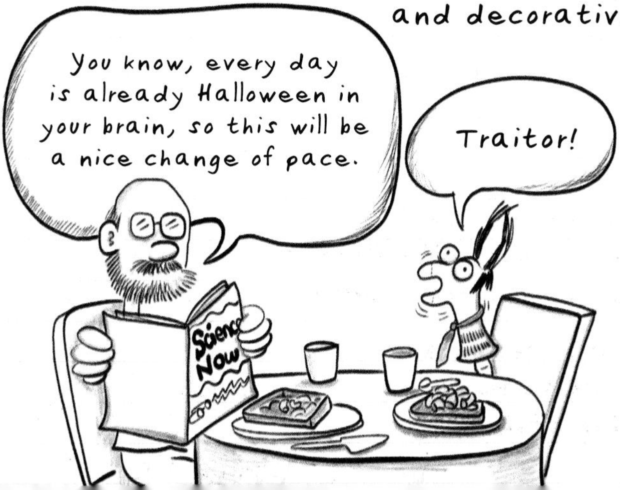
You know, every day is already Halloween in your brain, so this will be a nice change of pace.
Traitor!
Science Now

Some comfort he is.

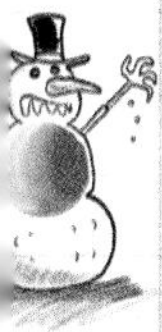

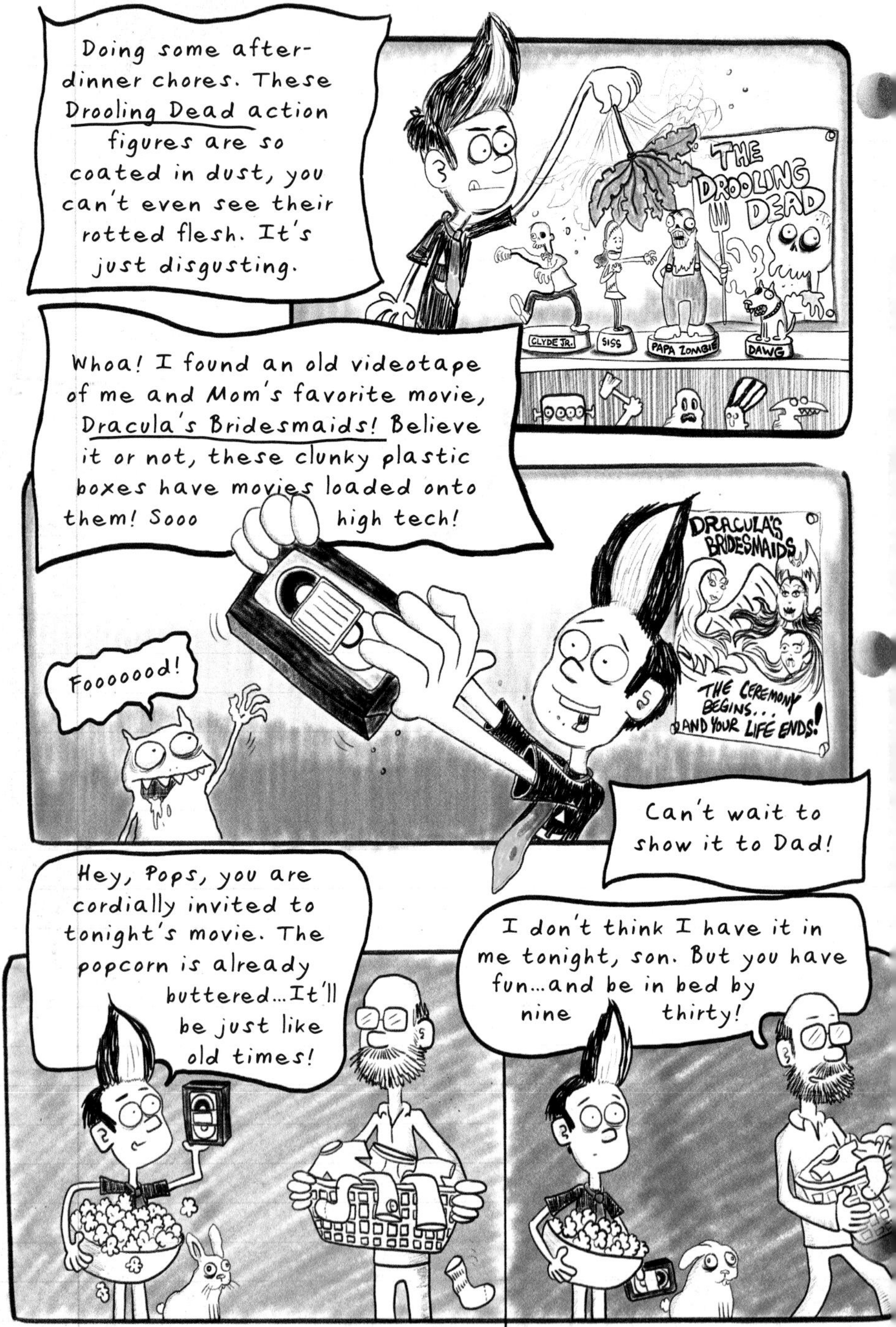
Doing some after-dinner chores. These Drooling Dead action figures are so coated in dust, you can't even see their rotted flesh. It's just disgusting.
THE DROOLING DEAD
CLYDE JR.
SISS
PAPA ZOMBIE
DAWG
Whoa! I found an old videotape of me and Mom's favorite movie, Dracula's Bridesmaids! Believe it or not, these clunky plastic boxes have movies loaded onto them! Sooo high tech!
DRACULA'S BRIDESMAIDS
THE CEREMONY BEGINS... AND YOUR LIFE ENDS!
Foooooood!
Can't wait to show it to Dad!
Hey, Pops, you are cordially invited to tonight's movie. The popcorn is already buttered...It'll be just like old times!
I don't think I have it in me tonight, son. But you have fun...and be in bed by nine thirty!

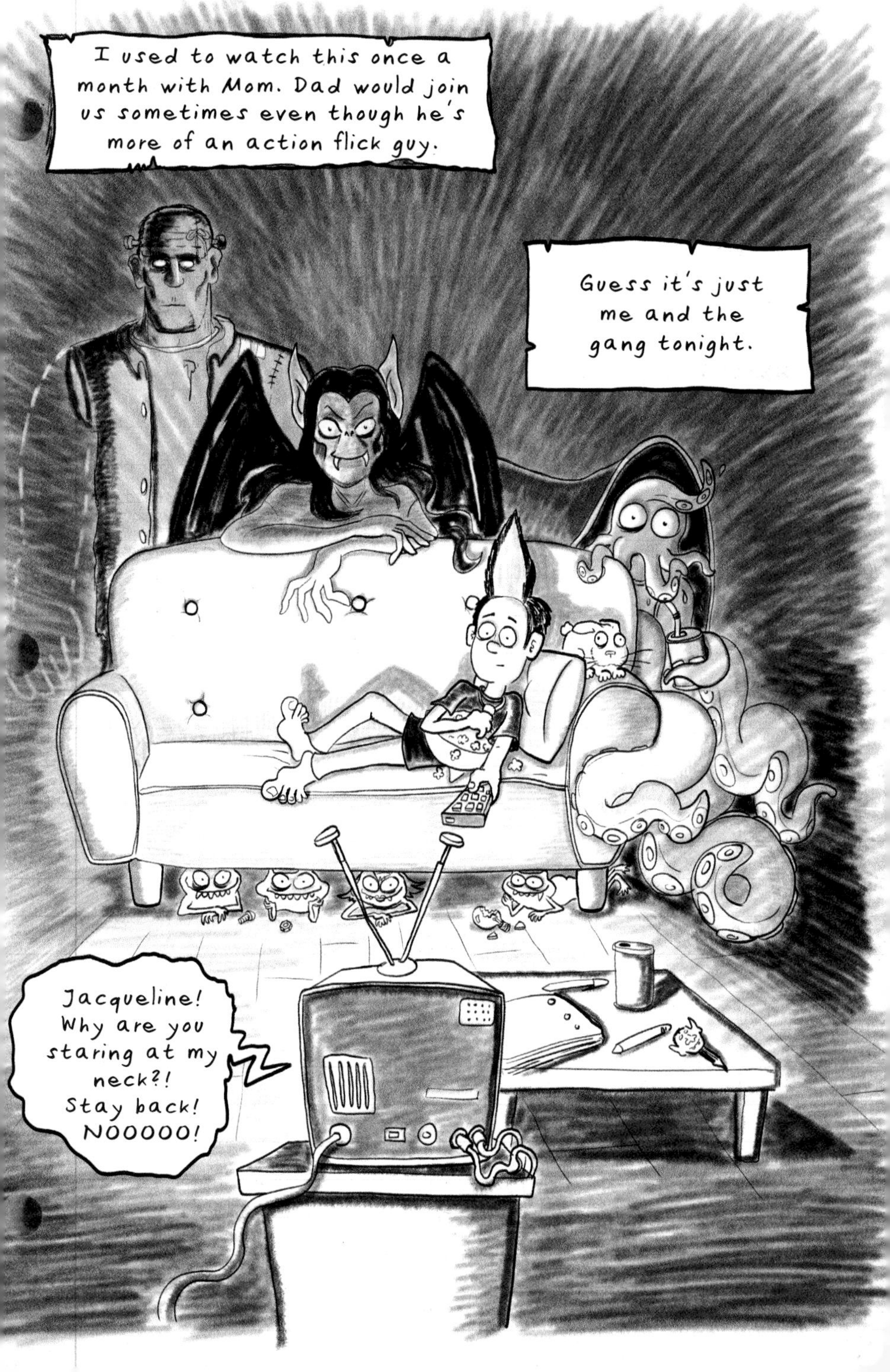
I used to watch this once a month with Mom. Dad would join us sometimes even though he's more of an action flick guy.
Guess it's just me and the gang tonight.
Jacqueline! Why are you staring at my neck?! Stay back! NOOOOO!

THUR.

Curious. This was taped to my locker when I got to school today. It's from that weird umbrella-totin' new girl. (The wizard tape is hers B.T.W.)

DEAR CASEY,

I FOUND A MONSTER!
IT NEEDS YOUR HELP!
THIS IS TOP SECRET, SO
PLEASE DON'T TELL ANYONE.

MEET ME AFTER SCHOOL
AT THE SNACK 'N' GAS.
PLEASE! A LIFE DEPENDS
ON YOU!

ZANDRA

monster
(not actual)
size

High Fever

Okay. I'll bite. She found a monster? Probably a hairless labradoodle or something. But I'll meet her. Just gotta make sure it's not some kind of set u

HELP SAVE THIS MONSTER (BY READING THE REST OF THE BOOK) COMING IN JANUARY 2021!